Winged Victory

M.P. Hough-Greene

Year of the Book
135 Glen Avenue
Glen Rock, Pennsylvania 17327

Cover design by Lydia Lura Harmer

ISBN 13: 978-1-942430-25-4
ISBN 10: 1-942430-25-6

Library of Congress Control Number: 2015948517

Chapter head quotations from *Country Cross Stitch Calendar 1984*, by Laura J. Conley.

For my family

I would like to thank the following family and friends who have helped me along the way with their careful reading, editing, and proofreading skills. Their encouragement and faith helped me to keep writing.

George A. Hough, III, my father, gave invaluable advice about geography, missiles, and island social dynamics.

Mary Lu Hough, my mother, provided editing tips and comments.

Lydia Lura Harmer, my daughter, created the cover that captured the essence of my story.

Neil Greene, my son, a thoughtful reader, always there to settle me down.

Bonnie Snow provided helpful insight into fashion and morés.

Shelly Carew Palczewski encouraged me through the years, and provided good observations that helped me describe characters and events.

Terry Palczewski, playwright, offered guidance for plot and pacing.

Rose Buscarini read the manuscript with skillful editing and encouragement.

Susan Hilkevitch read, reread, and reread the manuscript. A comma chaser and fact checker extraordinaire.

Maureen Beck kept me safe.

Demi Stevens, CEO of Year of the Book, brought my thirty-year project to conclusion. Without her guidance and assistance, *Winged Victory* would not have made it into print.

All remaining errors are my own.

PROLOGUE

WHITE HOUSE
New England Fishery Management Council
Assembled to Sign Agreement
1986

"Walleyes like a dark day and a chop on the water."

"I don't. I prefer a clear shot at the bottom and warm sun on my back."

"You get a little white-capping on a lake and everyone heads for protected water. Get yourself out on that windy shoreline and you'll find some exceptional fishing. Exceptional. Baitfish and oxygen are blown to the banks."

"Fishing in a head wind. You can have it."

The senator turned to his colleague. "So what do you think of the Siberian Connection?"

"Trout Unlimited? Damn spunky little group."

"A gaggle of gentlemen from Virginia wanting grander horizons for their sport fishing. Amazing, when you think about it."

"That agreement was signed in Moscow."

"Fishing in Siberia. No thanks. As I was saying, I like sun. Fishing is challenge aplenty without adding unique weather conditions."

"Trout Unlimited takes these fishing tours to Siberia and fish for *taimon*, the largest species of trout, I gather, and weighing as much as a hundred thirty pounds."

"What do you use to catch something like that?"

"Heavy weight fly fishing equipment, they tell me."

"In a snow mobiler's outfit to ward off arctic frostbite. How the hell's he going to raise his arm to cast?"

"Part of the challenge."

"Good morning, Senators," The President's aide interjected.

"Good morning, Ed. Is the President ready?"

"He'll be with you in seven minutes."

"Not five, not ten. What an efficient government you're running."

"Got the news media to settle," the aide replied.

"Of course," the Senator said.

The two senators moved ahead while the President's assistants continued counting heads, searching for the key members of the committee invited for the ceremony.

The senator continued, "Back in' 76 the Fisheries Conservation and Management Act was passed to add quotas to what foreign fishermen could keep within 200 miles of the U.S. coast."

"Yup. Now they're hauling in 50,000 metric tons of fish a year."

"And in return we get one or two 130-pound Siberian taimon."

"That's détente."

"That's bullshit."

The senator turned his attention in the direction of the Director of the National Federation of Fishermen. Her hair fanned out in a fuzzy perm. She was wearing a slate gray suit with a crisp white blouse. Pretty little thing, he thought. She looked like a caddis fly.

"Good morning, Susan." the Senator drawled.

"Morning, Senator." The Director replied briskly.

"My good friend the Senator from Maryland and I were just discussing the angler's coup—opening up Siberia to sport fishermen."

"Interesting, yes. But I doubt many Russian fisherman can afford sport fishing," the Director replied.

"Not trading Siberian taimon for pollock?" the Senator responded in mock surprise.

"Curbing vacuum sweeps of the ocean. That has restricted the activities of foreign vessels by placing fixed quotas on their fleets. And we monitor them effectively, too."

"Oh, I see." Funny, he thought, a woman turning God-given corn silk hair to permanent wave straw.

"Of course, the Canadians would like to see more quotas," the Director added gravely.

She was all business, he thought. What a pity. "And the Canadians would like to see the United States out of the Georges Bed, ah Bank. Right, Susan?" he winked at her.

The Director turned her attention toward the President's aide. "If you would all come this way," he said. Ten men hesitated. The only woman in the group led the way, stepping over the camera cables spread across the floor, avoiding the bright floodlights, and escaping further conversation with the Honorable Senator from Maryland.

The group filed into the Oval Office and spread out into a horseshoe shaped line behind the President who was already sitting at his desk, a Presidential smile spread across his face.

On his desk a row of pens was neatly lined up against the freshly printed agreement set squarely in the center for the television lights. Eleven times the President changed pens on the up-stroke of his signature. Each participant would have a pen used to sign the historic agreement that sent Russian fishing trawlers out of the Barents Sea and into the North Atlantic to once again fish the rich Georges Bank.

MURMANSK 1994

A group of gray stern trawlers set a course from Murmansk, spreading across the open seas. Viewed by satellite, their wakes looked as wispy as kite tails. Watched from the stern of the trawler *Zori*, the cold waters churned a broad trail.

In the gray light, Dmitri paused to watch the black waters diffusing silver light then smoothing again to onyx. It was a cold April day, but even in Murmansk the smell on the wind was sweet, scented with a hint of the spring *rasputitsa* thawing the Arctic land. The woolen cap on the man's head began to warm his brow. *Slava Rybakan*, glory to fishermen, he mumbled. Got a mission to complete.

Inside his quarters, Captain Alexandrovich Rubinov spread a chart across the navigating table to study the Eastern most part of the rich fishing zone. He was eager to fish the Georges Bank. These were the grounds his father fished, bringing home tales of giant and meaty fish, swimming so thickly a man could walk across their backs. Now they had to content themselves with the bottom dwellers, the fish the Americans ignored, considering them "trash."

Rubinov commanded a floating factory ship. No matter, he consoled himself. He would see how grand the fishing was off the Eastern coast of the United States of America. He can only keep the bottom fish. At least he will see with his own eyes the fish his father remembered.

Rubinov sighed heavily. He carried orders to be opened on the third of July in the presence of one of the crew, Dmitri Alexi Korsomakov. He was no ordinary fisherman. There are no ordinary men in Russia. Remember the Romanovs. Remember the USSR.

The trawler carried a crate of fishing labels brought on board separately from the other crates. Sealed, it was stored in the safe, and meticulously watched by Alyonso Orlov, an intelligence officer.

The Captain wanted no part of it, but no Russian was free from entanglements. Rubinov dreamed of a hold full of fish, nothing more.

LUNENBURG, NOVA SCOTIA
June 1994
International Convention of the Northwest Atlantic Fisheries

Seth McCalister breathed easily in the cool Canadian air. Lunenburg, Nova Scotia was a refreshing break from the early spring heat wave hanging over the East Coast. The FBI believed he could find the out-of-place face in the crowd of disgruntled fishermen listening to the bosses of the maritime fishing companies. The international boundaries drawn between the United States and Canada meant more than fishing rights. The U.S. fishermen wanted higher duties on imports of Canadian fish. They were still grumbling over the World Court decision that excluded U.S. fishermen from a large part of the Georges Bank, the rich fishing ground stretching 100 miles east and south of Cape Cod. The unions worried about the highly mechanized foreign fleets subsidized by the Russian government. Arguing their positions, on and on they droned. McCalister hadn't spotted any Russians—fishermen or government officials.

BOSTON 1994

Tom Sullivan inhaled the stale air. He wasn't thinking about 50,000 tons of fish allotted to the Russians. He was watching a man he suspected was an operational for the Federal Security Service, the former KGB. He was a tall man with a paunch spreading out before him, lessening the impact of his height. He liked bagels and cream cheese. A lot of cream cheese.

McCalister and Sullivan shared the credit for snaring a minor spy passing secrets in the woods outside of Washington, D.C. It was an insignificant victory, a small disruption in the delivery system of a highly complex espionage ring. The Soviet Union traded the spy for a journalist. Their version of a catch-release conservation program, McCalister concluded. Then the USSR went belly-up and everyone blamed the FBI for not seeing the downfall coming.

Somehow this man sipping coffee in a corner donut shop in Boston while he stared past Sullivan, this man was the link between adversaries. McCalister and Sullivan merely had to follow the chain.

1 | Everybody is Wise After the Event

1994

Captain Alexander Rubinov scowled at the sunset and watched as the water soaked in the pink-gold rays. In a few minutes the sun would slip below the horizon and the sky would merge into murkiness matching his mood. He had no place to go. He was the captain of a fishing trawler with nothing to do. He turned his back to the ocean and glared at the pilot house. He'd yearned for the day he would fish the Georges Bank. Now the sight filled him with anger and disgust.

A skeleton crew maintained the vessel, and the recreation area was crammed with taut muscled men hunkering around a tiny television. They were entertaining themselves, devouring scraps of American life, each man filling his head with strange illusions of an alluring country.

Two wizened fishermen sat hunched forward, ignoring the television.

"So who's this Korsakov? He's no fisherman."

"He's young, but his father was a big shot in the USSR's efforts at diplomacy."

"Alyonso Orlov—he's no diplomat. Something's going on."

"What do you think is in the crate Orlov keeps his eye on?"

"Something they need to get into the U.S."

"I saw Fyordorvitch in Murmansk last winter. He's an angry old man with a grudge. I heard he's gone to the U.S. as part of a coalition on fishing treaties. Didn't think he had much interest in cod. I do know he liked the old ways better. A lot of bitterness in that guy."

Captain Rubinov calculated the odds of a mutiny with so much plenty dangled in front of them on the screen. It was not his charge to stop them. The first mate, Alyonso Orlov, an intelligence officer when the Soviets were in charge was still in charge. He, the captain, was not in command. The vessel was crowded with men who were not fishermen, some not even sailors, and one was not even Russian.

Derrick Washington turned his face to the wall and tried not to move the rest of his six-foot-two-inch frame, squeezed into the rack that was his bed, his life-line, and his instrument of torture. Sweat beaded his upper lip; the inside of his mouth was dry. His stomach had taken on an entity of its own, and lunged like a huge formless creature throughout his body, freezing his toes, numbing his arms, swelling his abdomen until he thought it would explode; then curling into a hard little nut at the very core of him, threatening to pull Washington, a weightless, powerless shadow of himself, to the bottom of the sea. He was seasick.

Trying to get control, he forced himself to dredge memories of who he was. During his radical youth, he'd mocked his forefathers for not returning to their homeland in Africa. He thought now of the suffering they must have endured, packed body to stinking body in slave ships over months of cruelty beyond that of a gently rocking trawler. Of course, few chose to get on a ship again. Would any intelligent man go to sea?

And that brought him face to face with his present predicament. Derrick Marcus Washington was a marine biologist with a Ph.D. in oceanography. He was the American representative aboard a Russian stern trawler, his job to count and to monitor fish harvested by the Russian vessel. Any fish not allowed by permit had to be thrown back dead or alive. Washington was there to keep them honest—that and the threat of sudden Coast Guard intervention and inspection. But the trawler had caught its huge nets on a bottom-fisherman's pots, the pots had to be cut free, and the nets repaired. During the repairs, Washington developed an incapacitating seasickness. It had never happened before.

He pictured his grandmother, a devout Baptist who believed in evil spirits, menacing ghosts, and hovering entities. Her conversations were punctuated with gestures—a knock on wood with an arthritic knuckle, an imagined pinch of salt tossed over her shoulder, or a lick of her finger then etching the wind. He'd often scoffed at her superstitious hedging, but now his thoughts kept turning back to his own preoccupation with the idea that this trip was jinxed.

When he'd accepted the job he knew it could be unpleasant. The factory ships were dehumanizing, smelled bad, and old and rusty. Getting seasick hadn't occurred to him. It hadn't bothered him when the usual ship-to-ship transfer by way of a cargo cage had been cancelled, or that instead a lifeboat had been dispatched to pick him up in rough seas. He managed to scramble up the Jacob's ladder without being splashed by a wave. Then, as he watched a crewman raise his gear, midway a sudden gust of wind slammed the ropes against the side of the ship. His Russian phrase book, observer's manual, and personal comforts plummeted to the depths. He wasn't a sailor, but he knew his knots. It shouldn't have happened.

His thoughts were interrupted by a loud thumping rap on the door.

"*Zdast vootye*, Derrick."

He recognized the first mate, Alyonso's, voice and pulled himself out of his bunk to open the door. Alyonso thrust a glass into Washington's hand. It smelled like warm apple juice.

"Thanks," Washington mumbled as he took a sip. It tasted like apple juice, too, only much sweeter. Puzzled, he wondered how they knew he was sick. What the hell, it was a kind gesture. He took another sip. The sweetness was overwhelming.

"We ready to fish?" he asked.

"*Nyet. Nyet*. The gears… she is jammed," the mate responded.

Washington took another sip of the drink. Maybe if it were cold it would taste better.

"The men must be getting pretty uptight about reaching their quotas," he said.

"Nooo problem. They do okay. They are good fishermen. We will make it up," The Russian paused as if he were weighing whether to tell him more. Derrick looked down at him expectantly.

"There is another ship that is having trouble. We are going to help. It's drifting toward the territorial waters. What you think they do about it?"

“Who?” Derrick asked. The sweet drink and the rocking trawler were triggering another wave of nausea.

“Your American Coast Guard. If one of our boats drifts into your Boston Harbor.”

Washington spit the warm liquid back into the glass. “Boston? How the hell could we get way down there? You’ve got to be two hundred miles off the American coast in international waters, and we couldn’t be close to Boston. This other boat, it’s informed the Coast Guard it’s disabled?”

“Oh, they know. We’ve been talking to them for a couple of days on the short wave. You guys listen to all that.”

“A couple of days? How long have I been out of commission?”

“A couple of days.” So they knew he’d been sick, and he was surprised at the length of time he’d been out of it.

“So what’s the problem?”

“Don’t know. If they knew, they’d fix it.”

“So what can the *Zori* do about it?”

“Ah, we can find the trouble, fix it, and by that time we have our nets fixed. We get our quota. We go home.”

It sounded like a good plan to Washington. “Where are we now, exactly?”

“You better ask the captain. He’s got the charts.”

Washington stood up from the wall where he’d been leaning. His legs buckled as he followed the first mate to the captain’s door. After a short rap and an acknowledging grunt from within, Alyonso opened the door and Washington wobbled in. The captain looked up from a chart spread across the table in front of him.

“You feel better, Mr. Washington?” he asked without looking up.

“Yeah, I guess so. Sorry about your problems with the nets. We would probably all feel better if we were fishing.”

“Now the *Poyma’s* got problems. We go to fix it.”

Washington sensed the hum of the engine. The trawler was traveling fast for a fishing boat, but he welcomed the smoother ride. His stomach was calming

“Where exactly are we?”

The Captain stabbed at the chart and Washington stared hard at the location. They had indeed moved down the coast. He must have been out of commission for longer than two days for them to be so close to Massachusetts, and they must have been traveling at a high speed. He was certain the Coast Guard was paying attention.

"If you get within two hundred miles of the American coast, you're going to be escorted further out to sea."

"Good," the Captain snorted.

"Where exactly is this other boat, the *Poyma*?"

"Near some islands. Massachusetts? New Hampshire? Somewhere along there."

Washington was a marine biologist, not an expert on international boundaries. He knew if they kept the wrong fish on board, they could be fined or lose their permits. He hadn't considered the possibility of being aboard a Russian trawler caught invading his country. With the new regime in Russia, it probably wouldn't be considered an invasion. Just a mistake.

"You play chess?" the first mate asked Washington.

"Sure."

"Good. Let's play a game. Then we fix the *Poyma*, then we fish."

"Sounds good to me," Washington agreed. Alyonso opened the door, and Washington followed him out into the corridor.

The captain stared after them. What kind of a ship was he running—a cruise ship or a fishing trawler on a covert mission? The captain resented the intelligence officer's presence, the constant reminder that some things never changed. Had the American biologist needed a nurse-maid or a guard, he wondered. The man would not have become a marine biologist, the captain considered, if he got seasick in light seas.

The radio dispatch team brought on board the *Zori* specifically for this trip was busy talking to its counterpart on the *Poyma*. Their conversations were intentionally detailed to inform the Coast Guard of the troubles aboard each ship. These problems were technicalities that would be cleared up after the trawler drifted as close as it could to the American coast before the U.S. Coast Guard intervened. Then the captain would be back in command of his trawler, they would catch their quota and go home.

Dmitri paced his quarters. It was ten o'clock. The moon would not come out until after one in the morning, and if he was lucky, it would stay hidden in a cloud cover. The wind was picking up.

He stripped off his clothes and pulled on the jeans and t-shirt purloined from the hapless biologist's bag. A second, transparent line had held it secure as it plunged into the ocean allowing it to be retrieved, emptied, and thrown back overboard after the American was on board the *Zori*. He studied the driver's license picture. Washington was black and Dmitri was not. At the last moment there'd been a switch of biologists. He could depend on the intelligence officer keeping the American out of sight. Washington would have no way of suspecting anything unusual was taking place. The induced seasickness had been an additional precaution. The driver's license was useless. He pocketed the wallet with the other IDs that did not include pictures. In Murmansk he'd been given American money and a fake passport. The passport wasn't much use now either. He was going ashore as an American.

Dmitri opened the door and headed for the deck. He passed the recreation area where the off-duty fishermen sat entranced in front of the television. The sights and sounds of America were coming in strong. Those taking their place on duty were busy at their posts, each trained to do exactly as he was told and not to think about anyone else's duty. They might no longer be communists, but the old ways would not easily be discarded.

He regarded the captain standing at the bow, arms stretched on the rail. The man would not look back. He saw nothing. He knew nothing. Once Dmitri was gone, he would be back in command of his fishing trawler. Dmitri wished him a good catch.

Out from the shadows, Alyonso Orolov appeared carrying a small crate. He stood watching Dmitri pull the sides from a larger crate that contained a mini-sub. They would launch the mini-sub from the vessel's ramp. In the distance, Dmitri spotted lights from the *Poyma*. He scanned the skies for lights from aircraft. He saw none. He lowered himself into the mini-sub, and the agent handed him the cargo he was to deliver to Fyordorvitch on the shore of a small island near the coast of the United States.

It was now the third of July. The *Poyma* was drifting into American territory, with the *Zori* allegedly in hot pursuit. The radio dispatch man from each ship kept the other informed of the difficulties. The *Zori* had been shut down repairing the huge nets that had snagged on a bottom fisherman's pots. The *Poyma's* engine had stalled. The dispatcher droned on about how the *Zori's* sonar detector malfunctioned. The sonar detector was a sophisticated piece of equipment designed to display the ocean bottom and to identify schools of fish on a screen, pinpointing their depth and location. It could reveal details of the ocean floor, including lobster pots, if it were working properly. But an unknown blip in the machine kept it from revealing the pots. The Russians added a few degrading comments about the Canadian fixed-gear fishermen. Then they switched to discussing the Russian engineers who designed the engines improperly and allowed complicated equipment to make decisions fishermen used to make. It was a prolonged script meant to reassure anyone eavesdropping that the problems were frustrating, but solvable and the fishermen were eager to get back to fishing in open waters.

The Americans were sure to be amused by the inadequacies of the dilapidated Russian system. The *Poyma's* crew, unable to fix the engine, requested assistance from the *Zori*, as the boats moved into American territory.

Beyond the *Poyma* the horizon sparkled with lights from American boats poised for the festivities, fireworks, and general frivolity marking the Fourth of July. Aboard the *Zori* the radar screen did not pick up any sign of approaching aircraft. If Dmitri waited until it did, it would be too late to launch his craft. But the closer to the coast the boat drifted, the easier it would be for Dmitri to land on the island's beach unnoticed.

The captain of the *Poyma* interrupted the dispatch man. He wanted to talk to the captain of the *Zori*. "It's an American holiday. Tell your captain to come aboard. We share some borscht, *pilmeni*, and some vodka? Yes? You invite your American, too. Okay?"

"The American is not so good. He has lost his sea legs."

"When you come, I send our American back to keep him company. Her legs are pretty good."

Aloynso Orlov passed the word to Dmitri. He would watch from the starboard side. It was only a matter of time, despite the mindless prattle of the fishing trawler dispatchers, before the Coast guard would intervene. Dmitri said a prayer that the scripted denigration of the Russian engineers did not apply to the sub. He had to get close enough to the island to surface and launch his specially designed craft. As it drifted toward shore with an American flag waving from the stern, he'd be just another amateur sailor who sailed too far from the beach.

2 | A SMOOTH SEA NEVER MADE A SKILLFUL SAILOR.

Dmitri surfaced beneath a hazy cloud covered moon and set his course for Jellicle Island. By the time the sun burned through the fog, sailboats, wind-surfers, yachts, and fishing vessels crowded the ocean. A soft breeze carried the festive sounds of music and laughter within range of Dmitri's craft. He'd made good time, but now he slowed to a speed fitting for a rubber raft with an outboard motor.

He assumed a casual pose as he steered toward shore. With his legs stretched out before him, one elbow crooked over the starboard side and his hand loosely guiding the throttle, he whistled a Russian sailing song. Then, feeling the excitement build, he burst into a chant. Knowing he should be singing in English, he stopped to consider an American repertoire.

"Row, row, row your boat," came to mind from his English language courses. He started up again, louder, feeling his way into his new guise, that of an American college boy on vacation. The red, white, and blue coloring on the craft glistened. The American flag snapped in the headwind as the motor sped through the water. He would deliver the small package resting in the stern to a man named Fyodorvitch, who would be waiting in the woods at noon on Tuesday, the fifth of July.

"A piece of cake," Dmitri thought as he admired the first-class example of modern Russian technology showcasing speed and engineering. The mini-submarine brought him close to shore, emerged and Dmitri inflated the rubber raft and climbed into it with his cargo. The sub he sent out toward the open sea, and Dmitri created an illusion of leisure for himself aboard the raft.

When he heard the whistling release of air, the rapid searing noise of ripping canvas and rubber, and the surge of water, it was too late to ponder the source. The weight of the motor was now too great for the raft to bear. Like a child's balloon released unknotted into the air, the raft burbled and spun around in circles at an ever-increasing speed. Dmitri saw the crate flip into the ocean. Pieces of the raft spread across the water while Dmitri struggled to stay afloat in the frigid sea.

The current caught the crate with its vital content and it bobbed toward shore as if propelled by a tiny motor. Dmitri's mind raced through a shortening list of probable conclusions. If he could reach the crate, which obviously was buoyed by a sharp intelligence officer's contingency plan, then he and the crate could maneuver to shore and his appointed rendezvous.

The jeans and sweatshirt weighed him down. He struggled to remove his sneakers and to tie the shoe laces together so he could slip the shoes around his neck. The crate, a distant blur, hurried on without him. The numbness in his arms and legs forced him to give up his plan of following the crate. He swam swiftly now, checking the distance to land on each upswing stroke.

The crate angled toward shore. Dmitri could see the land as it curved toward the sea. Ahead, the shore appeared uninhabited. No houses, docks, or people interrupted this barren stretch of beach. But on the other side of the point, Dmitri knew a New England town nestled near the harbor and would complicate retrieval of the crate. He would know shortly whether he was a rising or falling star in the new Russian order. Maybe he would never smell the *rasputitsa* again.

***

"Hey, guy. You all right?"

Dmitri opened his eyes to look up into the face of a youth bending over him as he lay in the sand. The young man carried an ax.

"You're not allowed to swim here. You know that?"

"My boat… it capsized."

"Oh, yeah?"

Dmitri struggled to get his bearings. Exhausted when he reached the beach, he'd intended to shut his eyes a moment before he went in search of the crate. He wondered how long he'd been lying there. Where was the crate? And why did this kid have an ax? The long swim in the frigid water had exhausted and disoriented him. He rolled over and sat up.

"I'm off duty now," the youth said. "You want a ride to town?"

"What time is it?" Dmitri asked.

"It's about five. Come on. This nature preserve closes at five."

The caretaker for the nature preserve had been watching Dmitri sleep. There were rules against swimming and building fires and picnicking, but people sun-bathed.

The guy spread out on the beach all afternoon looked harmless, if weird. He needed to get him off the Sanctuary property.

"It's closing time, man," he said again, repositioning the ax on his shoulder. He carried the tool to remove branches and vines obstructing the numerous trails that wound around the rocky cliffs, through the woods, and near the beach. It was a summer job. Pruning shears would have worked as well with the underbrush, but not with the summer people who were disobeying the rules.

Dmitri had no choice but to follow the young man. He'd missed his rendezvous. He had no idea where the crate had floated ashore. He didn't want to cause any trouble. He already had trouble.

"I can drop you off at the Coast Guard station. You can file a report on your missing boat. What kind of a boat was it, anyway?" Without waiting for an answer, he turned and started to walk toward a path in the beach grass.

"It was just a skiff. I don't think the Coast Guard would be concerned. She was an old boat. I just wanted to row up the shore a bit for exercise." Dmitri felt the phrases fall clumsily from his mouth like the useless phrases in language class. Not wanting anyone to remember the raft, he'd changed the description.

The caretaker took giant steps, moving up the sandy path, his ax slung over his shoulder. The sun cast a long shadow for Dmitri to follow. His body ached. His scalp felt sandy, and his mouth was dry. Salt burned his eyes.

He had to mark this place. He searched the shore for a landmark, but the sand and the grass stretched into a seashore reminiscent of those of his childhood along the Caspian Sea.

Then he saw it. A burst of orange in a blur of splintered beige. His heart raced. So, it might be simple after all.

"If you don't mind," he called after the receding figure, "point me in the right direction, and I'll find my own way."

The caretaker heard him, but his mind was on quitting time and the girls waiting at the bar in town. He wasn't leaving any stragglers. He didn't want to be chewed out by old man Norton, and he didn't want to chance losing favor with the actress who owned the property on the other side of the Sanctuary and guarded her privacy. He kept walking, but pulled the ax from his shoulder and holding it close to its head, he pointed in the direction of the Sanctuary's entrance. He heard the sound of barking dogs and turned to stare back at the beach.

"Better step on it," he shouted. He saw the man turn and stare toward the sound of the dogs. The caretaker continued walking, confident the man would follow.

To the right of the path, Dmitri saw a NO HUNTING sign posted. He tore a zigzag corner from it. Then he hurried to stay in the sight of the young man with the ax.

The path ended in a sandy parking lot. A rusty red sedan was parked near a large wooden sign with a map attached to it. YOU ARE HERE and an arrow marked the spot. Dmitri let out a deep breath. He would have to accept the ride to the Coast Guard station. Then he would double back to the Sanctuary.

Now that he knew precisely where he was, and where the crate was pressed into the sand, he had to make contact with Fyordorvitch. Once he handed over the contents of the crate he was certain that traveling up the coast to Nova Scotia and rejoining his ship in Lunnenberg would not take long.

The caretaker had disposed of his ax and was leaning over the open door of his car. Dmitri quickened his pace. He opened the passenger door and sat down.

The gravel road was steep and the sedan's tires spun as the caretaker raced the engine and landed with a thud on a paved road.

Trees lined the road as it curved right and then left. They passed a farm and a vegetable stand. A group of bicyclists spread across the road in front of them and the driver muttered to himself, but he did not honk the horn. The group formed a wobbly single file line as the car swerved around them. Dmitri checked the odometer. They'd gone farther than he'd anticipated.

A moment later, they came over a hill and Dmitri saw cars and buildings and boats beyond. He realized they'd gone in the opposite direction from the town near the harbor.

"Over there's the Coast Guard station. There's a snack shop and a telephone in front of the grocery. See ya." The grin on the caretaker's face told Dmitri he was younger and less threatening than he'd believed. He checked the odometer again. Seven miles.

"Thanks for the ride," he said and pulled his stiff body from the small car. If he walked back up the shoreline to the Sanctuary, he could get to the crate in an hour and a half or two hours at the most.

He stepped onto the porch of the small grocery store where a large bulletin board caught his attention. Dozens of messages on brightly colored scraps of paper flapped in the breeze. He thought of the map and the large arrow pinpointing his position near his landing point. Perhaps a similar map could be found here.

He read the notes. Wanted: Tickets off-island for Labor Day. Wanted: Tickets to Carly Simon concert. Found: Black Lab with red bandana. Dmitri pulled at more notes hoping to find a map beneath. Then he saw a stack of glossy magazines beneath the board. They were travel guides. Flipping through the pages he found in the center what he was looking for, a two page map of the island. America lived up to its promise—The Land of Freedom and Opportunity.

He pulled out the map, stuck it in his pocket and entered the store. It was darker inside than he'd expected. He was startled to see a woman behind a barred window in a caged cabinet. Above the window, the sign read U.S. Postal Service.

His stomach muscles tightened as he took in the smell of fresh baked goods and spicy but unfamiliar odors, which reminded him of how hungry he was. He found a refrigerated case and chose a small package of cheese. He gathered some bread, a carton of milk, and looked for cigarettes.

He worked his hand under his shirt and pulled out a wallet. It was soaked as was the money in it. The cashier stared vacantly at a little girl who was buying stamps. She never glanced in Dmitri's direction as she pushed buttons on a register and mumbled the price. Dmitri handed her a soggy twenty dollar bill and waited for his change. She placed a few pennies in his hand, and only then did she look at him.

"Have a nice day," she said absently.

"You have a nice day, too."

Outside, a group of teenagers lounged on the steps. Dmitri studied them, weighing their usefulness as he stared at the purple streak in the boy's hair and the jagged short cuts of the girls' hairstyles.

"Do any of you know if you can walk up this shore to the Sanctuary?"

"The what?" one of them asked. Dmitri produced the map and pointed at his destination. "Can you walk up there from here?"

"I guess so. Who's to know, right?" one of the girls said.

"It's all private property from here to there, and it's really rocky in places," the purple-haired boy added.

"Nobody'd care," another of the girls said.

Dmitri thanked them and headed to the beach. He opened the milk carton. The first whiff reminded him all milk does not taste the same. He wished he'd bought a Coke, but at the time he'd been in a hurry to get started back up the shore. He poured the liquid down his throat. The bitter salty taste lingered in his mouth as he pulled apart the bread. The cheese, he realized, would taste no better than the milk.

He knew Fyordorvitch would be waiting for him. He had to get back to the crate in the sand. The beach was filled with children running back and forth, women shouting at them, and out in the water a few swimmers moving slowly back and forth in the gentle surf. It wasn't long before he'd left the public beach. The sandy stretch gave way to uneven patches of pebbles and then to fist-sized rocks spread out across the shore as far as he could see. He picked his way cautiously looking for signs posted NO TRESPASSERS and steeled himself for the possibility of encountering fences or dogs or ax wielding caretakers.

3 | To Teach Another Is to Learn Yourself

The weather in Chicago was irrelevant. Standing in the classroom doorway, Beth Norton stared beyond the bare bulletin board in the back of the room, ignoring the squirming class of third graders who hovered over their chairs, ears straining for the sound of the dismissal bell that would send them charging forth into summer vacation. Picking at a small flap of skin on her finger, Miss Norton was ready to peel away the carefully maintained persona of a tough inner-city school teacher and settle into the sand along the beach of Jellicle Island for a well-deserved summer vacation.

Getting to that destination was one tedious chore. She planned to leave her car in the suburbs with her friend Tess, spend the night in Prairieview, and in the morning Tess would drive her to O'Hare.

She looked forward to the evening with Tess, and yet she dreaded it, too. Her childhood friend would serve a fancy and delicious gourmet dinner, her handsome husband would be solicitous toward Beth and obnoxiously tender and helpful toward his wife. After dinner he would prepare a pitcher of margaritas and excuse himself saying he knew they were eager to chat the night away. Tess would pry delicately, but relentlessly for details of Beth's love life. She would reveal more than she'd intended, thanks to the margaritas, and by the time the plane was flying over Buffalo, she would wish she'd talked less and listened more.

Then she'd turn her thoughts to her friends on Jellicle Island. Margaret never asked intrusive questions and Alicia was introspective and aloof. Beth would fill them in on Tess's life. Then, Beth would compare her life to theirs to make the inevitable judgment as to who was happiest, most successful, or, at the very least, most content with her lot.

Throughout their childhood, the four girls had been inseparable, summering on the Island, slumber parties providing the intimacy for shared secrets and dramas, until college had scattered them: Margaret ending up divorced in Ohio, Tess happily married in Prairieview, Beth single in Chicago. Alicia alone had remained on the Island, where she had developed into an artist of some renown.

Beth and Tess lived within ten miles of each other, but Tess's suburban life complete with husband and children, was far removed from Beth's hectic life as an elementary school teacher in the city. If Beth hadn't needed a place to store her car during her annual visit to Jellicle Island, she knew the friendship would have faded to a birthday telephone call and a Christmas card.

By the time Beth reached Boston, she would forgive herself for being envious of Tess's life. When the shuttle landed on the Island her father, Dr. Franklin Norton, and her mother, Sue-Ellyn, would be waiting for their only child. While her father scooped up the luggage, eager to get back to his garden, her mother would drape an arm around her shoulder and tell her how thin she looked. By morning she would be suggesting a new diet.

The ride from the airport would be filled with small talk—how had the school year gone, dinner plans for the following week, how was Tess managing with two small children, and had she made plans yet to see Margaret, who was there for the summer, and Alicia? By the time the smooth blacktop road narrowed to a gravel one, the family conversation would run out. Neither parent would broach the subject of her love life, but her Mom would bring it up in the morning.

The gravel road ended at the back of the house. A wide grassy path took up the course to the beach, then narrowed by a row of beech trees lining a mossy ledge. From there the path disappeared as the undergrowth spilled out beneath it and branches provided a canopy. Within yards of the densest growth, the ocean roared, the sea mist met the cool woodland air, and within seconds open space invited the inland traveler onto the shore.

Each summer the shoreline was different. Sometimes winter storms wracked the shore, throwing up great quantities of stones and drawing the sand back into the ocean. Other winters, waves brought heaps of sand up onto the beach and rewarded the summer visitor with miles of easy walking.

Beth's first trip to the beach each summer was not completed when she reached the open shoreline. She headed up the beach almost to the Point. There she made an abrupt turn inland. In the distance the rise of ridge deep in dark forest green rimmed the summer sky. The contrast was sharp and clean.

From the beach it was impossible to see a pond hidden by the beach grass. It was her private sanctuary. Protected all around, even against the ocean breezes, the surface barely rippled. No boat, no skipping stone, no hungry bird broke the surface. The hill beyond, too steep, too deep within private property to climb, provided a rear guard.

Beth visited the pond each summer on her first trip to the shore. It was an annual pilgrimage. There she shed the last insult of city life and attempted to heal the hurt of another year slipping away.

The dismissal bell blasted the daydream. Beth flattened herself against the open door as twenty-seven squealing children shouted goodbye to the third grade by throwing their arms into the air and trampling pell-mell toward freedom.

By the time she reached the office, it was three minutes past twelve. The office was deserted except for the principal, who sat at her desk and the clerk, who waited for the last teacher to collect her paycheck.

Beth reached into her mailbox and pulled out her annual evaluation. She moved to the counter, signed for the paycheck, and mumbled "have a nice vacation" to the clerk. Her VW Beetle was one of the last cars still parked in the lot. She hopped in, locked the door and ripped open the evaluation report and quickly scanned the columns of checkmarks. She tossed it in the backseat knowing all along what it said. She was a superior teacher.

Turning the key in the ignition, she heard a dull thud. The car would not start. Quickly she estimated the amount of time since the clerk announced the checks were waiting. She raced through the teachers' roster. She grabbed her purse, jumped out of the car, slammed the lock down, shut the door and ran toward the front of the school. The side entrance had locked behind her when she'd left.

In the front of the building she caught sight of Alan Craine's Jeep, and then she saw him coming out of the school.

"Alan," Beth shouted.

He turned and stood, watching as she ran toward him. Her skirt flew up in her face and she batted at it with her hand.

"My car won't start. Will you give me a ride to the corner service station?"

He cupped his hand to his ear, not hearing her. Caine was the only man on the faculty. He enjoyed the status. Most of the instructional aides, some of the faculty, and a few of the mothers knew where his tattoos were inscribed. Beth called him Mr. Caine, treated him professionally, and kept her distance.

"Could you drop me at the corner service station? My car's in the parking lot and it won't start."

Caine smiled all the way to the corner.

"I'll stay 'til you get it started," he told her.

Beth weighed the offer. By now her car was the only one in the parking lot in the middle of a school yard in the middle of a Chicago housing project. She was, without a doubt, at twelve thirty on a Friday afternoon of the last day in the school year, the only white woman in at least a three-mile radius.

"You really don't have to."

"Yeah, I do."

Beth turned to face the station manager.

"Hi," she stated gamely.

The black man continued to wipe grease from his hand and stared through her, waiting.

"My car's in the school parking lot. It won't start. Will you jump-start it?"

"Got to tow it first."

Beth reached for her wallet. "All right."

"Bullshit." Caine was out of his Jeep. He stretched his hand over Beth's, shielding the credit card she was already holding. "Get out of here, man. You can see the school from here. The car's in the parking lot—ain't nobody else there."

"Don't matter. I ain't sendin' nobody in there."

"Get the cables," Caine countered.

"Too risky."

"All she needs is a jump-start. It's a Bug."

The two men stood eyeing each other. Caine, muscular with his black skin glowing in a white and navy blue running suit. The garage mechanic, blacker and dressed in overalls. Caine's dark skin was radiant, the mechanic's skin sucked in light. He was the invisible man—facial features obscured by a layer of grease, his body lost in dirty, baggy dungarees.

He could be any one of a number of men Beth observed through her tightly closed car window as she drove down the street each morning on her way to school—father, husband, dope dealer, chop-shop operator, or pimp.

Beth didn't blink. Neither did Caine. At last, the mechanic backed away.

"You do buy some gas. I seen you once or twice," he acknowledged.

He eased into his tow truck. Beth put the credit card back in her wallet and followed Caine to his Jeep. For this insurance, Beth purchased gas at this station once or twice a year, just as the man said.

The battery in a Beetle is under the back seat. The perfect ghetto car. It is impossible to steal the battery without breaking into the car. Beth and Caine were the only two faculty members who had not had their car batteries stolen over the years.

Caine pulled his Jeep up behind the Beetle. The mechanic pulled his truck up alongside it. Within seconds after attaching the cables, the Bug started with a familiar portable mixer whir. Beth jumped into the driver's seat and stepped on the accelerator. She waved to Caine and started up the street following the mechanic.

Leaving the motor running in the gas station driveway, she leaned over the passenger's seat to collect her purse. She drew in her breath. She'd left the purse in the Jeep. Caine was probably on the Dan Ryan by now. Twisting and turning back and forth, checking the floor in front, pulling at the still up-ended back seat, she caught sight of him sitting in his Jeep watching her. A smile spread across his face.

"This must be your lucky day," he said. "I just happened to see your purse on the seat before I headed to Tennessee."

This could cost her. She was relieved beyond words to see the purse, but sensing the frozen status of her indebtedness, Beth checked herself before implying too great a reward waiting for him in September.

"You are a knight in shining armor, Mr. Caine. Thanks again. Have a great summer."

He handed her the purse through the open window and sped out of the station. Beth unzipped her purse and reached for the wallet containing her last paycheck for three months. Her only cash was a ten dollar bill folded behind a mirror—an emergency stash.

Jabbing behind the mirror for the money, she caught the edge of the glass between her nail and the flesh at the end of her finger, and blood squirted out across the edge of the credit card she needed to give the service station attendant. Quickly she wiped it across her skirt, sucked at the finger, and handed the card and the bill to the waiting mechanic. Without expression he pocketed the ten and headed into the station with her credit card to pay for the jump-start.

"I'll wait here," she said. "I don't want to turn off the car."

As long as the car was running, it would get her back to her apartment on the north side of the city. When she reached the street in front of her apartment building, she was rewarded with a parking space near the entrance. Leaving the engine running she struggled with a box of school supplies she'd brought home for the summer for safe keeping. She dropped the box in the front entrance and went out to turn off the car. If it didn't start in the morning, she'd have to take a cab to Tess's house. To hell with the car.

The school year was over. She poured herself a glass of wine. What a year. Her students had been outrageous. Her student teacher had had a nervous breakdown, and materials lent to her were returned in disarray by an agitated mother. The mother seemed to think it was Beth's fault the young woman had come undone.

She picked up a photograph of a man smiling broadly and set it down on the coffee table in front of her. She hadn't seen him since their last date in February, but she'd bet her paycheck he'd show up before school opened in September.

In the morning, the car started. A quick trip to the pharmacy for an allergy prescription ended when a car rammed the back of Beth's car as she waited in the left turn lane. She hit the cab in front of her.

Stunned, she sat passively in the car until the driver she hit began pounding on the hood of the Bug. She thought the pummeling would stop the car for good, and when she took her foot off the choke it burped and stopped running. Now she was angry. She jumped out of the car.

"I didn't run into you on purpose. The guy behind me hit me first," she screamed into the face of the raging cab driver.

They both turned to stare at the driver behind her who had pulled his car away from her bumper and eased into a parking place in front of Walgreen's. The driver was leaning into the engine. The open hood hid him from view.

"Fuckin' idiot," the cab driver said in a thick accent.

Beth's sliced finger ached, her nose was stuffy, and the only man in her life was a cad. An assessment she made only in moments of extreme self-pity. This was the moment. She began to sob.

A traffic policeman ambled over, blew his whistle and swung his club at the cars behind her. They began to rush ahead.

"Lady, are you hurt?"

Beth shook her head no, tears streaming down her face.

"Stop your cryin', then. Get back in your car and get out of here," the cop said. "Nothin' happened. That car over there hit you. Nothin' happened. You hit this cab here. Nothin' happened. You're blockin' traffic. Move along. There's not a scratch on ya."

Beth climbed back in her car. Her legs trembled so she could barely push in the clutch. The Bug started. She pulled into the traffic, hesitated at the end of the block and turned west toward her apartment. She drove slowly. The plastic seat made her back perspire.

"Son of a bitch," she screamed and banged on the steering wheel. No one in the car next to her bothered to look. There wasn't a parking space on her street, and she turned the corner to park in a grocery store lot. Once inside her apartment she threw her purse and keys down and reached for the telephone and dialed Tess's number.

"Hello? Nick? Is your Mommy there? Oh, hi Michael. This is Beth. I thought I'd come out a little earlier than I'd planned. Is that all right?"

Tess's husband, Michael, was always so cordial. Must be nice, she thought.

Within the hour, Beth pulled into their driveway. Tess stood on the porch waving an exaggerated wave at her. "I hope you haven't eaten lunch," Tess shouted toward her as she got out of the car. "If I don't get out of this house in the next ten minutes, I'm going to lose my mind."

"And I was thinking if I didn't get into your house in the next ten minutes I was going to lose *my* mind," Beth replied.

"Well, come in for a minute. Do you have to go to the bathroom? Listen to me. Once you're a mother, all you do is ask prying questions."

They laughed, hugged, and walked into the house arm in arm. "How was the traffic? Saturday, not so bad I suppose. I thought we'd drive over to the shopping center and have lunch."

From another room, Beth heard a child shriek. "I wanna go, too. Don't leave me."

"Nick, your father is here."

"I don't care. I want to go, too.

"No."

Beth escaped into the bathroom. She could still hear Tess negotiating with her son.

"I'll bring you a surprise."

"A toy."

"Maybe."

"I don't want nothing to eat."

"Anything to eat."

"No."

Tess turned as Beth entered the room. "Can you believe I have a child who doesn't like to eat?"

"He's awfully cute. Where's the baby?"

"She's out back with Michael. We'd better slip out before she notices. Go find Daddy, Nick."

"No."

“Nick. I’m going to count to three.”

“Hurry, Beth. Let’s get out of here before they’re all in here.” Tess grabbed her purse, kissed her son, and Beth followed her out the door.

“We don’t have quaint little places like you have in the city. Sorry to rush you out of there like that, but you can see he’s at that stage. Neither of them wants to go anywhere without their Mommy, and they don’t want Mommy to go anywhere at all. I was so happy when Michael said you were on your way. I was down in the basement sitting on a pile of laundry just boo-hooing. I can’t go to the bathroom alone. I can’t sit down in a chair for ten minutes of solitude.

“Michael came home last night, plops down in his chair and tells the kids not to bother him because he wants to read the newspaper. Then he smiles at me and says ‘TGIF,’ as if it made any difference to me. Tuesday. Thursday. Saturday. I don’t get a weekend. Every day is the same for me. Wake up too early, kids don’t nap at the same time. By the time they’re asleep at night, I’ve got to pick up the house. And if I try to stay up and read or something adult-like, Nick wakes up with a nightmare, or the baby gets sick. I don’t have one second for me.”

Beth listened without interrupting. Tess pulled into a shopping center parking lot and turned off the ignition. “This is as good as it gets. It’s almost two o’clock. It shouldn’t be busy.”

It was a French café with red checkered tablecloths, a blackboard on an easel displaying the day’s specials, and a long glass-encased sideboard filled with cheesecakes, tarts, quiches, and croissants. Neatly stacked rows of bottled fruit juices stood nearby. Beth’s stomach growled. She didn’t remember eating anything after the wine the night before.

“My treat. I’m so happy to see you. I wish you’d come out more often, Beth. Why, huh? To see an old friend who’s become a raving maniac.”

It was too much for Beth to concentrate on her choice of food and respond with the appropriate words of sympathy as Tess chattered. She told the woman behind the counter she’d have the same thing Tess had chosen.

They moved to the cashier who rang up the orders. Beth tried to pay, but Tess shoved her aside. “My treat. You’re a poor, starving teacher. Save the money for your strike fund. Let's go back where we can chat and nobody will notice us."

When they were settled and Tess had removed the trays, they laughed at the large stack of napkins Tess had pulled absent-mindedly from the holder on the counter.

"I'm just so used to mopping up after everyone. Tell me all about yourself. How was school this year, or dare I ask?"

"It wasn't so good. I—"

"Oops. I forgot to get forks. I'll be right back." Tess jumped up from her seat. Beth went ahead and answered to the empty chair. "It was lousy. Really lousy."

Tess returned. "I'll settle down in a minute. I honestly think I forget how grown-ups act. I heard you. It was lousy. Are you still seeing Ricky-Ticky?"

Beth chewed the roast beef croissant slowly. She didn't want to talk about him.

Tess went on without an answer. "I know. I know. I shouldn't say things like that, and you know I can't stop myself. We've been friends for too many years for me not to be candid. I can appreciate your need to find someone, but character, Beth. Think about character." A tear tickled down her cheek.

"Tess, what is it?"

"Nothing. That's the stupid part of it. Here I am trying to tell you how to live your life and I don't know how to live my own."

"Is something wrong with you and Michael?"

"I don't think so. It's just I don't do anything. I mean important things. I love my children, I love being able to stay home with them, but sometimes I feel like I'm going to miss out on being me."

"I don't have a lot of important me time either, Tess. I just do lesson plans all weekend and struggle to get through the week and into another weekend. Then I spend it grading papers."

"I would like to be a brain surgeon. Part-time, of course. Just once at a cocktail party filled with women lawyers and MBAs and yes, school teachers, I'd like to say, 'why, yes. I AM a nuclear physicist. Why do you ask?'"

"Oh, Tess. You'll always be sane, sensible Tess. Lighten up. You think too much."

"You just wait. You'll meet somebody and have a couple of kids and wish you were getting dressed up and going to work every day. But not Rick. Promise me that."

"Tess, let's go. I want to see those adorable kids of yours and stare at your handsome husband."

"First, let's walk around and look in the stores. I can't do that with the kids."

They spent the next couple of hours engaged in happy conversation, commenting on shoes and fashion. When they returned to the house, Michael was in the backyard lighting the grill. They ate hamburgers and potato salad from a carton. Beth thought about the gourmet dinners she'd remembered Tess preparing before Nick and the baby arrived. They agreed that the wine at lunch had been enough. Michael drank a beer, and Beth was actually glad the pitcher of margaritas she'd been looking forward to never arrived. She didn't feel like any more heart-to-heart conversations with Tess.

In the morning, everyone went to the airport. Michael drove because Tess admitted she didn't like to drive on the expressway. Beth sat in the backseat wedged between two car seats. When they reached O'Hare, she blew them all a kiss and pulled her luggage into the airport.

She didn't think about Tess over Buffalo or even when she landed at Logan. The shuttle took off with a roar. She opened her eyes briefly to see a pointillist's vision of colored sails looking like pieces of confetti floating across the water and she wondered why the sails across Lake Michigan were mainly white. From the plane's window, she studied the dense dark green abruptly pocked here and there with aquamarine in the rectangular and circular patterns of swimming pools. Then an expanse of sparkling open water, more green from the island's trees, and the plane landed on Jellicle Island.

From the plane, Beth could see her parents standing near the fence. By the time she'd passed through the gate and into the tiny terminal, they were standing at the entrance to the parking lot.

"How was the flight?" they chorused.

"Bumpy over Buffalo. No one told me Air New England doesn't exist anymore."

"You bought the ticket," Dr. Norton reminded her.

"Yes, Dad. They just didn't mention the name of the airline. It's a commuter shuttle."

"I've invited the Cunninghams for a cocktail. Margaret's here with her son."

"I know. I talked to her last week. And Tess sends her love."

"You must call Alicia. We never see her. Her art is selling very well, I hear."

"Yeah, I'll check in with her, too. But what I really want is a nice long quiet walk along the shore. I want the weather to stay warm and sunny my entire vacation."

"You know what they say, 'if you don't like the weather wait fifteen minutes'."

"Yeah, well, the weather is relevant to my relative contentment."

* * *

The first hour of Dmitri's hike back up the shoreline toward The Sanctuary, he admired the rocky shore, enjoyed the salty breeze, confident he'd recover the crate marked as it was by the orange buoy. Each time he rounded a curve on the shore, he was confronted with another long rocky beach. After four hours, when he'd expected to be at the recovery point, and the shore stretched on, he pulled the map from his pocket and concluded it wasn't drawn to scale. It was then he heard the two giant dogs growl.

4 | Don't Ask Questions About Fairy Tales

In New England, the wild wood lily doesn't grow in the woods. Preferring solitude, it stands alone in the meadows and thickets. The flower is a brilliant vermillion as long as it is left unpicked, but once the stem is snapped it fades and withers.

Alicia spotted the brilliant petals blazing in the midst of the thick beach grass near the pond. She wanted to get back to it before it disappeared because she'd tried to paint the lily from memory the previous winter only to discover the colors she remembered were nothing like the real plant. In the meadow, the lily fired a memory of firecrackers or Christmas, but translated to paper the color had mutated into something bland. She wanted to sit next to the flower with her pallet and mix and blend until she found the exact shade that would instantly be recognized.

To get the proportions right, she did not need to stand with her arm outstretched saluting the sky with the tip of her brush. She most assuredly did not want an audience. She needed time and solitude and her unerring eye to capture the hue so she could transfer its exact shade of brilliance to paper.

She preferred winter solitude for serious painting. She could not imagine setting out her paints among the ebb and flow of strangers visiting the island in summer. She was delighted to catch sight of the lily basking in the obscure thicket near the pond on a warm June day.

Alicia knew the seasons and the shapes of the land as a spectrum of sunlight and shade. It was true that the island was forever on the move. The beaches varied from tide to tide and were radically altered from storm to storm. Alicia calculated the changes by the measuring of shadow and illumination and captured the essence of Jellicle Island in her paintings.

When Islanders viewed her work, they recognized the rocks and beaches as easily as a tourist identified the Harbor Light on a postcard at the end of a tour. Alicia Barrett watercolors were beginning to appear in homes throughout Jellicle Island. Her summer patrons requested duplicates to carry home with them to mainland houses. That, of course, was not possible. She could not, would not, try to replicate a painting.

Her first gallery show for the summer would be a sell-out, the gallery's owner assured her. Together they had gone through the odd assortment of paintings left in the studio, gathering the remaining works to supplement the show. Alicia worried about the price she might pay for fame and fortune. She took back the sketches of the lily, arguing they were not true and rebuffed the gallery owner's suggestion that an "off-islander" wouldn't know the difference. She was building a reputation for veracity, and she wouldn't have it sullied.

Alicia wedged a bottle of water between a box of paints and her sketch book. She checked the brushes, rolled them into a reed mat, and nudged them between a peanut butter sandwich and a bottle of ginger ale. She gave the backpack a little shake to see all was tight, then she pulled it up onto her back.

Her dogs, two large black Labrador retrievers, sniffed the backpack. Then they paced the room in anticipation of a romp through the woods.

"I hope there aren't a lot of people down there," she told them.

Betta wagged her tail sympathetically. Browning took a long slurp of water. Then the two of them stood impatiently at the door.

"I should call Beth. No, I should get to the beach, right pups?"

Alicia walked the quarter mile to the Norton property line without making up her mind whether to stop. Beth would be there for several weeks, she thought. The lily might be gone by evening. At the fork in the road, she adjusted the backpack and continued the trek to the beach. The dogs trotted ahead, circling back occasionally for a second sniff here and there.

Alicia concentrated on the woodsy smells, savoring the sweet odor of wildflowers and wrinkling her nose at the pungent whiffs of skunk cabbage. The woods were cool, and she did not walk fast enough to work up a sweat. She would break out from the trees at the end of the path, walk up the shoreline to the spot where she'd observed the lily in the open field near the pond, and if all went well, instinct mixed with sunlight would correctly match the elusive flower with a mixture from her palette. Then she would stop and see Beth on her way home. If not, she would sit there all day until she concocted the bright orangey red and made it her own.

Stepping out of the woods, she felt the ocean breezes brush across her face. She gazed up and down the shore, pleased to see no one. She rarely wore sunglasses because they changed the light, so she shielded her eyes to stare out to sea, memorizing the play of sunlight upon the quiet water. When she looked down the shore, she saw the lone figure walking toward her.

From this distance, she could only assume it to be a man, the broad shoulders swinging forward and back as the figure made its way up the shore, pants rolled to the knees, shoes in hand. She could have stayed ahead and disappeared up into the dune to the thicket and the lily. Instead, she pulled the backpack from her shoulder and set it in the sand. She squinted into the bright sunlight, watching his approach.

She could see now that it was a man. He walked faster than a beachcomber, slower than a jogger. The shoes he held looked expensive. Leather. Not the usual beach wear.

"Howdy," he said as he approached. He was wearing a raw silk suit, a rough weave. Armani, she thought. She liked it.

"Good morning."

"I had no idea this island was so charming."

"You don't read travel brochures."

He chuckled in an odd, grandfatherly way. Yet he was about her age, she estimated.

"Do you live around here?" he asked.

"Yes, I do live here. All year."

"I'm from the West Coast. I was in Boston when I thought I'd see what the islands around here are like. At least one island.

"You chose the best, but perhaps we should encourage people to tour the others."

"Then you don't rely on us pesky tourists to earn a living?"

Ah, but she did, though it was cheeky of him to inquire. "And how do you earn your living?" She could ask cheeky questions, too.

"Would you care to stroll down the beach with me?" he replied ignoring her question.

She glanced toward the thicket, wondering what had made her sit down in the sand. She had to admit she was hungry for conversation, yet she hadn't stopped to see Beth. Maybe she was spending too much time alone. Normal, friendly conversation eluded her.

Here was a man as rare as the wild wood lily—no running shoes, no pullover sweater with its obligatory worn elbows. She hadn't adequately psyched herself up to experiment with tints anyway. All the way to the beach, she'd been telling herself it would be too crowded to paint, and she'd been right.

"Let me show you something special. You can't see it from here."

"I'd be delighted."

The dogs flanked her with their ears cocked, as if they understood the conversation. They understood it to be friendly and charged off again, in and out of the water that slowly rolled onto the shore, barking at the waves as they broke onto the beach.

"I have a favorite view most people miss."

"The view here is as good as Carmel."

Silenced by the absurdity that anyone would compare this place to anywhere else, let alone the West Coast, she hoisted her backpack onto her back and set out ahead of him.

The Point and her beloved pond were protected as a natural land preserve. People had access to the woods from the Sanctuary's parking lot. They could strike out for the well-marked trails curving around the rim of the pond, but Alicia doubted many of them noticed the quiet pool of water. Some people brought binoculars and searched for birds, but most tromped through the woods discarding wrappers and cans, continuing past the markers clearly pointing in other directions, noted the uninhabited beach and ended up in the ocean for a prohibited swim. It was the job of the caretaker for the Sanctuary to keep them moving.

When they neared the Point she turned inland toward the tall beach grass. He followed, walking carefully in his bare feet. She walked over the tight strands of seaweed, dry and crunching under her step. The tall, slender reeds of grass reached her shoulders. They were a protected species. Their roots dug deep into the sand, holding it there in a conservation effort to block the island from collapsing more rapidly into the sea.

Until the last moment, the view was the same: a long stretch of sand and sea, the deep green rising from inland, the cloudless blue of the sky above. Then up over one last rise in the sand and there it was, nestled in the hallow of a glacier cut-lagoon, Norton's Pond.

He smiled. She studied the sheer glaze of the surface. He searched the deep line of trees enveloping the other three sides of the pond.

"A perfect, timeless scene. I'd never have found it without you. Thank you." He swept a low bow in front of her. "Frederick J. for Joseph Lewis."

"Alicia Barrett."

"Alicia, I'd like to invite you to lunch, but I see all the tables are taken. A careless oversight on my part. I should have made a reservation."

The dogs, who knew all along where she was headed, reappeared from the woods and took short slurps of the brackish water, and then lay down in the warm sand which stretched like a miniature beach into the water.

"I've interfered with your plans. I really would like to take you to dinner. Is that," he paused, "possible?"

He was right. There was no bistro. A charming, romantic island this was if one traveled *prêt-à-porter*. Here they were, a chance meeting by the seashore, five miles from the nearest exotic bottle of wine. What was needed was a fade-out to dessert, but what remained was a long hike up the beach, or one peanut butter sandwich and a warm bottle of ginger ale.

She considered the invitation. She'd shown him a piece of the island she considered her own special sanctuary, and he'd rudely compared it to Carmel. But he'd recognized the spectacular beauty of the quiet pond, and she liked him for that.

"How about a glass of wine and some bluefish paté at my place?" She could even surprise herself. This was not Alicia Barrett, the quiet artist who had no time for anyone. For this man she had all the time in the world, and he seemed to sense it.

"I'll bring the wine."

"Unless you have a cellar in the trunk of your car, you'd have to drive to the other side of the island to find a liquor store."

"I'm from California. I'll drive an hour for a bottle of Voslau."

"Where is your car?"

"That way." He pointed toward the parking lot at the entrance to the Sanctuary.

"Then you saw the pond coming down the trail."

"Not your pond. I had my eye ahead, on the ocean. The effect comes, as you showed me, from coming up on it from the shore. It is miniature perfection, an unspoiled scene from eons ago."

"For someone not knowing anything about the island, you picked the best day trip."

"I can't take any credit. I was waved off the boat by the ferry operators and found myself in a bumper-to-bumper procession out of town. I followed the road and it led to a dead-end circle around a magnificent old oak. I circled back; around the previous bend in the road, I saw the sign for the Sanctuary. The path to the beach was well-marked. Shall we get the car?"

"I have the dogs."

"It's not my car. It's Mr. Hertz's."

"Then by all means. Anyway, they're very well-behaved dogs."

It was an easy walk to the parking lot, a graveled section of flat land at the entrance to the nature preserve known as The Sanctuary. The way out to the main road was a steep climb up the ridge that made the dogs sit back on their haunches until the compact car reached the paved surface of the road. "Turn right and drive back to the oak," Alicia directed.

"I saw the row of mail boxes. There must be a lot of houses back here."

"Only a few. Just go straight ahead and you'll turn right… right here, that's it. Go slow or you'll tear out your muffler. Now stop a minute and look over here."

"Extraordinary," he said as he stroked his mustache.

"Sometimes I can see a snippet of water from my house, but not often. It depends on how the trees are blowing in the wind."

The road ended abruptly in her yard. The dogs barked a salutary yip and waited impatiently to be released from the car. Alicia opened the front door to her house. The first floor was divided in the center by the stairway leading up to her bedroom and studio. To the right was the kitchen and dining room and to the left was the living room.

The dogs pushed in around them and headed for the kitchen where loud gulping noises soon were heard as they emptied their water dishes.

"Sounds good. Could I trouble you for a glass of water?"

His eyes scanned the dining room table, which was piled with papers, various sizes and all blank. Alicia gestured toward the living room and went into the kitchen for the water.

"I think you'll find this tastier than Voslau. It's Jellicle Island well water."

He was standing before the mantel. "An interesting *gouache*," he observed.

"Ah, then you know something about technique?" she smiled.

"Materials, yes, but not technique. A local artist?"

"Yes," was all she said.

"Can you think of a restaurant where I could take you? The bluefish paté sounds interesting, but I'm starving. While you think, could I use your bathroom?"

"Yes, of course. It's at the top of the stairs."

As soon as he'd disappeared up the stairs, Alicia searched the living room, her eyes darting from wall to wall. Another woman might check her face in the mirror, but Alicia knew her house reflected more of her spirit than her face did.

"You're an artist!" he shouted as he bounded down the stairs.

And you're a snoop, she thought as she turned to confront him. Then she remembered the coffee can of brushes she'd left in the bathroom sink.

He stepped lightly from the last step and headed for the living room, searching the walls now for more evidence of her work. A couple of watercolors hung above the light switch just inside the room, but the majority of the work belonged to artists she admired. A Turner poster from the Tate Gallery dominated the space above the sofa. The *gouache* he'd spotted was hers, but she was disinclined to mention it.

He walked around the room, stopping before the watercolors, skipping over the prints, and moving past the originals signed by other artists. He stopped by the light switch and bent forward studying the work carefully.

"You're good. Water is difficult to get right."

"You said you were from Carmel. Are you an artist?"

"No, but I've seen a lot of watercolors depicting the Pacific. Let me see some more of your work."

She had always worked with watercolors, and she had always been satisfied to limit herself to that medium. She was surprised that she was struck by a sudden desire to be an artist of monumental works. At this moment she wished she could point out the window to a huge beamed sculpture stretching forty feet in the air.

"There are some paintings on the dining room table, under the newsprint. I paint watercolors and a few *gouaches*."

"I thought that might be yours." He turned back to the painting he'd first noticed. "If I knew the area better, I'm sure I would look at it and name the spot where you painted it. Even brief patches of water in the hands of a master show uniqueness."

Alicia was pleased, but she said nothing and thought of the wide open space in her front yard.

She tried again. "So, what do you do?"

"I'm working on an MBA. The company I work for cheerfully picks up the fees, so I am more or less cheerfully taking them up on their generosity. I don't know about you, but I'm really hungry. Name the place, and we'll be off."

"I'm going to change out of my woodsy clothes. The Island is very informal. Formal dress usually means you must put on your shoes."

She looked down at his feet, at the expensive leather shoes he'd carried through the sharp grass. She'd been right to think he was a banker, she thought as she ascended the stairs. She chose a bright pink gauze dress with a full skirt and an off-the-shoulder gypsy neckline, the silver necklace a friend had made, and a pair of earrings purchased at Bloomingdale's in celebration of the first major sale she'd made. The outfit would help camouflage the banker's silk suit—definitely not the standard Jellicle Island style. It'd been a long time since she'd worn anything but jeans and over-sized shirts, she thought as she returned to the living room.

"You look lovely. Maybe I should put my jacket back on?" he asked.

He'd returned to his car while she dressed. The crisp white cotton shirt with the fancy monogram was hidden beneath a sweater.

"Life's fairly casual around here."

"And where are we going?"

"The Wapatoo Inn."

"The wapa who?"

"It's the most popular restaurant on the island. Good food, nice atmosphere. We have to take our own wine, but there's a bottle on the mantel." She'd purchased it in the fall to take to a small gathering of friends, but she'd come down with a cold and the bottle had been sitting on the mantel ever since.

He held the car door for her, then moved swiftly around to the driver's side and hopped in, started the engine, and sped out of her front yard at an alarming rate. The gravel road slowed him down a bit, but he picked up speed as soon as the car moved on to the blacktop. He sped around the curve at the entrance to the Sanctuary Trail. She worried about the geese that would be wandering in the road by the farm around the next curve.

At an intersection she pointed down the road. "There used to be a gallery down there. I exhibited my work there one summer, but I never sold anything. People who are headed up here are generally going to the Sanctuary to hike, and don't stop to buy art."

Alicia agreed that the island roads were just as he had described them. There was a main blacktop road with side roads joining it, and private drives hidden in the trees that lined the way into town.

"Turn left and turn again into the A&P lot. We're between ferries, and it's about the only place you can find a parking spot in this town."

He followed her directions, parked, and moved around the car to open the door for her. She was part way out of the car by the time he got there. They crossed the street. He touched the small of her back gallantly, and she felt comfortable in his presence.

The Wapatoo Inn did not take reservations, but they were guided immediately to a table on the porch. He held her chair for her and then settled into his own.

"What do you recommend?"

"Fish."

He looked at the menu and chortled.

"You do eat fish, don't you?"

"Yes. I guess you'd be out of luck on an island if you didn't."

"You'd be surprised at the number of Islanders who won't touch it."

The waiter appeared and stood attentively, pad in hand.

Alicia hated the taste of mesquite, but she loved swordfish, and at $17.98 a pound, she didn't buy it often.

"I'll have the swordfish."

"I'll have the swordfish, too."

The waiter nodded. He lifted the bottle of wine they'd brought and showed the label to her companion as if he'd brought it to them from the wine cellar. Frederick studied the label intently while Alicia tried to recall what it was. At last, he nodded.

"This will be fine," he said as he winked at Alicia.

Alicia was relieved to see the waiter start to uncork the bottle. For all she could remember, it might have had a screw top. The waiter handed the cork to Frederick. He sniffed it appreciatively, then handed it to Alicia. Next, the waiter poured a small amount of the wine into Frederick's glass. He swirled it around, and the waiter, having shown off his *sommelier* skills, moved to another table. Frederick set the glass down untouched.

"I really enjoyed the view of that pond. Can you walk from the town back up to that beach?"

"You can. I've done it. But most of the shoreline is very rocky and, of course, private property. You keep thinking you've arrived, and then there's another bend in the shoreline. It takes forever to get back to where we met on the beach near the Sanctuary parking lot.

They tapped glasses.

"Thank you for having dinner with me," Frederick said.

She took a sip. He took a longer one. He choked, reached for his napkin, and removed his glasses. An acidic sting filled her mouth.

"It appears to be a tad dry."

"Islanders believe the only liquid good enough to drink with local swordfish is local water."

"I think the natives know what they're talking about."

Both of them were hungry, and they set about eating the fish with total concentration. The Wapatoo Inn was filled with noisy chatter. Too bad about the wine, Alicia told herself. It was probably a touch of reality. Picking up strangers on the beach was out of character. Frederick plunged his fork into the last bit on his plate.

"I have to make a phone call. I'll be back in a jiffy." He stood up and disappeared before Alicia had time to comment.

She settled into finishing the fish, the creamed potatoes, the cole slaw, another piece of bread and then a long drink of water. The waiter refilled her glass. Where could he have gone? And what was she doing here when she barely had time for her friends? She promised herself she would call Beth in the morning.

The waiter arrived with a triple decked slice of chocolate cake with a four-inch layer of whipped cream on top.

"I didn't order this," Alicia said.

"The gentleman ordered it for you. He had to make a phone call, and we don't have a public telephone."

"Oh, so where did he go?"

"I, ah, I don't know."

"In that case, I'll have the cake."

It was like intermission at a good play. She had time to analyze the day's events up to now. Whatever possessed her to take him to her favorite spot on the island, and then to her favorite inn? He would have to drive her home, but she didn't have to invite him in.

The dining room was beginning to empty. She checked her watch. It was nine-thirty. The Inn closed at ten. She checked her watch again. Some day she'd laugh about how she'd been stiffed for a large bill on a small island.

She wondered if they took credit cards. She thought her Shell Oil card was all she had with her. Was she sufficiently well-known on this Island to settle this gracefully? On the other hand, was she wanting to remain an anonymous tourist?

The bottle of wine. It had been an omen. She always saw patterns too late when it came to judging people, especially men. She had a muse. There were days when her paintings burst onto the paper. She merely touched a spot here and there. She worked quickly, painted for long hours, and was surprised at the detail in her work when she finished. On other days she couldn't paint a stroke. The white paper looked back at her, and the brush was heavy in her hand. Her muse did well for her artwork but was damnably silent when it came to men. She couldn't blame her muse. It was Alicia who had boldly set this scene.

"Excuse me, but ah, we're getting ready to close."

"Yes, I see. My friend must have had problems finding a working phone."

"The waiter stood tapping the bill on the palm of his hand, a nervous expression on his face. He set it on the table in front of her and turned away.

She opened her purse and pulled out her wallet. She had brought her MasterCard after all. The waiter returned and took the tray with the bill and the card without looking at her. She let out a sigh. He probably thought it was a scam and she was part of it. MasterCard reassured both of them. It was ten o'clock when he returned with her receipt. He'd waited as long as he could. She picked up her purse and walked out of the inn.

It was a warm summer evening. The salt air smelled sweet and familiar. She'd been trying to find a way to dump him, and he'd dumped her very nicely. Served her right, she thought. Now she had to find a way home. She certainly wasn't going to walk up the shore.

"Alicia!" She turned to see Frederick. "God, I'm so sorry. I thought I'd slip out and buy us a bottle of wine. I didn't realize they don't sell liquor in this town, and the traffic was awful. I figured I'd be ten to fifteen minutes at the most. And I didn't think they'd close at ten o'clock on a Saturday night. Sorry. I owe you for dinner."

She was relieved to see him. He was an odd mixture of wrong-era formality and California cool. She was amused to see his distress. She laughed, her pride restored. Reaching for his hand, she found herself in his embrace.

"And where is this bottle?"

"In the car, which is probably being towed as we speak. There are no parking spaces on this island. May I drive you home, assuming I still have a car?"

"Please do."

He ushered her into the car, made an illegal u-turn, and sped out of town. Alicia settled into her seat with a smile. He looked over at her, and gave a short burst of his odd laugh. Then he rolled his shoulders back and forth and twisted his neck, moving his muscles to release the tension.

When they entered her yard, the dogs set up a howl. She hurried into the house to reassure them. The fog was thick, and in the distance the fog horn let out its mournful warning.

He produced the bottle and handed it to her. "I've bought a bottle of Geneva. Can you find a couple of glasses?"

She studied the label. She couldn't read a word of it. "What is this?"

"It's Dutch. Made from juniper berries."

She took a sip. "This is … strong."

They settled down next to each other on the sofa, the dogs stretched out before them. Betta scratched her ear, and her leg made a loud thumping sound on the bare pine floor.

"You have a delightful house. And you are a lovely lady."

"I think I'll exchange this for some bourbon," she replied.

When she returned he was pulling a ferry schedule from his pocket. "I'd better check the departure time."

Alicia took a sip of the bourbon. "The last ferry left an hour ago," she said.

5 | When in Doubt, Shut Up

"Frodo. Frodo. Come here this instant."

Dmitri looked up on a dune to a woman who stood with her hand on a wide brimmed straw hat. The dog put its tail between its legs and slunk off in her direction.

"You're all right, aren't you?" she called to Dmitri.

"Fine," Dmitri said, but he held his hand behind his back. The woman turned her back on him for a minute, talking to someone Dmitri couldn't see hidden in the beach grass. Then a girl appeared and scooted down the dune and stopped in front of him.

"He bit you, didn't he? The dog is a nuisance, but he was Grandfather's, and now that he's gone no one dares tell Nana she should get rid of him. Please come up to the house and let's have a look at it."

"It's okay. I'll get it looked at when I get home."

"No, I'm afraid that won't do. Grandmother wouldn't want someone walking around the island telling people he was bitten by one of her dogs. My mother's a doctor, but she's off island at the moment. And my father's an attorney, and you're on our property, so you have to do what we say."

Dmitri had no choice. He followed the girl up a wooden stairway implanted in a dune. A house stood five hundred yards back from the beach. A dirt road disappeared into the tree line.

"Come on. Let's get some peroxide on that," the grandmother called out.

Dmitri followed the girl. She had long brown hair tied in a braid that started at the crown of her head and ended midway down her back. When she reached the house, she opened the door and stood back for Dmitri. She held out her hand toward her grandmother. "I'll put Frodo in the library," she said.

"You'll do no such thing. He has to apologize." She marched along with a walking stick in her hand and the dog followed meekly behind her.

"If it's any consolation, he's never bitten the same person twice," the girl said.

"Dmitri entered the house and found himself in a large kitchen. It was a bright, sunny room, with one wall pushed back to make room for a greenhouse filled with plants. The grandmother motioned with her walking stick to a closed door.

"There's the bathroom. Wash it off carefully, then let me take a look." The woman followed him into the bathroom and stared at his hand. "Oh, dear. This is very bad. You're a most taciturn young man. I think we'd better run you up to the hospital for stitches."

Dmitri pulled his hand from the running water. "It's not bad. A little peroxide will do, and I'll be on my way."

"No, my son-in-law is an attorney. He'd have my head if I didn't handle this properly. Don't worry. I'll pay the hospital bill. I practically have a running account."

Dmitri had the identification purloined from the hapless observer aboard the *Zori*, but he had no idea what kind of questions the hospital might ask. She handed him a white towel. "Wrap it up," she said. "If you don't mind, please go out the kitchen door so I can lock it after you."

With a dog like Frodo, it seemed an unnecessary precaution, Dmitri thought. He saw a white sedan parked in the driveway. He thought about refusing to go, but it would only draw more attention to him.

The old woman took a long time getting into the car, but once they were on the road she drove quickly. They pulled off the main road and headed up the driveway to the hospital and followed a sign that read EMERGENCY.

The Emergency Room was crowded with people wrapped in bandages or towels; children howled, and men and women paced back and forth. Dmitri turned to the granddaughter who'd accompanied them.

"What's going on here? What happened to all these people?"

"Oh, it's nothing. Just Fourth of July on the island. Most of them fell off their mopeds. The island is trying to get them banned, but my grandfather used to say it would be easier if they just killed themselves off. Actually, this isn't too bad. I've seen it much worse." She held a clipboard that had been handed to her.

"So, what's your address?"

Dmitri reached for the identification in his rear pocket.

"I'm left handed. Can you fill it out?"

She took the ID and attempted to read through the plastic which was crumpled and wet from time in the water.

"I can't really read this. What's your name?"

"Peter Smith," Dmitri said.

"And your date of birth?"

"April 7, 1960."

"You don't look that old."

"How long is this going to take? I've really got to get going. Tell your grandmother everything is ok. Thanks for the help." He turned, but the room was so crowded he couldn't move quickly. She reached out and grabbed his arm.

"Look, I know this is a pain in the ass, but you're going to have to go through with this. The damned dog is important to my grandmother, and my family spends a lot of time getting it and my grandmother out of trouble. As my father would say, 'We live in an age of litigation.' You walk out of here, and the next thing we know you're suing us. Sorry. Here comes the doctor, anyway. My grandmother has a bit of clout."

"Are you Mrs. Tenner's house guest?" The woman peered over her glasses. A stethoscope hung from her neck. "Follow me."

Dmitri followed her down a corridor crowded with gurneys. They entered a less crowded corridor, and the woman pulled back the curtains around an empty bed.

"Have you had a tetanus shot lately?"

"I was in the Army. I've had them all.

"Okay, but just to be on the safe side, I'm going to give you another."

* * *

A child was crying. Somewhere in the distance, Dmitri heard a woman laugh, and when he opened his eyes he was lying on a gurney. The doctor with the stethoscope was bending over him, taking his pulse.

"Take it easy. You sure you had a tetanus shot before? You had a pretty strong reaction."

"What time is it?" Dmitri struggled through a haze of rising panic.

"It's about six-thirty." Dmitri closed his eyes. How was he going to get a message to Fyordorvitch? He had to get back to the crate. He retraced the events that had led him to this moment.

He felt his body swaying with the rhythm of the sea on the raft. The raft collapsed, the crate floated toward shore, and as Dmitri swam hard to keep it in view, the current pulled him out to sea. He felt the undertow and was forced to swim parallel to the shore to keep from drowning. He'd collapsed on shore, thought he'd rest a minute and apparently slept until the strange young man with an ax had forced him to leave the crate behind as he drove him to the fishing village. As he lay on the gurney, he struggled to stay with the chronology of events, but his exhausted mind and body pushed him back further and further into his past.

Dmitri's father trained as a diplomat and served in the early '60s at the Soviet Embassy in Nairobi. The Soviet Union failed to accomplish its goals for Africa. The diverse tribalism of Africa rejected Soviet domination. African socialism did not mesh with Soviet Marxist ideals. His father returned from Africa with a phrasebook of Swahili proverbs and a growing bitterness. Then he'd spent five years in Cuba. He was there when Khrushchev was forced to withdraw the missiles. His father died a disillusioned and bitter man.

Dmitri drifted back again into deep sleep. The swaying of the raft took hold again. Dmitri could hear his father chanting songs he'd heard in Kenya, and he envisioned the Union of Soviet Socialist Republics as a crumbling wall, seeing the faces and hearing the languages that were splintering into factions. Like the tribes of Africa, each of the nations of the former USSR passed on the history of their people—parent to child, weaving the warp of ancient hurts and slights, invasions and defeats with the weft of victories and triumphs until the fabric of their individual histories was stronger than the collective political policies of the ever changing present. He could hear the sadness and regret in his father's voice.

"Okay, pal. Why don't you sit up a while. Walk around. Then we'll release you."

"What time is it?"

"About six-thirty."

"The doctor who gave me the shot said it was six-thirty about an hour ago."

"That was twelve hours ago. You fell asleep on the gurney and we've been busy. The Fourth of July is a big night around here. Mrs. Tenner paid your bill. She's almost got an account here because of that dog of hers."

The orderly turned to talk to a nurse. The waiting room was more packed than it had been the night before. Out in the morning sunshine, there was nothing for Dmitri to do but to start hiking.

6 | The Early Morning Has Gold in Its Mouth

Alicia stood by the mailbox examining her mail. She stood in the warm sun tapping the unopened MasterCard statement. She didn't have to open it to know the charge—eighty-two dollars and fifty cents, and a whopping twenty-five dollar tip. The tip had been meant as a bribe, a pledge allowing her a dignified exit from a humiliating scene.

There'd been an apology, an explanation, a promise to re-pay her, and an evening worth remembering. Had it been worth it? He hadn't called.

She gave the unopened envelope one final tap. What the hell, she'd picked him up. It was good she'd paid for dinner. The commission for paintings sold at the opening of the Watermark should have been delivered by now. She wanted the check. She wanted to stop thinking about Frederick J. Lewis, who like sand in a shoe, irritated her, ruining her concentration.

The dogs returned from an investigative romp to see what was keeping her so long at the mailbox.

"Come on guys. Let's go to the beach."

Alicia walked quickly down the road, then broke into a trot. She ran until she reached the end of the gravel, and where the road narrowed to a grassy path, she slowed to a fast walk. Her heart pounded. She drew in her breath and let it out slowly. It wasn't the physical exercise that agitated her. She couldn't let go of the indignity of the charge on her MasterCard.

What she needed was a project. Something big. It was time for sculpture. She was in a mood to twist steel.

Snapping the green wood from branches that fell across the path, she set her mind to creating something monumental. She thought about the form the sculpture would take as she bent back the branches. In the past, she had stooped beneath or squirmed around the branches, not wanting to disturb them, but today she tore out and broke off the intruding growth.

The path widened by a row of beech trees growing so uniformly close together that at first glance they appeared to be a fence. Here the woods grew especially dense, and a fine green moss covered the path. Then, where the path seemed to give in to the intruding underbrush, clumps of sassafras stood sentry to an opening that led directly out onto the open shoreline.

The sun was shining brightly as she stepped out onto the beach. She pulled off her sweatshirt and wrapped it around her waist. Her t-shirt was wet from the hike, and the ocean breeze chilled her. She gazed up and down the shore. It was one of those rare summer days when no one was there. It was an occurrence she normally applauded, a reminder of her childhood, before the area around the Point became a nature preserve and a well-visited hiking and bird-watching attraction. The trails were built and maintained by The Sanctuary, but the paths belonged to the families who lived along the ridge. Some of the paths had been created and traveled secretly by Alicia, Margaret, Beth, and Tess when they were children.

She scanned the shore for a figure. Then she admitted her pace through the woods was quickened by eagerness to meet someone. This had been no idle stroll for thoughtful contemplation.

"Damn. Damn and damn again," Alicia shouted to the wind. The dogs joined her, then circled her as she swore. Betta cocked her head and made a sympathetic whine. Browning sat in the sand and scratched her ear.

She still hadn't called Beth. She'd be going back to Chicago in a few weeks, invigorated by the sea air and salt water, ready to return to her job teaching inner-city kids. She smiled thinking of how Beth always described herself as "a basket-case," and that was precisely what Alicia was thinking of herself.

There was nothing to do but to throw herself into her art. The medium would be metal. The sculpture would be huge. It would be overpowering and prepossessing. As a child, when she faced disappointments, she hid herself in her room and painted delicate watercolors, recited lines from Edna St. Vincent Millay, and tried to imagine being Emily Dickinson. Not this time. She was going to buy a butane torch.

And a soldering gun. She didn't know about the fireproof mat. Maybe a sand pit would do. She'd need scissors—no, metal cutting shears—epoxy, and some kind of heavy glove. The shopping list forced her to reconsider the thought she'd been squelching.

"I want my money back, Betta. He never really made an effort to pay for dinner." The dog thumped her tail in the sand.

Alicia started toward the pond with the dogs in the lead. She stopped abruptly. She was angry. Why had she shown him the pond? She couldn't go there now. She turned around and headed in the opposite direction.

Giant boulders studded the shoreline. One, a giant slab of pink granite as flat as a sidewalk, had been a favorite picnicking spot for Alicia, Beth, Margaret, and Tess.

When the sun hit the tiny specks of quartz, it sparkled. Alicia liked to think those tiny specks were memory banks and the monolith stored the laughter and secrets of the little girls who'd long since grown up.

The sand was rutted by streaks of water coming from springs, burbling to the surface from sources deep within the island. Toward her pond, the cold streams stayed underground and broke open in the ocean. Swimming here was never warm, but gliding into a pool of spring water made the surrounding waters seem so.

Fishing was good here. She could catch blues from the shore. She could catch scup, or flounder, patiently dangling a line from Dr. Norton's tiny skiff. Alicia loved that tiny boat when they'd anchor it not far from shore. She'd study the shades of green, varying from minute to minute with the changes of light and wind and the speed of the water. A school of fish, a bottle, or a jellyfish just below the surface brought out new shades for her to memorize.

The shoreline was more interesting here, too. Whelks, moon shells and slippers were everywhere. Periwinkles covered the rocks, and great strands of seaweed stretched from the tide line into the water. Tiny hermit crabs scuttled about in the pools of water among the rocks. Alicia stopped to study a horseshoe crab shell.

When she stood up she saw the box in the sand. It was probably trash dumped overboard or left behind on the beach by a thoughtless intruder. It was the fifth of July. Maybe it contained fireworks. She made her way up the shore slowly. The fist sized rocks made it difficult to walk, and the little streams breaking through the sand forced her to stop and look for alternate routes so she could keep her shoes dry.

Finally, when she reached it, she could see it was a crate. It was sealed, but one end was badly damaged. A rope and a float still stretched out into the ocean. She picked at the splintered corner with her foot. It didn't smell. A chunk of the corner fell away.

A streak of bright orange shocked the snowy white exterior. Alicia sat down in the sand and pried off the lid. The box was filled with labels. She pulled out one, her artist's eye drawn to the bright red-orange background. A nicely rendered fish etched in coppery browns covered the center. Foreign writing was printed across the bottom. She pulled out a stack of them and stashed them in the kangaroo pocket in her sweatshirt.

The sun came out from behind a cloud and beamed across the open crate. Alicia saw a glimmer and dug around the labels with her fingers. A shiny metal object sat in the middle of the box, well padded by the labels. She pulled it out.

"Interesting," she exclaimed. She held it at arms length and examined it. The dogs circled the crate, sniffing at it, and then, tired from their run, lay down beside it.

"Betta, it's perfect. It's just what I needed to get started. I wonder what it is. Whatever it is, it's a gift. It's the cornerstone of the monumental work that will make Frederick J. Lewis think twice about trifling with Alicia Barrett, renowned sculptor. Right, pups?"

The dogs barked and wagged their tails. "Come on, pups. We've got work to do." Alicia's spirits soared, her mind filling with plans and designs. The creative spark was lit again. Her work would be no superficial bauble.

When she reached her house, she stood for a minute deciding where to put the cornerstone to her creation. She considered setting it on the front step, but a fog was starting to roll in behind the row of trees below her. She didn't want the salt air corroding it. It had already acquired a certain lovable quality, cradled in her arms, and wrapped in her sweatshirt as she lugged it up the ridge.

She unlocked the door. The dogs rushed in, jumping around her to reach their water dishes, and the phone was ringing. Her eyes darted around the living room, and she settled on the mantel as a temporary resting place for her *objet trouvé*.

"Hello, Alicia? It's Beth!"

"When did you get here?"

"About a week ago, but you know. The usual basket case. Just been lounging around trying to forget about kids and schools. Mom says your work is selling like crazy. We'd love to have you come over for a drink. She's upset that we've gathered a piece of your mail by mistake. It was in our box, and Dad didn't notice it until he got back to the house. It's from a gallery."

"Is it from the Watermark?"

"Yeah, I believe it is."

Alicia turned again to check the mantel, as if the little chunk of metal might have walked out when she turned her back. She was eager to work, but obviously she needed materials and money to buy them.

"Ok. Give me a half-hour. I just came back from the beach. I know the cocktail hour starts at five. I'll be glad to see you."

* * *

Alicia hung up the telephone. She'd been at the beach longer than she'd realized. She climbed the stairs thinking how Mrs. Norton dressed for cocktails, frilly feminine clothes, and she served elegant hors d'oeuvres.

Removing the barrette that held her hair, Alicia bent forward to brush the long blonde strands up over her head, then she stood straight up again moving her head in a circular fashion letting it fall back. She applied an outline of red to her lips. It was too bright, or she was not used to the sudden burst of color. She rubbed part of it away.

Mrs. Norton would wear a skirt, but Beth would be in jeans. Alicia pulled on a clean pair of jeans and a bright turquoise sweater.

Beth's mother always made her feel as if she were being judged. She'd known her since she was a child, but the same childish insecurities rose up in her when she went to the Nortons'. Alicia told herself it didn't matter, but she knew Mrs. Norton was the kind of mother whose very flicker of an eyebrow indicated that it mattered very much.

Alicia attached a pair of gold hoop earrings. She slipped into a pair of *huraches*, and then out of them. It was summer, but it was still cool after dark; she knew Mrs. Norton would probably invite her to stay for dinner, and she'd walk home in the dark through the wet grass. She pulled on socks, tied her jogging shoes, and went down to the kitchen to pour some dry food into a bowl for the dogs. She peered into the living room at her prize on the mantel and went out, locking the door behind her.

* * *

One of the routes from Alicia's house to the Nortons' was along a path so overgrown only those who knew of its existence walked it. She passed an old vernal pool, the water a dark reddish-brown puddle, surrounded by nettles and chicory. She cut across what used to be Beth's grandmother's rose garden, now cluttered with scrub oak. She stepped out onto the road that led to the Nortons' house.

Dr. Norton started out as a college professor in a small southern college. He'd made money consulting in Washington. Beth grew up near D.C. in Virginia, where Mrs. Norton used to say she felt as if she had encamped on the edge of enemy territory. To Sue Ellyn, Virginia had been a compromise with her heritage. Yet each summer, the Nortons returned to Dr. Norton's ancestral home on Jellicle Island.

How Beth's mother and father found one another was often discussed during summer slumber parties with Tess, Beth, Margaret, and Alicia. Beth's Dad was a taciturn New Englander, and her mom was a chatty southern belle. An invitation for a "simple supper" usually involved many courses laid out on a mahogany table set with a minimum of three silver forks.

Alicia hiked up the road, remembering the time she'd been asked to set the table and forgot the salad forks. Mrs. Norton liked to serve the salad course after the main course, "in the French way," she'd informed the girls. Alicia could still hear her voice at the end of the meal as she asked whatever became of the salad forks, as if she'd been inquiring who had let the cat out to be run over in the road.

The house was large, the living room on the second floor overlooking the ocean. The back of the house faced the woods, and anyone coming up the road was at a disadvantage. A long screened porch allowed those sitting there to hear and see anyone walking in the direction of the house long before they realized they were being observed.

Conversation travels in the woods, and idle chatter drifted onto the porch disembodied. The previous summer, while Beth and Alicia sat silenced by Mrs. Norton, they listened to the conversation of two approaching trespassers. Just as Dr. Norton was about to shout at them that they were on private property, Beth recognized Margaret and her son. Alicia had made a note never to say anything as she approached the Norton house.

"Welcome," Mrs. Norton called out. "We've started without you."

"Good for you," Alicia shouted back.

She continued up the road and across the front lawn, past the porch where the three of them were sitting. By the time she reached the front door Beth was standing there with the door open. They hugged and patted one another on the back.

"Another year," Alicia said.

"I'm afraid so," replied her friend.

By then Mrs. Norton was standing there, too, dressed in a soft denim blue circle skirt and a white lacy blouse with long full sleeves.

"Where have you been keeping yourself, Alicia? We always hope to see you when we go to the beach."

The entrance hallway was wide, like a Southern manor, and it led to an oak stairway with an ornate newel post. The landing window looked out across the woods toward the rose garden Alicia had just passed through. With the summer foliage, the road was hidden, but Alicia imagined that at night the headlights from a car in her own yard could be seen from here.

At the top of the stairs, another wide hall led to the living room, the Nortons' master suite, Dr. Norton's study, and a guest bathroom. The living room was long and narrow with a fireplace at one end and a wall that was mostly windows that provided a view of the ocean in winter when the trees were bare.

"Please come upstairs a minute, Alicia. The sun is bright now. Every summer I say I'm going to put up Roman shades, but I can't bare to cover up the windows. I want you to look at these photographs here by the fireplace. What do you think?"

Sue Ellyn Norton's conversations were like walking through a mine-field. If you ever relaxed, you could get your foot blown off. Alicia guessed she was asking about the arrangement.

"Those are interesting frames," Alicia responded hesitantly.

"Frank spent two weeks going through old family pictures, found the frames at the thrift shop, and matted them himself."

"They look great. Maybe he can frame some of my work," Alicia said with a laugh. "I'm glad you have my mail from the gallery."

"I'm so embarrassed. Beth should have brought it right over to you." Mrs. Norton pursed her lips, and Alicia recognized it as a sign she was about to charge forth in a new direction.

"Not to worry. I'm glad for the excuse to get me away from... from ..." Alicia turned to see whether Beth had followed them upstairs. She had not.

"That girl," Mrs. Norton said with a sigh.

Alicia re-entered the hallway before Mrs. Norton could launch into anything personal, either commenting about Beth's life or inquiring about Alicia's.

"What can Frank get you to drink?" Mrs. Norton hurried to take the lead. She held onto the rail with one hand and raised her long skirt with the other. Her nails were polished and her rings sparkled.

"Before we forget…" Beth stood at the foot of the stairs holding the mail for Alicia who took it from her and tore it open. Inside was a check for five hundred dollars. From the bottom step Mrs. Norton looked over her shoulder.

"You've sold another painting!" she chirped.

"I've sold all my paintings," Alicia said.

"I hope you get a lot of money," Mrs. Norton said in a tone that implied she would like to know exactly how much.

Alicia felt better. "I certainly did. This is for the last one. Five hundred dollars."

"Frank, Frank. Come fix Alicia a drink. She's rich."

Dr. Norton appeared good naturedly and placed his hands on Beth's shoulders. "Alicia, what would you like?"

"I'll have a gimlet."

Mrs. Norton scurried past the three of them into the kitchen. She picked up a tray of hors d'oeuvres and set them on the table on the porch. Beth and Alicia followed her and settled into wicker chairs as Mrs. Norton settled into hers. She raised her martini glass.

"To your success, Alicia. May we see more of you."

"Thank you."

Alicia studied the tray of crackers and cream cheese spread with red and green jelly. It looked awful, kind of Krafty, but Mrs. Norton would never serve anything like that.

"Hot pepper jelly. It's the thing in the South."

Alicia selected a cracker. Dr. Norton appeared with her drink. He stood patiently in front of her as men do who are accustomed to waiting for women. She took a bite and reached for the glass.

"Thank you. Hmmm. This is good. What did you say it is?"

"The green jelly is sweet pepper and the red jelly is hot pepper. You can't find it here. I'll bring you a couple of jars next summer."

"The drink is perfect." Alicia raised her glass. "To summer. Welcome home, Beth."

Beth started to reply, but her mother did. "She's been here for weeks. She hasn't done one thing. Not gone to the beach, not walked in the woods, not called her friends. Just mopes around."

"Now, Sue Ellyn," Dr. Norton protested. "Alicia, tell me about your paintings at the Watermark."

"You've very talented, Alicia," Mrs. Norton added as she glared at her daughter. "Where is the Watermark? I don't know it."

"It's in Beech Grove—you know, the fancy part of Jellicle Island. Maybe I've discovered the trick to making money, Mrs. Norton. I'll tell you. It isn't technique. It's size. I was running low on paper, so I began to tear the standard sized in half. It seems that's a better size for a yacht's interior. A man came into the gallery and bought five. I'd have charged five hundred apiece if I'd known to."

"So who bought them?" Beth asked.

"The gallery owner, Karrie Griffith, doesn't let fame go to my head. She said a guy wandered into the gallery, scurried around as if he were in a grocery store. My paintings were hanging in a little group at the end of the room. Karrie said, 'not to demean your talent, but it must have been the size of the wall in the head.'

"He stopped abruptly, pointed across the gallery at them and said, 'I'll take 'em.' She told me she wasn't sure what he meant, and said, 'The Barretts?' and he said, 'Yes. The boats.'

"She said she started taking them from the wall waiting for him to say which one, but he pulled out his wallet after she'd removed all five of them and simply asked, 'How much?'

"Only one of them had boats. I'm not that good with them. I'm best with water and flowers. Anyway, she wrapped them up, and he walked away with the Barrett collection. She was afraid he'd come back when he saw only one had boats in it, but I guess she decided he's going to keep them all, and now I have five hundred dollars."

"You paint water very well, Alicia," Dr. Norton said. "May I freshen your drink? My daughter has already requested another."

"To think, Frank, Alicia's money has been sitting up here all day." Mrs. Norton said as she handed her husband her empty glass.

"To be honest, I'd kind of forgotten about it," Alicia said as she thought about how Frederick J. Lewis, the mysterious object on her mantel, and her sudden desire to work in metal instead of paint occupied her thoughts.

"Forgotten about five hundred dollars! My, my, Alicia. How far you've come."

Alicia wished she'd been less open about the amount. Mrs. Norton managed to make more out of things than was there to begin with.

"Will you stay for dinner?" Mrs. Norton asked.

Alicia had counted on it, but suddenly she felt tired. Dr. Norton made stiff drinks, and she rarely drank gin. It was a festive thought when she saw the check, but now the burden of her moping friend, Mrs. Norton's chatter, and Dr. Norton's good natured attention were too much. She wanted to go home.

"I'd love to, Mrs. Norton, but I really must go."

"A date, perhaps?"

"I saw Tess," Beth began. "I leave my car at her house, and she drives me to O'Hare. Her kids are cute. She seems to be a bit bored with being a stay-at-home mom.

"That's too bad. I'd think it would be a great life."

"Beth, I'm going to Boston tomorrow. Want to come along?"

"No, I don't think so. I'll be going back to Chicago soon, and I think I'll try the salt water my mother keeps recommending."

"Oh, Alicia. Come see my find," Mrs. Norton interjected. "We took the path behind the house to the beach today. It was late, and we just wanted to go down and back for the exercise." Mrs. Norton led the way through the kitchen to the laundry room.

"Aren't these wonderful?" Frank says they must have fallen off one of those Russian fishing boats."

Alicia stared at the piles of labels stashed in a berry box on top of the washing machine. She'd contented herself with a handful, but Mrs. Norton must have emptied the crate.

"Fishing labels, oh, I'd wondered." Alicia stopped. She had no intention of mentioning what she had found in the crate. She said her good byes, then headed out to the road. She took the long way home in the moonlight.

7 | Fair Faces Go Places

Frederick J. Lewis sat in Butch McGuire's on Chicago's Division Street and contemplated life. His life. He was a little toy train on a little toy track, going round and round, passing the same plastic station and the same paper tree. Ten years had passed, and here he was again in the same bar in the same city thinking about the same woman.

He remembered the first time he saw her. She was sitting in the grass in the botanical garden at the university. The sun shining on her hair held him transfixed, and before he could think of the ramifications, he was sitting next to her. They'd dated, but something deep in his brain always sent a warning. She was a centered personality, and he was a man without a center. Yet he was drawn back to her, again and again.

He looked her up when he moved to Chicago after getting out of the Army and accepting a job with Continental Bank. Casual dating. The same deep, resounding warning roared in his subconscious. One thing led to another, and instead of finding his own place he'd moved in with her. He took life day-to-day, trying to chisel out some kind of career. She began talking about marriage. When he got fired, she cried, still insisting they should marry. Things would work out, she'd said. He had to get out.

An Army buddy found him a job in D.C. They don't have bars like Butch McGuire's in D.C. Fred finished his beer and looked at the crowd. The people were loud and chatty. A three-piece suit was an oddity here, not the suit of armor demanded by the lobbyists and advisors in the nation's capital. Here, people stopped in for a drink and some company. Men and women talked football or baseball, depending on the season.

In D.C., men were circumspect and chanted the hours they'd put in, while women inquired within ninety seconds of conversation about GS status.

Lewis's career hadn't gotten off the ground in D.C. either. He never got the hang of what it was he was supposed to do. Up at five a.m., work until two the next morning, then hail a cab for a two-and-a-half-hour rest. In Chicago, the bars were full of people who were happy to have a philosophical conversation at two o'clock in the morning. In D.C., he couldn't find a grocery store open after sundown.

Next stop, Boston. A lobbyist suggested the position, and he jumped at the chance because he recognized the signs he wouldn't last much longer in the nation's capital. A merger swallowed that company within three months of his arrival. Still, he'd managed to hang on for another year and a half. It'd been like working in a tank of feeder fish. The employees ran around checking the receptionist's directory, looking for associates who'd been scratched, worrying they'd be scooped up in the net next. Considering his late arrival to the company, he'd been lucky.

He talked himself into a job with the take-over company. That landed him on the West Coast. He'd have stayed there forever if he'd been given the opportunity. Unfortunately, the son-of-a-bitch who hired him just wanted someone to tidy up. Six months in the California sun walking soft white beaches, then, bam. The company merged, consolidated, liquidated, and dissolved.

* * *

So here he was again in Chicago, looking for the missing piece of luck in the puzzle. There were so many good pieces—a college degree in foreign affairs, an Army job where he'd learned Russian, a job, a job, a job. But not a career.

He was thirty-eight years old. He liked to wear Hickey-Freeman suits, order a second round of filet mignon for dinner if he felt like it, and drive solid cars like BMWs and Jaguar sedans. He wanted an office and a phone that rang constantly with people at the other end eager to talk to him.

Hard work didn't scare him. He just naturally gravitated to four-star restaurants for lunch, midnight toasts in front of custom designed fireplaces, and waking up in a rich but lonely woman's bed.

Frederick ordered a Russian Mule. When the bartender set it in front of him, he wished he'd stuck with the Miller's. Why in hell had he driven to Chicago? It broke one of his cardinal rules. Twice. Every time he got within five hundred miles of Beth, he was drawn like the proverbial moth to the flame.

In Boston he'd pulled out a map, studying it to find the location of Jellicle Island.

He hadn't known if Beth would be there on her annual summer vacation at home, but he wanted to walk the beaches she walked. Instead, he'd discovered an enigmatic woman named Alicia who intrigued him. Whether she had money, a lot of money, he wasn't sure. He had to get himself a job, or find a lovely lonely woman to spend his time and her money on the finer things in life.

* * *

"Excuse me." The woman eased in between the bar stools and placed an icy hand on top of Frederick's. Rubies sparkled from three fingers on her right hand. On her left hand a gold and diamond band hovered on her little finger.

Frederick moved the stool back to give her room, and looked down at the leather shoes with the intricate tooling. Costly, he thought, as he followed the legs back up the slim body to the expressionless face.

"Hello," he said.

"I need help, and I overhead you talking to the bartender about being a Vet and all. I know that's no character reference, but you look nice."

"Oh, I am. What can I do for you?"

"I'm not feeling well. I've taken something I probably shouldn't have, and I want to go home."

"I'd be delighted to… ah… escort you, safe and sound, but why don't you call a cab? I'll find you an English-speaking driver, if you'd like."

"I've got my car, and I've got to get it off the street. If you know about Chicago cabbies, you know about Chicago tow-trucks. Look, I'm really starting to feel pretty rocky."

She turned, putting her hand on the bar, head lowered, and waited. Frederick stood up and put his arm around her waist and gripped her so if she stumbled she wouldn't fall on her face. At the entrance, he pushed open the door with his free hand and they stepped onto Division Street. The sidewalk was jammed. A group of teenagers hovered around the entrance to the bar. Too young to get in, they contented themselves by making lewd comments about those who did. At the corner, several sailors stood trying to decide which bar to enter.

The woman seemed to walk stably, Frederick thought, for someone who was having a fainting spell. With drugs, it was hard to predict what a person would do. They passed the sailors and turned on to State Street. Frederick searched the street for signs of an accomplice and was beginning to wonder if the con had been conned when she stopped in front of a red Jaguar parked in front of a fire hydrant. It didn't have a parking ticket.

"I see what you mean," Frederick said while she fished into a small purse and pulled out a set of keys. He took them and unlocked the door. She slumped into the seat and put her head back on the headrest, eyes shut.

A car was waiting for the space, the driver unaware of the fire hydrant until the last moment when it pulled ahead just as Frederick started to move into the traffic. He braked, the other car rushed on and its driver flashed him an insolent wave. Frederick's passenger didn't open her eyes.

"I don't live far from here," she directed.

"What's the address?"

"It's on East Walton. The first building. Pull into the garage."

The car hummed along with mechanical perfection. Frederick wondered why anyone would keep a car like this in the city. He stopped in front of the closed garage by a ticket-taking machine. She pulled a plastic pass out of her purse and handed it to him. He took it and shoved it into the machine. The garage door curled up. He drove in.

"Number twenty-two," she said. He pulled into the stall and switched off the ignition. He turned toward her. Now she did look limp. He opened his car door and went around to her side. He helped her out of the car.

"The elevator's over there," she mumbled.

As they walked toward it she leaned against him. She was tall but light. Frederick figured if he had to, he could carry her, but there was probably a doorman or a security guard. Maybe this happened all the time, and no one would notice.

She gathered more strength as they approached the public lobby. By the time they reached the elevator she was standing on her own. The color had returned to her cheeks. Maybe it had been there all along. The bar wasn't famous for its bright lights.

The elevator door opened, and they got in. She pushed the button for the twelfth floor. They rode up in silence, and when the door opened she stepped out. Frederick hesitated a moment, the car key still in his hand. If he handed her the key as the elevator door closed, he'd wonder for the rest of his life what this had been all about. He hurried to catch up with her.

At her condominium door she reached into her purse and pulled out a key on a ring with a shiny gold emblem. He stood, warming the car key in his hand while she opened the door.

"May I offer you a drink" She said it in a weary, obligatory tone. It was not an enticement.

"That would be nice, but perhaps another time when you're feeling better."

"Come in then, just for a minute while I turn on the lights. I'm feeling better. I get frightened."

She opened the door and reached for the light switch. It ignited a master switch, flooding the room with bright light. She stepped in, and Frederick followed her, drawn by the intense light, curiosity, and a desire to hand back the key to the Jaguar, which she hadn't yet asked for.

The room was impressive. A thick charcoal gray carpet covered the living room floor, shadowing a rich chartreuse drapery along a wall of windows. Two black lacquer *étagères* divided the living room from the dining room. The shelves were filled with imaginative works of art, some hand-blown glass, some copper and brass. A *papier mache* sculpture looked to Frederick like a Dubuffet. A tall, graceful African mask towered over the top shelf, casting an eerie presence over the room.

The walls of the living room were covered with huge enterprising modern pieces in fluorescent colors. Frederick recognized an artist he'd seen at the Art Institute's show of recent acquisitions. Ed Paschke was the artist. This was a portrait of a muscle-bound tattooed woman with long wavy hair. In the distance, a corridor lit up with smaller, more traditional appearing paintings.

Frederick stood transfixed. She switched off lights. As his eyes fought the sudden change, the drapes opened and the shoreline appeared glittering before him. The condominium angled so that a part of Lake Michigan was visible. The edge of the city sparkled with neon lights, car headlights, and apartment windows casting shafts of creamy brightness into the night.

Frederick let out a low whistle of breath. It was he who liked to do the impressing. She cleared her throat.

"I've seen a lot of views of the lake," Frederick began, "but this is by far the best. You get up in the Hancock, or Lake Point Tower, and most of the time you just see fog."

"You've been a gentleman, and I want to thank you. Would you be my guest for brunch in the morning? The Ritz Carlton serves a wonderful brunch with lots of smoked salmon, oysters, good country ham. Identifiable food, not the mystery sauces swimming in silver tureens that other places serve. What do you say?"

"It really isn't necessary." Frederick paused, trying to sound sincere. "I'm happy to prove chivalry isn't dead."

"That's my intent. I'd like to reward your… rarity." She smiled briefly.

"Sounds good."

"I'll meet you in the lobby on the twelfth floor of the Ritz at ten-thirty."

"Your key." Frederick held out the key to her. She took it without responding. She looked fragile again.

Frederick headed for the front door to let himself out. He glanced at a small painting hung over the security intercom. The frame covered the artist's signature. He was almost certain it was a Pizarro. Crazy to hang something like that so close to the front door.

Before leaving the building, he checked the directory. The twelfth floor listed R.N. Scully. On the street again, he took a deep breath. It was a hot night, but close to the lake the air was cool. He felt invigorated. She had money. She'd picked him out. Maybe his luck was turning around. He walked the four short blocks to Michigan Avenue. He thought he'd like a drink. He was low on money, but it looked like that wouldn't be a problem in the morning.

Doubling back to the Hancock Center, he took the elevator to the bar. The doors opened onto a balcony overlooking the dining room on the floor below. He stood at the rail staring at the diners, admiring the women in their expensive dresses and sparkling jewelry. He noted that the men were mostly in their fifties and sixties, and most of their companions were easily in their twenties.

He walked down the hallway to the west side of the room, where the view from the bar overlooked the major arteries crisscrossing the city. Tiny threads of light stretched to the horizon. It was better than the view from the air. Sitting at the bar in Big John, a man could shave his gripe list down to nothing.

He ordered a Moscow Mule. While he waited for it, his eye followed the bright lines of the city streets. He liked this city. It was rational, clear cut. When a woman said she was from the west side, or the south side, or the north side, you knew her life story. Same with a man. If he said he was a Cubs fan, he was loyal, worked hard to get ahead and didn't give a damn if his team ever won a game. If he was a Sox fan, you could bet the bar tab he had a bungalow, a mortgage, a wife, five kids and a fat dog. You knew he didn't like his sports events interrupted by any news announcement. Frederick was happy to be back in Chicago. No bullshit.

Frederick finished his drink, left no tip, and felt better about his future. On the walk from the Magnificent Mile to Clark Street, the shiny sedans were replaced by rusty compact models. Fashionable jeans and sweaters were no longer the apparel worn and the light springy steps of the people on the Avenue were replaced by the slow trudges of a tired workforce waiting for a bus.

The number 22 bus rolled up. Frederick waited for the others to board. The kids who'd been necking in a doorway headed to the back seat, an old man dropped into the first seat, and a scruffy looking bearded man took his time selecting a spot. When the bus started, he began making strange puppet-like motions with his hands as if they were being jerked by invisible strings. The silence on the bus was broken every few blocks when he burst into short snorty hoots of laughter.

Staring out the window, Frederick watched as New Town replaced Old Town as he headed back to a small room in a shabby hotel. In the part of the city known as Old Town, the authentic folk music, improvisational theater, and great steaks kept the ambiance real. In New Town, as the name implied, the area was the new trendy part of the city, but the atmosphere was lousy.

He wondered if Beth was in town. He was about to call her when the mysterious ailing woman changed his plan. It was just as well. He wanted to get comfortable. He didn't want his mode of transportation to be the city bus, nor did he want to hang around the newest new town at two o'clock in the morning for the rest of his life. He wanted to stay on the Magnificent Mile of life with expensive cars, tall women, and breakfasts at the Ritz.

When the bus reached his stop, he got off, telling himself this was the last time he'd be taking this route. You bet, there was something about him that attracted women with style, class, and, sorry Beth, m-o-n-e-y.

In the morning he showered, shaved, and put on his Hickey-Freeman suit. Maybe she'd spill something on it and buy him a new one. He walked to Sheridan Road so he could avoid the working class bus route and take the number 151 which would let him off in front of Water Tower Place. The ride would put him in better company than his companions on the bus the night before.

The breeze picked up as he walked toward the lake. He wondered why he ever rode the number 22 with its odd assortment of old, tired, and poor passengers. Even the old ladies aboard the number 151 dressed in expensive clothes and wore hats, and their wrinkled hands flashed large diamonds.

Hopping lightly from the bus, he headed for the Ritz. On the elevator to the Ritz Carlton's restaurant, he adjusted his tie in the mirror, combed his hair, and turned back to stand with his hands clasped behind his back when the door opened.

The aroma of tasty food filled his nostrils. His stomach growled. From the lobby, he studied the brunch tables and scanned the people moving reverently toward them. An octagonal fountain spilled into a blue-bottomed basin in the center of the main lobby. A flock of bronze cranes hovered overhead. On the far side of the fountain, a bar partially obscured by pots of tall grasses and miniature palms, looked tropical beneath a skylight.

He saw her walking toward him from a wide hallway to the left of the bar. She didn't see him. He took his time studying her. She was tall, maybe five feet nine or ten. Her dark hair, which had hung loosely about her shoulders the night before, was pulled back in an elegant knot at the nape of her neck. She wore a simple linen dress, bright pink with an appliquéd design in black. She reminded him of a Matisse.

She wasn't carrying a handbag. He was relieved to see she hadn't stood him up, but he hoped she wasn't going to expect him to pay. He had twenty-two dollars in his wallet. He wasn't going to worry about it until after brunch.

"Good morning," he said cheerfully as she approached him.

"Good morning," she replied. "We're already seated. I didn't explain last night, but it's kind of a family affair. My brother will be joining us."

"Terrific," Frederick said and he meant it. "Frederick Lewis," he added. He decided not to extend his hand, but bowed slightly for the charm of it. "And you are?" he asked.

"Renata. Renata Scully." She smiled and took the arm he offered. He wondered what her brother would add to this budding relationship. For openers, he'd pick up the tab. Frederick could relax and enjoy himself.

Her brother was tall, big boned, with chunky wide hands. Except for the height, they didn't look much alike. It wasn't the kind of thing he needed to inquire about. The brother looked up at them as they approached the table. He didn't get up, but he extended his hand and smiled broadly.

"Antonio Scully. Glad to meet ya. My baby sister tells me you saved her from a bad scene last night. Great. Thanks a lot. I keep tellin' her not to take those damn antihistamines with a cocktail."

Frederick smiled. Things looked good.

"They got the best food in the city here. Some of these brunches are real pretty, but the food tastes like crap."

"Tony," Renata hissed.

"It's true. What can I say?"

"Shall we?" She rose and the two men followed her to a stack of white plates. Tony gestured for Frederick to start ahead of him. Standing behind him, he pointed out the highlights on the buffet tables.

"Omelets are good here. Fresh. Hot. You can see the guy make 'em, so you know they use real eggs." Frederick nodded as he checked to see if those standing in front of him were listening.

The omelet chef was busy preparing his specialty in a copper pan. Dishes set out before them offered a variety of ingredients; cheddar cheese, fresh parmesan cheese, tomatoes, green and red peppers, onions, mushrooms, chopped ham, and bacon.

"You can get Eggs Benedict, but you gotta ask. They don't let 'em sit around and coagulate."

Frederick placed his order for an omelet and moved down the buffet table. A silver bowl filled with fist-sized shrimp, another filled with chunks of crab, and trays of fresh oysters on the half shell brought a smile to his face. Smoked salmon and platters of lox, bagels and cream cheese made Fredrick think about just how much food he could consume. At the next table, Renata was carefully selecting pieces of fruit. Tony set one plate on their table and returned with an empty one and began to pile it with shellfish. No matter how much he ate, he'd never match Tony's voracious appetite. The waiter served the omelet. Renata looked up at him, fork in hand, and smiled. She took a nibble of fresh pineapple.

After the eggs and shellfish, Tony and Fred helped themselves to medallions of veal, fettuccini, breast of turkey, stroganoff, and meatballs. Renata selected a few raw vegetables; peas, long slender green beans, and cold white asparagus tips.

For dessert she chose several small cubes of *camembert* and apple slices. Frederick observed she didn't eat the cheese. Tony consumed two chocolate *éclairs*, a pecan sticky bun, and a large slice of walnut cake with icing as high as the cake. Frederick perused the dessert table with mixed emotions. He selected a piece of Black Forest cake and pushed some of the whipped cream to the side. He hoped Tony wouldn't see it and sweep it onto his own plate. Tony scooped whipped cream and sour cream with imaginative abandon. He'd emptied a silver bowl filled with cream cheese, clanked the spoon against the side as he piled a pound of it onto a bagel.

Conversation was limited to Tony's brief pronouncements on how hot or how sweet or how fresh whatever he was attacking at the moment tasted. Renata ate delicately, smiled vacantly, and chewed slowly. She sipped a cup of tea and watched the strollers in the lobby beyond the café.

Frederick relaxed and savored his good fortune. He had only to murmur in agreement now and then to Tony. He did not try engaging Renata in conversation. After the last plate was cleared and only two cups of steaming coffee lay before them, Tony leaned back in his chair.

"I like this guy, Renata. You could have gotten yourself a real Dove Bar, but you didn't. Nice suit, too. You mind if I take him fishing with me, Renata? I'll bring him back to your place later tonight."

He hadn't been consulted, but Frederick approved of the direction the plans were taking. Observing them, he noted that while Tony was as rude and crude as they come, his sister was classy and alluring.

"I got some clothes you can borrow. Don't want to get that fancy suit messed up. Hey, I didn't even ask your friend, Renata. Fred, you do want to do some coho fishing, doncha?"

Frederick wasn't at all interested in fishing for salmon in Lake Michigan, but he was very interested in the possibility of reeling in Renata Scully. He'd been sport fishing a few times. It could be deadly dull, or if the water was rough it could be unpleasant. Being dropped off at Renata's condominium was the best part of the plan.

"Sounds great," Frederick said, trying to sound enthused.

The check arrived. Frederick made a faint effort to reach for it. His gesture was grander than it might have been if he hadn't been certain Tony would pick up the tab.

"Hey, no way. Like I said, I'm grateful to ya for rescuing my baby sister. And I like you. We'll have a terrific afternoon. You'll like the fishing. I've got a great boat, don't I, Renata? Eh, she don't care."

He dropped a couple of hundred dollar bills on the leather folder. The three of them watched in silence as the waiter retrieved the bills, placed them inside the folder and retreated.

"I'll meet you by the elevators," Tony said. Renata rose, and Frederick followed her.

"I hope you don't mind going fishing with my brother. He likes you. He's kind of like an over-grown puppy. It never occurs to him people might have other plans."

"It sounds terrific. I've done a lot of sport fishing on the West Coast. This should be interesting. And will I see you this evening?"

"No, Tony's afternoons run rather late. I have things to do myself. Perhaps we could have dinner later in the week. I'm tied up until Thursday. Would Thursday be all right?"

"Thursday would be great," Frederick conceded. "What time should I pick you up?"

"Seven o'clock would be fine." She smiled that distant smile again.

At the elevators, Frederick stopped but Renata continued walking toward her brother who was adjusting his pants as he lumbered toward them. She walked past him, ignoring him. He said something to her Frederick couldn't make out, and she gave a flutter of fingers wave over her shoulder and continued walking in the direction of the ladies room and the Coco Cabana Bar.

"So, you ready?"

"I'd better meet you at the harbor. I'm a little overdressed for fishing." Frederick was beginning to dread the afternoon's activities. Especially now that he knew it wouldn't end with Renata. "Say I meet you in two hours?" He hoped that would convince Tony to go on without him.

"It's your lucky day. My kid-sister, Renata's half-sister, she sent me this stuff for my birthday. She figures it's the gesture that counts and

I can always take it back and get what I want. Not at all like Renata. Renata's a shopper. She don't go in a shoe store and say where are your red shoes. She says, 'Show me your Ferragamos.' She goes in to those little shops up and down Oak Street, not the big fancy ones everybody's rushin' into. She just sits in a nice soft chair and the sales lady brings her fancy designer clothes for twice the price as the department stores. She goes through them, sends half of them back and takes the rest of 'em home. Never tries nothin' on. She knows what she likes, and she knows how to get it. You understand I get this info from my kid sister. She sure as hell wouldn't take me in those places with her." He snorted.

Frederick wondered if he ever shut up. "I don't want to hold you up. Maybe you should go fishing without me."

"Like I said, it's your lucky day." He turned into a small building wedged between two taller ones. The smells from a carry-out pizzeria next door repulsed Frederick. Tony started up the stairwell. Frederick followed him. On the third floor Tony lumbered down a narrow stuffy hallway. He stopped at the end and unlocked a door.

The room was small and hot. A tiny kitchenette looked as if it had not been used in a long time. The bed was neatly made. There were no dirty ash trays, Styrofoam fast food boxes, or empty bottles. That surprised Frederick. Tony did not appear to be the fastidious type. The room wasn't any classier than his own in New Town, but he knew the rent was four times greater.

Tony opened a closet door, blocking Frederick's view of the contents, and began to toss boxes on the bed.

"It ain't your birthday is it?" Tony chuckled.

"No, I don't think so."

"So what have we got here? Everything you need, right?" Tony pulled open the lids and gathered up pants, a sweatshirt, socks and boat shoes. All Frederick's size. All expensive.

Tony turned back to the closet. He took off his sport jacket and hung it in the closet. He unzipped his pants and hung them on a hook after struggling with a hanger. Frederick stood holding the shoes. He was thinking he should get the hell out. Tony peered out from behind the door.

"You need a dressing room?"

“No, I’m just a bit overwhelmed.”

“Eh, forget it.” Tony said. He disappeared into the bathroom but shouted back, “Like I said, it’s your lucky day. My kid sister just sends stuff, never thinks about the size. Saves me the trouble of sendin’ it back.”

Frederick grabbed a hanger and put his suit on it, stashed his tie in the pocket, and pulled an empty wardrobe bag over it. He lay it on the bed intending to take his good suit with him. He didn’t know much about sport fishing, but he was an expert on quality brands. He was going to look as if he were trying out for the America’s Cup. They were good clothes, his size, and he liked them.

Tony reappeared. “Hey, maybe the kid’s not so dumb after all. Maybe I should tell her what size I am. What’d ya think? Ya look good.” Tony snorted a laugh, picked up his keys. “Let’s get goin’. The boys should have her ready.”

On Michigan Avenue, Tony hailed a cab. “You can’t keep a car in the city. Tell that to my crazy sister.”

The drive to the harbor took less than ten minutes. The driver sped north on Lake Shore Drive. The cab’s windows were rolled down. The air felt cool, but the sun beating down on the cab was hot.

Tony paid the driver when they reached Diversey Harbor Marina. Frederick could see two young men standing near the dock, watching them. One raised a hand and shouted to him.

“Hey, Tony. Where you been? We’re all set.”

“Yo. What’s the hurry? The fish don’t bite ’til I get there.”

“Okay, Tony. You’re the boss.”

Frederick followed the three of them to the dinghy. One of the kids got in and sat down by the motor. The other began uncoiling the line tied to a cleat on the dock. Tony stepped into the boat heavily and it began to rock unsteadily. Frederick waited for the boat to calm as Tony arranged himself in the middle seat, starting it rocking again. The kid at the throttle stared after a couple of girls strolling the sidewalk edging the harbor. Frederick eased himself into the boat, and the other kid slid in after him.

The short ride to the power boat was smooth, the lake was quiet, and in spite of it being a Sunday afternoon in July, there were only a few other boats moving about in the water beyond them.

Frederick wondered whether Tony owned the boat. He didn't show much grace getting aboard, and once on board, he didn't pay much attention to his surroundings. Usually boat owners were hovering over loose cleats, or picking at specks and nicks their companions hadn't noticed. Maybe he was a fisherman, not a boater.

Frederick studied the dark line of buildings growing smaller as they headed into Lake Michigan. His catch was waiting on shore. Tony settled into the chair next to him after handing him a beer. He spread his knees and hunched forward as disinterested in the ride as a commuter riding the El train. After the third beer, Tony stood to survey the water.

"This'll do," he shouted. "Cut the engine."

He pulled two rods from a box on the deck and handed one to Frederick. He squatted over the bait well, digging around, pulling up bits of bait. He threw some back, tugged at a piece of fleshy meat, threw it back, and shoved his hand deeper into the box.

Frederick watched a couple of sailboats becalmed, sheets stretched for a sail full of wind. Tony tossed his line into the water and secured the rod to a holder attached to the rail. Frederick pushed up the sleeves of the new silk blend sweatshirt and took the first piece of bait he touched. He wrapped it around the hook, secured a second hunk and cast his line out into the water. As he shoved the handle into the holder, he felt a tug on the line. There was no mistaking it. He'd hooked something big. He let out the line. He could feel the pull. He locked the reel. The tip of the rod bent toward the water. He fed it more line.

"Son of a bitch," Tony said. "Hey, kid. Start the engines."

Not much of a fisherman, Frederick thought. "Wait a minute. Let me do this myself," he said aloud.

Tony appeared indifferent. "Hold it," he shouted to the kid. Within an hour, they'd each pulled a coho onto the deck. That seemed good enough for Tony, and Frederick was eager to call it a day, too. Tony returned with another beer and handed one to Frederick. He didn't appear to be in any hurry to get back to shore. An uneasy feeling swept over Frederick."

“So what kind of work do you do, Fred?” Tony asked as he took a long swig of beer.

Frederick J. Lewis proceeded slowly. He offered a textbook definition of a consultant. He labored over details of his work in the nation’s capital, then launched into a monologue on the current rage of mergers and buy-outs. He inferred he was hot, in demand, but was playing it cool. Biding his time, trolling for the best deal. He was taking a breather, his work consolidating the Boston company had been brilliant, he implied modestly.

“I like Boston,” he concluded. “Food’s great. Easy to get to great fishing. They’re taciturn people. Don’t chat much. When I want to relax I come to the Midwest. Chicago, now that’s my kind of town.”

“You said it,” Tony agreed. I love this city. The greatest city in the world. My grandmother used to say it all the time when I was a kid. I used to think she was crazy. She’d get on the El and just ride it around. By the time I’d figured it out for myself, she was already dead, or I’d a told her so.

“Hey, maybe I could hire you. Maybe you could so some consulting for me.”

Frederick took a long drink from the bottle he’d been holding. Things had started to get a bit weird for a while, and he’d have preferred to have this conversation over drinks at the Hancock Center. Then again, thinking about Tony at the Ritz Carlton, maybe this was more Tony’s world.

“I’ve got important papers to send to Boston. Can’t trust the mail, or Fed Ex. Can’t fax ’em. Too big and bulky. Got to get ’em right back. Can’t stand to go myself. Hate that city. Full of damn little bumpy streets. I got blueprints sitting on my desk right now that have to be in Boston tomorrow. Used to let a kid in my office take ’em. He stops off at that Funnily Square and leaves ’em on a oyster bar, he’s got the nerve to tell me. So I got these prints to send to Boston tomorrow, and I got a meeting here in Chicago and nobody I can trust to take ’em.

“So what’d ya say? Can you help me out? You don’t have to consult with nobody. What do you charge for consulting? By the hour, I suppose. Like lawyers. So stop by my office in the morning. I’ll give you the prints and a round-trip ticket to Boston. And expenses, of course.

"Don't leave 'em in no oyster bar. I saw you pass up them oysters at the Ritz."

Frederick walked over to the cooler for another bottle of beer. One of the kids had cleaned the cohos and was baiting the hook. He wondered how long it had been dangling empty in the water.

"Go ahead, Mario," Tony shouted. "See what you can catch."

8 | Where Doubt Ends, Peace of Mind Begins

The Chicago El was crowded at seven o'clock in the morning. Frederick stood in the aisle all the way to his stop, trying to keep the pocket of his suit from brushing against the chocolate donut being consumed by the passenger seated next to him. There was no room to move. When the unintelligible intercom mumbled again, he pushed his way out of the train, down the stairs and across Wabash Avenue to Scully's office.

He took the elevator to the tenth floor and stepped out into a dark, narrow corridor lined with closed doors with frosted glass windows. Halfway down the corridor, he found the door marked thirty-two in chipped black paint. No light was visible from within. He rapped on the glass and turned the knob. The door opened.

Frederick walked into Tony Scully's business organization. He'd been hoping for a spacious room with a receptionist. What he found was no larger than a closet. Tony was leaning out an open window.

"Hey, come on in. I was just lookin' at all the food vendors up the street. They didn't used to allow that. Now they got 'em every few feet—hot dogs, pretzels, ice cream. You name it.

"Sit down. There's a chair under all them phone books." Tony sat down behind a messy stack of papers so high Frederick hadn't noticed the desk. The arms of Frederick's chair were dark and greasy. Frederick picked up the phone books and dropped all but one on the floor. He sat down on the last one and hunched over, putting his elbows on his knees.

"So here's the package. Take a cab directly from the airport. I don't need to tell you. I can relax." Tony leaned over the desk and handed

Frederick an oversized envelope wrapped in Bubble-Wrap with a name and address attached.

This wasn't where Frederick had intended to be, but life took strange twists. He'd had offices with fine mahogany desks, and they'd led nowhere. He'd had titles with detailed job descriptions, and they'd led up blind alleys or out the door.

"I should get myself a real office. S'that what you're thinking? That can wait. I just need a place to show up to once in awhile. A mailing address. I know too many s.o.b.'s with mile-high carpets. When they go bankrupt, it don't mean so much."

"So what's the project?" Frederick didn't want to push, but he needed to know how much Tony Scully was worth.

"Yeah, these are some specs for somethin' we're puttin' together in Boston. Haven't hit the big one yet. The Shopping Mall. Maybe someday. Those are big operations. Maybe you're what I need to pull it together. You could talk real nice to civic leaders. Romance the environmentalists."

Tony handed Frederick the familiar envelope of an airline ticket. It was heavier. Fred could feel the outline of several bills behind the ticket.

"This should tide you over. I don't mind telling you it makes me sleep good knowing you're delivering these. I hope I can persuade you to stick around; so take a few days. See the seashore. Then next week, well, I'll see you before that. Renata likes brunch at the Ritz on Sunday mornings."

Frederick read the name and address on the package. "I just give this to J. Smith?"

He wanted to know the name of the company.

"Yeah, and tell him to give you a receipt. When I get it, we'll settle up on your expenses. Hey, I'll walk down with ya. Want to get me some of them pretzels."

Frederick stood up and walked into the dark hallway. His new boss, Mr. Scully, locked the door and lumbered toward the elevator. Frederick needed to find a place where he could count the bills, check the contents of the package, and assess the ambiguity of his assignment.

They rode to the main floor with an elderly woman who peered suspiciously at each of them as she wagged her cane menacingly. When the door opened, several octogenarians tottered forward. Scully charged ahead, ignoring age and shaky gaits. Frederick held the door open and waited for the last of them to enter the elevator.

Scully slammed the back of his hand against Frederick's chest. "Stay away from the oysters." Then he lunged toward a red-and-white striped umbrella and the warm, yeasty smell of pretzels.

Frederick headed toward the Palmer House and the privacy of a stall in the men's room. He checked the contents of the envelope. A round-trip ticket to Boston and ten hundred-dollar bills. The package was securely wrapped in plastic. His stomach muscles tightened. He turned the sealed package over and over. He didn't know what he was getting into. It was unlikely the previous courier was paid a thousand dollars to deliver a package.

On the other hand, if you needed a well-dressed, well-spoken young man to represent you, and you wanted to be assured your bid, or contracts, or blueprints or whatever the hell was in the package were delivered on time and to the right man, why it was worth the money.

And then there was Renata. Men hired men to keep an eye on their women. Better a brother than a husband. She'd set a date for Thursday evening, which assured his return to Chicago. She was cold and gave him the impression she knew he was meant to be an escort, not a boyfriend. If this was all a set-up to assure that Frederick would keep an eye on Tony's sister, so be it. He'd need plenty of cash for Renata. Tony knew that, too.

Frederick stashed the money in his wallet. He'd dole it out carefully until he knew how much and how often the payments would continue. He'd prefer a cab, but the bus to the airport was loading outside the Palmer House. He hurried to get on board.

The trip to O'Hare took forty-five minutes. The late Monday morning traffic was light, and he was at the United Airlines departure gate twenty minutes ahead of schedule, with no line for check-in and plenty of seats to choose from. No infants wailing or toddlers sprawled across the floor, and a bar around the next corridor. It was tempting, but he thought he'd better wait for a drink until after he'd delivered the package. He had no idea what he was getting himself into.

The flight departed on schedule, an unusual event. Frederick settled into his seat, listened to the beverage cart clinking toward him, wavered in the direction of one Bloody Mary, but decided against it. He shut his eyes and tried to figure out where he fit in with Tony and Renata Scully.

Renata Scully obviously needed someone to look after her. He didn't know what it was—drugs, alcohol, gambling? On the other hand, Tony Scully needed a minder, too. Renata was not as fragile as she'd first appeared. And Tony was the proverbial bull in a china shop. Frederick could see that he would be a big help to both of them. Tony had the money. Frederick J. Lewis had the *savoir faire*. Money can be made when you have the right timing. The pieces were starting to fit together.

Frederick wiggled his shoulders forward and back to massage his back muscles. The captain announced the approach into Boston. Not this trip, but maybe the next one he'd take the ferry again to Jellicle Island.

Inside Logan Airport, Frederick found himself surrounded by kids, college kids. American airports all looked the same, the food tasted the same, but people in different cities dressed distinctly. In Chicago, people dressed up when they traveled. Frederick enjoyed checking out the expensive wardrobes. In Boston, with its permanent college-aged population, the airport was filled with an androgynous crowd clothed in jeans, sporting long hair, duffle bags, and guitars.

Frederick stepped out to the curb and hailed a cab. He read the address from the package label to the cab driver. "They've had a lot of trouble with that building," the driver responded.

"Is that so?" Frederick could use any information he could get.

"Yeah, electrical fires. Where you coming from?"

"Chicago."

"They got tall buildings there, too. Tallest in the world. Sears Tower. Windows fly out of that sucker?"

"Not that I know of. I used to work in there. You can feel the building sway."

"Is that right?"

In his mind, Frederick pictured Scully's office. He needed to upgrade. He could appreciate Tony's lack of interest in spending money on an office he rarely used, but Frederick would like an office with a view. Part of the game.

"Here we are, buddy."

Frederick stared up at the tall expanse rising before him. He paid the cabbie, pocketed the receipt, and walked into the lobby, stopping in front of the directory. He knew where he was going, but he hoped for more information. The offices were listed alphabetically, not by floor. He searched up and down the board for names on the seventh floor. A lot of initials. Nothing helpful.

On the seventh floor, a guard looked up from his desk.

"I'm looking for J. Smith. Suite 777."

"Don't know the name, but 777 is around the corner. There's a lot of office space for rent up here."

A secretary smiled nervously when Frederick pushed open the door. An open bottle of nail polish occupied the desk. She held the brush awkwardly in her hand and hurriedly put it back as Frederick walked in.

"I'm looking for J. Smith," he said.

"Yeah?" She turned to her telephone and pushed a button. "There's a guy here to see you." Frederick glanced around for a chair. There was none.

The door behind the secretary opened. A scrawny little man peeked out. Frederick walked forward and extended his hand. The man stared at him for a moment but didn't extend his hand.

"Scully sent you?"

"Yes. I have a package for you." Frederick didn't offer it to him. "I'll need a receipt."

"Oh? Well, then, follow me."

Frederick followed the man into the room behind the secretary. It was a cavernous space divided into small cubicles with shoulder-high modular walls. He hurried after J. Smith, who scurried down the maze. Frederick tried to peek into cubicles as they went along. There were men, women, plants, telephones, and computers. He had no idea what anyone was doing.

At the end of the room, the rear wall supported a row of offices with doors and a wall that extended to the ceiling, providing privacy and perhaps, designating a higher rung on the corporate ladder. He wished he'd figured out how to check the contents of the package. Maybe he could get the guy to open it before he accepted the receipt.

J. Smith opened a door, and Frederick followed him into a room with a window. The blinds were shut. The desk was shoved against the wall, leaving a lot of space in the center but also leaving the impression it had merely been moved to clean the floor. A huge painting hung on the wall behind the desk. It was a copy of an old oil painting of Boston Harbor in an elaborate gilded frame. It was too large and heavy for the wall. The copy was too poorly reproduced for its expensive frame, and it looked as if it could lean forward and topple the pre-fabricated wall with it.

"Can I have it?" J. Smith squeaked.

Frederick handed him the package. The man reached for the parcel and hesitated, smiling at Frederick as he accepted it. Frederick felt relief when it was out of his possession.

"Scully doesn't trust conventional delivery systems. He's right, too. Like the commercial says, sooner or later it's going to fall off a truck and into a lagoon." He pronounced it lay-goon.

"You can't be too careful. Want to check the contents and give me a receipt?"

"So how's the weather in Chicago?" He didn't sound interested.

"It's a beautiful summer day in both cities."

"I'll probably be going out that way in a couple of weeks. Keeps us employed, right?"

The man seemed out of sync, but Frederick was focused on the idea they were working for the same company, that his coming and going might be a routine. "You want to check the package and give me a receipt?"

J. Smith squeezed his way back behind the large desk and opened one drawer and then another. "You headed straight back, or are you going to take in the sights?"

"I've got to head back. Lot of work to do." Frederick felt out of sync, too. "If you'll check the package and…"

"Nah, that's okay. I don't have a receipt book so here…" He turned and pulled a sheet of paper from the printer behind him. He scribbled across it and handed it to Frederick. Frederick looked at it. The man had written "Got it! 4:15 PM 7/18/94 J. Smith."

Frederick had no choice but to find his way back through the labyrinth of cubicles to the receptionist. She sat slumped before her telephone, chewing gum, and stared after him. He could hear the bubble pop as he shut the door.

The fresh salty air smelled good as Frederick pushed his way through the revolving door. When he reached the street, Tony Scully's right hand man, conduit, *chargé d'affaires*, and all around general manager needed a good lunch and a stiff drink.

Boston. Home of the Ritz. He hailed a cab.

9 | A GOOD CAT DESERVES A GOOD RAT

When the ferry left the dock, Alicia wished she hadn't had the second gimlet with the Nortons. She sat in the center row of empty chairs on the deck. She preferred the old days when canvas backed "director" chairs lay scattered about and each passenger could set her chair in any odd space, at any angle she liked. Alicia hated watching the island disappear from view. She'd be back in a few hours, yet she always feared something would happen and she would be trapped on the mainland.

She sipped hot coffee from a paper cup, planning her stops, weighing the importance of a visit to the MFA against the instructional value of stopping at one of the galleries on Newbury Street.

She didn't want to be influenced by another artist's work. She intended to create something substantial, but the watercolorists kept returning to visions as light and airy as a kite bound to the earth by a long thin line.

Swallowing the last of her coffee, she tossed the cup into a trash receptacle. In the distance, she could see another ferry headed toward the island. She turned her attention once again to planning her stops. She could buy art supplies at a store near the Museum of Fine Art and spend an hour there. Then she thought of the supply store on Newbury Street.

She recognized the hostility of her mood. The ferry would be docking shortly. People began gathering their belongings, and heading for the stairwells leading to their cars or lining up by the pedestrian exit.

Back in her car, she felt like a horse trapped, waiting for the sound of freedom in an opening gate. The ferry doors opened with a grating screech. She put the car in gear and drove over the gangplank and onto the mainland.

She checked her watch and noted she could be at this spot, but headed back to the island, by five o'clock that afternoon. The traffic intensified as more and more cars sped toward Boston. She hoped she could find a place to park on the street, avoiding an expensive parking lot.

On Newbury Street, she was rewarded with a parking space. She fed the meter and headed to the art supply store. Once inside, she wasted no time looking for an illusive tube of paint as she used to, but went straight to the counter.

"I need these items," she said as she thrust her list at the clerk. "I've parked up the street, and I'll need someone to come out and put the supplies in my car when I pull up."

"No problem," the clerk replied. "We should have all this in stock."

He disappeared into the supply room with Alicia's neatly printed and precisely detailed list, which included code numbers from the supply catalog. Now she wondered why she hadn't had them sent by UPS. Because, she answered herself, she did not want to wait. And, she added, she wanted to be part of the whole process of selection, accumulation, and delivery.

"We don't have the Werindus," the clerk shouted from the supply room door.

"Do you have any sheet metal sheers?" Alicia asked.

Just then the store's manager appeared. He held her list. "We probably have them at our other store. We could ship them to you."

"I don't want to wait. I'll just have to drive over to Beacon Street and pick them up there." Now she would have to find two parking spaces in Boston. That settled it. She would visit the MFA.

"The shears will be at the desk for you. Everything else is here. How did you want to pay for it?"

Alicia handed over her credit card and watched as the assistant stood waiting to put the supplies in her car. It was hot. She was thirsty. She wished Beth had come along, but she appreciated her desire to remain on the island when she had so little time there. She lived in a city.

As promised, the Werindus were waiting at the counter when she arrived, happy to have found a second parking place easily. The shears turned out to be much heavier than she'd anticipated. What was she going to do with the sheets of metal, the wire, the self-flux soldering wire—whatever that was? She'd culled the list from an art supply catalog. She was glad she'd added a book—a book for beginners working with metal.

Certain her luck couldn't hold Alicia, once parked in a lot next to the MFA, walked up the stairs and presented her membership card to the guard. Trying to free herself from the brooding mood that had crept over her, she tried to dismiss the doubt that had crossed her mind as she'd carried the heavy shears to her car.

Thomas Hart Benton. That's a painter she liked. His style was straightforward, solid, and masculine. It could not confuse or influence her own style, but it inspired her and filled her with energy and eagerness.

Except for the guard standing with his hands folded in front of him and his eyes staring into the next gallery, she stood alone before the painting. Her eyes followed the thick lines, absorbing the muted grays and ochre, seeing in the solid face a pair of eyes as familiar as those in a family portrait.

"Hello, Alicia."

He was standing next to her, almost touching her, his arms folded like the museum guard's, yet she had been unaware of his presence until he spoke. His voice did not startle or surprise her. She turned to face him casually, as if she'd been expecting him.

"Frederick, how are you?"

"Fine, thank you. Now I know why you haven't been answering your phone this morning."

"I..." she paused. She had no intention of explaining her trip.

"How about a guided tour? Share your observations with me, for example, on this painting."

"I don't really have much time. I have a ferry reservation."

"What a coincidence. So do I."

"You do?"

"You don't think I'd have business in Boston and not make time to visit my favorite artist, do you?"

Several responses occurred to Alicia, and each seemed more nagging and reproachful than the last. If he annoyed her so, why was her mood changing to pleasantly surprised?

"Have you been to the MFA before?"

"No, this is my first visit."

"Is there anything in particular you'd like to see."

"I think I've found it."

There it was again, his wonderfully charming, completely unbelievable smile. She needed to get back to the island.

"Why don't we walk quickly through a couple of galleries? I don't want to miss the ferry."

"Nor do I."

"You really are on your way to the island?"

"Unless you can be persuaded to spend the night in Boston."

"No, I don't think so."

"Then can I persuade you to accompany me to a lovely little restaurant on the island? I owe you."

"Not that again, please." She was laughing now, much too loudly for the Museum of Fine Art.

"You pick the restaurant."

"Anthony's." It was the most expensive restaurant on the island.

"Sounds fine to me. Now about the cars." He placed his hand on the small of her back and nudged her forward toward the exit. The cool air of the museum turned to heat outside as they walked down the stairs.

"What about the cars?" she asked.

"Is this to be a parade, or may I abandon mine and ride with you?"

"Abandon your car?"

"It wouldn't be difficult. I haven't picked it up yet from the rental agency."

"On one condition."

"Any, my dear."

"You drive." Alicia tossed him the keys as they approached her car. She hated Boston's traffic.

He drove fast, easing in and out of gear. If he could maintain the speed and the traffic diminished as they left the city, they would reach the ferry ahead of schedule. They could eat by the dock, he could take a shuttle back to Boston, and she could go on alone to the island.

As he drove, Alicia had time to think about the next steps she needed to take. Roger, or someone from his lumberyard, would have left a load of sand in the front yard by now. She hoped the extension cord for the soldering iron would reach it. He'd mentioned some scrap metal and volunteered to give it to her. That would help. The large flat sheets of metal in the back seat did not inspire her. A successful watercolor painting evolved from relationships of colors and objects. Painting a boat and a lighthouse and a wave did not assure a composition. For the painting to succeed, each part had to become a part of each other part. However, she never analyzed her paintings. She simply painted.

Reaching into her bag, Alicia pulled out a small sketchbook. She uncapped a charcoal pencil and drew a square. She could not imagine cutting the square into interesting shapes and welding them together. Her brushes flew across the white space of paper, colors appeared, shapes took on depth and shadow.

Now the pencil felt awkward as she dragged it across the sketch pad. She had no idea where to push it, what line to draw first. Her paintings were an intuitive act, a drawing in of all she saw about her, all she felt. It was not that different from the poetry she had read in her girlhood. Like Emily Dickinson, she took little truths and made them clear to others. But sculpting. She would not be a creator so much as an assembler. Even as she envisioned herself in her protective goggles, torch in hand, she saw the destructiveness, not the art. It was an explosive act—a pugilistic attempt to re-create the universe. To realign. To tame.

When they reached the ferry landing, Alicia told Frederick to avoid the line for the ferry and park on the street.

"I thought we were all set," Frederick said.

"We're early. Let's eat here. I'm hungry."

It felt good to be close to the ocean again, closer to her island. The air was cool and smelled salty. Seagulls circled overhead. Alicia took a deep breath and let it out slowly.

The bar was filled, but the dining room was practically empty. The walls were covered with ship wheels, fishing nets, starfish and lobsters. In the center of the table, a candle burned in a lantern.

The waitress appeared, pad and pencil ready to take their order.

"I'll have a lobster roll and a cup of chowder." Alicia requested.

"Sounds good. Bring me two lobster rolls and a bowl of chowder."

"The rolls are pretty big, sir."

"Oh, it's not for me. It's for the lady. She's hungry."

Alicia shook her head. "What do you have on tap?"

"Michelob and Strohs."

"We'll have a pitcher of Strohs," Frederick ordered.

"So, you're working in Boston now?"

"Actually, I'm commuting between Chicago and Boston. That's why I haven't called. I've been in Chicago. I should have called before I left, but something came up all of a sudden. I'm working for a Chicago-based company intent on redesigning the entire East Coast, I think. I'm the advance man. It's a construction company. From the look of the back seat of your car, it appears you're going into bridge building."

"Something like that." Alicia thought he'd said he was in banking.

The waitress returned with the beer and chowder and assured them she'd be right back with the lobster rolls. Alicia started on the chowder. It was hot and creamy. The rolls arrived with large chunks of lobster meat sliding out over the plate. She grabbed one of the morsels and popped it into her mouth.

"I'm glad we don't have to share," Frederick observed. "This is tasty."

"What do you mean we don't have to share? I thought you ordered only one for you."

Frederick laughed again. It was a strangely high-pitched giggle. Alicia continued eating. She'd only had coffee on the morning ferry. She'd been thirsty all afternoon, and the beer had merely whetted her appetite.

"There, we have plenty of time," she observed as she stared at their empty dishes.

"Does that mean you'd like dessert?"

"Oh, I'll have that at Anthony's on the island."

"You're intending to eat again?"

"I thought you invited me." Alicia cocked her head to one side and gave him a wink. Her long blonde hair was braided, but a strand had come loose and hung touching her collar bone. She felt it brush against her skin and reached back to secure it.

When the waitress appeared with the bill, Alicia pulled lipstick from her purse. Frederick placed a hundred dollar bill in the leather folder.

Okay, she thought. He can come with me to the island.

"Let's go," he said unaware that he might have been disinvited.

For the return trip, Alicia liked to sit so she could watch the island zoom back to full size, its blurry green coming into focus, blots of white turning to sharp architectural forms—a church spire, a widow's walk, a high-pitched roof. On the hill overlooking the harbor, a water tower extended above the trees, edged in the darkening blue of the approaching summer evening.

"See that water tower over there?" Alicia pointed. "Do you suppose it really is a water tower, or do you think it's part of the Star Wars Offensive?"

"Looking at this idyllic New England landscape, that never occurred to me."

"Going to Boston always leaves me grumpy. Once, on a particularly hostile trip, I looked at it and thought maybe it's not at all what we think it is. Perhaps it's a missile tower disguised as a water tower. It gave me a great sense of satisfaction to think we islanders could obliterate the entire East Coast if it didn't shape up."

"I'll bear that in mind."

Alicia finished the last swallow of coffee and stared at the empty Styrofoam cup. "Take this cup, for instance. As flimsy as it is, it's indestructible. The fast-food containers tossed out on the mainland would sink this little island. Think about those barges of garbage floating up and down the coastline searching for a place to dispose of their trash. We've always had to be careful on this island. Pieces of plastic like that around a six-pack strangles birds who get entangled."

Alicia stopped talking, aware her conversation was disjointed. It wasn't the beer. It was the man. He was not trustworthy, she felt, yet she found him irresistible. She'd become aloof, insular, and detached. She'd started to back away from her grand designs, fearful of cutting into metal. Then, once in Frederick's company, she felt recharged, energized, and ready for action.

She was eager to get to work. How long would the sculpture last when it was completed, she wondered. Someone had created the plastic, boiled it up in great vats, and molded it into disposable cups, and it turned out to be indestructible. The soft sea breezes would corrode steel, dissolve aluminum, and pit brass.

She thought of her friend Tess. It would be nice to have someone to share a life with, to hunker down by a seaside fire and talk in hushed tones about all the unimportant details of daily life with a husband and children. Instead, like the seagull, she'd slipped her neck into a plastic yoke and wondered why she felt stuck, yet unwilling to struggle.

10 | Sometimes the Best Answer Is No Answer

The telephone blasted Alicia out of deep sleep, but Frederick didn't move. He looked as inscrutable now as he had the night before, she noted as she yanked the receiver from its cradle.

"Hello? Oh, hi, Beth."

She continued studying Frederick's face as she listened. His eyes did not open, but the lids flickered slightly. He was listening.

"Dinner tonight? I'm not sure. I missed your company in Boston yesterday, but I can certainly understand why you wouldn't want to leave the island. I thought Roger was going to deliver sand for me, but it's not here. Could I let you know about dinner later this morning?"

When she'd hung up the phone, Frederick opened his eyes. "Good morning," he said.

"Good morning to you." She settled back on one elbow, not knowing whether she wanted to get out of bed or to settle down next to him.

"I wish I could continue to interfere with your social life, but I have to get back to Chicago. I'll take the shuttle back to Boston."

Alicia opened her mouth to speak, then shut it again, pulling in her lips like she used to do in school to stifle a giggle. Only now it wasn't laughter, but indiscretion she wished to avoid.

"That was a friend who's home for a visit. She lives in Chicago, too."

It was Frederick's turn to weave words carefully. It worried him to know Beth was close by.

“I wouldn’t say I was from Chicago. The main office is in Boston, and I seem to be spending most of my time in planes shuttling back and forth between the two cities.”

Alicia turned and stood with her back to him as she pulled a robe over her bare body. She left the bedroom, and Frederick moved swiftly from the bed and stepped into his shorts and pulled his pants from the back of a chair. He could hear Alicia brushing her teeth in the bathroom.

“Is your friend coming over?” He stood outside the half-open door.

“If you’re interested, I’m going there for dinner tonight. I’ll ask if I can bring a friend.”

“If I could stay, I’d rather spend my time with you. Unfortunately, I’ve got to be in Chicago for a meeting.”

“You’d better check on the shuttle flights. It’s not always easy getting on and off the island by air.”

Frederick finished buttoning his new monogrammed shirt and started down the stairs. He calculated the odds of Beth appearing at Alicia’s door. The dogs followed him into the kitchen, sniffing at his pant legs and wagging their tails. He found the telephone directory and looked up the number for the airport. He punched the number rapidly, then waited impatiently as the phone rang on and on. Checking his watch he was surprised it was only 7:30.

“Yeah, what’s the next available flight to Boston? Good. Book me on it. Name’s Lewis. That’s the last name. F. J. Lewis. No, I’ll pay cash. Save the seat.”

He hung up the telephone and called up the stairs.

“Could you get me to the airport in twenty minutes?”

Alicia appeared at the top of the stairs. Her long hair was pulled back and tied. As she leaned forward on the stairs to answer him, part of a loose curl slipped forward caressing her neck.

“Not even time for coffee?”

“Not even time for coffee. If I had time, it wouldn’t be for coffee. Will you meet me again in Boston next week?”

“I don’t think so. I’ve got a big project underway. I have to earn a living, too.”

He wished she’d hurry. He wasn’t sure how Alicia felt about him. She’d acted fairly indifferently. She was an artist, but he hadn’t seen the legendary artist's temperament. He'd been watching the dogs, hoping they wouldn't start barking at the sound of someone approaching the house. Next trip, he thought, he'd make sure Beth was back in Chicago. He didn't want to accidentally run into her. He knew she still cared about him, and she was the one woman who got under his skin. Renata didn't care, but he didn't want to cause any contention. He had a good thing going. He liked his action under the covers, not looking for cover.

Alicia grabbed her car keys and walked past him out of the house. On the main road, they passed a trio of moped riders weaving unsteadily. "They've got to ban those things. They have terrible accidents all the time," Alicia muttered.

"I'd rather ride one of those than a bicycle," Frederick said.

Alicia squealed around a corner and headed into the airport. When she pulled up in front of the solitary terminal, she left the motor running.

Frederick wasn't sure how to read her. "Thanks for the ride. Will I see you next weekend?"

"You'd better hurry. I think that's your plane loading."

Frederick thought about kissing her. He decided against it. He scrambled out of the car and hurried into the building. Alicia sped away. He liked her style.

He watched as the last passenger got on board and the attendant pulled back the stairs. The plane was taxiing down the runway when Frederick asked where he could get a cup of coffee. He had plenty of time. The flight into Boston didn't leave until eleven o'clock.

11 | What Gets into Your Eye Is Not Visible to You

"Roger? Alicia Barrett. Could you deliver the sand today?"

Leaning against the kitchen wall, Alicia stroked Betta's back with her bare foot. The telephone cord bounced in front of the dog's nose. "I want to get started welding, and I don't want to set fire to my front lawn. Yes, yes, I'd love to have some of that scrap metal. Set it near the wood pile."

Alicia stared out the window at the yard. Roger apologized for not delivering the sand by explaining his wife was pregnant and it was hard for him to keep his mind on business.

"When's the baby due? That soon? Sure. Thanks." She disconnected the line, listened for the dial tone and re-dialed."

"Hi, Beth. Is my dinner invitation still viable? Thanks. Roger Dutton promised he'd deliver sand, and I wasn't sure when he was planning on doing it. You're welcome to stop by this afternoon; otherwise, I'll see you around five. Oh, is anybody else invited? I just like to know if I should spend the afternoon researching some esoteric subject I know nothing about."

Alicia hung up the phone and walked into the living room to the mantel. She was thinking it probably wouldn't have been a good idea to take Frederick with her to the Nortons'. Mrs. Norton would be overly curious, and she didn't know if Beth was still wrapped up with the crazy guy who was always disappointing her. She studied the shiny object on the mantel.

The dogs paced about, perking up their ears each time she left the house, moping when she returned with each load of materials. She spread out the welding iron and its parts on the dining room table. Then she took the directions and a book about the art of welding and settled into a wing chair in the living room, where she could look up at the mantel for inspiration if her courage began to falter.

At four o'clock, she realized the day was gone, no lunch, no Beth, no sand. And no conviction she had any idea how to use the tools she'd purchased. She stood at the window, estimating the distance to the nearest trees from the center of her yard. She would need a longer extension cord for the soldering iron. A bucket of water or a fire extinguisher sounded like a good investment, too.

There was no point in delaying a shower to be followed by a snack of peanut butter and crackers so that she could enjoy a gimlet or two with the Nortons. A flared skirt and silk blouse instead of her comfy jeans and baggy shirt set Alicia to thinking about lives more formal and less solitary than her own. She wondered what it would be like to have to include someone else in her life.

She hoped she'd made her point with Frederick. She had no intention of perking up her ears each time the phone rang. Weekends in Boston were out of the question. At five minutes to five, she set out for the Nortons' house. She strained to hear conversation as she walked up the road, but sound traveled down the ridge toward the beach, not up the road. When she reached the bend in the road she could see the porch and hear Mrs. Norton sending forth a cheery hello.

"Come in, come in. Frank? Do we have ice? Beth? Beth? Alicia's here. Where *is* everyone." She made it sound as if the house was filled with people, but Beth had assured her she was the only guest.

Alicia continued walking around the screened porch, past the wall of windows by the dining room to the front door. By the time she reached the front step, Mrs. Norton was holding open the door. "Welcome. Come out to the porch and have a drink. Tell me what you've been up to. I'm absolutely starved for news."

Alicia doubted Mrs. Norton was ever starved for news but concluded she perhaps always thought she was. As they passed through the dining room, Mrs. Norton straightened a sagging candle on the elaborately set table. A piece of driftwood covered with the bleached shells of tiny whelks was surrounded by shards of sea glass and little vases of roses. Crystal wine glasses sparkled in the light of the sun which was slipping below the line of trees beyond the house.

"Sit here. You must keep your back to the sun for another half hour. Frank, where is Beth?" Mrs. Norton fussed.

"Right here, Mother. Alicia, you're all dressed up!" laughed Beth.

"Beth, you should have worn something better than those dreadful bell-bottoms," her mother intoned.

"They're so old they're new again. I'm sure Alicia won't be offended, and it's easier to keep a stash of clothes here than to carry a big suitcase."

"Absolutely," Alicia agreed.

"Well, Beth does look better. The sun and the salt water have done wonders for her, but it was an effort to get her to the beach."

Several times Alicia attempted to speak to Beth, but Mrs. Norton interrupted, answering, or slipping in her own agenda, messages only Beth would get.

"You could stay longer," Mrs. Norton said to her only child.

"I have bulletin boards to put up, name cards to laminate," Beth replied wearily. It must have been a daily discussion.

Dr. Norton appeared on the porch, standing in the doorway with his fingertips pressed together in prayerful yet professorial guise.

"Alicia, my dear, what could I get you to drink?"

"I'd love a gimlet."

"That's easy. Beth?"

"A spritzer."

"And you, Sue Ellyn?"

"A Manhattan, very dry."

"An agreeable group you are." He retreated around the corner to his bar.

"Did you tell her?" Mrs. Norton asked Beth.

"No, you go ahead." Beth shook her head and smiled again, with the same weary look in her eyes. Mrs. Norton could wear a person down quickly, Alicia knew.

"Come upstairs. You're going to love this."

Alicia patted Beth's shoulder as she passed her and followed Mrs. Norton back through the dining room to the stairs. She stopped before the bathroom in the second floor hallway. The door was shut, and Mrs. Norton stood with her hand on the knob, waiting for Alicia to reach the top of the stairs. When she did, Mrs. Norton flung open the bathroom door.

A bright orangey red burst from the room.

"Isn't it wonderful? There isn't another bathroom like it, I'm sure."

Alicia recognized the source of the color. Mrs. Norton must have confiscated all the fishing labels from the crate that held Alicia's treasure. She had to agree with Mrs. Norton. It did look wonderful. The fish in the center of each label looked right at home in Mrs. Norton's bathroom.

"I like it. It must have been hard to do. They're not very big."

"Patience. I am blessed with it. Beth pasted and I patched. Then when my arms got stiff, I pasted and Beth patched. Have you ever wall-papered a room? It's actually much easier with small pieces." Mrs. Norton stood with her arms folded in front of her, admiring her work.

Then she frowned and drew in her breath. She leaned forward in what Alicia had recognized long ago as Mrs. Norton's conspiratorial pose. "Do you know if she's still seeing that dreadful man?"

Alicia pushed forward into the bathroom and turned on the faucet. "I think these are Russian fishing labels. You'll have to keep vodka in here instead of water."

"Oh, Alicia. You're a gem." Mrs. Norton put her hand against the door frame and Alicia realized she'd allowed herself to be trapped in the tiny room. "So tell me, have you had a chance to catch up with Beth?" Mrs. Norton was going to push the inquisition.

"What's she up to? She won't tell me anything."

Someday, someone ought to tell this woman her prying and nosiness only left her more isolated from the daughter she professed to care so much about. Alicia swore she could shut her eyes and hear Mrs. Norton asking the same prodding questions when they were teenagers. She could almost hear the giggles from the slumber parties echoing in the shadows.

Alicia's silence forced Mrs. Norton to reconsider her position. She started from the manly pose she'd assumed, blocking the door. She straightened. "I'm happy you like my decorating. Let's not keep them waiting, although I doubt they've waited for us."

Mrs. Norton stopped at the top of the stairs, swayed slightly like a skater about to sweep across the ice. Then, gathering her skirt in one hand she descended the stairway. Alicia took one last look at the papered walls. She followed Mrs. Norton down the stairs.

"Frank, Frank. Wait until you hear this. Alicia thinks we should have vodka flowing from the bathroom faucet. Isn't that priceless?"

"Here you go, Alicia." Dr. Norton handed her a drink. "I hope this is to your liking."

"Thank you. It always is."

Alicia turned and raised her glass in salutation to Beth. "Boston is so congested. Is Chicago like that?"

"That's part of the fun. Finding a legal parking space and getting in and out without a scratch or a ticket. Tell me what you're up to."

"I'm going to try sculpture. It just occurred to me to do it. It's taking me a lot longer to get ready than I'd anticipated. Not at all like painting. Grab a palette, some water, and you're into it."

Beth and Alicia laughed, sipped their drinks and, in the silent spaces of the conversation, communicated the depth of their friendship. Mrs. Norton sat silently, listening intently to their words, unable to grasp the sympathy that passed unspoken between them.

"What material are you working with?" Dr. Norton inquired.

"That's part of the problem. I bought some sheet metal, and Roger Dutton has promised to give me some scrap metal, but I've got a special piece I'm trying to incorporate into the design, and I haven't the remotest idea how to do it. I don't know what it's made of, and I don't know if it's got an oxide on it that will prevent me from doing what I want."

"Could you get it tested?" Dr. Norton asked.

"I'm sure I could, but I'm too impatient."

"Someone in Boston, perhaps?"

"Oh, God. I'm in no mood to go back there."

Alicia didn't want to tell Mrs. Norton where she'd found the object. Now that she knew Mrs. Norton had collected the rest of the contents of the crate, she didn't want anyone to know where it had come from.

"Well, don't get in a glum mood. Dinner is ready." Mrs. Norton stood up and ushered them into the dining room. She served linguine in cream sauce with chunks of swordfish and a grape and walnut salad. While Dr. Norton poured the deep red burgundy, Mrs. Norton proclaimed it a suitable wine because swordfish is a meaty fish. For dessert, she scooped vanilla ice cream into silver bowls and liberally poured *cassis* over it.

After dinner, the four of them went upstairs to the living room because the porch was too cool. There she served strong coffee, and Dr. Norton brought out a tray of liqueurs. A fireplace with a wide mantel filled the north wall, and the interior wall was filled with paintings. The west wall, like the dining room beneath, was made up of windows. It was an inviting, cozy room.

"Alicia," Beth said when they were settled with their after-dinner drinks, "I used to work in a gallery in Chicago during the summer to make ends meet. I still keep in touch with the owners. Would you be interested in showing some of your work in Chicago?"

"I don't know if the windy city is interested in island scenes." Alicia's mind was on her sculpture.

"I honestly don't know either," Beth said. "They're big on surrealists and the kind of stuff that reminds me of the drawings adolescent boys doodle, but I've seen some beautiful drawings and sketches in the galleries, too. Barns, and buckets, and boats that suggest Lake Michigan marinas. Who's to know it isn't the lake?"

"I would know," Dr. Norton broke in. "Alicia Barrett is such an accomplished recorder of island life that I can identify the very rocks she paints."

"I wasn't meaning to insult. People see what they want to see. I was really thinking it would get you to Chicago and we could arrange a reunion with Tess."

"Now that sounds like a good idea."

"These are good galleries, Alicia. I could take back some photos and see what I could arrange."

"Don't bother with photos. Take some paintings."

"It would be good for you, too, Beth," Mrs. Norton chimed in. "You might just meet someone… interesting."

Alicia realized it was time to go before Mrs. Norton launched a new attack.

"Come over tomorrow, and we'll sort through some of the drawings and watercolors." Alicia was in the mood to clear them all out of her house.

"I would love to see what you're working on, Alicia," Mrs. Norton added. "You're quite mysterious about this sculpture."

"When are you leaving, Beth?" Alicia asked.

"Monday," Beth said with a hopeful smile.

"That soon?" Alicia turned her attention to Mrs. Norton, praying she could breeze over the obvious exclusion in the invitation for Beth to visit.

"What a wonderful evening. The dinner was scrumptious."

"It's almost August. You must come back. Even if Beth's not here, you could come see us."

"Of course, and..." Alicia paused. She was about to rush into an invitation to show Mrs. Norton her work, and she didn't wish to do that at all. "And I'll do it soon."

Alicia stood up. The strong coffee had not entirely worn off the effects of the wine and the *cassis* and the *crème de menthe*. She walked out of the living room, past some of her own watercolors, past the brilliant bathroom and down the stairs. As she stepped out onto the front step, she turned to say one last thank you.

"I'll turn on the back lights for you, Alicia. Haven't you brought a flashlight?" Mrs. Norton asked.

"Oh, no. I don't need one.

"But the moon isn't out yet. It's pitch black out here."

"It's okay. As long as a deer doesn't crash into me, I'll be fine. I go through the woods when it's dark all the time. The road is an easy walk."

"Well, if you think so, but I would want a flashlight. I keep one by my bed and one in my purse. I'd be happy to lend you one."

"Alicia," Dr. Norton added, "with the flood lights Sue Ellyn had installed, you'll think it's daylight all the way to your door."

"You'll be grateful to throw a little light on the road the night something comes creeping up here, Professor Norton," his wife retorted.

Feeling provocative, Alicia decided to cut through Grandmother Norton's old rose garden, taking the short-cut through the old path, to see for herself how far the light could shine.

12 | Sit, Ye, Rock and Think

"Damn," Tess mumbled as she turned on the kitchen light. "This is *my* Formica hearth. I have warriors to send to battle, a castle to fortify, buffalo to hunt. Monday morning. Yuck."

Her morning routine was automatic. She was no morning person.

The kitchen light, idiotically installed by the back door, forced her to walk the length of the room in the dark. Her bare foot crunched on a lost cat kibble, and her mouth puckered into a grimace. She did not have to think about this daily ritual of breakfast and lunch-making.

Turn from light switch. Open drawer. Pull out two sandwich bags, one brown paper bag, and one coffee filter. Set bags on counter, filter in coffeepot. Light gas under tea kettle. Measure coffee. Open refrigerator. Take out mustard, lunchmeat, juice and bread. Fill juice glasses. Put two slices of bread in toaster, four on cutting board. Spread sandwiches, put in plastic bags. Wash apples. Bag them. Toast pops. Back across room. Pull out toast. Grab soda for lunch bag. Set toast on stove while pouring boiling water for coffee. Take juice, vitamins, and toast to dining room table.

She could do this in her sleep. Mindless. Yet she was proud of her organization. No wasted movements.

She poured a cup of coffee and stood leaning over the kitchen sink sipping it, staring at the back yard. Her soft brown hair was cut shorter than she'd like, but she didn't have time to blow dry long hair. She was five feet tall and, in spite of two pregnancies, weighed only five pounds more than when she married Michael. She didn't exercise or diet or play any sport. She ran up and down stairs twenty times a day, ate the crusts from Nick's sandwiches, and chased Katy through parks, grocery store aisles, and shopping malls. She looked after her neighbor's children when they were ill and the day care center wouldn't take them.

Tess reached into the pocket of her seersucker bathrobe and pulled out a tissue. It was a hot summer. Her allergies were bad. She blew her nose, took another sip of coffee. She was waking up. She began to plan her day.

I'm going to start here, she thought. Wash the floor on my hands and knees with a nail brush. Get into all those damn grooves. Get out the jam and pickle juice. Seal it with that high-gloss plastic stuff. Spray Fantastic on every piece of chrome—the bread box, the rim along the stove, the piece that falls off at the bottom of the refrigerator. Clean out the cupboards. Throw out the mismatched glassware—football mugs from Shell, Pocahontas plastic ware from Burger King, long tall glasses from Pizza Hut. Dust, hell no, get out the ammonia and cut grease. Wash the kitchen windows.

After lunch, she thought, I'll take on the dining room. That won't take long. The breakfront is pristine. The kids know not to touch the glass on the relic case stuffed with wedding china, anniversary crystal, and great-grandmother's silver tea set.

The carpet. First, I've got to get down on my hands and knees and pick out all the scrambled eggs. Then, I'll rent a steamer and boil the sucker. Pity poor Neanderthal maid? She just tossed a little more sand around the floor of her happy home.

On to the living room. Dust the book shelves. Take out all the stuff stashed on top of the books—the thermometer I'll never figure out how to attach to an outside wall from the inside, the ten spools of thread on the top shelf out of the baby's reach (each pierced with a needle), and the cards waiting since Christmas to be answered.

Michael kissed her. "You look deep in thought."

"No, just planning my day."

"Take the cat to the vet."

The cat sat by Tess's feet with her head stretched forward like a camel. It coughed.

"Don't forget your lunch."

"I'm going out. I don't need a lunch today."

“You could have told me sooner. I wouldn’t have gotten up.”

“You have children to care for. And a cat.” The cat coughed again, an empty rattling wheeze. “I’m sorry, Tess, but the cat is sick. Do something about it.”

“I know. What kind of cereal do you want?”

“I have a choice?”

“Power Ranger Puffs or Temptations French Vanilla.”

“What happened to the fear of sugar?”

“That was before I had to spend five minutes in the cereal aisle looking for the package with the Wacky Spiders in it.”

“Temptations French Vanilla is full of spiders?”

“It just might be, and you know what female spiders are known for.”

“I’ll have toast.”

“It’s on your plate.”

“We need trash bags.”

Katy wrapped her fat baby arms around Tess’s leg. She looked down at her in surprise.

“Where did she come from?”

Michael pulled her to him and nibbled on her ear lobe. “I’ll be glad to show you.”

“Has she learned how to climb out of her crib?”

“Don’t get hostile. I brought her down with me. I didn’t have time to change her. There’s a diaper on the sofa for her.”

“Hi, baby. Want some juice?”

“Okay, I’m out of here. I’ll see you tonight. Bye, Katy. Be good to Mommy. Oh, do you have the water bill?”

Why did he always ask her for something just as he was leaving? Something he should have asked for the night before, after the children were asleep, when she had time to pick through the stacks of paper stashed in her desk. She was proud of her domestic engineering, household management, filing systems, accounting, banking, logging, and general retrieval skills. Why must he ask for something on his way out the door? It was in the desk, stuck between the coupon for Pampers and the notice for the homeowners tax exemption status. The minute he pulled out of the driveway, she’d find it.

"I'll take care of it myself this afternoon."

"Don't forget. I think it's due today. There's a five percent penalty if we don't get it in on time. "

"I'll find it. I'll pay it. Have a nice day."

Michael gathered his briefcase and umbrella. "Katy, your mother is really a very hostile person." At the door he turned and blew her a kiss.

"Mama, the cat's tryin' to throw up."

"Oh, good morning Nick."

"Can I watch cartoons?"

"You're going to day camp, remember?"

"Oh."

She set a bowl of cereal in front of him. "If you want a Wacky Spider, eat."

Tess stooped to stroke the cat's back. She hadn't been ignoring this poor creature. She was trying to deny what was happening. The cat was dying.

She remembered one of those rare evenings when the children went to bed without a struggle, and Michael dozed on the sofa in front of the television, Tess had crawled into bed with a mystery, a box of tissues, and a pad of paper to jot down the random thoughts that interrupted her reading. Pay the safe deposit fee, fabric sale ends Saturday, try looking under the bathroom sink for Katy's lost shoe. The cat had jumped onto the bed and nuzzled its nose on the corner of Tess's book.

Tess had looked into its eyes. One eye was nearly shut; a gooey discharge covered it. She felt her own eyes fill with tears. She shut the book. The cat was old. The cat was sick. It had stopped eating. It was going to die.

She'd owned the cat longer than she'd known Michael. She'd worried more about the cat accepting her husband than she had about her friend's opinions of Michael. They shared the lonely months waiting for Michael to come back from his mission in Desert Storm. She'd counted down the months, then the days, and finally the hours until the birth of first Nick, then Katy, under the watchful companionship of the cat.

At first she tried to tell herself it was only an eye infection, but Tess knew better. When she forced herself to look up the symptoms in the cat care book, the words *this condition cannot be ignored* taunted her like a double-dare. She tried to ignore its listlessness, the untouched plates of food, the silence when there used to be meowing. When Tess picked her up, the body rose too quickly as if the bones had hollowed. It was when the rattling cough began Michael finally noticed something was wrong with the cat.

Every day started too soon, ended before she accomplished much. There were Christmas cards on the bookshelf, and it was the middle of July.

And now her baby could walk. Life moved too quickly. It would be suppertime before she'd cleaned the breakfast dishes. She'd be forty-three years old when Katy started kindergarten. She'd be an old woman rocking in a chair before dawn.

"If you were a Neanderthal, you'd be ten years dead," Michael reminded her when she worried about being mistaken for Katy's grandmother. "Their life expectancy was about twenty years," he'd guessed.

There were times when she wished she had not jumped from the career track. She reassured herself those women chasing stock trends to stay ahead of the competition didn't hear the hum in the beetlebung. That was an expression she'd coined after she and Michael had honeymooned on Martha's Vineyard where they called the tupelo tree a beetlebung. Now it seemed so very long ago.

People who rushed about all the time simply didn't notice the tiny hints the universe dropped all around. She sensed a hum to life, a background static, a camaraderie with seen and unseen forces.

The first clue came in the nursery one night, when she held her infant son. When she was too tired to cry any longer, she rocked him at a furious pace. The chair slowed as if by an unseen hand. Her tight hold on Nick lessened. She took a long, slow cleansing breath and felt a maternal embrace in the darkness. She was not alone with this baby who had torn her body asunder, never let her sleep, and whose shrieking hastened her husband's retreat out of the house for "necessary" overtime. In that moment, she sensed a timeless unity with women everywhere, and it brought her peace. It was the hum of the beetlebung.

There was truth in the adage, "She who rocks the cradle rules the world." Tess lost the resentment she'd felt when she was no longer a part of the professional world. The minds of mothers could be better utilized, she concluded. All those brains clicking away. As mothers stood waiting in small clusters outside school on rainy days, the droplets sliding from their umbrellas into tiny pools around their feet, she could sense the kindred spirit of busy minds solving problems. There was bread to be made when an ingredient was missing and another trip to the store was impossible. There was a birthday present to be manufactured when there was no money left in the "revolving funds" jar.

What had been resolved in any of the "think tanks" scattered around the country? Mothers ought to be consulted. Balance the budget? Mothers had to do it everyday.

Although Michael was perplexed by malfunctioning computers, garbled messages, and tumbling stocks, and shared his daily battles at the office with Tess, she was less inclined to tell him how delighted she had become to discover a complex universe that was sending her clues to eternal quagmires.

Wait time had a lot to do with it. She waited in grocery lines, doctors' reception rooms, and traffic while Michael's secretaries typed faster, garage mechanics found the mysterious squeaks sooner, and Walmart opened a new line for the executive on his lunch hour errand. His time was limited, defined, and structured in a manly, worldly way.

Her time was flexible, fluid, and unpredictable. For Tess there were no exact hours, weekends bound by optimistic Friday nights and pessimistic Sunday evenings. No personal business days.

Fourth of July weekend, Katy caught a fever, and Tess's day was measured in the four-hour cycle of Tylenol's relief, starting over again as the fever crested, ending with its defeat. She hovered over her tiny daughter, praying her brain was left undamaged by a one hundred and four degree temperature. There was nothing else that mattered beyond the confines of a rainbow-muralled nursery where cold baths alternated with soothing rub-downs punctuated with bright red drops of modern miracle drugs.

Downstairs the television blared and when, at last, the fever broke, Tess stumbled off to her own bed. In the distance, she heard the Canadians had a new fishing rights treaty with the Russians, and the President would address the United Nations 49th Year Assembly. While she had hovered over Katy, Nick had watched eight hours of cartoons.

She would like to see some of those CEOs MBAs, and PhDs forced back to the cauldron where the foamy brew that started it all still whispered clues, hinted secrets, and flashed omens. It they were forced to wait once in awhile, they might learn something.

She still felt guilty that Nick had watched so much television when Katy was sick. But she knew he was bored by simple stories about cats and mats when he absorbed exciting cartoons about inter-stellar cultural events.

"Mommy, when do I go to day camp?"

"In a few minutes. I have to find the water bill and then we'll leave."

"You've been looking at your desk for a long time."

"I'm waiting for Katy to finish her toast."

"Is the cat going to die?"

"She's very, very old and very, very sick."

"Can David come over?"

"We'll see."

When Tess arrived at the school, a line of cars stretched the length of the block. She took her place behind a station wagon and inched her way forward.

"How come it's raining?" Nick whined.

"I don't know. Maybe it will stop."

"It smells in the gym," Nick whined.

"It would smell worse in a tent." She inched her way forward until she reached a point where she could see Nick walk safely into the school. "Okay. Get out. Have fun."

"I can't go in by myself," Nick wailed.

"Go on. Hurry. Pleease," Tess implored.

"No, you have to come with me."

"Nick, I can't get out." Tess whined. "Katy's in her car seat. Just go."

"No."

They were at a familiar impasse. She turned off the ignition, pushed the buttons on Katy's car seat strap, pulled her from it and, grabbing for Nick with the other hand, stepped out into the rain. She avoided the eyes of the driver behind her. It had happened to every mother in line. A car pulled ahead of hers and the car door opened. A regiment of legs under a rising umbrella rushed past them. She gave Nick a little push.

"Follow them. You'll be fine."

He ran toward the door, but it shut just as he reached the bottom step. Nick let out a howl that thundered across the school yard to the street. Tess adjusted the child on her hip, brushed a clump of wet hair from her eyes, and hurried to the door. She bent down to give Nick a kiss.

"Now get in there." She stood holding the door while a group of children rushed around her.

Tess returned to the car, buckled Katy into her car seat, and rejoined the line of cars that had left their cooperative passengers out at the curb. At the corner stop sign, she buckled her seatbelt. The alarm stopped its unrelenting beep.

There were library books on the floor in the back seat to be returned. She would have to hurry to the grocery store while Katy was still cheerful. Then, on to the Borough office to pay the water bill, home to call the vet. It wasn't possible. By the time she'd finished buying the groceries, it would be time to pick up Nick. After the rough morning start, she didn't want to be late picking him up.

She knew the day was coming when she would not be able to see all things and be all things in his world—the door shutting in his face, the scratched knee from a nasty tumble, the snotty little comment from the neighbor's child. But for now she would rush to hold doors, stop hurts, dismiss and smooth over all acts of unkindness.

And before she had completed her list of errands, she was back in line in front of the school. The cars moved forward slowly as children raced through the puddles and struggled with car doors. Tess searched for Nick's little yellow raincoat, which looked like a dozen others, but she knew she would pick him out instantly.

The cars crept ahead and Tess stopped in front of the school. "Nick, over here," she shouted. The small boy thrashing about in the yellow slicker came alive with a smile and jumped toward the car. He was too little to open the door. She reached over the seat, squeezing her breast on the head rest, and gave the door a shove to open it. He fell into the car splattering water.

"We have to go pay the water bill, and then we'll go home. How was it?"

"Okay." He said it slowly, the pain of his morning sliding through the vowels stretching into a howl.

"My day hasn't been so great, either. Want to tell me about it?"

"No."

By the time the groceries were put away, dinner started, the table set, and she had settled into a chair to read the magazine she'd just purchased, Michael walked in. He observed the domestic tranquility, and as he started up the stairs, he muttered something about how it must be nice to be able to spend the day reading.

"Daddy's home," he said to Nick who sat engrossed in a cartoon show.

"Hi, dear. You're early."

"The air-conditioning shut down. I had to leave. High-tech sealed windows. It was too damn hot."

"Supper should be ready in about half an hour."

"What are we having?"

"Pollock. Lake Perch was seven ninety-five a pound."

"Pollock's fine. Why don't we have a drink? It looks like the kids are under control."

"But of course. I always have everything under control." She pulled a bottle of vodka from the cupboard and fixed them each a Bloody Mary.

When the cartoon ended, Nick kindly switched the television channel to the news and wandered into the dining room to play with a Transformer. Katy slept soundly on the floor, tuckered out from all the errands that didn't leave time for her nap.

As Michael came down the stairs, he said, "I didn't know Margaret's divorce was final."

"What?" Tess asked.

He held up the note from Margaret she'd pulled from the bookcase at the crack of dawn. "Michael, that note is two years old."

"I thought you left it on the dining room table for me to read."

"I pulled it out of the bookcase because I was planning on picking up, but instead I spent the day struggling through errands. I just got home ahead of you."

"Why did you save this?"

"The design on the paper is the Marimekko print I want to make curtains with for Katy's bedroom. I just haven't been able to get to it."

"Is Margaret on Jellicle Island this summer?"

"Yes. And at the moment so are Beth and Alicia. I'd love to see them."

"A funny thing happened to me today. I ran over to Marshall Field's on my lunch hour. I wanted to find a tie for my red sport coat."

"Terra-cotta."

"Whatever. I couldn't remember exactly what shade it was, so I went into the coat department. There was this guy in there trying on expensive sport coats. I wouldn't have paid any attention, but I heard the sales clerk telling him it was an Armani. We watched that movie last weekend where you pointed out to me the Armani jacket. You're always talking about coincidences, so I hung around to see what happened.

"I hear the clerk tell him it's a $1,200 jacket and he's talking about how he isn't sure of the fit. I take a look at his face, and its Beth's friend Rick. The guy you don't like. I heard the clerk call him Mr. Lewis.

"Beth thinks he's working for a bank, but doing something clandestine because he's so secretive."

"That's what I heard her tell you."

13 | Today Must Borrow Nothing from Tomorrow

Things appeared to be looking up for Frederick. When he returned to Chicago, Renata acted happy to see him. A new nightclub was opening and she wanted to be there. Later in the week, she'd informed him, they had reservations for dinner at a tony restaurant in a small town west of the city. Then, she'd explained she would be out of town for a few weeks at a spa in Palm Springs. When she returned, perhaps, if he was interested, she'd like to go to New York and see some plays.

Lunch with Tony brought more animated conversation but less satisfaction. Frederick would have liked to see the dining room of the Urban League Club, or the view from the First Chicago's private dining room. Apparently, Tony did not have access to the very good, very old "good old boys" network. In fact, Frederick had not met any of the partners Tony peppered his conversation with.

It was eleven o'clock when Frederick opened the door to Tony's small office.

"Hey, Fred. How ya doin'?" He stood up from his desk and backed Frederick out of the room. "I'm starved. Been on the phone with New York all morning. Didn't even have time for a danish. Let's get over to Berghoff's before the Yuppies and Fluffies get there."

Berghoff's, the Chicago men's club for men with no club, was a short walk from Tony's office. The men-only restaurant now served women, but the sentiment remained.

Male waiters rushed about with white dish towels draped over their arms, white aprons wrapped at their waists. They carried large trays piled precipitously with white ceramic plates held high over their heads and at the last second they swooped them down onto tray stands, flinging dishes onto tables with the learned precision of fly fishermen. The aroma of roast beef, creamed spinach, and hot apple strudel filled the air.

Frederick and Tony gave their orders to the waiter, who scribbled them on a plain note pad. Behind Tony, Frederick watched two women lean conspiratorially toward each other, Marshall Field's shopping bags tucked beneath their chairs.

"Move the mustard," snapped the waiter. The brunette quickly complied just as a large plate dropped in front of her.

The waiter slid a roast beef sandwich in front of Tony and a wienerschnitzel in front of Frederick. He wasn't impressed. He preferred the restaurant in the Webster Hotel across from Lincoln Park Zoo. He liked their sweet and sour cabbage soup and the creamy cole slaw, the basket of warm onion rolls served with every order.

"This is terrific. You're not hungry?" Tony gestured at Frederick's plate and wiped his mouth with the back of his hand. "Eat. Then we talk on the way to Angelo's."

Tony ordered a second beer. Frederick admitted to himself that the bread was good, thick and chewy. He'd barely swallowed the last bit when Tony, standing over the table, gulped the last of his beer, dropped the exact amount of the bill onto the table, hesitated, then added a tip, and headed for the door.

Frederick took one last look at the women who were eating dessert. The waiter hesitated at their table, a pot of steaming coffee held aloft like a standard, then turned away from them without refilling their mugs.

Back on State Street, they entered a building similar to the one where Tony had his office. The Loop was filled with such buildings, a warren of unadvertised shops—jewelry stores, hat makers, dress makers, doll repair shops, shoe repair shops, tailors. Up and down the corridors, small businesses sold uniforms, lingerie, party supplies or kinky aids.

Tony took the elevator to the tenth floor and stepped out into the dimly lit hallway. Frederick followed him around the corner and half-way down the back side of the building to a doorway with a frosted glass window and a chipped sign painted in black—Figaranni's Fabric.

The doorbell was answered by an elderly man, barely five feet tall, his white hair meticulously combed into a back sweep held in place most certainly by hair cream, not mousse. A tape measure draped about his neck.

"Mr. Scully. How are you today?"

"Just fine, Angelo. Meet my business partner, Frederick J. Lewis. Fred, meet the best suit maker in the city of Chicago. Probably New York, too."

The old man protested, but held out his hand to Frederick.

"How do you do," Frederick said. His mind raced. He was Fred to some, Frederick to others, and Rick to a chosen few. He didn't remember mentioning the "J" to Renata or Scully.

Business partner. Now that had a nice ring to it. So Scully was going to do something about his wardrobe. He'd expected Renata to get around to that. Business partner. He had a funny feeling in the pit of his stomach. Whenever he started to feel his luck was with him, odd chunks fell out of it like a hole in a jigsaw puzzle that gave better clues than the assembled pieces. Why was Scully buying him a custom made suit?

"So, listen up, Fred. Angelo's makin' you a suit. He'll get the measurements while we talk.

"You know we got to make out a better business arrangement. It's great for me you delivering contracts, pickin' up blueprints. It makes me sleep good. But it doesn't make me sleep so good knowin' you're probably feelin' like somebody's delivery boy, and on one of these trips somebody's going to offer you one of your consulting jobs and I'll be back to not sleeping so good."

Scully settled into a chair and popped a piece of gum in his mouth. "So here's the deal, Fred. I put the nice suits on you. I make you my partner. Renata says you're a great dinner companion, so I say you go to dinner with the big shots I'm dealin' with, and we put us together a mall. Whaddaya say?"

"You kind of caught me by surprise, Tony." He didn't know a damn thing about shopping mall construction. And Tony had never asked him about it. He'd been playing a game he was good at with Renata.

"You making me a business partner?"

“Think it over. For now, concentrate on fabric. Take your time. We can talk about salary and pension later.” Tony snorted a whistling and wheezing throttle as he said it, then walked out of the shop.

Frederick pondered the equation. Who gained the most in this arrangement? Frederick J. Lewis knew how to wheel and deal with the best of them. He’d been waiting for an opportunity, but this caught him off guard. Scully needed him. He could see that. He had money but no finesse.

Frederick followed the tailor to the back of the room. He stood still while the tailor measured him. A memory floated back. He remembered a long time ago when he’d stood for uniform measurements, a little boy going off to boarding school. The misty image of his mother standing out of view, the pungent smell of perfume more clearly pronounced than the features of her face.

“I have some pictures for you to look at for the style,” the tailor said. “Do you want to look at the pictures first or cloth?”

He gestured to the wall behind them and Frederick turned to stare at the neatly arranged bolts of wool and silk. He was uncertain what to do. Trying on expensive suits in high end stores was a hobby of his. It never bothered him to walk into the men’s department and keep a salesman busy for an hour or longer while he examined merchandise he could never afford. Then, rejecting each for a tightness in the chest, a pull across the back, or a faintly visible change of shade in the weave, he’d express regret that he didn’t find what he was after. A quick look at his watch, a Rolex purchased from a pawn shop, and then he’d mumble about a meeting with the board, or a plane he had to catch, and then he’d exit.

He liked to take women to expensive dress shops and insist they try on designer evening clothes and one of a kind furs. He paced about before deciding none of them was what he was looking for. Most of them loved the game, too. Only Beth had embarrassed him when he’d tried the game with her. “This is nuts,” she’d said too loudly. “We can’t afford this stuff, and where would I wear it anyway?” The sales clerk had given them a haughty look, and Frederick had escorted her from the scene with a hold on her arm that had left a bruise.

Renata had the money to buy the luxury items, but he'd never gone with her. She'd tell him to meet her at a specified time in a tiny Oak Street dress shop, but when he arrived she was finished with her shopping and waiting for him to carry the packages.

Angelo pressed the scrapbook into Frederick's arms. His selection would be made from one of the pictures. He studied them carefully.

"You want double breasted or single?" Angelo asked.

"Single. My shoulders are broad," Frederick replied.

The tailor squinted up at him, licked his finger and turned ahead several pages in the book. He slapped his hand across a picture. "Then, this is what you want. You want top stitching?"

"No." If Scully wanted him to wear tailored suits, and he was willing to pay for them, Frederick was ready to please. "I'll need shirts, too."

He ordered half a dozen custom-made shirts with his initials on the cuff. Next, he began thinking about the suit he'd pick out when he returned after checking out the ready-made suits at Brooks Brothers or Marshall Field's to be certain of the current fashion.

"Everything is in the construction, from the cloth to the buttons, the interfacing, the lining…" Angelo gathered several slips of paper together and slipped them into an envelope. He wrote "Mr. Lewis" in an elaborate, old-fashioned script.

"Finished?" Scully reappeared and stood with a bag of pretzels in one hand while he chomped noisily. "I'll get back to you one of these days, Angelo, but it's too hot to think about it today."

"Okay, Mr. Scully. Mr. Lewis will have a good suit. It will take me about six weeks."

"Great," answered Scully. "We got business to do, Fred." He slapped him on the back and shoved him toward the door.

"I got something for you to take to Boston," Scully told him when they were back on the street. "There's a lot of opportunity out there. You'd think there wouldn't be a square foot left to develop, but there is. Lots of places. Old places falling down, new ones going up. Still some good buys, but damn, property's expensive on the East Coast. No bargains.

“You got to talk turkey to those patriots—turkey and cranberry sauce,” he snorted at his wit.

They passed through the revolving doors leading to the elevator and rode up to Scully’s office in silence. Like the building they’d just left, the corridor was lined with doors with frosted glass windows, and a chipped painted number was often the only identifying mark.

“Who are these people?” Frederick wondered briefly as he brushed away any doubts he had about Antonio Scully and his generosity.

14 | Work Is Fire for Frozen Fingers

Beth stood on the corner of Michigan Avenue and Huron Street, a cardboard portfolio of Alicia's paintings gripped in her hand. She noticed the fine leather portfolios some men and women carried and thought she ought to buy one. She shifted the folder from under one arm to under the other, worried about bending the contents, and concluded she'd never thought about how difficult it was to handle such a bulky envelope when a gust of wind caught it.

She was headed for Leslie Crane's Gallery on Erie Street. Two years previously, the city schools had closed early because the Chicago Board of Education said it was out of operating funds. To pay the bills, Beth worked as a temporary secretary. An agency for temporary workers had placed her with Leslie, who needed someone to type gallery listings, write painting descriptions, and assemble artists' biographies. She enjoyed the experience, and even though she and Leslie were very different, they had become friends. When schools failed to reopen as scheduled for the fall semester, Leslie had kept her on as a gallery assistant.

The gray concrete building where Leslie ran her gallery was three stories tall. Each floor contained a separate gallery, and the work displayed in each represented starkly different styles. Outside, a chain linked each sign identifying the three: The Leslie Crane Gallery, Down's Gallery, and R.N. Rieneke Gallery.

Leslie Crane and Gloria Down hated each other. Beth had been surprised at how coldly Leslie directed people to Gloria's gallery if they entered her gallery only to ask where Gloria's gallery was located.

Sometimes she simply ignored them as if she had no idea Gloria had a gallery above her own. The galleries competed for the attention and money of the city's affluent art collectors.

Gloria was from New York and exhibited mostly New York artists. Leslie loved the Chicago School and openly spoke of her disdain for what she called the over-rated East Coast group. Roy Rieneke padded about his gallery in argyle socks and appeared startled whenever Beth had occasion to deliver misguided mail or messages to his third floor salon. He sold tapestries to corporations. Beth thought he'd run out of lobbies to decorate sooner or later, but the gallery flourished. Leslie had a keen eye for young artists who found their way into the Art Institute's permanent collection. Gloria advertised exclusive rights to well-known artists, and Leslie feigned indifference to what was shown there.

As Beth climbed the stairs, she wondered what kind of a mood Leslie would be in. If she were in a bad mood, there was little point in showing her Alicia's work. It was a long shot anyway, but for sentimental reasons Beth thought she would ask Leslie if she would exhibit the watercolors.

She was met at the doorway by a huge bearded man who was waving his hands in the air and shouting, "This wall can't stay. It is all wrong. It was not here before. It cuts the light. It meets the eye—bam." He slapped his large hand against his forehead.

"Andrew, the wall stays. It's a small building. I can't take out walls. This is not MOMA."

"I'll have to think about it." He stormed past Beth who flattened herself against the wall so that he did not knock her back down the front stairs.

She could see Leslie in the rear of the gallery in her office. She was wearing an orange dress with a wide leather belt with a huge silver buckle that caught the sun from the open doorway and shot a bolt of light this way and that as she swayed back and forth on her high heels in a spirited agitation Beth remembered well. There was no point in showing Alicia's delicate watercolors to Leslie.

"Hi, Leslie. I just dropped by to say hello, but I don't think it's such a good time," Beth shouted across the gallery to her.

“Oh, hello dear. Of course it’s a good time. Do you remember Edward Gilson? Just as big as that fellow. Carried all his own work in, looked at the gallery space, worked all night hanging his pictures. The sun came up in the morning. He looked at the way the light hit his paintings, took them all down, rearranged them, and then worked all day and into the next night getting it just right. He didn’t utter a word. When he finished he sat down in the center of the floor and hummed some damned incantation. And you know, I had yellow dots on nearly every work by the end of the opening, and red dots by the end of the week. Now he only exhibits in New York. And this fool can’t hang one lousy painting without a major explosion of drama.”

“I’ll come back.” Beth adjusted the cardboard portfolio under her arm.

“Still teaching?” Leslie asked.

“Ahuh, I was just in the neighborhood.” Beth knew she was angling for some volunteer assistance.

“He’ll come raging back in here, and I’ll have to stay all night while he hangs the show. I wouldn’t dare leave him alone. He’d take down a wall.”

“Bye.” Beth turned and exited the gallery. Perhaps Sand and Struthers Gallery, a couple of blocks away, would be a better place to begin her pitch.

The wind caught the cardboard portfolio, pulling her along like a sail. Her arms began to ache as she waited for the light to change. She watched an old man on a bicycle, a messenger “boy” and wondered what it would be like to deliver messages to earn a living. Most of the men were old and wiry. She imagined them going home to tiny rooms in one of the seedy hotels along LaSalle Street, eating food cooked on a hot plate after a long day moving in and out of traffic, walking in and out of spacious lobbies with miles of thick carpets and offices filled with massive desks of mahogany or walnut.

The light changed, and she crossed Michigan Avenue. Auturo Rodine’s gallery was on the other side of the Avenue, in the next block, on the top floor of an office building. She would stop in there to rest. It was too great a struggle to continue to Chestnut Street in the strong wind.

She stepped inside the building and walked into an open elevator. On the top floor, the doors opened directly into Arturo's gallery. It was a surprising entrance for a first time gallery browser. Arturo kept large, immovable statues cast in bronze positioned near the entrance.

He specialized in paintings from Eastern Europe, lithographs from Yugoslavia and what had recently become the Czech Republic, large angry acrylics from emigrants recently resettled in the West. These oversized paintings always seemed cramped and ready like jack-in-the-boxes to be forced back into smaller spaces. Alicia's work would not be suitable for Arturo, but he had always been kind to her when he attended Leslie's gallery openings. She could catch her breath. He had a security sensor system and stood in front of the elevator door when it opened into his gallery.

"Welcome. Come in and look at the beautiful paintings." He held his hands cupped in front of him. He was a tiny man with wire rimmed glasses in round frames. He had a mustache, and he wore brown wool suits even in the summer. They always looked as if they must itch, Beth thought.

"Why if it isn't Beth Norton who has come to grace my gallery. How nice to see you, my dear. I don't believe we've seen you for quite some time now. Come, come. I was just fixing an omelet. But, of course, you want to see my lovely paintings. Such mastery. Such suffering. You look. I'll go back to my omelet. You will have one with me, won't you?"

Beth nodded in agreement. It was the last thing she wanted, but even on this hot summer day the wind was cold by the lakefront and her fingers were stiff.

"You have given up teaching and taken up drawing?" Arturo's head nodded in the direction of the portfolio she held.

"Oh, no. I have the work of a friend of mine. I'm trying to find someone who would be interested in exhibiting it. I came here to see you, not to show it."

"Come, come. Let me see. Oh. First, the omelets. You look at my paintings and tell me what you think, and then I'll look at your friend's work."

Beth leaned the portfolio against the pedestal of a bronze nude. She began to circle the gallery with its vaulted ceiling. The paintings screamed in jagged streaks of red and orange and black. She didn't like them.

She studied the smaller pieces near the screen Arturo had disappeared behind. Lithographs and *gouaches*. She read the biography of the artist. It said he lived in Yugoslavia. She realized, as she looked more carefully, they were all erotic scenarios.

"Come. Eat. Tell me what you are doing these days. Such a beautiful girl. The children of Chicago are lucky to gaze at you."

She followed him to the back of the gallery, where he had laid out two plates and two sets of ornately decorated silverware on a tiny table with a stiff white linen cloth. She sat down and watched as he slid an omelet from a copper pan onto the plate in front of her.

He cracked two more eggs and beat them in a bowl, added milk and chopped chives, humming an aria. "It's the milk that makes the difference. Great controversy, but it's the milk. Eat now. Don't wait for me. It's no good cold."

Beth ate the omelet quickly. Arturo smiled at the empty plate. He sat down and dropped a linen napkin on his lap.

"I just stopped in to say hello. I didn't expect lunch."

"Always my pleasure. Leslie, of course, would never eat one of my omelets. She should learn how to enjoy the simple pleasures of life. What about my beautiful paintings?"

"They're... bold." Beth thought about the tiny drawings and the many warnings Leslie had given her as she sent her off to Arturo's with page proofs for the Art Society's newsletter. He'd always been a gentleman, and she'd always enjoyed his old world charm.

"So let me see your friend's work." He clasped his fingertips in front of him expectantly.

"They're watercolors. She lives on the East Coast on an island. She's been successful there, and I thought maybe I could find someone in Chicago willing to exhibit her work."

She slipped one of the watercolors from the folder. Arturo studied it.

"She knows the ocean."

Beth was disappointed to hear that. She had thought she'd pass them off as paintings of rough water on Lake Michigan. Maybe Alicia was better than she'd realized. Maybe this was a very silly thing for her to be trying.

"I wish I could display them here for you," Arturo said as he put the painting back in the folder and pulled out the one behind it. "They are beautiful."

"Oh, Arturo. I never expected you to. I just wanted to say hello."

"I am sure someone will make room for them. They will sell."

She tied the string around the portfolio. She wouldn't mention Sand and Struthers as the gallery she had in mind. Arturo was less competitive than most gallery owners she knew because no one else exhibited Eastern European artists exclusively as he did. However, she had learned as her brief stint as a gallery assistant they were all competing for sales and prestige.

The Chicago art community had a developing art scene further west, but she did not know any of the people there. Leslie referenced the district as not being part of the established art world of Chicago. Arturo often said his paintings were more authentic, less derivative than those exhibited "off the Avenue."

Beth felt emboldened by her visits to Leslie and Arturo. Time to drop the beleaguered school teacher offering a friend's art persona and assume the guise of a tough art agent. By the time she reached Sand and Struthers she'd be ready to pitch Alicia's work as a commodity.

"Goodbye, Arturo. Good luck with the exhibit."

"They are all sold," he replied with a smile.

Alicia stepped into the elevator. She wondered who bought his paintings. She knew that the Sand and Struthers Galleria was popular with the people living in the high rises along Lake Shore Drive, and even though Leslie spoke derisively of it, she always invited the owners to her openings and smiled gamely at them when they appeared.

When she reached the gallery with its wide, old-fashioned glass showcase entrance, she rushed in without stopping to see what the artist's work displayed there looked like. Once inside, she looked about and discovered the room was filled with delicate watercolors—rural scenes of barns and buckets and trees.

A woman rose from the Italian provincial desk and walked toward her.

"Good afternoon. May I help you?"

"Is Martin Struthers here?" Beth asked familiarly.

"No, he's in New York. Mr. Sand will be back shortly." She peered at the portfolio Beth was holding. "Mr. Sand doesn't do any acquiring. Only Mr. Struthers.

"We really aren't taking on any new artists at this time," the woman replied coolly.

"Well, that answers that. Thank you."

It would be a long hike back up Michigan Avenue. How did all those people on the Avenue look so elegant and graceful carrying huge leather portfolios? She was exhausted. Her hair was a mess, and her arms were too tired to raise. She stepped back out on the Avenue. She was too worn out to weave her way through Water Tower Place to the Ritz for a cup of tea. Instead, she headed toward a little coffee shop a few blocks farther south on the Avenue, where the tables were tightly packed, and she'd make a mess of things trying to maneuver her way to a table. What she needed was an expensive leather portfolio with a handle. And an artsy wardrobe.

Preoccupied with her thoughts, she hadn't noticed the man on the street who was peering through the window of a shop. Now she brought him into focus. Something about him seemed familiar. He looked like Rick. It couldn't be. Her heart pounded.

If it were Rick, then he'd lied to her, and she should do nothing. She hurried to catch up to the man, trying to get a look at his face. There was no point to this, she told herself, but still she hurried. She was about to call out Rick's name when the man turned abruptly and began walking rapidly away from her. She turned too, trying to keep him in sight.

This is nuts she told herself. It's probably not him. He was almost at the corner when he stopped and bent to unlock the door of a fire red sports car. If she ran she could catch up to him before he got into the car. She would glare into the car and settle this fantasy she perpetuated. She took off at a trot, but a gust of wind caught her and like a giant hand pushed the cardboard portfolio against her bringing her to a stop. The car turned into traffic and disappeared.

“That was absurd,” she said aloud. But she’d caught a glimpse of the man’s face before she’d been whacked by the portfolio. She knew it was Rick. Sooner or later he’d call. She’d take him back without any questions. It wasn’t smart, she knew. It didn’t matter. There was no passion like the passion she felt for that scoundrel.

The energy of her thoughts made short work of the walk down Michigan Avenue. Back on Huron Street, she marched half a block to Prints and Posters. She walked down the concrete stairs to the ground level door and pushed it open. Mark Lyndonfeld, the owner, was on a ladder. He looked down at her and hurried back to the floor.

“Hello, there. How are you, Beth? Haven’t seen you in quite a while. You working at Leslie’s gallery again this summer? Man, July is the pits in here.” He pressed his arm to his forehead.

“Mark, do you think you could do me a favor?” Beth asked.

“Just ask,” Mark said. He sat down on the last rung of the ladder.

“I’ve got a friend back East, and I thought I’d see if I could place some of her watercolors in a gallery in Chicago. She’s really good. She sells well on the island where she lives. We’re childhood friends, and actually I’m trying to get her to come out here. We have a mutual friend in Prairieview, and we’re trying to get up a reunion.”

“Why doesn’t she just fly out here for a reunion?” he said with a laugh.

“I guess that would be too simple.” The sighting of Rick had squelched her enthusiasm for the art project.

“People make life too complicated. You’ve probably concocted this whole fable just as an excuse to see me,” he said with a wink.

Beth walked over to a wide table and dropped the portfolio on it. She was glad to be relieved of it. She swung her arms back and forth and wiggled her fingers to get some feeling back. Mark pulled out a watercolor slowly, set it aside and pulled out a second one. He nodded and looked at the third, the fourth, and then he pulled the fifth one out and walked to the window with it.

“She’s really good. Not the usual easel by the sea stuff. Sure. I’ll put some of them up. I’ve got some space on the print rack. Look at this one. I really like it. You got a price list?”

Beth produced the price list.

"Sure you do. You're all set. Great." He read over the price list Beth and Alicia had arranged. "Dumb titles. I'm glad she didn't write them on the work itself," he added.

"Thanks, Mark. The titles were my idea. I thought it might sell better with titles that sounded more like Lake Michigan than the places on Jellicle Island."

"Whoa. Jellicle Island. That's high-end territory."

"Not if you live there full time."

"There you go again, making life complicated. Lake Michigan never looks this good. The prices are… realistic. I'll put them up. You check off what I'm taking. Do you have another copy of this list?"

"Yes. We made several copies. Unless you want to keep them all. Exclusive rights, you know," she said wearily.

"Hey, this isn't the Leslie Crane Gallery. How come she didn't take them? I'm sure you went there first."

"She was in a fit when I got there, and I decided not to show them to her."

"Aha, I knew I wasn't first on your list!" He winked at her again.

"I thought you didn't complicate your life with second-rate emotions," Beth said and winked back at him.

"Point for you, Beth. Why don't I see more of you?"

"Probably because you lead an uncomplicated life."

He set to work sliding the watercolors into a print rack, turning the frames in search of empty spaces. Beth checked off the titles he selected. She wished they had been placed next to each other, but as he turned the rack, Alicia's work popped. The other works looked artificial, their colors not as true, the images less original.

"Okay, I've got five. Right?"

"Right." Beth felt relieved to have placed some of Alicia's art. She was sorry not to have lent at least one of her paintings to Sand and Struthers. She wished she'd shown them to Leslie.

"Want a soda?" Mark asked.

"Do you have chocolate?"

"I knew you were a connoisseur. Of course, I have chocolate soda."

Beth settled onto a bench by the wide table. She sipped the soda and listened to Mark's business woes. If she stayed until after five, she could slip back over to Leslie's.

The next hour and a half passed easily. Beth watched the pairs of feet scurrying by Mark's basement window. She observed the high heels, sandals, jogging shoes, and wing tips. When the pedestrian traffic began to thin, she collected the portfolio and said goodbye. For Alicia's sake, she hoped his business picked up.

Beth knew that while Leslie appeared to be in a high frenzied state or a cool aloof state most of the time, when it came to her artists she knew how to handle them, when to be sympathetic, and when to recognize a temper tantrum as counter-productive. She calculated that by the time she returned to the gallery, the artist would be seriously at work assembling his show, and Leslie would be standing nearby watching.

When she entered the gallery the artist was gone, his work was on the walls, and Leslie was sitting in a chair drinking a cup of coffee from a china cup.

"See?" She gestured to the paintings. "Isn't he wonderful? He's one of Sammy's artists. I talked them into letting him do a Chicago show. What do you think?"

Maybe this was a good sign. If Leslie was showing New York artists, just maybe she'd show a New England one, too. She scrutinized the canvas of the painting closest to her. It looked like graph paper—huge expanses of perfectly spaced monochrome lines. And he worried about the lighting? Well, on second thought, she concluded he should. Without sufficient light the canvases looked blank.

She preferred the wild inventiveness of the pugnacious Chicago style. "Leslie, you do stretch the limits, don't you? Give me the little comic characters running around with little deer feet, or great big ugly men in tights and tattoos."

"You don't like it. It's big in New York. He'll sell here. The opening's tomorrow night. Are you coming?"

"I might, just to see your favorite customers struggling."

"You're wrong. A collection needs variety. He's going into the permanent collection of the Art Institute in the fall."

"He is?"

"Seth Koch has been negotiating with Sammy over a small one. I'll get him to buy a big one from me instead."

Beth moved from one painting to another. They all appeared exactly alike to her. The colors were so faint it was difficult to see any variety from canvas to canvas.

There was a loud knock at the front door.

"I'm closed," Leslie shouted fiercely.

"Perhaps I could have a look about."

"Persistence pays," Beth suggested.

"I hope you're right," Leslie responded as she released the lock from a switch under her desk. Leslie's voice took on a rich entrepreneurial resin as the man walked into the gallery.

"Perhaps you could come back in the morning."

"Unfortunately, I'll be in San Francisco by morning. I was told you were an excellent gallery with interesting work on the cutting edge."

He gazed across the room at the huge canvas paintings. As Beth had, he moved forward to see what was on the canvas and then back to see if it made a difference. Beth suppressed a smile.

She had nothing to lose. She pulled the watercolors from the portfolio and spread them across Leslie's wide table. Dismissing the cutting edge work he headed toward the smaller room beyond. He moved quickly across the highly polished pine floor, making a loud clicking. Beth noticed he wore boots.

Inside Leslie's office, the shelves were lined with small Italian sculptures. Here she kept whimsical pieces that moved with noise or light. The man looked at the prints on the wall and then turned his attention to the sculpture. He picked up a Plexiglas piece that jutted out in sharp planes and housed a small intricate moving center. He set it on her desk.

"I'll take this one. How much?"

"That's a Marco LaRosa. A very solid investment for $1,000."

"Okay." His eyes searched for something else. He could have been looking for red peppers at the grocery, Beth felt. Then he saw Alicia's watercolors. He marched loudly over to them and held one up. He drew in his breath, then let out a low whistle. "These I like. I will take them, too."

Leslie looked perplexed. Beth stepped in. "These are acquisitions the gallery is just now considering. I don't know whether they are for sale, yet. I was just conferring with Mrs. Crane.

Leslie's eyes were on the $1,000 sculpture. She wanted to sell it. She looked at the paintings and only Beth caught sight of the slight curl of her lip. "They usually are sold in a series," she said smoothly. "Five hundred dollars for three of them, or one hundred and seventy-five dollars apiece."

"Okay," said the man in boots.

Beth wasn't sure what he'd agreed to, but Leslie moved swiftly to her desk and began to write up a bill of sale. "That will be fifteen hundred dollars. How did you intend to pay for them?"

"Travelers check."

"Beth, will you wrap these up for the gentleman?"

Beth gathered the watercolor he had whistled over and chose two more—a Jellicle Island boulder at the water's edge with a wave rolling back toward the sea and a view of the ocean painted from the ridge above Norton's Pond. She left the two remaining paintings on the table. Leslie wasn't wild about flowers, but maybe now she would agree to keeping them in the print cabinet for awhile.

In the back of the office Beth found a box suitable for the sculpture. She gathered some Styrofoam packing and returned to pack the object. She carefully rolled the watercolors and inserted them into a tube and handed the two parcels to the art collector.

"Here you are, sir. Thank you so much." Beth smiled gamely.

"Great. Thanks for letting me in."

He left without looking at the immense canvases in the front salon.

Leslie said nothing until the man had disappeared down the front entrance stairs. She picked at the edge of one of the two remaining watercolors as she slid it across the table. "It's not bad. Of course, it's not the sort of thing my gallery handles. Who did it?"

"A friend of mine. I'm trying to find a Chicago gallery to exhibit her work. She's very popular on the East Coast."

"Not my gallery."

"I wasn't going to ask you. I was just going to show them to you. I wanted your opinion."

"Well, your friend has just made five hundred dollars." Leslie said as she shook her head in disbelief.

"Less your commission," Beth added.

"No, I'll write you a check for five hundred. I don't want to be associated with it, and he won't remember where he bought them."

"So who do you think that man was?"

"Somebody who just made some money in the Commodity Exchange, or finished a film in Chicago. It's been happening a lot lately. He obviously didn't know much about art. He was just looking for a trinket to commemorate the day," Leslie said with an air of contempt.

"A thousand dollars, just like that. And then the watercolors."

"Don't be surprised. He could have had one of these for eight thousand." Leslie waved in the direction of her one man show.

"Or more watercolors."

"You know perfectly well I don't carry gentle little watercolors with ocean views."

"But could I please leave these two with you? Look at this pitiful portfolio. I don't want them to be ruined. I need to buy a proper leather portfolio."

Leslie looked again at the paintings. "If anyone looks as displeased as you seem to think they will at my opening, I'll give them a peek."

"Thanks. I'll stop in next week to collect the money." Beth knew even though it was a traveler's check, Leslie wouldn't write her a check until it had cleared in the bank. Maybe she would show the other watercolors to her clients.

"I'm sorry you gave up on us, Beth. You could have had an excellent career in the art world. Anytime you change your mind about teaching, let me know. That was a pretty smooth move you made there."

"You, too. A series… hmm. You've got a couplet now. Hope you can sell them.

"Come back for the opening. Free champagne. Maybe you'll meet a nice young art collector."

"I tried when I worked here. Never happened," Beth said without a smile.

When she was back on Huron Street, Beth looked toward Michigan Avenue. She saw the red sports car. It was blocking the alley behind Saks. She was free of the portfolio, and she began running toward it.

A woman seated in the passenger's seat blocked her view of the driver. The traffic cleared and the car sped off, but not before Beth saw a familiar gesture—the driver flexed his shoulders back and forth to relieve tension.

15 | SING ALL SUMMER, WEEP ALL WINTER

Frederick saw Beth on Michigan Avenue, his eye drawn to her as if she were the narcotic and he the addict. She was sweet, too forgiving, and trapped in the fantasy they had something good going. She brought out the best in him, and that wasn't what he was after.

What man would not have noticed the pretty woman, skirts blowing, nearly airborne by the portfolio that flapped against her as she struggled with it? He'd watched, charmed, but the instant he recognized her he felt a wrench deep within, angst, or regret, or foreboding. It was real, and it hurt.

He was killing time, waiting for Renata to complete one of her shopping expeditions. Sighting Beth, he was forced to acknowledge his current situation. He was a gigolo to a passionless shoe-tree and a partner in a company he knew nothing about. It was quite possible he was simply being bought by Tony to watch Renata.

Six times he'd flown to Boston, carrying blueprints or material samples or bids, though for what and to whom, Tony never explained. The packages were well sealed, and he never attempted to open them. After each trip, like a remorseful drunk, he'd sworn it was the last. Yet once in Boston, he was drawn to an island and an artist. Then, back in Chicago, Tony paid him well to keep his sister distracted from her cocaine habit. He must be doing a good job because he never caught her using.

He was living dangerously. The sight of Beth reminded him of that. It was time to quit playing games, join the real world, and get a real job. Frederick walked to Renata's car and drove back to Huron Street to the side entrance to Saks Fifth Avenue. Thinking about Beth, he didn't see Renata until she climbed in the car.

"Let's go to The Lemon Tree," she said to him with as much emotion as if directing a cab driver.

"I thought you didn't like loud music," Frederick said in an effort to personalize the conversation. He'd turned his head to check for traffic and caught sight of Beth in the rear view mirror. He pulled out on to Huron Street.

"Tony told me to tell you to meet him at That Steak Joynt at seven o'clock tonight. He said he hadn't been able to reach you. The Lemon Tree is close. You can walk from the club in five minutes."

Frederick wondered whether he should have spent the weekend on Jellicle Island. He pulled up in front of the club. An awning reached out to the street. A doorman in a bizarre uniform grabbed for the handle of the car. Renata got out and walked into the nightclub without looking back. Frederick slipped five dollars into the man's hand and followed her inside.

The music rushed at them like hot air escaping from a pressure sealed container. The room was cold, the air conditioning filling the atmosphere with dampness which had not yet been absorbed by the crowd of hot, gyrating dancers. Frederick checked his watch. It was a quarter to six. The place would be packed shortly.

A waiter approached them wearing an outfit as silly as the doorman's was bizarre. Frederick considered his choices. "The lady will have Campari on ice. Bring me a double bourbon."

"Hard day?" she asked in her usual distracted manner. He knew she didn't give a damn what kind of a day he'd had.

"A Moscow Mule is too sweet when it gets this hot," he said. The music began another blasted beat, heavy on the bass, and they were relieved of attempting further conversation.

Frederick was beginning to regret he hadn't been more prudent with the cash Tony supplied him. He didn't have much left. He shouldn't have spent it so freely or so fast. He always did. The ant and the grasshopper. He was a grasshopper, and it was time to hop.

He checked his watch again. Six-thirty. The music throbbed, the dance floor filled, and Frederick stared at the tiny bodies in short shorts and at their partners with muscles that bulged from time spent in athletic clubs, not loading docks. Neither he nor Renata fit in here. Other than being close to That Steak Joynt, he wondered why she'd chosen it. She sat stiffly in a three hundred dollar linen frock, a diamond tennis bracelet on her wrist, and stared at the dance floor.

"Would you like to order something to eat?" he asked. It was his job to be solicitous. She shook her head no. "Then we'd better get going. If I'm to meet Tony at seven, I'd better get you home." He was ignoring her suggestion that he could walk.

She didn't finish her drink, but picked up her purse and sat waiting for him to move the table so that she could stand. On the street, the humidity was oppressive. The sun was hanging low on the horizon, and the sidewalks steamed. There was no breeze from the lake. When the car arrived, Renata surprised him and walked around it to the driver's seat.

"I'll drop you at the restaurant. He always acts easy going, but he doesn't like it when he's got business to do and his partners are late."

Frederick walked back around to the passenger seat and got in. Partners, he thought. Then there were others. So at last he would meet them.

It was only a couple of blocks from the night club to the restaurant. She stopped in front. Frederick got out. He hesitated, feeling he should say something to her. Nothing came to mind. She didn't suggest that he stop by later for a nightcap or to return a key to her car. He shut the door, and she shot up Wells Street without uttering a word.

Inside the restaurant, the rich décor startled him: red flocked wallpaper in an 1890's motif. The thick red carpet was worn thin by the maître' d's desk, and waitresses moved about in black lace tights.

"May I help you?"

"I'm dining with Mr. Scully. Is he here?" Frederick attempted to look beyond the man into the dining room.

"Just a minute, sir." He scanned the guest list. Apparently, Tony Scully was not known here by sight.

"Yes, sir. Right this way."

Frederick followed the maître d' to a table near the back of the dining room. Tony looked up from a salad, his fork dangling over it dripping dressing. “There you are. I was beginning to think you couldn’t make it.”

Frederick sat down. It was an odd remark, he thought as he double checked his watch. It was exactly seven o’clock. The waiter handed him a menu. It was long and too awkward to ignore.

“I ordered already. You want a drink?”

Frederick hadn’t enjoyed the double bourbon with Renata. He didn’t want another, but he ordered one. He turned his attention to the menu. He considered filet mignon, T-bone, strip loin, strip steak with bacon, sirloin—8 oz. or 16 oz.—and then there were chops—pork veal, lamb—and calves’ liver.

Scully continued munching his salad. The waiter arrived with the bourbon. Frederick took a swallow. Tony chomped noisily on the spinach, his shoulders hunched toward the table. Drops of dressing were beginning to spread across the tablecloth.

Frederick set the menu on the table.

“You’re not hungry?” Tony said through a mouthful of spinach.

“It’s too hot,” Frederick replied.

Tony returned his attention to the salad plate, scraping the glass for the last strip of green.

“Are you ready to order, sir?” the waitress in the lacy tights and the short skirt asked.

“I’ll have the filet mignon, rare.”

“Baked potato or cottage fries?”

“Baked potato.”

“Sour cream, bacon, or butter?”

“Bacon”

“Will that be all, sir?”

“Yes.”

“You shoulda ordered the apple pie,” Tony said after the waitress had departed.

Frederick had no response.

The waitress returned as Tony was pulling an envelope from his breast pocket. She set a large, aluminum-lined wooden plate with a huge piece of sizzling meat in front of Tony. His eyebrows arched in appreciation. He handed Frederick a photograph.

Frederick looked at the picture and back across the table at Tony, who was slicing through a three-inch-thick slab of red meat, the juice burbling out across the platter, sizzling as it touched the hot plate.

Frederick stared at the photograph. Perspiration began to appear in tiny droplets across his lower lip. Tony stabbed at the meat with his fork and severed a hunk with the steak knife and shoveled it into his mouth.

Frederick set the photo down next to his plate. He was in deep shit. He knew it now. He saw Renata's cold eyes as she sat in the driver's seat. Nice move, Renata, he thought. If he was to be dispersed piece by piece into load luggers throughout the city, she would not have to trouble herself about the whereabouts of the keys to her Jaguar. Renata was good with details.

He looked again at the woman in the photo. How the hell did Tony find out he was two-timing his sister? The thought sent fresh pangs of fear through him.

Tony waved his fork in the direction of the photo. "Nice looking."

Frederick winced. Tony continued, "I knew I'd picked a winner when I picked you. You did real good in Boston. Now, I got something for you to take care of on this little island."

"For Renata?" Frederick was lost.

"Forget Renata," Tony replied. "She's a whore."

"You're talking like that about your sister?" Frederick was groping for an explanation.

"She ain't my sister. She's a whore who can be had for the price of a fancy pair of shoes."

"What's this got to do with Alicia?" Frederick fought for control. He wiped his brow with the oversized linen napkin.

"Alicia? You know this broad already? You are the man, Freddy. My man.

The waiter placed a plate of seared filet in front of Frederick. His nostrils flared at the smell of the charred meat. He took a long slow sip of bourbon and set the empty glass back on the table. He studied Tony, who without the ornament of Renata's grace looked shabbier than he had on first impression. If she was a whore, what then was Tony?

“This woman is an artist. What possible interest could you have in her?” Frederick was moving back from the sea of panic, but he was still adrift.

“I got no interest. The men I work for think she’s got something they want. You’ve been groomed, my man. You got class. You can move in the fancy circles in fancy places without making any waves. That’s an important part of this. They figure she don’t know what she’s got. They just need to get it back. Soon. Real soon.”

“What does she have?”

“Can’t tell you.”

“Then how am I supposed to find it and get it back?”

“Girly, I’d like some coffee and a piece of that apple pie. Make it two pieces and some whipped cream. You want some, Fred? Hey, you ain’t touched your meat.”

Frederick grimaced. “How do I fit into all this?”

“You’ll have it all laid out for you. I told you we’d be partners. There’s someone who wants to talk to ya.”

Partners. The word taunted him. He’d rejected friends, family, lovers, any relationship that suggested permanency, intimacy and belonging. Yet he’d been suckered by a word that encompassed them all. Partners. He’d thought it was the key to power, wealth, and independence. Someone had control over his life, but it wasn’t Frederick J. Lewis.

“If you’re going to eat that, you’d better hurry.” Tony shook his fork at the filet growing cold in front of Frederick.

“What if I’m not interested?” Frederick suggested.

“Oh, you’ll be interested.” Tony finished the water in his goblet and reached across the table to drink Frederick’s water also.

The waitress appeared with the check and set it on the table between them.

“You want to get this?” Tony laughed, mocking the wiggling fish on the hook. He dropped several bills onto the table, scooped up the mints and walked toward the front of the restaurant.

Frederick followed him out onto the street. The gas street lights flanking the front door cast a ghoulish yellow haze in the dark. Tony looked up and down the street, a toothpick dangling from his lip. He stood close to Frederick as if he intended to grab him if he should walk away. Tony sniffed the air. "Hot," he declared. "This way, Freddy, my man."

Frederick followed him, watching him, watching the street. He observed that he kept one hand in his jacket. He didn't recall Tony wearing a jacket very often, and it was a hot night. They turned the corner and the street quickly disintegrated into the tough neighborhood that surrounded Old Town. High rises, townhouses, and restored row houses were supposed to have stabilized the community that sat in the shadow of the Cabrini Green Housing Project. The raggedly dressed black kids on shiny bicycles, weaving in and out among the cars, indicated otherwise.

In the next block, Frederick saw a dark car parked along the empty street. "That's them," Tony said. Frederick thought about bolting, but he walked with Tony to the car. The door opened and Frederick, with a slight assist from Tony, got into the back seat. Tony said something to the man in the passenger seat and laughed.

As the car sped away, Frederick looked back to see Tony pop a mint into his mouth. A shiny piece of foil fluttered to the curb.

"Who are you?" Frederick asked.

"We do the talking. You listen."

The man sitting next to him stayed in the shadow. The street lights were mostly shattered, but he handed Frederick a photograph. The car was moving fast now and when the light improved Frederick could see he held a picture of a small cone-like object. A ruler positioned next to it indicated that it was about eight inches long and two inches wide. The man handed Frederick another photo. It was the same one Tony had shown him in the restaurant. Alicia was standing on a dock, but the picture was taken in profile as she stared out toward the ocean.

"We have reason to believe this woman has this little bauble. Mr. Scully has persuaded us you are the man to get it back." The man spoke with an accent.

"And why is that?"

The man passed a packet of photos to Frederick. He shuffled through them as the car sped along Lake Shore Drive under the bright lights. There was a picture of him coming out of the tailor's shop, at the

Ritz, with Renata in several expensive restaurants, and a photo of him with Tony smiling over the coho salmon he'd caught. Then there were four photos of him at Logan and O'Hare, holding the packages of contracts and blueprints.

"So what's this? A bunch of pictures of me enjoying myself." Frederick tossed them back at the man seated next to him. He made no attempt to take them and they fell to the floor of the car.

"But how did you pay for all this? These fancy restaurants. You wear expensive suits. You live in a two-thousand-dollar-a-month rental on Dearborn. Where did you get that kind of money? How did you earn it?"

The man handed him another photo. This one was larger. Frederick recognized the man he'd delivered the first package of prints to, J. Smith. The large gilded frame he'd thought looked out of place in the tiny office was missing and in its place hung the flag of the USSR. Smith's hand was outstretched as Frederick was handing him the blueprints from Tony. He remembered a moment of hesitation before the man had taken the package.

"What the hell is this? Some kind of doctored photo? This is an office in Boston. I was there. But there wasn't any fuckin' Soviet flag, which by the way doesn't represent anything anymore. It was an American contractor's office. I can give you the address."

"I'm sorry, but if you should go there, you would find there is no such office, no such person. You were around the corner in the Russian consular's office.

"I know where I was, Mack. If this is some kind of fuckin' attempt at entrapment, it's not going to work." Frederick pulled at the door handle, but the car was moving fast and the door was securely locked.

"You have been in the employment of the Russian people for some time now. You have provided us with a great deal of useful information. We are most grateful for this, and it was you who came to us. Androveb Sclovich will remind you of that. You needed a job, you needed money to support your expensive taste and, with your background you were just the man. We paid you very well."

"It won't hold up, jack-off. I'm a veteran of the US Army. I'm a law-abiding American citizen. Stop the fuckin' car. I'm getting out."

Frederick pounded on the glass partition that separated the back seat from the driver in the front.

"Please, calm yourself, Mr. Lewis. I am sure when you've had time to think about it, you will see it our way."

"Not on your life. I'm going straight to the FBI—the CIA—the police."

"They will be happy to see you. In fact, they have already begun to look for you. After the Ames affair, they are rather sensitive about informants; a man who fits your description, a veteran down on his luck, selling information to support an expensive lifestyle, they'll jump to it quicker than they used to."

Frederick slammed the photos in the man's face. "I'm sorry, Mr. USSR. You are the one without a government. I can go to my government and expose you. We've got laws against this sort of third-rate entrapment."

"Your legal system moves very slowly. It will take a long time."

"I got a long time."

"Unfortunately, we don't have a long time. We need your assistance."

"Well, you're not getting it."

The car left the Lake Shore Drive and headed for the Dan Ryan Expressway.

"Mr. Scully has informed us you already know this woman. Talk to her. Find out in your smooth way what she has done with this little piece of flotsam that drifted up on the beach. When you hand it over to us, that will be the end of it."

"Why don't you ask her yourself? Cut the crap, stop playing spy games and go ask the woman nicely for your toy. I'm sure she'd be happy to cooperate with you."

"That is why we collect men like you. It is our insurance program. Then, when we have unexpected complications like this missing piece of property, well, then we have people we can call on to help us out."

The sedan had not gotten on the Dan Ryan, but turned back up Michigan Avenue. They rode in silence and stopped in front of Frederick's apartment building on Dearborn Street. "One last thing, Mr. Lewis," the man said. "There is ten thousand dollars in the Lake Shore

Bank in an account bearing only your name. You deposited it there for Mr. Scully a month ago. Your picture is in the bank's files. It would be very hard to explain to your government why it got there, don't you think?"

The lock released. Frederick opened the door. "Keep your fucking pictures," he shouted as he slammed the door shut and hurried toward the welcoming lights of the high rise.

He hurried through the lobby and passed the elevator and bolted up the stairs. When he reached the fourteenth floor, he was out of breath, but he felt better. He shoved his key into the lock and pushed open the door.

The air conditioning was running. He left the door open and snapped on the light. The studio wasn't large. The kitchenette was clearly visible from the front door, and the bathroom door was open, the door flat against the wall. No one else was in the room now.

Frederick shut, locked, and chained the door. On the kitchen counter lay two packets. One held a set of the pictures he'd been shown in the car, and the other contained an airline ticket to Jellicle Island. United Airlines flight #212 leaving Chicago at 8:40 AM, arriving in Boston at 10:50 AM, with a connecting commuter flight to the island leaving at 12:10 PM. A rental car slip was stapled to the flight envelope. They'd thought of everything.

He grabbed a bottle of Jack Daniels from the cupboard and didn't bother with a glass. He took a swig and then he spread out the photographs.

Yes, there he was on the boat with Scully. Behind him, propped against the bait well, was Scully's briefcase. He hadn't remembered seeing it that day, but he'd seen it often after that, and as he flipped through the photos he noticed it or one identical to it in each of the prints.

There was a picture of him shaking hands with the man who had dropped into Scully's office, and in the next photo he was handing Frederick the briefcase. He remembered the man telling him about his purchase in Florence, and Frederick had taken it from him to admire the leather. But now in this photo, it looked as if the briefcase was exchanging hands. Frederick to this man, or this man to Frederick?

He studied the photo taken in the dark corridor outside the tailor's tiny shop. Scully had encouraged him to buy suits from his tailor, although Frederick realized he'd never seen Scully in anything that looked hand tailored.

He had a dresser full of underwear from Brooks Brothers and a dozen silk shirts with his initials on the sleeve. Once he'd admired an ad in Town and Country displaying an open armoire filled with sweaters in a dozen shades. He'd purchased a shelf full of them at Marshall Field's. He had three pair of running shoes, in addition to the pair Scully had handed him the first time they'd met.

Renata chose the restaurants. They'd flown to New York and San Francisco when the mood struck her. Always Scully had kept him well supplied with cash. His baby sister, he'd explained, had taken up with the wrong crowd; and it had been a long, slow recovery from a cocaine habit. It was a miracle she'd asked someone like him for help that night in the bar when she'd started to slide from her cleaned up lifestyle. Scully was happy to provide Frederick with the funds to keep his sister clean. The odd jobs and hint of a partnership with Scully had sealed the deal.

How had they been so sure of him? How long had they been waiting to set the trap? He'd enjoyed a sensitive position in the Army. He'd had a high security clearance. It would never occur to him to abuse it. He wasn't a traitor.

He'd been dealing the photos out across the counter when the last one in the stack surfaced. He stared at it in disbelief. A woman, standing by a picnic table, held a small child. It was his sister and the nephew he'd never seen. She lived in a small town in Wisconsin. She was a nursery school daycare teacher. Her husband was dead. Cancer.

Frederick hadn't talked to her since his nephew was a baby. Once in a while, when he had money, he'd send her some. He'd sent her a hundred dollars the week Scully told him he was finding a place for him in his business. Making him a partner. Their own mother had died when they were young, and Frederick and his sister had lived with his father's second wife, who had never been much interested in either of them.

When did they take the photograph of his sister? Who was the man standing behind her smiling broadly into the camera? There was a lake in the background. He could almost smell the mud. He could almost remember the sound of his mother's voice. A rush of long-abandoned childhood memories cried out from deep within him.

The telephone jarred him back to the present. He picked up the receiver and waited for the person on the other end to begin the conversation.

"Fred? Everything in order?" It was Scully.

"You son-of-a-bitch. If you think I'm working with your fucked up friends, you can think again."

"Careful, pal. You live a charmed life. No reason to stop. You already know this broad on the island. Know her real well, I'll bet. And that's real lucky for all of us. Now these nice gentlemen are real concerned about retrieving their property. I'm sure you can figure out a way to get it from her before she knows it's gone. It's gotta be done soon, Fred. You get it. We'll tell you where to deliver it."

"The hell I will."

"Your sister's got a new boyfriend. She even let him move in. Big step. He'll kill her if you forget to do your job, pal." The phone went dead.

16 | Patience Is the Greatest Prayer

Alicia turned up the flame and melted the tallow and sal ammoniac. She dropped metal strips into place and watched the forms sketched in charcoal explode into three dimension in the sand pit in her yard. It was hot and smelly work, and the metal proved to be far more unyielding than she'd anticipated.

The *objet trouvé* did not cooperate. Like a mother surprised to discover her child had a mind of his own, she struggled to transform the conceptual into the real. Failing to do so, she turned angrily against the glistening object.

She screamed. She kicked sand. She threw a wrench into the woods and then spent an hour searching for it, mumbling and sputtering all the while. The dogs, unused to such outbursts and empty language, at first wagged their tails, then thinking they were to blame hunched down and whimpered. Finally, they ambled off into the woods.

She meant for the object to serve as a starting point for a much larger—monumental was the word she liked to use—work of art, but the solder wouldn't hold. The metal strips fell apart overnight.

After several days of cutting, her hands were blistered, her fingers ached, and her eyes burned from the searing odors. Sliding a large piece of metal underneath the uncooperative object, Alicia altered her plans to build from it and began reforming her vision.

She was used to delicate brush strokes, colors swimming eagerly out of her mind and onto the paper, and images floating into focus as effortlessly as a Polaroid snapshot developing. Watercolors were her vocation, her signature, her fortune. Easily, she gathered samples of her work and sent them to Chicago with Beth, to island galleries, and to friends, but this sculpture was to be a bold statement. She loved and hated the sculpture with an intensity of emotion she did not associate with her brushwork. With its independence, its refusal to be melded into her vision, it forced its importance on her.

The object became the core of the sculpture, and there, caged, its identity known only to her. At last she succeeded in creating a piece of some size with interesting curves and hollows. It was tiresome, physical labor. She admitted it would never be monumental in size, as she had envisioned. It wouldn't be visible to the commuter planes swooping over the island, and it wouldn't rise above the tree line in her front yard, as she had planned. Yet, she concluded, it was a good idea brought down in scale. Something she was proud of creating but, nevertheless, separate from her professional work. A secret folly, Alicia's diversion. She wondered how successfully her watercolors were being received in Chicago.

After weeks of hauling sheets of metal, cutting, hammering, soldering, and fluxing, Alicia's original version, a structure at least eight feet tall, had been seared and twisted into an object four feet tall and two feet wide. It didn't soar. It sat like a toad hunkering on the ground, its beady eye on an owl.

It was the middle of August, the summer more than two-thirds gone, and her body ached from the weeks of struggle with the metal. Her hands were nicked and callused from cutting with the heavy shears, her eyelashes singed from staring too closely at freshly soldered buttresses that tended to collapse overnight.

When she compared sketches to finished paintings, she could see the brief lines transformed by color and shadow into the essence of the island, alive with smell and temperature. The preliminary sketches she had drawn for the sculpture were abandoned, and she had worked from instinct. Now, when she looked at the bold lines of those sketches and then studied the hard, unyielding mass in her yard, she saw only a mean and alien blob. It had no life force. It had sucked her energy, muddied her visions, and bothered her dreams.

She was relieved to be finished with it. Like any good exercise, it had sharpened her skills, and now she eagerly sought her paints and brushes and once again thought about the wood lily. The time spent grappling with space and mass left her yearning for choices of greens and blues. The startle of red would yield its composition this time, and as surely as the seasoned batter connects with the well pitched ball, Alicia would capture the essence of the wood lily growing in the thickets by the pond.

The sun was disappearing below the trees, a cool wind suggested fog might be evident before evening, and the dogs reappeared trotting out of the woods. Alicia pulled the unused sheets of metal to the side of the house and dragged a canvas tarp over them. She traced the long extension cord to the door and followed it into the kitchen, unplugged it, tugging the end through the open door.

Deer flies as big as blueberries buzzed through the house. The door had been left open a crack for the extension cord. She slammed it shut, swatted a fly, and lamented that flypaper was no use against these creatures. They'd eat it. She was starving. She was exhausted.

Outside again, she picked up her tools and carried them into the house. The dogs followed her, hungry; they waited for her to settle down and notice them. She sighed as she stared at the nearly full bag of dog food. Too tired to lift the bag, she tore at the opening. After a day dragging heavy metal about, she was stronger than she realized and the bag ripped wide open spilling kibbles across the floor.

Two hungry mouths gobbled them up. She watched their tongues dart out about the bottom of the bag, searching for the scattered food. Who cares, she thought. She pulled at the torn bag and watched as more kibbles fell to the floor. She took a can of soup from the shelf and worked her way around the animals to the kitchen counter.

While the soup cooked, she spread out her sketches and studied them. She knew she'd feel better if she cleaned up before she ate, but exhaustion was creeping over her. She dumped the shears, pliers, hammer, and sandpaper in a box and sat down. She didn't want to look at that stuff any longer. Her legs were wobbly.

This really hadn't been about art, she admitted. It had been about expunging Frederick from her life. He'd gotten under her skin, and she'd thought the sculpture would be the cure. If she'd only gone after the wood lily in the meadow instead of the beach, she'd have saved herself a lot of mental anguish.

She stared at the watery imitation chowder in the pan. Were there no clams in the clam chowder? She read the label to confirm its identity. She turned up the heat under the pan. Then she poured the chowder into a mug and drank it lukewarm without stopping until the mug was empty.

She climbed the stairs for a bath. When she looked in the mirror, she smiled. She hadn't removed the bandanna she'd wrapped around her head. "Good evening, Rosie the Riveter," she said as she grabbed a tube of cleanser and smeared it across her face.

The tub filled with water, burbling and gurgling it came through the faucet. She'd never installed a shower, preferring the old cast iron tub with claw feet. For a while she'd strung a plastic hose up along a bamboo pole for a make-shift shower, but more water went on the floor than in the tub. She didn't want to add a shower curtain and hide the beauty of the tub. Besides, she preferred baths.

Sliding into the water, she shut her eyes. She was going to enjoy the next winter, working in her studio. The ease of it beckoned her as she began to wonder if there were enough days left in August to complete her grueling project. She flexed her fingers, suddenly aware of how foolish it would be to permanently damage her hands. What if she developed arthritis and lost her magic touch?

It would be better to sleep than to drown. She pulled herself out of the tub, feeling the soreness in her arms. She slipped into her nightgown and pulled the covers over her, certain she'd be fast asleep in a minute.

Downstairs the dogs growled. Someone was knocking on the door.

17 | Patience Wears Out Stone

It took Dmitri longer than he'd calculated to walk back up the shore to where he'd left the crate. Standing over it now, he drew in his breath and let it out in a slow, anguished sigh as he considered the enormity of his failure. The crate was empty. One corner of the crate was damaged. It lay at an angle firmly planted in the sand. The cover had been pried off. The buoy he'd followed to shore was gone. The bright orange marker he'd spotted before being chased from the beach was gone. His anticipated two-hour hike back up the beach had turned into a forty-eight-hour setback. It was the sixth of July. Dmitri Alexi Korsomakov had big problems.

He felt the presence of someone and turned to see a small boy standing beside him.

"It's empty. I could carry it if you'd help me get it out of the sand," the child said.

"You saw this crate before?" Dmitri asked.

"Sure. I was down here yesterday with my uncle. He was catching blues. I saw it first. It was full of treasure. I know it was. My uncle said it probably had Spanish gold in it, but I couldn't open it up, and when I got back here it just had paper with weird writing on it, and then when I finally got my uncle to come look, it was empty. He wouldn't help me get the crate out of the sand. I want it. It's neat."

"You saw this crate, here, with the top on it?"

"Sure."

"It hadn't been opened?"

"Nope. Do you think it was full of gold?"

"I don't know," Dmitri said slowly, figuring his next move. Finding treasure on the beach was a boy's dream. It was Dmitri's dream, too. What the treasure was depended upon the dreamer. Maybe this boy could help him find the precious cargo he was supposed to have delivered to Fyodorvitch.

"Are you sure the crate hadn't been opened when you found it? Maybe it was open but turned over." Dmitri had to be absolutely certain someone on shore had opened the crate. There was a chance he could retrieve the cargo if it was on the shore, but not if it had been lost in the ocean.

"I tried to open it with a rock, but it was nailed shut. It's pretty sturdy wood. Not like the stuff you usually find, like plastic. It must be real old." The boy stared lovingly at the empty crate. "I went home for a hammer, but my uncle wouldn't come with me because his girlfriend was with him and when he did come it was like this. But I came back once by myself, and it was full of paper. Paper with different writing on it. Probably code."

"Code? Yes. Maybe. Who do you think opened it up and took the paper?"

"Do you think the paper is money? Oh, no!" The boy began hopping around kicking sand into the air. "Do you think it was old dollars?"

"I don't know. I'd have to see some of it. Usually, where there's paper money, when you're talking about treasure, there's gold. You didn't see anything that looked like gold, did you?" The boy shook his head. "Who do you think opened the crate?"

"I don't know. Could have been anybody. Lots of people walk along here. They're not supposed to, but they do. You have to get down here real early after a storm to find anything interesting. And I've never found anything this neat, except once when I was little my Mom and I found a ship. Well, I thought it was a ship. She said it was a garbage scow. Looked like a ship to me. It was huge. I can take this home."

Dmitri looked at the crate. Maybe he could help the boy dig it out. If he could go home with the boy someone might know about the missing contents. "What I need is a shovel, but a flat rock would do."

"I could ask Dr. Norton." He was an eager, happy child and he bolted down the shore, jumping over rocks, hopping over tiny streams that rippled through the sand. Dmitri sat down on a boulder to wait. He was running out of time.

Soon the boy reappeared, moving slowly and dragging a shovel. He met the boy and took the shovel. "Great," Dmitri said and set about freeing the crate from the sand. He worked cautiously, letting the boy see he was being careful not to hurt his prize. The empty crate was his only chance, his only clue to the whereabouts of its cargo.

"Did your friend with the shovel know about the crate?"

"Yeah, Mrs. Norton said it was full of labels and she had them all." He emphasized the word labels, his voice filled with disappointment.

"She did?" Dmitri's heart quickened.

"I don't think she found any gold, though."

"What makes you think that?"

"Would you be sitting on the beach eating fish for breakfast if you found gold?"

Yes, Dmitri thought. If he could find this particular piece of "gold," he would like to think he could end up on a beach eating fish. If the woman had the labels, surely she had what he was looking for.

He put the shovel down and brushed sand from the crate while he considered his next move. "Why don't you ask her? You're a nice boy. Don't say it so… you know, don't ask her if she found gold because of course she'd say no. Say, did you find anything shiny in the crate? Maybe she'll forget herself and tell you."

He pulled the crate free from the sand and set it upright. The boy danced around it with pleasure, squatted to examine it, then jumped into the air, and squealed with delight.

His skinny arms punched at the sky. "Yes!" he shouted.

Perhaps the woman had pitched it. Perhaps to her it had not seemed as interesting as the labels. He looked at the dune behind them. The beach grass was sparse there. The sun might reflect off it, if it had been tossed into the sand.

"I'll carry the crate home for you. First, you return the shovel and ask the woman if she saw anything shiny. Remember, don't mention the gold. I'll wait here for you."

"Okay," the boy said as he eagerly took the shovel. He watched him lug the tool around the curve in the shoreline and out of sight. Dmitri turned his eye to the sandy rise. It was not possible to climb to the crest of the sand dune. It was fragile and would crumble. He saw nothing.

When the boy returned, Dmitri waited for him to speak. He didn't want him to think he was too interested. "They'd left," he said at last. "I put the shovel next to the boathouse where Dr. Norton told me to."

"Where do they live?"

"Up there." The boy pointed to what appeared to Dmitri to be an impassable row of trees.

"It's not far from my grandparents. I'll show you if you want after we take the crate to my grandparents' house. We'll go this way."

Dmitri positioned the crate on his shoulder. The boy looked up at him. "You're strong. Do you live around here?"

"It's not so heavy when there's no sand in it. Lead on."

The boy was off with a bound, his question forgotten as he led the way to what had previously been an unseen path. The narrow path widened and eventually they came to a fork in the road. "The Nortons' live that way," the boy said pointing. They continued along a gravel road until it broke into a wide lawn.

"Hey, hey! I got it," he shouted as he ran toward a screened porch.

Dmitri could hear manly cheers. There were people sitting on the porch. He could hear the high-pitched chattering of the boy, but he could not see who he was talking to.

"Welcome," a man shouted. "You've earned a beer. Come on in."

Dmitri set the crate in the yard and followed the boy onto the porch.

"This is my friend," the boy said triumphantly. "He dug it out and carried it all the way up here for me."

A man sat on a chair with one leg extended on a straight back chair. He looked about sixty, his hair almost gone, and a stubble of gray beard covered his face. He reached up to shake Dmitri's hand. "Bob Cunningham. And this worthless bum over here is my son, Robert."

The younger man stepped forward and offered his hand to Dmitri.

"Peter Smith," Dmitri said as they shook hands.

"Thank you, Peter." Robert stepped back to pull a chair forward. "You've saved me from the haranguing noise of my nephew. His mother's bringing you a beer."

A young woman appeared and smiled at Dmitri. She handed the beer to Dmitri and went out into the yard to examine the crate. Another, older woman, stood behind the grandfather rubbing the back of his neck.

"The child has been so excited about that box," the grandmother said. "You were so sweet to help him bring it up here. It has made his summer."

"No trouble," Dmitri said. He took a long sip of the cold beer. "It was empty."

The grandmother laughed. "When we first saw it in the sand, there must have been five hundred labels in that box. Every person on the island probably has one. It will be interesting to see where they turn up over the summer."

Dmitri cringed. He'd thought the beach was remote.

"I know where most of them are," the boy's mother said as she returned to the porch.

Dmitri sat hunched forward, the cold can between his palms, his elbows resting on his knees. He waited for the conversation to continue.

"I saw Mrs. Norton at the mailboxes, and she said she had carried up a basketful. She was going to put them in her bathroom," the boy's mother said.

"For toilet paper?" the uncle chortled.

"She was going to paper the walls with them."

"What kind of labels were they?" the grandfather asked.

"They're beautiful," the boy's mother continued. Beyond her, in the yard, the boy danced around the crate.

"You saw them?" Robert asked.

"Yes, brother dear. Some of us are not too lazy to leave the porch. I would have carried the crate for Justin, but it was half buried in the sand." She smiled at Dmitri.

"And you're telling me you saw the labels at the Nortons'?" her brother asked incredulously.

"No, not at the Nortons'. Alicia Barrett has some. So do the kids at the Clayton house, I'd bet."

“Hey, Justin. Did you get any of those labels that were in the box?” she called out to the yard.

“No. Nobody would go with me. And I wouldn’t have gotten the crate if it wasn’t for this guy.”

That brought the conversation back to Dmitri. He crushed the empty can in his hand.

“Maybe we could get some of those labels for the boy. He could put them on the crate.”

“Hey, that’s a great idea. Can we, Mom, can we?” Justin stood outside with his face pressed against the screen door.

“Well, I suppose we could ask Alicia.”

“Cool. Let’s go.” He charged back into the yard.

Dmitri stood up. He needed to locate these houses. Nortons, Claytons, Barretts. He needed the boy’s help.

“You coming, Mom?”

“I guess so.” She turned to Dmitri. “Want to come with us, or stay here for another beer?”

“I’m curious about the labels, too. If you don’t mind, I’ll go with you.”

“Great. Are you staying around here?”

Dmitri hesitated. He needed to get his hands on the cargo. He’d need some assistance finding the houses they’d mentioned, and he didn’t want to make anyone too curious about his motives.

He was taking a risk, but forty-eight hours on Jellicle Island had led him to believe it was easier for some people to accept outrageous possibilities than to settle for mundane details leading to less interesting conclusions.

Justin had run across the wide lawn toward the trees in a different direction from the one they’d come. He stopped and shouted at them, “You said you were coming, so COME!”

“Your son is very bright. You and your husband must be very proud of him.”

“I am very proud of him. His father… doesn’t see much of him.”

“He’s a fisherman?”

“He is… we’re divorced.”

“Sorry.”

“Don’t be. I’m not.” She smiled coyly as they walked down the road. That’s it, Dmitri thought, he was going to take a big chance.

“I am a fisherman,” he began slowly. “A Russian fisherman.”

“Oh, really?” She gave him that coy smile again.

“I had a little trouble with my boat.”

“Oh you did, did you?” Now she was smiling broadly.

“Our fishing trawler ran into some rough seas, and some of our crates fell overboard. I volunteered to come ashore and see what became of them. If it’s just a crate of fishing labels, it’s no problem. If it’s a crate of television equipment that’s come ashore, it could cause an international incident. And it shouldn’t, because the crew just wanted to hook into American cable TV. If someone finds all this television equipment, then the next thing you know we’ll be accused of spying, and then we’ll lose our newly acquired fishing rights along the East Coast.”

Dmitri had kept his head down kicking at a root while he spun his tale. Now he looked at her and smiled.

“So you’re kind of an illegal alien, but not a spy?”

“You won’t tell on me?”

“And risk being laughed at? And for your information, there is no cable TV on this island. And Russian trawlers aren’t allowed to fish along here.”

“We got a little off course.”

“Of course you did.”

“Mom. Come on.”

They stood in the road staring at each other. Dmitri smiled at her. It was a sweet smile, a warm and inviting smile, she thought. She was surprised to feel the glow, to find herself enjoying basking in the utter nonsense of it all. Guys had tried some lines on her, but this was a good one.

“No, Mr. Peter Smith. I won’t tell a soul.”

She turned and hurried to follow her son. The road curved, the trees were thick, and Dmitri tried to get his bearings. The road led directly into a lawn. A gray shingled house sat at the other end of it, with more woods beyond. Dmitri followed across the grass, trying to determine which direction led to the beach, the Sanctuary, and the Norton house.

"Alicia, it's Margaret Eastman." The front door opened and a woman appeared and smiled at Margaret who stood on the stone step, Dmitri not far behind her, and Justin who was playing in the sand.

"I hope we're not interrupting your work," Margaret said. "You know those labels you found at the beach? Justin saw them, but when he went back they were all gone. Could he have some of yours?"

"Mrs. Norton took the lion's share. I wonder where I set them. Come in." She looked at Dmitri, but Margaret didn't introduce him.

In the front hallway, they stood awkwardly for a moment. Justin pushed past his mother to stand by Dmitri. A man appeared in the doorway to the living room. He was dressed in a cranberry colored blazer, and he stood stiffly observing the three of them. Dmitri bristled.

"I'm sorry," Margaret began. "I didn't realize you had company." She began backing toward the front door, backing into Dmitri. The man in the living room did not move, his arms behind his back, his posture straight and military. Dmitri searched the blazer for insignia. He put his arm casually over Margaret's shoulder.

"Oh, this is my…" Alicia stopped. "This is Frederick."

"How do you do?" Frederick extended his hand, first to Margaret and then to Dmitri.

"Peter Smith," Dmitri said.

"Join us. We were just having a glass of wine."

"I should have called first," Margaret protested. "Justin was so insistent, and we just started out to see if we could track down some of those labels."

"They are wonderful. Very brightly colored, and with foreign writing. You'll die when you hear where they've ended up. Beth's mother has plastered them all over her bathroom."

"Beth told me when I saw her at the mailboxes. She told me you had some, too."

Dmitri waited. The man in the blazer said nothing. Alicia brought glasses from a corner cupboard and set them on a wooden chest in front of the sofa. Margaret sat down and Dmitri sat down next to her. She poured the wine and turned to hand a glass to Frederick, who stood stiffly by the fireplace.

"Cheers," Alicia said as she raised her glass. "To old friends, and new."

Dmitri's stomach growled. He hadn't eaten, but he'd drunk a beer, and now he had a glass of wine in his hand. He picked up the knife on the board in front of him and cut a large hunk of cheese.

Margaret reached over and took it from him. "Thanks, dear," she said. "Alicia, Nana says your work is selling like Picasso. She went to the opening at the Watermark, and she said everything was sold. I think she'd like to commission you to do a painting of the house."

"That could be arranged."

"I've been thinking of taking Justin to Chicago to visit some of the museums. We could stay with Tess. Do you hear from her?"

"No. Beth stays in touch with her. It would be fun to get together, wouldn't it?"

Dmitri wanted to get the conversation back to the labels. The man in the blazer made him nervous. Someone rapped softly on the front door, and he remembered Justin had not gone out.

"Mom," Justin shouted as he was admitted to the house. "You should see what the Clayton kids found!"

Dmitri stood up.

"Justin, your manners. You shouldn't burst in like that."

"Mom," he moaned.

"I'll go with the boy," Dmitri leaned over and kissed Margaret lightly on the cheek. She was surprised, and now she wouldn't want Alicia to think they'd just met. "I'll join you in a minute, hon," she said as she took a sip of wine.

"Let me look in my backpack for those labels," Alicia offered.

Margaret studied Frederick. He was certainly overdressed for Jellicle Island. He must not be a boyfriend, Margaret concluded. Probably an art dealer.

"Now that I've pushed my way into your house, my son doesn't seem interested in the labels. I keep telling myself not to get involved with small boys' games," she said with a nervous giggle.

"This is the best I can do, Margaret." Alicia pulled a couple labels from the backpack.

“They are colorful. Thanks. Now, I won’t interrupt any longer. Thanks for the wine and cheese.”

“You just got here. Don’t leave.”

Margaret finished the last swallow of wine and headed for the door.

“Nice to meet you,” she called to Frederick as she stepped out onto the front step.

The Clayton house was only a few hundred yards further down the road, but it couldn’t be seen from Alicia’s house. She crossed the circle of sand in the front yard. An odd place to put a barbecue pit, she thought. She jogged up the road around the bend and into the Claytons’ yard.

Behind the house, a barn projected against the clear summer sky. In its doorway she could see Justin and the Clayton boys bending over a box. Dmitri stood outside the doorway, one foot resting against the side of the barn.

“What is it that you’ve found?” she called out.

“A dog.” Dmitri sounded disgusted.

“A dog?” Margaret inquired, puzzled. Everyone had a dog.

“Puppies,” Dmitri replied bitterly.

If the artist didn’t have the cargo, and the Clayton boys knew nothing about labels, then the Norton woman must have it, Dmitri concluded. He would rekindle the boy’s imagination to get into the Norton house.

“Okay, Justin. The next thing I know you’ll be wanting a puppy, and the answer is no. Here are the labels you were looking for.”

“Let me see them!” he exclaimed. His mother held out a handful of labels. She turned to the man she knew as Peter Smith. “What do they say, fisherman?”

“Cod.” Dmitri replied. “Packed in America.”

He turned to Justin. “I think we should go check out your neighbor’s bathroom and see what else she might have found. What do you say?”

18 | Enough Is as Good as a Feast

"*Eto bardak*," Dmitri muttered.

"What did you say?" Margaret asked.

What a mess, Dmitri was thinking. Fyordorvitch was philosophical about Dmitri's botched landing on the beach when Dmitri assured him he knew the whereabouts of the crate. There'd been contingency plans but they had a deadline. The President's speech was the first week in September. They'd given themselves lead time, but it was being sucked up as Dmitri was caught in a desperate scavenger hunt.

Margaret reached out and took Dmitri's hand. The path disappeared, and reedy grasses reached her shoulders. Dmitri pulled a burr from her hair. In the distance a gull cried out, and close by a dragonfly landed on a leaf, bending it down and sending it flying upward when it flew off.

When they reached the road again, their clothes were covered with pods, burrs, and bits and pieces of leaves and twigs. Margaret brushed at her shoulders. "I guess nobody ever takes that path anymore," she said.

The road forked, and she guided him to the right. Dmitri tried to make a mental note of the path, but the gravel and the trees and the winding roads all looked alike. He was close to finding it, he was sure. Whether Mrs. Norton had it, or the artist, or even the kids with the puppies, he did not know.

Margaret stopped short, reached up and put her arms around his neck. She kissed him solidly. "A few more yards and the Nortons can hear and see us clearly," she cautioned.

They continued walking. The house jutted out from the woods and Dmitri heard a woman's voice. "Frank, Frank. Someone is walking up the road," she shouted.

"Oh, for God's sake. I wish people would learn to read. How any one could mistake this road for one of the trails to the beach is beyond me. I've got to talk to the Sanctuary about putting up more markers," he replied gruffly.

"Oh, that looks like Margaret, the Cunninghams' daughter. The young man we saw at the beach with Justin must be her boyfriend." Sue Ellyn determined.

"How do you know?" Dr. Norton inquired.

"Well, they're holding hands, dear."

"How nice."

Margaret winked at Dmitri and released his hand. Dmitri wondered why Dr. Norton was so concerned about security, about markers.

"Mrs. Norton?" Margaret called out. "It's Margaret Cunningham."

Justin raced past them and trotted up to the front door, and then circled back to walk behind his mother.

"Is that your son? How big he is. Come in. You've missed Beth. She's gone back to Chicago." Mrs. Norton left the porch to walk through the dining room to the front hall and open the door.

"This is my friend, Peter Smith. Justin has been collecting treasures from the beach. He was wondering if you found any labels. They are bright red and floated up onto the beach in a crate he has claimed."

"Found any! Oh, my. Come in, and we'll get you something to drink." Mrs. Norton held the door open wide.

"We were just taking a walk, when I thought I'd stop and ask. I don't want to impose on you," Margaret said.

"Not imposing at all. I love it when you young people remember us. Justin, would you like some ginger ale?"

"Frank, Frank. We need drinks." She led them to the screened porch, where Dr. Norton sat reading his newspaper. He peered up at them over his reading glasses. Then he stood up and held his hand out to Dmitri. Dmitri shook it. Next, he turned his attention to Justin. "Well, Justin. Did you get that crate out of the sand? Thank you for returning my shovel."

Justin nodded. Dmitri waited for the boy to ask questions, but he appeared to be shy in the Nortons' presence and slunk back behind his mother.

"Peter, is it? Can I get you a little bourbon?"

"Maybe he'd rather have a beer," Mrs. Norton suggested.

"No, bourbon would be fine," Dmitri said.

"Margaret, what would you like?"

"Do you still make gimlets, Dr. Norton?"

"I certainly do, young lady." Dr. Norton peered over his half-glasses at his wife. "And what could I interest you in?"

"A dry martini." Mrs. Norton turned to her three guests. "Please, sit down. It's been a lovely day. Rather warm at the beach, but nice and cool as usual in the house.

"Justin, I've got a few extra labels upstairs. I want you all to come up and see what I've done with them. It took Beth and me all the Fourth of July weekend to do it. I'm glad I didn't use them all. I'd hate to have to peel some of them off the walls for you, Justin, but I would. They probably belong with a boy, not a bathroom, but I think it came out rather well."

"Do you find many interesting things washed ashore?" Dmitri began cautiously.

"Before there were so many people walking the beach, I did. It depends on the tide and the storm. Years ago, there were so many starfish. One year I spray painted dozens of them silver and hung them on our Christmas tree. You don't see starfish anymore."

"And other people, have they found things this year?" Dmitri swallowed the bourbon.

"Oh, I don't know. I'm the only one around here who gets excited about finding things on the beach."

"Justin was pretty excited to discover the crate," Dmitri pushed on. "It was empty when we got to it. What was in it when you saw it?"

"It was filled with labels. Come see what I did with them. Frank will get you another drink while we look."

Dmitri rose, and Margaret and Justin followed her up the stairs to the bathroom.

“Voila,” Sue Ellyn said as she flicked on the light. A brilliant orange illuminated the small room, and Dmitri stared in astonishment. He calculated the number of labels on the wall. Except for the few Alicia had given them, he was convinced she must have taken the rest. She must have the cargo, too.

“Looks like they’re some kind of packing material,” he began. “Whatever else do you imagine could have been in the crate?”

“Frank said they were fishing labels. Fell off one of those Russian trawlers fishing the coast now.”

“And you found nothing else?” Dmitri risked.

“What else do you think there could have been?” Mrs. Norton seemed defensive.

“Well, caviar, perhaps,” Dmitri smiled at her.

“Oh, I never thought of that. I’ll bet Alicia found it. She got to the crate first.”

Dmitri winced. It’d been his hunch she knew more than she let on. Her friend appeared more menacing than he let on, too. His relaxed military stance betrayed him. He needed to get back to the artist’s home for a better look around.

Were Margaret and Justin an asset or a distraction? With Justin he could ask questions that might not make anyone curious about his motives.

“We’re having clam spaghetti for dinner. Why don’t you stay? Margaret, you must tell me what you’ve been up to. And you Peter, I don’t know anything about you.”

Margaret did not care for Mrs. Norton’s inquiring mind. She’d been subjected to Mrs. Norton’s curiosity her whole life. She was aware that Beth’s mother had made disparaging remarks about Margaret’s failed marriages. Honestly, it was nobody’s business.

Not curious about his past, she simply wanted to have a happy summer. He liked Justin, and Margaret liked him even more because he seemed to enjoy her son’s company. She was going to put Mrs. Norton on the wrong track.

“Oh, Peter and I have been friends for years. He went to St. Mark’s He’s studied abroad. Russia, wasn’t it, Peter?”

Dmitri was stunned. He had no idea what or where St. Mark’s was.

"No, no. I've just always had an interest in Russian iconography."

"He's been telling such wonderful stories to Justin ever since Justin discovered the crate on the beach."

"Yes, I've got him convinced there must have been more in the crate than labels. What do you think?"

Mrs. Norton shook her head. "I would have loved to have found something valuable in that crate. I'm quite happy with the labels. I made plans to use them creatively."

"And we have plans, Mrs. Norton," Margaret said smiling at Dmitri. "We've taken up enough of your time. It's always nice to enjoy a summer drink with you."

Relieved to end the conversation, Dmitri stood, shook Dr. Norton's hand, and followed Margaret out of the house.

19 | A MAN IS NOT GOOD OR BAD FOR ONE ACTION

Tom Sullivan sat at his desk in an FBI field office in Washington, D.C. He was reviewing a Coast Guard report about a curious incident with two Russian fishing trawlers in the Georges Bank. When Seth McCalister breezed in, he tossed a pile of fishing manuals on his desk.

"How was Nova Scotia?" Sullivan asked.

"Boring, but the weather was good."

"Gotta take the good with the bad. Boston was hotter than Tophet."

Nodding at the fishing manuals, Sullivan asked, "You planning on joining Trout Unlimited on a fishing trip to Siberia?"

"No. What's up?"

"Not sure. I have a report here on two Russian trawlers having engine problems near the Gulf of Maine. They were briefly in U.S. territory but allegedly explained themselves and got back out into international water.

"Androveb Sclovich, calls himself Tony Scully—he's been passing tidbits to the Russians. He's handling an American, Frederick J. Lewis. Lewis has spent the last couple of months flying in and out of Boston delivering packages, and making trips to Jellicle Island. The President is going to make a stop at the National Marine Fisheries Center in Woods Hole—on Cape Cod, before he flies to New York to speak before thc United Nations."

"Hand me the file."

McCalister flipped through the report. "The *Zori* and the *Poyma,* I saw those two ships in Lunenburg. Had some engine trouble and were escorted to the shipyard."

“Think any of those Russian fishermen could have slipped into the country?”

“To do what?”

20 | Living Is Like Licking Honey off a Thorn

Beth stood in front of an arts and crafts shop on Clark Street. She'd passed it many times on her way to the bus stop. Through the display window crammed with a variety of paintings and ceramics, she could see the dusty interior. It was filled with curious objects—oil paintings of poorly proportioned, but clearly anguished souls, jewelry made from feathers and peach stones, and sculpture that showed distressed signs of hammering and chiseling. She had often studied the contents of the window while waiting for the bus. On this day, much to her surprise, she noticed that a peculiar painting of a naked man sitting on a tree branch was missing. She'd never seen anyone enter the store, or noticed that much of the merchandise disappeared, but only rearranged when another object was added to the collection.

She didn't want to think about Rick, but Rick was all she thought about. He was back in the city. She was certain she'd seen him. She'd been walking the streets forlornly, debating whether to go to Leslie Crane's gallery opening on the off chance she'd meet someone new.

She felt like shopping, but she didn't have much money left as she waited for her first paycheck at the beginning of the new school year. She wasn't hungry, but she decided to head for the Jewel.

Wandering the aisles, she picked out a package of extra-lean sirloin. A salad would go with the meat, but it seemed too wholesome now that Beth was beginning to feel good about wallowing in self-pity. A carton of chocolate-mocha ice cream, a bottle of vodka, Beefamato juice, raspberries, Cap'n Crunch, and a copy of Cosmopolitan ought to get her through the evening. Checking her watch, she realized she'd managed to spend over an hour coming to terms with her loneliness.

She could hear the telephone ringing when she stepped out of the elevator and rushed forward, dropped the grocery sacks to the floor, pulled out her keys and unlocked the door. She grabbed the phone.

"Hello? she shouted into the receiver.

"Ah, you're there. I was about to hang up," Alicia said. Beth felt the disappointment crushing her mood again. She bit down on her lower lip, realizing the disappointment of not hearing Rick's voice blurred her attention. She wasn't listening.

"Well then, what do you think?" Alicia was saying.

"Think? About what?"

"You did such a great job with the paintings, and I've sent half that money back to you, by the way. Don't you think you could find a place for the sculpture?"

"Sculpture?" Beth stammered. "What sculpture? What does it look like?"

"I honestly can't explain it. It's bigger than a bread box," Alicia laughed.

"How big is it?"

"Maybe four feet by two. Not solid. It's… it's kind of hard to describe, actually impossible to describe." Alicia laughed again. Beth wondered if she'd been drinking.

"If it was some kind of paperweight size, Leslie likes that sort of thing. Is it heavy?"

"Yeah, actually, it is. I don't know what I was thinking. I just want to get rid of it."

Beth couldn't lug a hundred pounds of indescribable metal up and down Michigan Avenue, but she was thrilled Alicia had shared the commission for the paintings with her. She could have a glorious shopping spree.

"Let me think about where I might take it. You never mentioned it or showed it to me when I was on the island."

"It's a long story. I got myself emotionally involved with the most annoying man and decided to refocus my attention on a project. At the moment, I seem to be stuck with both. Oh, and our dear friend Margaret has another hunk following her around."

"She'll probably be married for the third time before I can get myself married once," Beth said.

"There's nothing wrong with being selective, Beth."

"That's what Tess tells me. I'll see what I can come up with. You figure out how to ship it out here, and I'll find a place to show it. School starts at the end of August, so we've got to do it soon."

Beth hung up the phone and turned her attention to the groceries she'd dropped on the floor. Tearing the cellophane wrapper from the sirloin, she pinched a hunk of raw meat and ate it. Shouldn't eat it raw, she thought. It was probably contaminated with PCB's, antibiotics, virus and bacteria. That's what the vodka is for. She took a tall glass from the cupboard, filled it with ice, poured in the Beefamato and the vodka. A sprig of parsley or a lemon wedge would have been nice, but a squirt from a plastic lemon was all she had.

She sat down on the sofa and took a long swig of the drink. How long was she going to wait for Rick? How could Tess complain about her happy married life? So even cool and aloof Alicia could get snookered. And Margaret, how lucky could she be? Beth finished the drink and fixed another.

The second Bloody Mary went down quicker than the first, and Beth thought about a third, but a plan was beginning to form. She grilled the hamburger, ate a few raspberries, considered whether to try the Viennese coffee or to fix some regular. There was a delicate balance between the first-rate confidence of just another vodka and the inertia of too much.

Now to think about what to wear. This wasn't Michigan Avenue. New Town had its own dress code—jeans, a racer back T-shirt, flip-flops, and a pair of silver earrings would be just right.

She dressed quickly once she had her wardrobe figured out and left the building before dark. She walked quickly, not wanting to lose her nerve. The building was lit up, and the man she'd seen a hundred times as she'd walked by sat on a stool surrounded by "works of art." As usual, there was no one else in the store. She opened the door and stepped in.

"Hey," he said.

"Hello," she replied.

"Seen you go by a few thousand times."

"I… I take the bus." She motioned toward the bus stop.

"The Clark Street bus or the Broadway one? That's the crazy one, isn't it?"

"It can be."

"See something you like? Got a lot of stuff here."

"Yes, I've noticed."

"You interested in jewelry or painting or what?"

"Actually, I was wondering if you'd be interested in showing a piece of sculpture. I have this friend. She's a famous painter. She's got work in downtown galleries. She's trying something new, and she doesn't want to use her name." Beth wished she'd skipped the second Bloody Mary.

The man did not reply. The room was hot, and the vodka made it worse. She wasn't sure what she'd said. She began again. "It's crazy, I suppose, but I pass your… gallery…" Wrong word, she thought. "I see you have different kinds of art in here, and I thought maybe you'd be interested."

"Sounds good." He stood now, away from the table where he'd sat on a stool, and his arms hung limply at his sides. Nobody stands like that, she thought.

"Really? I don't have a photo. As I said, she usually does watercolors. Leslie Crane's Gallery carries them."

"Whatever." He continued to stand with his arms at his sides. She thought he was swaying, but it was probably only the vodka that made her think so.

"I could work up a contract. What kind of commission do you usually take?"

"Commission?"

"How about twenty percent? When you sell it, you take twenty percent. Is that all right?"

"That's cool. How much you think it will sell for?"

"Five hundred dollars." She had no idea. She'd save the money Alicia had split with her on the watercolors. She just didn't want to peddle the sculpture.

“Five hundred dollars!” he fairly spit the words back at her. He looked around the room and laughed, rubbing the back of his neck. His long hair was tied back in a pony tail that reached to his shoulder blades. “I don’t know if my insurance will cover it.” He laughed again and Beth wished she’d thought this through.

“I don’t think it will melt if you have a fire, and I don’t think anyone can walk off with it.”

“Nah, I was just joking. How big is this thing?”

“About four feet tall.”

“Is it a horse or something? What’s it made out of… chrome?”

“No, I don’t think it’s representational. Now that I have a gallery to represent her, I’ll get you a photo. And I’ll let you know when it will arrive.”

“Where did you say she lives?”

“It’s an island. Jellicle Island. It’s on the East Coast.”

“And she sends her stuff to Chicago?”

“She sends her work all over. I represent her in Chicago.” Suddenly, Beth felt sober. She wondered whatever had possessed her to do this. “Do you have a card? I need the address.”

He walked over to the table where he’d been sitting and wrote an address on the edge of a Chinese menu. He tore off the corner and handed it to her. “I’m just out of business cards. Sorry.

Ronald watched Beth as she scanned the room. “I get a lot of stuff from the pottery guild that meets in the Presbyterian church around the corner. And some students from DePaul, they bring in their work. I need to get this place better organized.”

“You had a painting in your window…”

“Yeah?”

“The oil. The one of the man in the tree.”

“Oh, that. Where is that?”

“I thought maybe you’d sold it.”

“Holy shit.”

He went to the window and moved a display of earrings on a poster board. “She’s going to be really pissed when she finds out it’s missing.”

“You think someone stole it?”

“I know somebody stole it. That goofy guy who sits around in the doorway, he’s been staring at it for weeks. I never saw him come in, but he hasn’t been on the street lately.”

“Maybe you should put one of those bells on the door so you can hear when people come in.”

“Yeah. Catch you later.”

Beth stepped out into the warm summer evening. She would go home, have a cup of coffee and some ice cream and read Cosmopolitan. She’d call Alicia in the morning and give her the address. Alicia seemed awfully eager to get rid of it, and Beth was, too.

21 | Any Ache but Heartache

Ordinarily, Alicia didn't paint in the summer, but creating the sculpture had worn her down and made her feel on edge. Matching the color of the wood lily revived her spirits and her thoughts turned to painting to relieve her downcast mood. But the painting did not go well. The brushes, which she expected to feel light and comfortable in her grip after weeks of working with the soldering iron and metal sheers felt awkward. It worried her.

She paced back and forth in her studio. She stopped to stare out the window at the sculpture in the yard. Just looking at it, she was annoyed. She checked her watch. It was eleven o'clock in the morning, and she should wait until the phone rates went down at five, but she couldn't wait another minute. She called Beth.

"Did you find a gallery for the sculpture?"

"Oh, Alicia. I don't think so. I talked to someone in the neighborhood, but it's all wrong."

"Did they say they'd take it?"

"Yes, but…"

"I don't care, Beth." Alicia's voice was shrill. "I want it out of here. Off the island. Gone."

"I don't think this place is up to your standards."

"Who cares. I'm not a sculptor. Give me the address."

Beth fumbled with the telephone cord searching her pockets. "I'll have to call you back. I don't know where I put the address."

"Fine. I'm going to go ahead and send it to the lumberyard to get crated."

"How big did you say this thing is?"

"About four feet high. I hate it."

Beth couldn't imagine the urgency. The phone had woken her and she wanted to go back to sleep. To be left alone.

Alicia hung up the phone. Beth sounded sleepy, but there was no point in apologizing. Her artistic powers were being drained. She had to get rid of the sculpture. Fast.

She stormed out of the house to the car, opened the back door, and turned to charge at the massive hunk of metal. She struggled to get her hands around it. It was heavy and awkward. She tugged it off the ground and staggered to the car energized by adrenaline. A part of it tore the plastic lining in her car when she dropped it on the car seat and she cursed it as she slammed the door.

Her anger spent, she realized she didn't have a plan. Roger could crate it. She'd get UPS to take it. They took anything. They could pick it up from the lumberyard. As she drove along the main road her thoughts turned to Frederick. He just showed up. It was annoying. She hadn't a clue what to say about him when Margaret and her friend had come in search of the labels for her son. It was Friday and she'd bet her last dollar that he'd show up again.

It was foggy, but living up-island in the woods it was impossible to know whether it would be dismal in town as well. She pulled into the lumberyard. Roger the owner of the lumber yard, was leaning against a pile of logs. She felt like she was going in search of a casket.

"Hello, Alicia."

"Hi, Roger. I've got a piece of sculpture in the back seat. I'd like you to crate it. I'll have UPS pick it up here."

"Sure. I wondered what you'd done with the load of sand." He peered into the back seat. "I still don't know."

"How's Dora?" Alicia said, ignoring his artistic criticism.

"Big as a whale. Due any time now."

"Lucky you."

"She wants one more trip to the stores on the mainland. Every time we go she's got a list a mile long. The kid's cost me a fortune and it's not even born yet." He struggled to pull the sculpture from the car. "This sucker is hard to get hold of. Where did you say it's going?"

"Chicago. In a crate. By UPS."

"I'll get it crated for you, but I'll tell you right now it's going to cost you a fortune. Your best bet is to take it to Seaport to the Northern Moving Company. They'll ship it to Chicago for you."

"I knew this was trouble." She glared at the sculpture.

"They'll just add it to a load going west and it won't cost much. When does it have to be there?"

"It's not for a special show. I just want it out of here."

"Hey, we're going to Seaport tomorrow. If you'd like, I'll take it with me."

"That'd be terrific, Roger. Dora wouldn't mind?"

"She won't care. I'll drop her off at the mall to wander the baby shops and it will give me a place to go. She'll be happy not to have me peering over her shoulder muttering 'do we really need that?'"

Alicia pulled two twenty dollar bills from her wallet. "This is for lunch. Send me a bill for the crate. Now, how am I going to know what this is going to weigh and cost at the moving company?"

"Just give me the address where you want it shipped. I'll just put it on the Company credit card and bill you later."

"Damn it. I don't know the address. Let me call from your office."

Beth answered on the first ring, had the address ready, and Alicia was back in her car headed home in a much better mood. The car should have felt stuffy with the windows closed against the damp sea air, but without the sculpture the density exploded into airy freedom. Her relief was immeasurable. She held her stiff arms outstretched to the steering wheel and let out a shout. The day was hers. She had her life back. She would return to her studio and paint. She knew the results would be great.

When she pulled into the yard she looked toward the sand pile to enjoy the empty space. Instead she saw a car and beyond it, Frederick sitting on her doorstep.

He walked over to the car and opened the door. "I was going to call, but I was able to get right on a ferry, so here I am. Glad you showed up."

Liar, she thought. No one gets right on a ferry on a Friday in August. He wrapped his arm around her and pulled her to him and kissed her. Never did that quite so fast, she thought. The dogs howled and pawed at the door, sensing her return.

The fog had lifted, but the house was damp and cool. She'd left the windows shut and went from room to room opening them up again. Frederick helped himself to a glass of water.

"You look lovely, but why don't you put on something fancy and I'll take you to dinner."

She thought getting him out of her house was a good idea and didn't protest. He watched her go up the stairs as he drank the refreshing island water. He waited until he heard the bath water running and then he crept up the stairs and into her studio.

He shuffled through a sketchbook of drawings. He stared at the bright crimson patches on one page, each a delicate variation of the same color and yet yielding an entirely different hue. A skylight admitted graying light into the room cast a pall over the brushes. No works in progress here. No sketches strewn about the walls and floor.

The tape on the easel was beginning to curl up from the summer heat. The brushes were all dry, and the box of charcoal on the table was full. Only one piece had been removed and lay broken in half on a blank sheet. He hurried back to the first floor.

He saw the soldering iron on the dining room table, checked the living room, and went outdoors to the sand pit. He stared briefly at it before heading for the small shed at the edge of the woods.

Alicia noticed the front door ajar as she descended the stairs. A swarm of deer flies buzzed around the living room. As she reached to close it she saw Frederick open the shed door. She felt the competitive energy begin to stir again as it had when she'd decided to create a forbidding monolith in her front yard. If he was searching for clues about her, or her work, she had no intention of discussing either. When Fredrick came back into the house he offered no explanation for his prowling.

"Did the boy find his fishing labels?" he inquired.

"Justin? I gave him what I had when you were here. I haven't seen Margaret since that afternoon. I don't know if he found any more."

"What happened to the plumbing fixture?" he nodded toward the mantel.

"The what?"

"You know, that strange thing you found in the crate. It looked like part of a toilet."

"Is that what it was? No wonder it gave me so much… how awful."

"I thought it looked rather attractive on your mantel, a reflection of the comic touch of the serious artist."

"Would everyone know it was part of a toilet?"

"Maybe not the highly refined, but I'm not known for my household skills, and I knew it was a toilet fixture."

"You did? You didn't say so."

"Why don't you put your artwork back on the mantel. I thought it was rather intellectually romantic."

"I can't."

"Why not?"

"It's in Chicago."

"Where?"

"It's a long story."

"I'm not catching the ferry."

"I found it on the beach in the box of fishing labels everyone is so interested in. I thought it was unusual."

"Russian fishing labels? It's probably radioactive. Does it glow in the dark?"

"No, but it was a strange material. It wouldn't take to solder. Nothing would adhere to it. I wasted the entire summer with… a toilet fixture."

"Hey, I'll be in Chicago tomorrow. I'll take a look at it and let you know if you can tell its basic premise is plumbing."

"It just sat there, a lump, a toilet."

"So, in despair you shipped it to Chicago. I always wondered how islanders handled recycling."

"It was supposed to be a monumentally sized sculpture. I had to give that up. I built around it, burying it in the center. You'd never know by looking at it. You'd never recognize, or see, the little piece I found in the box of labels. No one will walk into a gallery and say 'there's a toilet.'"

"DuChamp's urinal made quite a hit."

"I'm not that kind of artist."

"Where did you send it?"

"I can't remember the name."

"Look it up. I want to see it."

From her desk Alicia pulled a plastic index card box and began filing through it. "I have paintings in the Leslie Crane Gallery, the Lydonfeld Prints and Posters, a possibility in the future at the Sand and Struthers Galleria, but the sculpture… hmm. I needed the address for the UPS label, but I had to call Beth. It's near where my friend lives. Park West Arts and Crafts. Now I remember. It's on Clark Street." Alicia had forgotten it hadn't been shipped by UPS as she'd planned.

* * *

Frederick poured some bourbon in two glasses. He handed her one. They clinked glasses. In the morning he'd take the commuter plane to Boston in time to catch an early flight to Chicago. Tonight he could relax. No one else knew where this little Russian gadget was. It was, he thought, a sure thing and so was she.

22 | Hope keeps the heart from breaking

Alicia looked sexy in her jeans and oversized sweatshirt. He'd thought she'd have put on a skirt and some fancy earrings. He'd suggested they have dinner at the Wapatoo Inn. He could relax. He had what he'd come for.

"I hate to tell you, but I think you'd better catch the commuter to Boston tonight. I'm really not in the mood for, as you put it, 'an intellectually romantic' evening."

Frederick looked surprised. He'd planned to tell her he had a business trip scheduled for Hong Kong, to tell her he wouldn't be back soon. Now she was giving him the boot.

He backed out of the yard onto the gravel road and hit the black top going fifty miles an hour. He spun around a curve, paused at the fork and sped down the main road to the airport. In the coffee shop he bought a Coke and thought about the steps he needed to take to get him back on track. Fly to Chicago, take a cab to the gallery, buy Alicia's sculpture, deliver to Tony and head for the West Coast.

He used the return ticket to Boston with a connecting flight to Chicago Scully's thugs had left for him. Outside O'Hare he hailed a cab. Maybe he'd suggest his sister visit him in California. He couldn't touch the money. The $10,000. There it sat in an account in his name. Damn. He needed money. The sculpture had better be cheap. He'd take a thousand. He needed walking around money. No, to take any of the money from that account would compromise him—if it came to that. It wouldn't. He'd deny everything. They had no proof. The pictures? So, he'd dated Renata Scully. That didn't make him a traitor. What the hell was so important about this metal object that Alicia had made into sculpture?

He looked at the scrap of paper Alicia had given him with the address on it. She'd printed "Arts and Craps" on it. He would miss that woman.

"Okay, mister. Here you are. 2860 North Clark."

Frederick paid the driver and got out. He found himself in front of an old building. There was no sign for Arts and Crafts, but the address was right and the windows were filled with an odd assortment, just as Alicia had said, crap. He opened the door and was met with the sweet smell of marijuana. Perhaps it was incense, or dust. He searched the cluttered interior for the sculpture.

"Yo, can I help you?" a scruffy looking kid said from a stool in the back of the room.

"I'm looking for a piece of sculpture."

"Hey, I must have something here." He scratched the back of his shoulders and looked vaguely across the room.

"No," Frederick said. "I'm looking for a specific piece by Alicia Barrett."

"Never heard of her. You sure you have the right place? Maybe I could show you something else."

"No, I have the right address. Alicia Barrett gave it to me. She's from the East Coast."

"Woah. No, man. I don't know. Most of the artists here are from around the block. Nobody from… 'The East Coast.'" He wiggled his eyebrows up and down as he repeated Frederick's words.

"She seems to think she sent it to you." He reached into his wallet and read 'Park West Arts and Crafts, 2860 North Clark Street, Chicago, Illinois.'

"That's this joint, but I never… hey. Wait a sec. There was a chick in here a week ago. Said she was representing some artist. I told her I'd save her a spot; hell, I don't care. But she didn't come back."

"Could someone else have received the shipment?"

"Received the shipment?" the kid looked serious. The words implied something else to him.

"Could I see the owner?" Frederick tried to keep his voice steady. He wanted to shove the kid's smart alecky face into the floor.

"You're lookin' at him," the kid smirked. "Ronald's the name."

"And you don't have the sculpture?"

"Hey man, look around. Maybe you'll see something you'd rather have. The chick lives around here. Maybe she'll bring it by. I could phone you."

Alicia had told him it had been shipped the day before by UPS.

"The artist is a friend of mine. She's changed her mind. You know how artists are. I'll call back at the end of the day. UPS should have delivered it by then. Put it in the back. You do have a telephone number, don't you?"

"Sure." He laughed again. "337-0219. I don't have any business cards."

"Got a pencil?" Frederick asked.

"Got a magic marker," Ronald replied.

"Write me up a bill of sale. I'll pay you when I get it."

"Maybe you should leave a deposit."

"Keep it for me," Frederick said and walked out the storefront door.

It was only a few blocks to Beth's apartment building. He pushed the buzzer in the code they'd shared. Three short rings, one long blast. Her voice came through the speaker, eager and surprised. "Hello?"

"It's me. Frederick. Back in town."

The lock release droned across the lobby. He pulled the door open and pushed the button by the elevator. The hall was dark and narrow, and he could see from the patch of sunlight that her door was open and she was waiting for him.

She stood there in bare feet and an old shirt of his. He bent over and kissed her. She embraced him tightly, pounding his back, and he kissed her chin, her forehead, and both cheeks. Then he picked her up, kicked the door shut and carried her into the living room searching for the sofa. She was always moving the furniture. The last time he'd been here, it had been near the balcony, but it wasn't there now. He set her down.

"Missed you."

"Then why haven't I heard from you?"

"Because I'm a rat. Now repeat after me. 'You are a rat.'"

"Frederick, you *are* a rat."

"Feel better?"

"No. I saw you downtown last week."

"I know. I saw you, too. But I was between flights between coasts, and that wasn't the time. Now is the time. Get in the bedroom. I've missed that beautiful body of yours."

"Frederick. You were with a woman. In a red car."

"Business associate. Not my car."

He kissed her again lightly on the forehead, and then more intensely on the lips, and then patted her behind. "Get ready."

Beth started to object, stopped, smiled. "You are a rat."

"I am a rat."

He was thirsty. In the kitchen he helped himself to a glass from the cupboard and filled it with tap water. He knew better than to check the refrigerator for spring water. He drank the water slowly, set the glass down and headed for the bedroom. He'd make love to her while he figured out what he should do next.

She said nothing, but rolled over on top of him and kissed his lips. He'd never told her much about his life, but he'd shared more with her than with anyone else, isolated memories, silly incidents, funny anecdotes that showed his vulnerability, which endeared him to her. The stories came out in choppy little fragments, interspersed among the weeks or months they'd spent together off and on for several years. His erratic comings and goings had convinced her he did something mysterious and dangerous for a living, and he'd let the biographical sketch work for him. She would have found meaning in the irony of it now.

"I've got to go out for supplies. As usual, your refrigerator is practically empty. When I get back we'll hole up here for a couple of days or weeks and see what the future holds… for us."

He got out of bed and dressed quickly. "Rest up. You won't get any when I return."

At the corner he found a telephone booth. He pulled out a roll of quarters he'd discovered in Beth's kitchen drawer and dialed Alicia.

"Alicia. Frederick. I'm at the gallery. They don't have the sculpture. I've got to make a trip to Hong Kong, and I really want to see it before

I go. I'm sure it will be sold by the time I get back. When did UPS say it would be delivered?"

"Hello, Frederick. It skipped my mind. I didn't send it by UPS. Northern Shipping, I think."

"A moving company? You sent it with a moving company?" Frederick struggled to keep his voice calm. "That could take weeks. Call them and find out when it's going to be here. I'll call you back shortly."

"I don't think it's necessary to rearrange your life around it. You didn't mention you were that interested in it."

"Was thinking of buying it. You know, maybe win my way back into your good graces."

"I'd have given it to you, gladly."

"Well, you didn't. And now I want it, sight unseen. I'll call you back in an hour."

The empty feeling in Frederick's stomach and the tight feeling in his wallet left a bad taste in his mouth. The thought of calling Tony Scully didn't improve it. On the second ring, Scully answered.

"Hello? It's Frederick."

"Freddy, my boy. You got it?"

"Not yet, but I know where it is."

"Where?"

"I'm going to need some cash."

"You ain't in no position for bargaining. Ten thousand in the Lake Shore Bank is it, my friend."

"I'm not touching that, Scully. I need walking around cash. It's been shipped to Chicago. I'm going to need some funds to pick it up."

"Freddy, my boy, you're too free with the money. Didn't your mama ever tell you about saving for a rainy day?"

"I'm talking insurance plan. I know where this thing is. And you, Scully, don't even know what you're looking for. It's been nicely disguised."

"So how much we talking about?"

"Thirty-five hundred." Frederick was trying to come in cheap.

"Come by my office. Maybe we can work something out."

Frederick hung up and redialed Alicia's phone number. The phone rang and then began to make a whirling sound. He hung up and redialed.

Nothing connected. He called the operator. "Operator, I'm trying to place a call to Jellicle Island, and I can't get through." He gave her the number and waited. At last she came back on the line and said "Sorry. The lines aren't working. They've had a big storm that way. The phones are out."

Frederick cursed and hung up. It was a hot day in August in the city. It'd been sunny when he'd left the island that morning. He walked the two blocks to the Arts and Crafts shop. He could see before he reached it that it was closed.

A bus lurched to a stop at the corner. Frederick watched the pathetic few toddling off. The last person on the pavement was Ronald, the guy who ran the shop. He stuck his hand in his pocket and pulled out a ring of keys as he whistled and walked up the street toward Frederick.

"Hi, there. I don't have the sculpture yet."

"I know. But I've spoken to the artist, and she expects it to arrive in the next few days."

As he unlocked the door, Frederick decided he was older than he acted. Frederick followed him inside.

"Man, it sure gets ripe in here," he said as he plugged in a fan.

"You ever been to San Francisco?"

"Not lately."

"I'll make you a proposition. You deliver the sculpture to me, and I'll give you a round trip ticket to San Francisco."

"And the price of the sculpture."

Frederick hesitated. He wasn't as spaced out as he acted. "Of course. And the price of the sculpture. By the way, what is the price?"

"I'll have to get back to you on that. You know how they are. Whimsical." The shop-owner snorted at his perceived cleverness.

"I'll give you the artist's telephone number. Call her and find out when she shipped it and when it's supposed to arrive. Then, call the agent, Beth something. Here's her number. Call her the moment the sculpture gets here. You do this right, bud, and there's some extra spending money for the trip to California."

Ronald tossed the paper Frederick handed him with the numbers written on it onto the table littered with papers and old Styrofoam cups. Frederick retrieved the numbers and handed the paper back to him. "Do me a favor. Keep this in your wallet. And call this agent the minute the sculpture gets here."

Frederick wanted to knock the guy across the room, but he winked at him. "Love makes a man do funny things. It's not a particularly good sculpture. I'm sure no one else will want it, but I wouldn't want her to know that. Remember, it's mine."

"Okey dokey," said Ronald.

Frederick left the shop and headed for the bus stop. He didn't look forward to the meeting with Scully. The air conditioning was working on the bus, and Frederick stared out the window as it continued down Clark Street to the Loop. The street was crowded, people were bumping into each other and stepping off the curb to get around the crowds. It was a Monday. Didn't anybody work any more?"

The street cleared as the bus moved past Bughouse Square, notorious for its drug dealings. It passed the drunks, bag-ladies, and then the squeaky clean sand blasted brownstones, and into the Loop before Frederick cooled off. He walked toward Scully's office and bought a pretzel before he entered the building.

Frederick tried the door. It was locked. A gruff voice within answered the rattle.

"Who's there?"

"It's me, Lewis. Open the door." A buzzer sounded and Frederick unlatched the door.

"You ought to put an 'Import-Export' sign on the door, Scully," Frederick said as he dropped the pretzel covered with mustard onto the desk. "I brought you a snack."

"So, Mr. Lewis. Nice to see you."

Scully sat behind his desk, his broad frame spread over the wooden chair, which creaked and groaned as he rocked forward to pick up the pretzel. He wiped mustard from the paper where it had splattered and licked his thumb. Frederick walked out of the office. Scully got up and followed him into the hallway chomping on the pretzel.

"I don't like cramped offices," Frederick said. "They make me claustrophobic, you know what I mean?"

"You gettin' suspicious in your old age, Freddy? Never mind. It's too damn hot in there anyway."

In the elevator, Scully asked, "Where is it?"

"You'll get it."

"You got competition. Things are heatin' up. Seems they got to have this thing by Labor Day."

"That's two weeks."

"You hand it over to me. I deliver it to them. You've got ten thousand in a bank account. Don't get cocky, Freddy."

The elevator door opened and their conversation stopped. Wabash Avenue was filled with shoppers. Scully zigzagged around them, taking a cut to the thigh from a shopping bag being carried by a large, brown-skinned woman with a shopping bag in each hand. "Aw, come on lady," Scully shouted after her.

He walked quickly, and Frederick hurried to keep up. Scully was in better condition than he looked, and Frederick had to admit he'd spent too much of the summer eating fine foods with fine ladies. Scully climbed the stairs to the El platform.

At the other end of the platform, a teenager stood with a radio blasting across the tracks. It was a good place to have a private conversation. It crossed Frederick's mind that the kid could be secretly photographing him with his "radio" just as Scully had apparently photographed him from equipment hidden in his briefcase.

"I want to know more about your business, Scully. Your 1.9 million square-foot shopping center—Woodfield Center for the East Coast. You tell me you're going to make me a partner in a construction company, and the next thing I know two goons are threatening me if I don't find some obscure piece of equipment they say fell off a Russian fishing trawler."

"They were a little heavy handed with you. They can't get used to the new 'open society.' It may be a new country, but it's an old way of operating."

"How do you operate, Scully?"

"I'm a broker, Freddy. Like I told you, I'm in construction. I build bridges between people. I got a bevy of cleaning ladies here in Chicago working day and night to get somebody out of somewhere. They bring me things they find in places they work. I pass them on to people who want them. Eventually, the cleaning lady gets what she wants—a husband or a mother or a kid out of Poland or Bosnia, or they get enough funds into Russia to keep some poor former communist from starving. The people I work for get little pieces of information they could pick up in any American newspaper. I make a living. You, Freddy, make a good living, too."

"You set me up. You think you own me for a few good suits? The Soviet Union doesn't exist anymore."

"Old grudges die hard, Freddy."

"And the Sears Tower waste-baskets are overflowing with national secrets?"

"You got to remember the psychology. What's more valuable, something you pick up for free or something you pay for? I don't deliver anything they couldn't pick up themselves. I just make them pay for it. They don't understand open access. They would rather pay me for a spreadsheet out of the trash than read it for themselves in the Wall Street Journal. You got to do a lot of reading for a little information. I give it to 'em in the right package."

"So how did I fit into this? I was just sitting in a bar, minding my own business."

"You're a profile, Freddy. A classic. You stand out like an emerald in the snow. You want the nice things, but you aren't real good at making enough cash to pay for them. You made a very pissy salary as a banker, but you liked to eat at Tavern on the Green in New York. You made diddly for an accounting company, but you go to work in Armani jackets."

"It doesn't make me a traitor, Scully."

"Will you cut the traitor bullshit? You're a high-priced messenger boy. You are an easy piece of insurance. When I run into problems, a guy like you can save the day."

"Entertaining lonely women who like to buy me nice things isn't the same as blackmailing me into finding God knows what for you and your Russian buddies. I was doing fine without you."

"Maybe. You were between gigs, as I recall. You enjoy the good life. You were pretty easy to get a handle on, Freddy. Relax. What's done is done. And it is done, Freddy. This time my contacts seem to have lost something they need real bad. You fit their needs to a T. Turns out you're a regular on this damn island I never heard of. Almost makes me believe in predestination."

"How about I find this thing, and I give it to them. On my terms."

"You don't want to do that. You've got a nice life style. Hand it over to me. No strain on your conscience."

"Where's the next Aldrich Ames? Let him help them out."

"You're beautiful, Freddy. Clean as a whistle. A few years back, when there was a big difference between East Germany and West Germany, they got some poor bastard, a West German, had an accident in East Germany. The Soviets then, same difference, pay him a visit in the hospital where he's lyin' with both legs and arms wrapped up and trussed like they were broken in forty pieces. They pay him a visit while he's hanging doped up. Tell him he's had a serious accident, caused a lot of trouble. They show him two reports of the accident—one accusing him of being drunk and driving, which is a criminal offense in East Germany, and the other saying he's not at fault.

"After they got him peeing in his plaster cast, they stamp the official version, saying he wasn't guilty of drunk driving, and they've got themselves a willing double agent."

"What's that got to do with me?"

"You're in now, my friend. Don't matter how it started. They got you all trussed up now, and they'd like their equipment back. And you're just the fellow who can do it without raising any questions."

A train screeched to a halt. A few people got on, a few got off. An inaudible message blared, and the train started up again. A gust of wind slapped a Burger King wrapper against Frederick's leg.

"You son of a bitch," Frederick said slowly.

Scully handed him an envelope. "Here's the package you asked for. Like I said, things are heatin' up, and I'm not sure what it's all about. Get that piece of equipment to me by the end of the week."

Scully turned and walked down the El platform steps. Frederick waited until he was out of sight. On the street, he hailed a cab. He'd spend the week shacked up with Beth, a block from the gallery, and only a telephone call away from one tight spot.

23 | Genius is only patience

Dmitri lay in the sand next to Margaret. A series of storms kept them in the house for a couple of days, and now Margaret poured on the suntan oil, rolled onto her stomach, unhooked her bikini top, and tossed the greasy tube to him. He massaged her back slowly, artfully, and then settled back on the towel next to her. He was either a lucky man or a dead one.

He'd managed to get word to Fyordorvitch who was busy on the other side of the island with his part of the plan. Dmitri had assured him it was a small glitch and he'd have the cargo within a couple of hours. Fyordorvitch wasn't happy with the report, but he reassured him they'd built in time for error, and they'd be on their way up the coast to Nova Scotia on the trawler headed for home shortly after Labor Day.

Margaret appeared to be napping and Dmitri forced himself to go over the details of the past six weeks. He'd landed as planned on the Fourth of July, but the crate had not. It was now the 20th of August. Now he knew the young man who'd stood over him with an ax on his shoulder was simply doing his job as a caretaker for the nature preserve known as The Sanctuary. And he knew hitching a ride with anyone who happened to be going your way was the common and acceptable mode of travel on the island, and his ride to the fishing village was the way the Sanctuary's caretaker got rid of anyone he didn't want left behind when the preserve closed.

What wasn't usual was for someone deposited in the fishing village to turn around and walk back to the Sanctuary along the shore. Lying in the sand next to Margaret, Dmitri marveled that he'd gotten through the past six weeks undetected. He replayed the screw-ups and the near misses, and yes, sheer luck that brought him to this day; the dog bite, hospital visit, long hike up the shore. Justin, the imaginative little boy with the naïve mother, had become his lucky charm. Fyordorvitch had agreed that it was just as well to leave the cargo where it lay until the day it was needed as long as Dmitri kept his eye on it.

* * *

Standing over the empty crate, realizing the severity of the situation, it was Margaret's son, Justin, who provided the luck that kept him in motion for the next six weeks. Margaret asked few questions but had invited him into her house, then into her bed. Justin, basking in the attention Dmitri bestowed upon him, looked for adventure.

Dmitri wove a tale of intrigue and mystery, suggesting that something of value was surely hidden in the crate of fishing labels. Possibly gold. Perhaps a Russian icon had been placed there to protect the boat from storms at sea and to assure the fishermen of a good catch. He convinced the boy something had been hidden in the crate and they needed to find it.

Curiosity and adventure held his attention. Drawn in by Dmitri's storytelling, he knew beyond a doubt the crate he'd discovered on the beach held treasure. Justin spent his summer days interviewing neighbors and seeking clues. Dmitri debriefed the boy each evening making certain no one heard the interrogation.

Justin was a good detective. When he discovered the sand pit in Alicia Barrett's yard, he informed Dmitri their neighbor was being visited by aliens. At first Dmitri was alarmed. He thought Fyordorvitch had come looking for him. Then he realized Justin was imagining extra-terrestrial aliens. They returned to the spot, sneaking through the woods, whispering. Margaret watched them leave, delighted to have the company of a man willing to spend so much time with her son.

They squatted undercover in the blueberry bushes watching Alicia. As she bent over the spot, her face was hidden behind a safety goggles that looked to Justin just like a space helmet. She blasted a strip of metal with a welding torch. Justin jabbed at Dmitri excitedly. Dmitri gasped as he realized what was at the center of the strips of metal.

By the time Dmitri had guided Justin's imagination from aliens and rocket ships back to gold, Alicia had finished welding a fourth strip of metal to the structure. The smell of hot metal drifted to them in the salty air. Dmitri was going to need tools to get at it.

* * *

Now Dmitri lay in the sun, again calculating how he was going to get his hands on his cargo, get it delivered to Fyordovitch, and make his way north to the trawler in Nova Scotia. Labor Day. That was the deadline.

Justin's shouts rang out from the woods before he reached the beach. Margaret grabbed for her t-shirt, and the two of them watched as the boy came into view, his words lost in the wind, his scrawny arms stretched out as if he were about to take flight, propelled by his own agitation.

"Peter, Peter. It's gone!"

"Oh, for God's sake, Justin." Margaret stretched out on her beach towel.

Dmitri stood up and reached for his jeans. "It's not there?"

"No, the tarp is pulled back against the shed, and the sandpit is empty!"

"Do you think she launched a rocket? Do you think she has the gold?"

"Rocket? Gold? Justin you are too much. Alicia Barrett is not launching a rocket. She's an artist. She's making sculpture. Mrs. Norton told me all about it."

"Mrs. Norton knows about it?" Dmitri had his suspicions about Mrs. Norton and her husband, who he thought had connections with Washington.

"Mrs. Norton knows about everything," Margaret responded. "Peter, you should see your face. Alicia would not be pleased if she thought you two were spying on her and thinking she was launching a rocket. So much for art."

She searched for the beach bag and removed a bottle of water. She offered it to Dmitri. He twisted off the cap and emptied the contents down his throat.

"Don't you ever do that, Justin. You'll choke," she said sternly to her son.

"So what are we going to do?" Justin wailed.

"I'm not sure," Dmitri said thoughtfully.

"I know," Margaret said. "I'll call Alicia and ask her where she is exhibiting her sculpture, and you two art critics can go get a good look at it."

"Good idea. Let's do it now," Dmitri said.

"Yeah," said Justin as he headed for the path.

"I'm going to take a quick dip, then we'll head for home."

Dmitri watched as she made her way across the rocks to a small sandy spot. She dived quickly, shallowly, into the chilly water and swam rapidly back and forth a few yards. Dmitri considered his timetable. He had ten days to find and deliver the cargo to Fyordorvitch. He'd lost it, found it, kept it under surveillance for the past six weeks, unable to get his hands on it. Now, when he'd thought he had almost completed his mission, it was gone again.

He watched Margaret inching her way through the sharp stones that made getting in and out of the ocean difficult. At last she'd made it beyond the rocks, through the seaweed, and onto the sand. Shivering in the sun, she dried off quickly and put on her jeans and sweatshirt.

"Let's go," he said trying to remain casual. "Your son has a great imagination. I didn't know what she was doing, but he was sure she was building a rocket. He thinks Mrs. Norton found gold in the crate. But I guess it was Alicia who had it all along."

"Thanks to your crazy stories, he's having a great summer. He's been so caught up in your tales, he'll be the center of attention in the fourth grade all winter long."

She gave him a look he knew well now, as she stopped to catch her breath as they climbed the hill to the house. He was relieved she hadn't believed his story about being a Russian fisherman. In six weeks, he'd become to her just an ordinary American on summer vacation, her summer romance.

"You're leaving soon?" he asked. He knew exactly when she would go. He'd heard her tell her brother she'd be leaving on Sunday, the 28th of August. Getting out before the Labor Day traffic. He'd been relieved to hear it. If he had to tear apart the sculpture, it'd be good for them to be gone.

When they reached the clearing to Margaret's house, Justin jumped from the stone step in front. "I went over to Alicia's and snooped around, and it's gone all right. I asked Alicia where she put the stuff she found in the crate and she just laughed."

"Justin, come in the house. It's our last weekend on the island with Peter. What would you like to do special?"

"I'd like to see her rocket and the gold."

That a boy, Dmitri thought. The sooner the better. "Your Mom's going to call Alicia," Dmitri reminded her.

"Would you, Mom?" his voice pleaded.

"Okay. I'll find out where she's exhibiting the sculpture if it will make you two happy. It's nice to see an interest in art blooming in you, Justin."

Justin screwed up his face and rolled his eyes. He held the door for his mother and then Dmitri and followed them into the house. The screen door slammed behind him.

"What would you two like for lunch?"

"Call her, Mom."

Margaret picked up the receiver and dialed as both of them watched.

"Hi, Alicia. It's Margaret. Justin is having a fit because he's been watching you work your wonders in the front yard and now he wants to see the finished product. He says it's no longer there. Is it on exhibit?"

Dmitri listened intently. Justin fidgeted with the fireplace poker.

"It's not on the island?"

Dmitri's brow began to sweat. He had a mission to complete. It was his father's dream for revenge, and his father's friends who had created the plan to settle the score. They might now be Russian again, but the comrades of the KGB were still running the country. A six-week flirtation with democracy on an American island hadn't erased his longing to return to Murmansk. He had a job to do, and he didn't want to fail. Justin let go of the poker. It crashed to the hearth.

"Ah, I knew it. She isn't going to tell anybody. My Mom is so stupid. She'll believe anything anybody tells her."

Dmitri strained to keep track of the phone conversation. "Why don't you come by for a drink? We're leaving Monday, and we're into the last minute crazies over trying to do all the things we haven't found time to do all summer. When we leave the island we're going to head for Chicago. I'm thinking we'll visit the galleries exhibiting your work. Now where's this famous sculpture—Justin wants to see it."

Dmitri spun around and grabbed a pencil from the table. He handed it to her. Margaret began to write on the back of one of Justin's Transformer brochures.

"Not on that, Mom. I've got to send that in so I can win a free Transformer!"

Justin grabbed the form and ran from the room.

She hung up and went into the kitchen to fix lunch.

"So," Margaret began. "There is no rocket for us to see on the island. She's sent the sculpture to a gallery in Chicago."

Dmitri took a deep breath. "Which gallery?"

"I'm not sure. She's going to get me the list of galleries where her work is on exhibit."

"Why don't I go with you? I've been thinking I don't want to stay on the island after you leave. I'll give you the cash and you can make a reservation for me."

Margaret spun around from the sink where she'd been washing lettuce. A smile spread across her face. "Really? I'd love that. Let's make the reservations now. Shouldn't be a problem getting the commuter flight to Boston. That's why I like to leave before Labor Day."

Dmitri kissed the back of her neck. Margaret began to cut up a cucumber for the salad. She hated traveling alone with Justin, dragging all their luggage. If she charged his ticket on her Visa and he gave her cash, she could pay it back all winter and spend some money on herself.

"Hey, Justin. Why don't you run over to Alicia's and get the list of galleries?"

Dmitri picked up the keys to Margaret's island car. "What we need is a bottle of wine."

Dmitri headed for the main road. He had to get a message to Fyodorvitch.

24 | If you would have a thing well done, do it yourself

"You got it?" Fyordorvitch towered over Dmitri and lowered his head, looking at the ground.

"It's a long story. The raft was a flawed concept. Not like sailing a fleet into Guantanamo Bay. I lost the crate, I found it, then I knew where the cargo went but I couldn't get to it, and now it's in Chicago."

"Chicago. How do you plan to get it to me by Labor Day?"

"There's someone at the Consulate who knew my father. I can get to Chicago, but I'm not sure how the hell I'm going to transport it back here."

"By Labor Day. We're moving along as planned over here." Fyordorvitch kicked a rock into the air from the sandy road.

"Looks good. A solar-heated, wind-powered home. I like the sign: 'Feel the power of modern windmills.'" Dmitri nodded toward the house and a group of men working on a windmill. "How many of those guys are ours?"

"Them? All ours. The environmentalists are headed back to college."

"That's convenient."

"We know what we're doing," Fyordorvitch snorted. Give me your latest excuse. It better be good."

"The damn thing got picked up by an artist. She incorporated it into a sculpture she was welding together. Lucky she didn't melt it. I had it under surveillance, and then damned if she didn't ship it off to a gallery in Chicago. I've been staying with this woman who's a friend of hers, I have a list of the galleries where it may have been shipped. I know what the sculpture looks like so I've made plans to go with this woman and her kid to Chicago. Good cover. I'll get it."

"How the hell you going to transport it back here? That's why we planned to bring it directly ashore where we needed it."

"I know. I know. *Eto Bardak*."

25 | When the Cat Is Away, the Rats Are Master

Dmitri, Margaret and Justin departed the island on a commuter flight to Logan Airport. Margaret cheerfully accepted Dmitri's help getting her luggage to her connecting flight into Chicago, but it had been filled and she'd booked Dmitri on another flight. He watched the approach to Chicago from the window seat. The lights of the city shone brightly, and he wondered if any Russian city would ever look as inviting.

The captain announced a short delay. Dmitri settled back in his seat to study the patterns below. He was content to be suspended in time for a few more minutes. Once Margaret and Justin left, he was truly alone, forced back to his Russian roots—champion of a new order, but defender of an older one.

After an hour circling the metropolitan area, Dmitri felt the tension building. He fought the suspicion the delay was intentional, that he would be met by US officials when the plane landed. He fiddled with the overhead valve for air. The thin, noisy squirt of air did nothing to relieve his anxiety.

The captain announced they were cleared to land. The wheels bumped down on the runway, and the plane taxied to a stop. Most of the passengers hurried, grabbing coats and packages from the overhead compartments. Dmitri waited. The woman seated next to him continued reading the book she'd been engrossed in over the entire flight. Dmitri wiggled his fingers. They tingled. At last the woman put away her novel, Dmitri followed her down the aisle and into O'Hare International Airport, Chicago, USA.

No one blocked the doorway to the terminal. He fell in step behind a group of people with leis strung around their necks, shouting and laughing, wearing straw hats and brightly colored shirts. Beyond them he saw an intersecting corridor, a travel checkpoint, and glass-enclosed shops. He studied three men in military uniforms, but they continued their conversation as he walked past them. He saw the darkness beyond the exit and walked into the humid night.

Dmitri raised his hand, and a cab pulled forward. "Where to, buddy?" the driver asked.

"Michigan Avenue." He pronounced it Mitchigan, but the cab driver pulled into the traffic with indifference.

"You got a hotel in mind?"

"The Palmer House." Margaret had suggested it.

"That's not on Michigan Avenue. You still want to go there?"

"Yes." Alicia had given Justin a list of galleries, but she'd failed to identify which one had the sculpture.

"Hot tonight. But I'd rather have it than the wind chill. Right?"

Dmitri mumbled in agreement, relieved he was quite alone.

* * *

"Hi, Tess. It's me, Beth."

"Hang on a minute." Beth could hear children shouting in the background. She looked at her watch. Five o'clock. Probably the worst time to call.

"Sorry, about that," Tcss said brcathlcssly. "Arc you coming out here for dinner before your school year starts?"

"No, I'm flying back to Jellicle Island at the end of the week. It's my mother's sixtieth birthday. Dad's trying to throw a surprise party, and the teacher's union isn't seeing much movement in negotiations for our contract. I don't think the schools will open on time. What's new with you?"

"Same old same old, I guess. So you're going to the island. Margaret called and she and Justin are going to stay with us and do some sight seeing in Chicago."

"Actually, I'm calling to ask a favor. I brought back some of Alicia's watercolors, and several galleries are showing them. Can you take over the job of being her agent?"

"Agent! What does that mean?"

"I use the term loosely. You really don't have to do anything but take the call when one of her paintings is sold. She's good, and she's making money. It just looks more professional to imply she has a local agent handling her work. As I said, I'm going to the island, and then hopefully school will start, but I can't give out the school number, and I'm not buying an answering machine."

"I don't have to go anywhere, do I? I mean, I don't think the galleries would be too excited seeing me with the kids spraying orange juice on their walls."

"No, you don't have to go to the galleries. Just answer the telephone. I just want the galleries to have a local contact—you know, art agent handling her work. It will ease you back into that professional life you claim to be missing so much."

"Okay. Sounds easy enough. But remember, I'm doing this for Alicia. Not you. It's time you added a life to your life."

"Yes, mother." Beth started to say something about being back with Rick, but she thought better of it. "I'll put a copy of her price list in the mail—and a list of the galleries that have some of her work. If anyone needs information about it, you've got it. When she sells something, you get a commission. Alicia insists."

"That's nice. Hold on a minute."

While Tess shouted at her kids, Beth congratulated herself for getting out of the gallery business. She'd already made postcards announcing the work of Alicia Barrett was being handled by Tess Pomeroy. She would send them to Leslie Crane, Mark Lyndonfeld, Arturo Rodine, and Sand and Struthers, even though not all of them actually had some of the paintings. She'd walk around the corner and give the goofy guy in the arts and crafts shop Tess's number.

"Sorry. Nick's having a tantrum because the Cubs game has replaced his beloved cartoon show, 'The Transformers.'" He shrieks, Katy cries, and the cat gags. Are you sure you don't want to stop by for dinner?"

"Maybe in a couple of weeks. If we go on strike, I'll be looking for a hot meal."

"Oh, Lord. The cat's throwing up. Talk to you later."

The phone went dead. Beth frowned into the receiver, then set it down. Rick was out. She never thought she'd see the day when she was glad not to see him, but the last two weeks of his constant attention, his fidgeting, and pacing and unexplained comings and goings had almost ended the romance.

Beth walked around the corner to the arts and crafts shop. The same garishly painted work on velvet graced the entrance. The feather jewelry and a pair of red silk slippers had been added to the showcase in the center of the room. The place smelled like an attic.

"Hi," Ronald greeted her. "Your friend's sculpture isn't here yet. Some guy was looking for it. How much did you say it was going for?"

"Two thousand." Beth made it up on the spot, thinking about the high prices at Leslie Crane's gallery. *Jeez*, she thought, had she mentioned the sculpture to Tess?

"Whew. That's a bit pricey for here. What if he wants change?" Ronald said with a grin. He picked through papers scattered on the table in front of him and pulled out a card with Alicia's name written on it. It was the card Beth had given him, but across the back was Alicia's phone number. She hadn't given him that.

"This is the name of the new agent who will be handling Miss Barrett's work." Beth handed him the postcard she'd artfully created.

"You think someone's going to pay a couple thousand for this sculpture?"

"We can always hope, can't we?" She glared at him as she peered over the top of her glasses. "Maybe you ought to tidy up this place." Beth walked out.

26 | Little Wit in the Head Makes Much Work in the Feet

Washington was hot and muggy. Seth McCalister loosened his collar and wiped his brow. The field office was air conditioned but smelled like a clothes hamper full of wet towels. He hated office work, but he hated it more when he had to go out in the August heat.

"What have you got?" he called across the room to the broadly smiling face of Tom Sullivan.

"I'm not sure. Chicago's seeing some action. We're not supposed to do anything about it yet. Just keep an eye on Scully. He and Mr. Gucci Lucci are up to something.

"Yeah, well, that's how we screw up. Let a few transcripts sit around unread for days until the deals are made, then when we read them say, 'by golly, we should have nabbed that fella.'"

"We don't know what they're up to. Scully's been scurrying around. Had a bit more direct contact with his Russian pals."

"Scully's minor league."

"He's up to something."

"So why don't we know what the scurrying is about?"

"Getting some intel right now. Got some curious visitor at the Russian Consulate in Chicago."

* * *

Dmitri walked up the stairs to the Russian Consulate and through the front door. At the main desk, he leaned forward and said, "I need to talk to Alexi Gavanavitch. Now."

A door opened to the right of the desk before the official could pick up the telephone. Dmitri followed Gavanavitch down a hall and into a room with a drawn curtain.

"You are?" Gavanavitch asked, for confirmation.

"Dmitri Alexi Korsomakov. I'm the man from the *Zori*. Due to a rather serious miscalculation, the raft took a gash that destroyed it when I landed on Jellicle Island. The cargo went one way and I another. I've got to deliver it by—"

Gavanavitch raised a finger to signal caution. "You must be the fisherman who wanted to see the American way of life. Did you not understand that our country has gone to great lengths to renew fishing treaties? One of these treaties is coming up for renewal. Thousands of our countrymen will not be able to share their catch with their countrymen if the Americans refuse to extend the agreement. I understand a crate of television equipment went overboard and you were sent to retrieve it so there would be no misunderstanding with the Americans. It was a stunt, yes?"

Dmitri realized the consulate was not secure. He reached across the table for a tablet. Swiftly he began to write.

Aloud, Gavanavitch replied, *Wapignanapo ndovu wawili ziamazo myasi.*"

"*Wengi wape.*"

Dmitri handed the list of galleries to him.

The sun was shining when Dmitri entered the consulate. It was pouring when he walked out. By the time he reached Huron Street, it was still raining, but the sun was shining. A curious place, Dmitri thought.

The sign Prints and Posters swung furiously back and forth in the wind. Dmitri stepped quickly down the three steps to the entrance and opened the door.

"Hello, there," Mark Lydenfeld said. "Got caught in the rain, did you? I love it when it rains and the sun's out."

"I am looking for the work of an artist by the name of Barrett. Alicia Barrett. Do you have any of her work?"

“I sure do.” Lydenfeld ambled over to the print holder and began turning the frames. Colorful paintings floated past Dmitri’s eyes, a whirl of color blurred as the gallery owner looked for the Barrett watercolors.

“She’s popular. I’ve sold almost all her watercolors.”

“It’s not a painting I’m looking for. It’s sculpture.”

“Sculpture? I don’t have any of her sculpture. I didn’t know she did sculpture. Take a look at her watercolors. They’re beautiful.”

“It’s sculpture I’m looking for.” Dmitri walked out of the gallery. He continued on Huron Street to the Leslie Crane Gallery and hurried up the concrete stairway. Inside the building, he was confronted by a closed door. He turned the knob.

Huge canvases hung from the walls, and at first glance they all appeared to be blank. But when he stood close to one, he saw tiny grids of pale color. He stepped back. The color all but disappeared. He looked at the label by the side of the painting. Eight thousand dollars, it read. He backed up for a better view. There was no discernible application of paint from where he stood.

“May I help you?” a woman said with a slight edge of disdain in her voice.

“I’m looking for sculpture.”

“That would be back here.” Her hand waved in the direction of a shelf of tiny blinking objects in motion. Some were cubes of Plexiglas, some chrome balls that moved up and down on wooden frames, and one a flashing work in purple neon. None looked remotely like Alicia Barrett’s enigmatic sculpture.

“The artist I’m looking for is Alicia Barrett. I was told she exhibited here.”

“No. You are mistaken. I don’t exhibit her work.” The tone was decisively icy.

“But…”

“Perhaps I could show you someone else. I have wonderful artists. These are from the Biennale. Mannicini.” Her voice took on a rich, Italian roll.

“No, I want a specific Alicia Barrett sculpture.”

“I’m sorry, not here.”

Dmitri walked the length of the gallery, his heels echoing loudly on the polished oak floor. Back on Huron Street, he pulled out a copy of the list of galleries Alicia had given Justin. Now the sky was overcast, neither sun nor rain falling on him as he walked toward Michigan Avenue headed for the Arturo Rodine Gallery.

He stepped into the building and took the elevator to the top floor. When the elevator door opened, he was startled to find himself in the gallery.

"Welcome. You will see such beautiful paintings—it will make your heart weep. This one, Mikel Listowski, does he not show the agony, the blood spilled?" Arturo Rodine asked.

Dmitri waited for his eyes to adjust to the wide, dim room. There was a skylight above, but the Chicago sky had darkened. He hoped it wouldn't start to rain again.

"I'm looking for a piece of sculpture. The artist is Alicia Barrett."

"Ah, Alicia Barrett. I have seen some lovely watercolors, beautiful seascapes, but no sculpture."

Dmitri looked closer at the paintings on the wall. Much better than the previous gallery, he thought. This was a dealer in Eastern European art. He had a slight, unnatural rhythm to his English.

"Do you think you could find out where the sculpture might be? It is important to me."

"But of course. A charming young lady was in here a couple of weeks ago with some of the artist's paintings. A delight. I will call her for you. Is it a particular sculpture?"

"Yes, I have not seen it completed. It is about four feet tall, I believe, but I cannot describe it."

"Excuse me for one minute. Perhaps you will look around?" Rodine disappeared behind a freestanding wall, peeked his head back out from behind it and asked, "Would you like a glass of tea?"

It sounded good to Dmitri, but not now. If he could sip tea and admire the sculpture that would be different.

"Ah, here. Oh, I have a postcard she recently sent me. Someone else is handling Miss Barrett's work now. I will give her a call for you."

Arturo dialed. Dmitri followed him into the private office and stood listening as the telephone rang and rang. At last someone answered.

"Hello," Arturo said. "Hello? Is your mommy home? Oh! Oops." He put down the receiver. "That did not work so good. It was a child. He hung up the phone. I'll try again in a couple of minutes. Please, look around my beautiful gallery."

"No, no. It is the sculpture I want."

"I see you are a man possessed. That is as it should be with art."

Dmitri lowered his head and looked into the gallery owner's eyes. Then he glanced away. He did not wish to say anything else.

* * *

The air in Washington was so hot and sticky that Seth McCalister leaned over a drinking fountain and let the water spray his face. He took a quick sip of the lukewarm coffee he held, and stepped into the field office where the frigid stale air hit him. He hated summer in the city.

Tom Sullivan saw him coming and jumped out of his desk chair. "I've been waiting for you," he said. He pointed his thumb toward a room in the back where the walls were acoustically secure.

"You mean you've got something?"

"Not yet, but our transcriber is working overtime. Your expertise is needed." Sullivan dropped a transcript on the table in front of McCalister. He read the pages, flipping each page back as they were stapled and numbered.

"Sounds to me like the official didn't know who the guy was. He knows they're bugged. Lots of rustling of paper or gesturing going on. Think they were writing stuff down. Nice speech though, about fishing treaties and international cooperation. I like the bit about sharing fish catches. Guess that's part of the democracy of not-so-Soviet but more Russian détente. It's the reference to cargo that stops him from speaking aloud." McCalister continued reading.

"So what's the gibberish in the middle?" Sullivan asked. "The wawadingo shit."

"Swahili. *Wapignanpo ndovu wawili, ziumazo nuasi*. When two elephants are fighting, the grass suffers."

"That clears it up for me. What the fuck does that mean?"

"I don't know. It might just be the link in the chain we've been looking for."

"You'll have to be more specific for your buddy, here."

"Two Russians speaking Swahili in the Russian Consulate. The official doesn't know who he is until he says something in Swahili. Then he answers him in Swahili. In the Sixties, the Soviets were trying to have some influence in East Africa. Not too difficult to trace who was working in Nairobi at that time."

"Not exactly a hot spot for the past thirty years," Sullivan considered.

"No, but it might be a connection. How many people do you know who speak Swahili?"

"Just bilingual you, pal."

"Apparently this guy comes cold off the street. We don't know who he is. Initially, neither does the Russian. He gets him to write down who he is and why he's there. The Swahili must be a pass code. He's pretty sure what he said aloud wasn't giving anything away, knowing the room is probably bugged. He's good. Bold, but not cocky. Knowledgeable, but not arrogant."

"You got all that from an African proverb?"

"Using Swahili, he was able to connect with the Russian official. And two elephants—the United States and Russia, the grass—the Russian people. I don't know, just a hunch." McCalister balled up his fist and tapped his chin.

"Other sources think something is going down by Labor Day. Scully and Lewis are mixed up in it somehow. Guy goes into the Russian Consulate and the consular makes a speech about the guy dropping a television overboard and going ashore after it. Doesn't make sense. Why would they want us to think it was just a stupid stunt by a Russian fisherman? Reading between the lines, I think this cargo is something that has to be delivered to someone on Jellicle Island. So how close is Jellicle Island to New York City?"

"President's making a speech to the UN right after Labor Day. And he's also stopping on Cape Cod."

"So we need to find out who the bwana is."

"I could go check out Jellicle Island," McCalister smiled as he thought about it.

"Don't pack your trunks yet, no pun intended. I think you're going to Chicago. Check out Scully. He's had Lewis delivering packages all summer to Boston. Jellicle Island seems to have been an extra-curricular trip for Lewis, who was making time with an artist there. Maybe Jellicle Island is more directly involved than we'd considered. And apparently this Russian came ashore there with something of value."

"I'd sure rather check out the breezes on an island than swelter in Chicago."

"Sit tight. I've got a call from the NSA."

* * *

Arturo Rodine dialed again, then he put down the telephone. "The line is busy now. The child has probably not hung it up properly. I'll give you the telephone number."

Dmitri took the number, shook hands with Rodine, and departed the gallery. He hurried toward Michigan Avenue and the next gallery on his list. The Sand and Struthers Galleria was near Lake Shore Drive. The wind from the lake offered no relief. The large display windows in the front of the gallery held several oils hung from invisible lines attached to the ceiling. In the largest painting, a child held a cat. The colors glistened, and the cat's fur looked soft and fluffy. Inside the gallery, the walls were hung with paintings of people and places. A middle aged woman stood up from a desk which had ornately carved legs and a large quill pen resting on the top.

"May I show you something?"

"I am looking for sculpture by Alicia Barrett."

"We do not carry sculpture."

On the street again, Dmitri stopped to look at a broad expanse of store windows that were draped in rolls of Mylar. The window stretched half a city block. As he studied the reflections made in the paper-like mirror, he saw the man he'd noticed when he came out of Rodine's gallery. He watched the man, who was unaware Dmitri was watching him in the Mylar reflection. Dmitri entered the store, saw the side entrance, and exited onto a side street. Down the street was a telephone booth.

He read the number written on the fine white paper with Arturo Rodine Gallery engraved across the top. As he dialed, he thought of Margaret, her warm smile and carefree laugh. He counted on her friend being as casual as Margaret had been.

"Hello?" a woman answered on the first ring.

"Excuse me," Dmitri began, "the Arturo Rodine Gallery gave me your telephone number."

"They did?" the woman replied in a quizzical way.

"I am interested in sculpture by Alicia Barrett. Could you tell me where it is?"

"Oh, that," the woman said with a laugh. "Just a minute. I just found out about the sculpture."

In the background, the sounds of guns and planes whirred and screeched. Someone was watching Justin's favorite TV cartoon show, 'The Transformers.'

"Sorry to keep you waiting. It's at the Park West Arts and Crafts Gallery. That's on Clark Street. 2860 North Clark Street. Do you want the phone number?"

"Yes, yes."

Dmitri hung up and dialed the number. "Is this the Arts and Crafts Gallery?"

"Yeah, man."

"I'm looking for sculpture by Alicia Barrett. Do you have it?"

"I wish I did. Had somebody else in here looking for it. It's supposed to be here by the end of the week, but it's sold already. Do you want me to get some more?"

"No, I want that one. You say it's sold?"

"Yeah, sight unseen."

"I need to see it before you sell it."

"No problem here, but I don't know when it's coming, and I don't know when this other guy's gonna show up for it..."

"Perhaps you could get another sculpture for this person."

"No. He really wants this sculpture. I can hardly wait to see it myself. What's it look like?"

Dmitri pressed on. "Did he give you his name? Maybe we could come to an agreement."

"Naw, I doubt it. He's been pretty persistent."

"I am persistent, too. How much did he offer to pay for it?"

"Four thousand," Ronald replied without hesitation.

"I will give you six." Dmitri thought of the bland canvases at the Leslie Crane Gallery.

"Six thousand bucks? No shit?"

"No shit," Dmitri replied.

"Ah, let me see what I can do. Give me your name and phone number."

"Peter Smith. I have not checked into a hotel yet. I will call you back. Don't sell it until I've seen it."

"For six grand, you just want to look at it? I can't hold it if this other guy shows up first with the money. But if you show up first…"

"Put it in the back room. I think you can afford to hold on to it until I see it," Dmitri suggested sternly.

"Man, this thing must really be something."

"It will make your heart weep," Dmitri quoted Arturo Rodine.

"No shit."

"No shit." Dmitri hung up and hailed a cab.

A block from the Park West Arts and Crafts Gallery, Dmitri left the cab and walked up the street in a headwind. He wondered who else was looking for the sculpture and why. He sat down in a window seat in the Night and Day Lounge, across the street from the shop. As he drank his coffee, he watched a man reading a newspaper at the bus stop. He didn't know much about the habits of Chicagoans, but he knew they didn't stand at bus stops reading a newspaper. Too much wind.

* * *

You could never know too many rats, was Scully's opinion. Not long after Dmitri's visit to the Russian Consulate, Scully knew about it, too. He put on a clean pair of pants and a Hawaiian print shirt and headed for the first gallery on his list.

Leslie Crane blocked his entrance. She stood in the doorway, an arm extended to the door frame and stared hard at his outfit. "May I help you?" she asked without moving to admit him to her gallery.

"I'm lookin' for some sculpture. Artist named Alicia Barrett."

"I do not carry her work. Ever," she replied icily. "Now, if you would excuse me, I was just leaving." She pushed him away from the door and shut it behind her. He could only step back, then down one step. She walked past him and down the steps and up the street.

Scully was inclined to think she must be hiding it, but he'd looked beyond her and saw the gallery was filled with unpainted canvases. It was a funny way to run a gallery, he decided, but artists were mad. Everybody knew that.

Mark Lyndenfeld was no more helpful, though eager to chat. "Are you sure you don't want her watercolors? They're great. You're the second guy to come in here looking for her sculpture. I'd like to see it myself."

Scully had nothing to say. He hurried up the steps to the street and headed for the hotel in the next block. He wasn't going to continue walking in the heat to talk to those nuts. It must make 'em itchy, sitting alone with that kind of stuff. He dropped a quarter into a telephone in the Allerton Hotel lobby and dialed the Sand and Struthers Galleria.

No, they did not exhibit sculpture, the woman said in a snippy voice. He called the last number on his list.

"My, my. She is very popular," Arturo told him. Scully scribbled the number for Tess Pomeroy and dialed.

"Hello?" A kid, Scully noted. "Get someone taller to the phone, will ya?"

"Hello?"

"Can you tell me where I can get this Alicia Barrett sculpture?"

"Who's calling, please?" Tess was trying to adjust to her new role. She was going to keep a list of everyone who called, get their telephone numbers, and try to make some sales. The kids needed a swing set.

"Ah, John Smith," Scully replied.

"Miss Barrett is showing her sculpture at the Arts and Crafts Gallery on Clark Street. 2860 North Clark Street. And what is your telephone number?"

Scully hung up.

"That was rude," Tess said into the empty line.

* * *

Frederick dropped a quarter into the telephone again. This time he didn't get a busy signal. "Hey, Ronald. Any word on the sculpture?"

"No, but there's another guy looking for it. Offered me six grand just to look at it."

"Then I'll give you six thousand. Did you tell him it's been sold?"

"Yeah, he's giving me six grand just to look at it before you take it away. Can't wait to see what this looks like. Must be more than big tits."

"Nothing like that. It's good art. I don't think you'd better let this guy look at it. He may be trying to copy it—like fall fashions, you understand?"

"I understand money. What gives?"

"Like I told you before. I thought I was the only fool. It boils down to a couple of old fools in love with a very sexy artist."

"I get that, I guess."

"I'll give you six thousand. You've got Beth Norton's phone number. Call the minute it's here. And don't let that guy at it. Put it in the back room." Frederick hung up. Who was willing to pay six thousand dollars just to look at it?

"I don't actually have a back room," Ronald said into the empty phone line.

Frederick placed a call to Tess Pomeroy.

"This is David Jones. Any word on when that sculpture's going to arrive at the gallery on Clark Street? I've been waiting over two weeks. Should be there."

"You're the fourth man who has called about it."

"Oh? Call Miss Barrett. I am most eager to purchase it. I'll call you back in five minutes."

"It's only four o'clock. I'll wait until the rates go down at five," Tess told him.

"I'm paying six thousand dollars for a piece of sculpture, and her agent can't make a phone call until the rates go down?"

“Six thousand!” Tess swallowed. It was difficult switching gears. One minute she was a housewife and mother tending noisy children and a sick cat. The next moment she was an art agent. She pictured herself decked out in a leopard jumpsuit and wearing dangling silver earrings. She was a fast learner. Her commission was going to buy a bigger swing set. “Where did you say I could reach you, Mr. Jones?”

“I’ll call you,” Frederick said as he hung up. He figured Scully was trying to beat him to it, and apparently so were the thugs who’d threatened him. Who else was on the trail?

27 | More Than Meets the Eye

"Alicia? At last. Do you realize your phone has been ringing busy for two days?"

Tess blurted into the phone.

"Tess. Oh, one of the dogs must have knocked the upstairs phone off the hook. What's up?"

"Did Beth tell you she was handing over the art agent job to me? Said she can't handle phone calls once school starts. Oh boy, have there been phone calls. This is becoming a full-time job. What kind of crazy sculpture is this? My phone has been ringing constantly with weird men asking me when the Alicia Barrett sculpture is arriving. Have you given up rocks and flowers for erotica?"

"Slow down, will you?" Alicia laughed. "Yes, I knew you were the art agent. No, I have not taken up erotica. How many phone calls? What makes you think they're weird?

"Of course, I exaggerate a bit, but four or five."

"Really? I think I know who two of them are. One of them is a quote unquote friend of mine. And the other is probably Margaret's latest conquest. Go on. I'm intrigued."

"You're intrigued? I'm intrigued. What does this sculpture look like, and where the hell is it?"

"I honestly can't describe it. Beth took some watercolors back with her, saying she thought some of her past acquaintances in the galleries might be willing to show them. On a whim, I decided to send this damn sculpture because I was sick of it. I was going to ship it by UPS, then Roger—you know the guy at the lumberyard—suggested when I took it to the yard for crating, that I ship it with a moving company. He thought it would be cheaper, and volunteered to deliver it to the moving company on the Cape. When he checked with them, they wouldn't ship it because it was just one piece. They recommended a company called GOD. He took it over to the mainland on the ferry.

"Too big, too small, so GOD took it."

"Guaranteed Overnight Delivery."

"I know there's some philosophical debate over how long God's days actually were, but we're talking two weeks of non-delivery Chicago time."

"I'll call Roger, and get back to you. In the meantime, get the names of those men."

Tess hung up and looked at the cat. It was dying, she knew, but it was hard to face the inevitable. It was time to get the children bathed and into bed before Peter, Paul, John or whomever called again. This short excursion into the art world settled one thing. She was happy just being a mom.

28 | You can't lose a cat

Sue Ellyn Norton moved the living room furniture, checking each chair, end table, and sofa, nudging some forward, some back, pushing a book further into a bookshelf, sliding candlesticks forward on the mantel, and spot-cleaning the crystal figurines.

Standing in the doorway, Dr. Norton muttered, "For God's sake, Sue Ellyn, the party's not for another three days. I am going to be comfortable in this room in the meantime."

"I know. I know. But every little bit helps. Every time I go up the stairs, I take something and put it away."

"Are you ready?"

"Yes and no. I want to call Alicia and ask a favor."

"I have a load in the back of the car for the dump, and I want to stop at the lumberyard."

"Of course you do." Mrs. Norton gave a satisfied nod to the room and went in search of her purse.

"I'll have another cup of coffee, while you talk to Alicia," Dr. Norton said.

"It won't take but a minute." Mrs. Norton turned to dial Alicia.

"Alicia, Sue Ellyn Norton. How are you, dear? Are you coming to my Labor Day party? Good."

Mrs. Norton settled into a chair. "I've invited practically the entire island; Frank insisted. Well, not that I invite so many, but that I have a party. I decided if I was going to celebrate a sixtieth birthday, I should do it right. He was planning a surprise. He should know better.

Mrs. Norton paused and then continued. "What I want to ask you is whether you'd let me display some of your artwork. Maggie Warner wanted to get over to the Watermark all summer long and never did. I'm sure she'd like to purchase an original Alicia Barrett.

"I'm not trying to decorate my house at your expense, of course. I think you could make some sales. I'd like to hang them along the foyer against the brick. I thought about putting them on the floor, but that wouldn't show them well. That is the fashionable way these days. But people might step on them or think we were packing up for the winter. Frank will need some time to hang them."

Alicia fought her way into the conversation. "That's very thoughtful of you. I don't have much left. Beth took most of the watercolors I had in the house back to Chicago with her. She is coming back for the party, isn't she?"

"Of course she is. I think she's still harboring the idea of it being a surprise."

"I'll be glad to see her. Other than when she came over for the paintings, we never got time to chat."

"Nor did we, Alicia. Nor did we. She doesn't have much opportunity to meet a nice young man, teaching. You may bring a guest if you'd like, Alicia."

Time to end the conversation. "Thank you, Mrs. Norton. I'll gather up a couple of my paintings and bring them over later today."

"Lovely."

Alicia hung up and went in search of a few watercolors for Mrs. Norton. Within the hour she dialed Dutton's Lumber Yard.

"Hello, is Roger there?" She listened to the background noises as the telephone clanked back and forth, swinging on the cord, while someone went in search of Roger. She could hear the screech of power saws, the rumble of men chatting. She thought about her sculpture and began to wish she hadn't been so impulsive about getting rid of it.

"Hello? Alicia? You're going to kill me."

"Why?"

"Dory had the baby. I'm a father. A girl, name's Ivy. I should have called you, but I've been real busy. Man, I didn't think these little things could take up so much time. I'm exhausted. We were on the ferry when

Dory went into labor, so we came right back on the same ferry, huffin' and puffin'. I was so scared. Then once we got to the hospital, it took another ten hours. She was exhausted. I was exhausted."

"So where's the sculpture now?"

"It's still in the back of my pickup. I guess it's been there damn near two weeks. I forgot all about it. The baby wakes up every ten minutes. I'm not getting any sleep."

"It's okay. Congratulations."

"I'll be with you in a minute, Dr. Norton," Roger shouted.

"Is Dr. Norton there now?"

"Yeah."

"I've changed my mind about shipping the sculpture to Chicago. Could you let me talk to Dr. Norton?"

"Dr. Norton? Sure."

Dr. Norton took the telephone with an amused look on his face. "Alicia? Hello. I've never been paged at a lumberyard before."

"Dr. Norton, Mrs. Norton wanted some paintings of mine for the party. How do you think she'd like a piece of sculpture?"

"I'm sure she'd be delighted. She's in the car. I'll go ask her." He handed the phone back to Roger, who spoke into it uncertainly. "Alicia? What's up?"

"Roger, the Nortons are going to take the sculpture. Take it out of the crate. He shouldn't have to wrestle with it. Put it in his car. He can carry it into the house, can't he?"

"I don't think so. That sucker is heavy. Anyway, I owe you. I'll drop it by their house later today. Glad you're not mad. I'll—here comes Mrs. Norton."

"That's all right, Roger. I'm sure Mrs. Norton can handle the arrangements. Bye."

Alicia settled onto her sofa and curled her legs under her. She felt great. The sculpture had a mind of its own. It didn't want to go off island. It deserved a welcome home party. It was going to have one. She dialed Tess.

"Tess, you won't believe this. The sculpture never left the island. Roger's wife had their baby sooner than expected. He forgot all about it. I forgot all about it. It's still sitting at the lumberyard."

"It's not in Chicago?"

"No, I'm happy to say. I'm quite attached to it after all. I sent it away in anger, but it refused to leave. I'm glad to know it's coming home."

"Kind of like owning a cat. I've got to go. I think the cat is throwing up."

The line went dead. Alicia shook her head as she settled back on the sofa. Life could be so peaceful, and she liked it like that.

* * *

It was seven thirty in the evening when the phone rang. "This is Peter Smith."

"You aren't going to be happy about this, Mr. Smith. I spoke with the artist, and she decided not to send the sculpture to Chicago, after all."

Dmitri's throat tightened. "It's still on Jellicle Island?"

"Yup." Tess wrote a number one and then "Peter Smith."

"*Eto Bardak.*"

"I beg your pardon?"

"Good God." The line went dead.

"Actually GOD had nothing to do with it," Tess said into the empty receiver. The phone rang again.

"Hello?" Tess asked, thinking perhaps Peter Smith had accidentally disconnected.

"Any word on the sculpture?"

"Who's calling, please?"

"David Jones. What about the sculpture?"

"Ah, Mr. Jones. The sculpture never left Jellicle Island." Tess added his name to her list.

"How do you know?"

"The artist told me."

"She told you herself?"

"Just a few minutes ago."

"Are you saying it was never in Chicago?"

"I am, indeed." Tess hung up.

Upstairs she could hear Justin turning on the bath water. She hurried up the stairs before Justin flooded the bathroom. He was busy tossing his toys into the tub when the phone rang again.

"Come with me," she said as she went into the bedroom and picked up the phone.

"Before she could say hello, a man asked, "You find out about the sculpture yet?"

"Miss Barrett has withdrawn from the Chicago gallery. The sculpture will remain on Jellicle Island."

"Son-of-a-bitch." The line went dead.

"Easy for you to say," Tess said as she hung up the phone, "I'm a mother. I have to content myself with little sayings like 'whoopsey daisy.''

"Who called?" Justin asked.

"I have no idea."

"How come?"

"He didn't say. And I don't think the caller before him was using his real name."

She underlined the names on the notepad. John Smith, Peter Smith, David Jones, Mr. Son-of-a-bitch. Earlier there'd been a call from a man with a foreign accent. And then she wrote next to each "Doe."

"Can I stay up?"

"No, it's bedtime."

"Can I have a story?"

"You always have a story."

"Are you going to take Miss Beth to the airport?"

"No, she's already gone. She took the bus."

"Last time we got to go to the airport."

"Well, this time she went on her own. It's her mother's birthday. She thinks it's going to be a surprise, but it's not. No one ever surprises Mrs. Norton."

"How come?"

"Nick, right now Mrs. Norton knows you're stalling for time. No bath, too many phone calls. Into your jammies, and I'll read you a story."

Tess picked up the notepad again and drew a box around each name. Her mind drifted to Beth. She had a funny feeling Rick was going with her to the island. He was such a loser. Why oh why couldn't she shake him and find a man who would make her as happy as Michael had made Tess? And cool, talented Alicia. The way she talked about that sculpture made Tess think Alicia should be looking for someone special, too. Then there was Margaret. Divorced twice, was she about to make the mysterious stranger both Beth and Alicia had mentioned Number Three?

"Mommy, read." Nick thrust a book into her lap. She set the notepad aside, but before she could begin the story the phone rang. She started the story, but the phone rang on and on. Whoever it was, he was persistent.

"Hello?"

"So, lady. Do you know where the sculpture is, exactly?" It was the voice of the man who had sworn at her earlier.

"Who's calling please?"

"Give me the telephone number of this artist."

"Give me your name and telephone number."

"Just give me the information, will you?"

Tess hung up. "That will teach you to call me a son-of-a-bitch."

"Mommy!"

The two of them snuggled back down on the bed. Tess looked grimly at the book Justin had chosen. Another Transformer story.

"Can I have a Transformer?"

"I think you have several."

"I want a big one. If you buy five, you can put them all together and make one giant Transformer."

"I'll think about it. Let's read about them." She studied the cover of the book. It was much more fun these days reading to Katy, who enjoyed hearing about bunnies who couldn't sleep when the moon was too bright instead of Rock Warriors, Power Rangers, and Transformers. When at last the story ended and Nick was asleep in his bed, Tess picked up the notepad.

One was probably Alicia's friend, although Alicia sounded as if she was no longer interested. The one with the foreign accent said his name was Arturo Rodine, he was the gallery owner. He was polite, and would have a legitimate reason to ask about the sculpture. And one, although he didn't have an accent, she was sure he was foreign. She listened to young children improving their language skills all day, and they stopped and stumbled in odd places searching for new words, struggling with their native tongue. The man who called himself Peter Smith hesitated in odd places. Even the rhythm when he said his name, it was slightly off. As for Mr. Son-of-a bitch, what in the world would he want with the sculpture? And then Mr. David Jones. There was something familiar about his voice that nagged at her.

Downstairs, she put the cat in its basket. Tomorrow, she told herself, they'd go to the vet. She glanced at Michael, who was half asleep on the sofa. She looked down at the floor at the puzzle pieces scattered there. Nick was terrible with puzzles, but he could wiggle his little fingers around a Transformer and change it back and forth from robot to car without being able to read the complicated directions that came with it.

She picked up the Penney's catalog and thumbed through the pages of toys. Five Transformers at ten dollars apiece. Fifty dollars? No way she could afford to buy Nick that. The Voltron Warrior had fifteen space vehicles that combined to form three different attack machines, or combine them all to make The Towering Voltron.

The set included a jet radar station, armored equipment carriers, helicopters, friction-powered space vehicles, a floating personnel carrier, fighter planes, space probes, multi-wheeled explorers, two all-terrain trucks and a space ship. All for sixty-nine dollars. She wondered if Justin could put it all together. Of course he could. He was five years old.

With Alicia's sculpture back on the island, she wouldn't be making any large commission. Maybe it was time to get some sleep. Instead of a grocery list, she had a list of phony names. The grocery store had a new contest, and she remembered the names of the winners posted—Laurie Hess, Milly Bosch, Jenny Farrell, Hope Davies. They were real names. As she pushed conscious thoughts away, she fell into a deep sleep, hearing the sound of her son singing the theme from "The Transformers," "Decepticons…more than meets the eye."

29 | You Are a Stone. I Am a Coconut

"Is this seat taken?"

"Rick!" Beth inhaled his name and sat straight up in the United Airlines terminal chair. "What in the world are you doing here?"

"Business."

"In Boston?"

"Jellicle Island."

"Why am I not surprised?"

"You're jumping to conclusions again."

"We weren't exactly getting along by the end of the week."

"Agreed. It's the point I've been trying to make for years. But as soon as you'd left for the island, I wanted to see you."

"You mean you had a few loose ends to tidy up."

"Let's go somewhere where we can talk." Frederick picked up her carry-on bag and walked toward the end of the corridor. Beth followed him. Along the row of windows overlooking the runway, he pulled her to him and kissed her. "You have a friend, an old friend, Alicia Barrett."

Beth sucked in her breath. "I knew you knew her. I knew you had some connection to her and her sculpture."

"You're jumping to the wrong conclusion. Your friend is mixed up in something, and I've got to get something back that she took, maybe unwittingly. I can't talk about my job; you know that. I'd rather not be sharing this, but it appears to be unavoidable. I love you, Beth. In my own, idiosyncratic way." He smiled at her.

"Just tell me who you work for."

“Can’t tell you. I thought over the years we’d kind of come to an understanding. When we get to Logan, we’ll cancel your shuttle flight and drive up the coast and take the ferry.”

“Not this weekend. It’s been filled for weeks. Probably months.”

“We’ll eat lobster rolls and drink champagne in the stand-by lane.”

“My mother is expecting me.”

“So call her.”

“What about Alicia, is she expecting you?”

“No. I can’t tell you any more than I have. Trust me.”

“If I’m not on that plane, my mother will kill me.”

“She’ll get over it.”

“She’ll never get over it. She never forgets a thing.”

“I felt bad about the way things ended in Chicago. I’ve said it before ‘familiarity leads to contempt.’ Let’s undo the damage; what do you say?”

“I’ll see if I can get a later flight, but I have to be on the island tonight. Over dinner, you can explain a great number of things to me.”

“We’d better get back to the gate.”

Beth felt his arm on her shoulder, then he moved away from her as they took their place in line waiting to check in. On the plane, they weren’t seated near each other. Frederick continued down the aisle when she found her seat, and she did not look to see where he was sitting.

He always got to her. She’d known Rick since college, slept with him, promised to forget him—and always, always glad to take him back. She really didn’t know anything about him.

When the plane landed in Boston, she stayed in her seat until Frederick came up the aisle. He hadn’t bothered to stand up until nearly all the passengers had left the plane.

“May I help you with your luggage?” he asked as he took it from her.

“It’d be nice,” she said curtly. He’d asked as if he’d never seen her before in his life. There was no one left in the aisle to notice.

Past the security check for oncoming passengers, he slowed and pointed to the United Airlines desk.

“Go cancel your flight.”

"It's not a United Airlines flight."

"I know, but they can handle it. You don't have to walk all the way over to the shuttle terminal to cancel a flight."

At the counter she handed the attendant her ticket. If Rick hadn't been carrying her suitcase, she would have marched straight to the terminal and boarded the shuttle.

"The lady would like to cancel a flight."

"Not cancel, just make it later," Beth corrected.

"Nothing open until tomorrow morning, I'm afraid."

"That's what she wanted," Frederick answered for her. The rebooking taken care of, Rick asked, "Which would you prefer, a bed and breakfast up the coast or a motel on Cape Cod?"

"I'd rather drive to the Cape, because it's closer to Boston and I don't want to miss my flight."

"We'll get a rental, then, and be off for the Cape."

She let him get out of the airport traffic and through the tunnel before she started asking questions. "Tell me about you and Alicia."

"Beth, what I do is top secret. Alicia's found something, and I've got to get it back. What I don't know is if she knows what she's got and she's involved, or it's a case of coincidental mass confusion."

"And you've been sleeping with her to sort it out."

"What a thing to say about a friend."

They drove along in silence. The summer weekend traffic intensified. Frederick drove fast, changed lanes often, and moved ahead of the congestion. As last the bridge to the Cape loomed before them.

"It's a great bridge," Frederick said. "Not the Golden Gate, but it's a good looking bridge."

He maneuvered through the rotary easily. It made Beth wonder how many times he'd driven this route. The radio music faded, then cleared. The hard rock made her feel on edge. Frederick drove on oblivious to it and her.

He took the highway toward Hyannis and pulled into a restaurant parking lot. The porch out front had a long expanse of green awning. There were tables filled with people eating. He turned off the ignition and smiled broadly. He reached over and caressed the back of her neck, then pulled her to him and kissed her on the nose, and then the lips.

“You’ve got to learn how to relax, Beth. Let’s get something to eat.”

She followed him into the restaurant. He held a chair for her at an inside table away from the rail, and sat down across from her. After the waiter had taken their order for live boiled lobsters, he stood up.

“I’ll be back in a minute,” he said and walked away. She’d gotten used to his abrupt comings and goings. What she hadn’t gotten used to was the idea he was involved with Alicia.

The waitress arrived with the accoutrements that went with a lobster dinner; a plastic bib, lobster crackers, and dishes for the shells. He returned to the table as she set them down. Beth wouldn’t have been surprised if she’d called him by name, but she smiled vaguely at the two of them and left.

“I’ve got a room at a motel up the road. Call your mother and tell her you’re shacking up with your lover for the night on Cape Cod. Don’t mention my name. I don’t think she likes me.”

“She never did. I’ll think up my own story.”

Beth walked into the lobby and dialed her parents’ home.

“Hi, Mom. I missed the shuttle. United was late getting into Boston. A lot of turbulence. Fortunately, I’ve run into a friend. She’s renting a cottage near Sandwich, so we’ve driven down to the Cape. Don’t worry. I’ll be there in time for the party. I knew you couldn’t be surprised. Love you. Bye.”

Beth’s hands were shaking when she hung up the phone without waiting for her mother’s next query. She might as well enjoy this strange twist in her long affair with Rick.

“Where’s the champagne?” she asked as she sat down.

“Don’t be petulant, my pretty.”

She tore apart the lobster with gusto. She pulled off each claw and set it aside. Next, she yanked each leg from the body and sucked out the meat. Then she broke its back, dividing the head from the savory tail. Finally, she picked up the cracker and snapped each claw open.

“You sure know how to handle a lobster.”

“I know how to handle a lot of things.”

“I hope so.”

“I’m still waiting for the champagne.”

"They don't have a liquor license." He waved for the waitress's attention.

"The lady will have a piece of chocolate-chip cheesecake."

"Rick, I don't want that."

"Sure you do."

Beth took a bite of the cheesecake and said, "Now what?"

"The motel's just up the road. We'll spend the night in passionate embraces, and in the morning we'll go our separate ways. That seems to work best for us."

Fredrick pulled into the motel driveway and went into the office. He was back in five minutes, picked up her bag, and they went to their room. It was small and smelled of the musty odor the damp ocean air left in rooms near the water.

She loved making love to him. He made her forget time and place. Or he used to. He wasn't the right man for her. She got seasick on merry-go-rounds, and he was a roller-coaster ride.

Later, they retreated into silence.

"Want to walk by the ocean?" he asked eventually.

"Want to tell me about Alicia and the sculpture?"

"Alicia Barrett made a sculpture with some material she found. She could be in danger if I don't get my hands on it. I don't think she knows what she's got. You can help me out, and her too, if you would call her and ask her where the sculpture is. I'll get you back to Logan and to your shuttle in time for the morning flight. You'll have a lovely time at your mother's party. I'm sure Alicia will be there. I'll give you a call and you can give me the information. Alicia will never know she was caught up in industrial espionage."

"I thought you were with the FBI or the CIA. I never thought you were an industrial spy."

"Beth, I can't tell you who I work for. Let's leave it at that. Find out what she's done with the sculpture. When I call, please be able to tell me where the sculpture is. I'm sure I don't have to tell you not to mention this to anyone."

He stood up and began putting on his pants.

"Where are you going?" she asked.

"The lady wanted champagne, remember?"

30 | Today is Yesterday's Pupil

"Am I going to Jellicle Island?" Seth McCalister inquired. The heat and humidity were unbearable in Washington, the thought of cool ocean breezes unbearably enticing.

"I don't know where you're going," Tom Sullivan replied. "You got that Russian bwana figured out yet?"

"No, but something's about to surface. It's going to ring a bell."

"Well, start chiming, buddy. This guy's up to something mighty important to a mixed bag of ideologies. That consular official let him walk out, which means they knew who he was. They're tailing him, which means he isn't necessarily on their side, but at this point the former USSR slash Russian Federation's got as many sides as a geodesic dome.

"Scully is trotting around at an uncharacteristically rapid pace and visiting art galleries. Not his usual recreation, I might add. Mr. Gucci Lucci has high-tailed it back to Jellicle Island. He had his teacher girlfriend with him for a while, but she went to the island on her own. Whether he's planning to meet up with her or that artist, I wouldn't hazard a guess.

McAlister began writing names on a note pad. Sullivan thumbed the edges of the report.

"If you go over the transcript of the conversation in the Consulate, your Russian bwana mentions delivering something to someone on Jellicle Island by Labor Day. How he got on the island I haven't figured out. There were Coast Guard helicopters hovering over those two Russian trawlers that were having some kind of technical problems. It doesn't make sense that he's a fisherman with access to Russian government officials in Chicago."

McCalister circled Alicia Barrett's name. "What do we know about this Barrett woman?"

Sullivan tossed the transcript to McCalister. "Speak, O Master of Obscure Languages."

"You honor me with faint praise. I'm not looking at a master plan. I thought we had a scrappy misfit who made a living trading basically trivial bits of information to the highest bidder. Scully's smarter than he lets on, but he's no Master of the Universe. He makes a living. No ideological concerns get in his way. Frederick J. Lewis is a ladies man, a gigolo, with expensive taste and a charming way with wealthy women. Scully got something on him, turned him into an operational for the FSS—KGB, whatever. The school teacher, she just seems to be an old acquaintance who goes back to his college years. When he's between wealthy lady friends, he wanders back to her.

"The artist. That's a piece of the puzzle I can't figure out. Did Lewis go to the island to meet her or the school teacher whose family has a home there? Seems the artist was just a diversion for Lewis until all of a sudden after Lewis meets with Scully's Russian buddies, and our bwana—or fisherman—or whatever he is arrives in Chicago and visits the Consulate, Barrett's name keeps popping up on our intel."

McCalister drew another circle around her name. Sullivan looked over his shoulder at the emerging flow chart. "Lewis knows Norton, Norton knows Barrett, Barrett knows Lewis. Where does the fisherman fit in?"

"Where does Scully fit in? Scully's cover is that he's a contractor. Contractors build things. Scully never built anything; he deals in paper. Bits of information. Gucci Lucci goes to Boston, then to Jellicle Island."

"Suppose he's delivered something to the artist?"

"The Russian's drop-sight in Boston is under surveillance, but Jellicle Island is a maze of back roads and trees. Lots of trees. And being a small island, everybody knows everybody."

"I guess that means it's your lucky day. Alicia Barrett shows her artwork at a gallery called The Watermark. You can start there and see if you can arrange a chat with the mysterious artist."

* * *

The owner of the Watermark regretted to inform McCalister that Alicia Barrett's watercolors were all sold or on loan. She had nothing to offer him until she suggested he could call her himself and see what he could arrange.

He called, and she answered. "Miss Barrett? My name is Seth McCalister, and I'm with the FBI. I'd like to talk to you."

After the third go around with directions, he thought he had it. At the end of the paved road, he slowed and cautiously drove on a gravel road, down a steep hill, and turned into the lane that led to Alicia Barrett's house. He got out of the car and walked to the house, past a sand pit and around a wheelbarrow full of flowers.

Alicia answered after the third knock. Her dogs stood behind her, growling.

"Could I see some identification?" Alicia asked.

McCalister handed her his ID. "Do they bite?"

"Only when necessary," Alicia replied. She unlatched the screen door, and McCalister walked into her house.

"What's this about?" she asked as she led him into the living room and gestured toward the sofa. She sat down in a wing chair in front of the fireplace.

"I'm hoping you can tell me. It seems you've created some artwork that has churned up quite a bit of interest."

"I'd like to think so. What piece did you have in mind?"

"I don't know. Do you do a lot of sculpture?"

"No. In fact I've only done one piece."

"That's good news. Can I see it?"

"It's not here. It's on loan to a neighbor. She's having a party. It was invited."

"I'd like you to call them and tell them you've changed your mind. I'd rather you didn't mention it's being confiscated by the FBI."

"You're going to take it?" Alicia moved to the edge of her chair in astonishment.

"Sorry. You'll be reimbursed."

"I don't want to be reimbursed. Why does the FBI want my sculpture?"

"Could you make the call?"

"They're not there. They left a while ago to pick up their daughter at the airport. I saw Mrs. Norton at the market this morning."

"Then she'll be back soon." McCalister checked his watch.

"I don't think so. She's angry with her daughter for missing a plane, and Dr. Norton will probably take them to the Wapatoo Inn for a drink and lunch to smooth things over."

"Then they should be back by, say, around three?"

"Probably."

"In the meantime, tell me everything you can about the sculpture."

"There isn't much to tell. I'm a watercolorist, primarily. I make my living painting. For some unfathomable reason, I decided in July I wanted to create a monumental work of sculpture. I went to Boston and bought an ungodly amount of supplies—sheet metal, a soldering iron, you name it, I bought it. It wasn't as easy as I'd envisioned. Eventually I was thoroughly sick of the project. Beth, she's the daughter I was just talking about, took some of my watercolors to Chicago to show. On impulse I thought I'd send the sculpture. It's a long story. It didn't get there, and now it's at Beth's parents' house."

"How big is it?"

"About four feet high. Maybe about seventy pounds."

"What does it look like? A tree? A nude?"

"It's quite indescribable. It looks like one of those beeswax free-form candles. Only a lot heavier." Alicia sighed at the thought.

"You bought the materials in Boston. Where in Boston?"

"An art supply store on Newbury Street."

"Anybody could buy them?"

"Of course. I did include something I found on the beach."

McCalister sat on the edge of the sofa. "Tell me more."

"I found a strange piece of metal on the beach. I decided to start with it to create the sculpture. While it was on my mantel someone suggested it was the ball cock assembly for a toilet. That made me mad."

"Who told you it was part of a toilet?"

"A man I met on the beach."

"Name?"

"Frederick Lewis"

"Frederick Lewis took a look at your found object and told you it was part of a toilet. Then what did he do?"

"Nothing."

"He didn't want it?"

Alicia looked at him skeptically. "No, he didn't want it. Why would he?"

"I don't think it's part of a toilet. That's why I have to get a look at it."

"Well, you won't be able to see it."

"Why not?"

"I couldn't get anything to adhere to it so it's embedded in the center of the sculpture."

"Where did you say you met Frederick Lewis?"

"On the beach."

"On Jellicle Island? He was just walking along the shore?"

"Yes."

"When was this?"

"The beginning of June. I don't usually pick up strangers on the beach. He was… charming."

"I'm sure he was. He was just walking along the beach, and he gave you this object?"

"Oh, no. He had nothing to do with it. I found it after the Fourth of July. It was buried in a crate of Russian fishing labels."

"How do you know they were Russian fishing labels?"

"Now that you ask me, I really don't know. I think it was probably Dr. Norton who said so."

"Dr. Norton? Your friend Beth's father?"

"Yes. That's who has the sculpture now. Dr. and Mrs. Norton."

"And he speaks Russian?"

"I don't know."

"Tell me more about the metal object in the box of labels."

"Around the Fourth of July I was walking along the beach when I saw the crate. I pried it open, and it was filled with colorful labels. When I began digging around in the crate, I found the metal piece. It was shiny, an unusual color, so I took it home. My neighbors collected the labels, and Mrs. Norton papered her bathroom with most of them. It was her husband who said they were Russian fishing labels that probably fell off one of those trawlers that got too close to the coast."

"What could you tell me about the metal?"

"Nothing. I'm a painter. I don't know anything about metal."

"And Lewis knows where it ended up? That it's in your sculpture?"

"I might have mentioned it."

"And he hasn't asked about it?"

"Well, yes. He called me from Chicago and said he wanted to see the sculpture. He's called a couple of times asking when it's going to get there."

"Has anyone else inquired about it?"

"Yes. One of my friends has been acting as my agent. She seemed to think several people were asking about it. One, I'm sure was Frederick. Another was going to Chicago with her boyfriend, and they wanted to look at it. Apparently some really rude guy has been asking about its whereabouts."

"Describe the metal again, the way it looked."

"It was a beautiful bluish shiny silver color. It wasn't lead and it wasn't silver. It looked heavy, but it wasn't. It was incredibly light. When I held it, it didn't feel chintzy, like aluminum. It was an odd color, unlike anything I'd ever seen. It was shaped like a shuttlecock—but metal."

"Do you think you could draw it for me?"

"Of course. My materials are upstairs. I'll be right back."

When she left the room, McCalister drew a deep breath and paced back and forth. He stopped before a corner cupboard and admired a shelf filled with wooden statues.

"I'll get started," Alicia said as she settled into the wing chair.

"These statues are interesting. They don't look like airport art."

"Oh, they're not. My grandmother spent a lot of time in East Africa when she was a young woman. The tallest one is particularly rare. You can see the arm actually moves, like a lever, and the spear will go up."

Alicia sketched quickly. When she was finished she handed the sheet of paper to McCalister. "Can't say I recognize this. You say it was a peculiar shade of silver. Could you find a color close to it?"

"I don't think I could. It was the metallic shimmer to it that gave it the unusual cast."

"*Maneo fedha, majibudhababu,*" McCalister shrugged.

"Beg your pardon?"

"It's Swahili. 'Words are silver, the answer is gold.'"

"You've been to East Africa?"

"Peace Corps. 1968. Would you call the Nortons? I've got to get my hands on that sculpture."

Alicia set down the sketchbook and left the room. The charcoal pencil rolled across the floor. The telephone was ringing when she reached the kitchen.

"It's for you," she shouted to McCalister. He picked up the pencil, handed it to her and took the phone.

"McCalister. Okay, that's possible. I think I can handle it. Will do." He handed the phone back to Alicia. "Try the Nortons, please."

She dialed the number and let it ring ten times. "I'm sorry. No one seems to be there."

"Perhaps I could order us some dinner. You're kind of stuck with me for a while."

"Jellicle Island doesn't have delivery service."

"I believe it. How about if I take you out for an early dinner?"

"I thought you were in a hurry to get my sculpture."

"Everything's under control. We've got a stake-out at the main road. Nobody's likely to come in or out unnoticed."

"Don't be so sure. What about the back road, the trails and paths to the beach?"

"I believe we've got that covered with some local help."

"And I'm under surveillance, too?"

"I'm afraid you are."

Alicia smiled. Her sculpture had turned out to be quite a work of action.

"Do you know how to use a grill?"

"Torture rack, no. Grill, it depends."

"Just a plain old ordinary charcoal grill."

"I can handle it."

She led him around to the back of the house and pulled a grill from under a tarp.

"Why don't you set it up over there in the sandpit. I used it when I was welding the sculpture. Might as well find a new use for it. There's charcoal in the shed over there. I hope it's not too damp to light."

Back in the kitchen Alicia pulled a package of swordfish from the freezer. She'd intended to serve it to Frederick, but he always managed to irritate her until it was too late for the fish to thaw.

"How does swordfish sound to you?" she called to McCalister who was checking out the bag of charcoal.

"Fantastic, but I don't expect you to feed me."

"It will be a couple of hours. Fish has to thaw. The chances of finding a meal without a reservation on Labor Day weekend are remote to nil. I make it a policy never to go anywhere on the island on summer holidays. Going to the Nortons' tomorrow is just as far as I care to travel.

McCalister would be going with her, but telling her could wait. He painted a bit himself. It helped him relax and forget about his job; sometimes when he was grappling with a problem, when his mind relaxed, solutions came more easily. He wasn't good at it, but it was fun. Alicia Barrett, he'd noted, was a very good artist.

When he found the Leonard Cohen tapes, he settled on the floor to listen to one. The swordfish grilled to perfection. Alicia was sipping bourbon, and neither the FBI nor Russian politics had entered into their intense conversation.

"I'll try the Nortons again. They should be home by now. It's nearly eight o'clock. If I don't get them soon, I guess you'll be contemplating spending the night on my sofa."

"Probably in my car. The FBI is an agency of gentlemen."

They both laughed. He didn't want to tell her he'd be taking a crowbar to her creation as soon as he got his hands on it.

31 | He who speaks, sows. He who listens, reaps

Tess couldn't sleep. The clock in the living room chimed on the hour at one, two, three, and at four o'clock she got up to check on the cat. Poor thing. It was so weak and thin.

The restless night's thoughts were all a jumble, and now that she'd had so little sleep she felt even more on edge about Alicia and Beth. Who were these men who were looking for the sculpture? She needed to warn her friends. But of what? She wasn't certain. Her intuition told her something was wrong.

It was five o'clock when she began to make coffee. When she didn't hear Michael moving about upstairs she poured a cup of coffee and went to wake him.

"You'll be late," she told him. Michael rolled over and looked at her.

"Tess, it's Labor Day."

"Oh, Michael. I'm so sorry I woke you up. I forgot. I'm so worried about Alicia and Beth."

"I knew you were preoccupied. I thought it was the cat."

"The cat, too. But something is terribly wrong. Men have been calling here all week asking about Alicia's sculpture. And they're lying about their names."

Michael sat up and reached for the coffee. "Please go on," he said as he sipped the coffee.

"I was excited to be Alicia's agent when Beth decided she didn't have time what with school starting and going back to the island for her mother's birthday. This week I began getting increasingly agitated queries about Alicia's sculpture."

"I thought she painted."

"It started out with the watercolors Beth brought back to the galleries. Then Alicia decided to ship a sculpture she'd made. That's when I started getting inquiries about the sculpture. A man called and asked where the Alicia Barrett sculpture was. I tell him I don't know. Then another man calls, and he's more intense. The third guy is just plain rude. He sounds like he's checking on a lost order of frozen steaks, not a work of art. Alicia's a good painter, and apparently she's only made just the one sculpture. I wrote down the names because they seemed phony."

"Why?"

"Peter Smith. John Smith. David Jones. One has a discernible accent and the other sounds like he's a truck driver."

"The frozen steak guy?"

"Yeah. Then the guy who says he's David Jones—something about his voice was real familiar."

"Did you ask Alicia what this is all about?"

"Of course. She had no idea. She thought one was probably Margaret's boyfriend and one a guy Alicia's been seeing. You know Alicia; she's kind of inscrutable when it comes to her love life."

"Maybe it's erotic. A nude."

"I asked her. She said it was just an inartistic lump."

"You know… hmmm." Tess took a sip of Michael's coffee. "The man who said he was David Jones sounded just like Beth's friend Rick Lewis." Tess studied the note pad where she'd written the names of the phone callers.

"A couple of years ago Beth and Rick stopped by here and he used the phone. He'd been fired from his job at the bank—he said he'd quit, but I figured he'd been fired. Anyway, he was calling some guy about getting him in to see somebody about a job. He didn't say 'Rick Lewis.' He said 'FREDrick Looisss.' It sounded so funny, so pompous. I could almost imagine a Rolls Royce waiting for him. Right then I had him figured out. He was little Ricky Lewis to Beth, sweet guy—all charm.

But when he wanted something, he used whatever name sounded best for the moment. Rick, Ricky, Fred, Freddy, FREDrick LOOiss."

"Interesting. He seemed like a user to me, too."

"When this guy called and said his name was David Jones, he said it just the same way. And I thought how pompous he made such a simple name sound. Yet he sounded as if he made it up on the spot. I've been trying to piece it together until now."

"What else did Alicia have to say about her sculpture?"

"She told me she found an interesting piece of metal on the beach, but when her boyfriend—she didn't call him that—when her friend suggested it was part of a toilet, she was incensed. She turned it into sculpture."

"Here's a thought. I know how your mind works, Tess. It's probably part of a satellite. Her sculpture is beaming messages."

"That's it, Michael! She's found a piece of something that belongs to something bigger. A Decepticon."

"I shouldn't have got you started. You've watched too many cartoons."

"Think about it. What if someone was building a missile and they lost a piece of it?"

"Who? What?"

"Exactly. Margaret had a summer romance with a guy who said he was a Russian fisherman, but she didn't believe him. One of my phone calls was from a man with a foreign accent. Actually two did, maybe three."

"Let's move on for the sake of argument because I have nothing better to do at five-thirty a.m. on Labor Day."

"The rude guy swore and was irritated when I told him the sculpture wasn't in Chicago."

"Sounds like a passionate art lover to me."

"No. He wasn't after art. That brings us back to David Jones who I now know is really Ricky Lewis. I think Alicia even mentioned her friend once with the name Frederick. Which proves I'm right."

"You think Alicia's friend is Beth's friend Rick? I'm hiring a babysitter. Got to get you out. And you're not allowed to watch cartoons anymore."

"I didn't tell you about the FBI agent."

"No, you skipped that part. How do you know he was an FBI agent?"

"Because he identified himself as one. And he had a real name. Seth McCalister."

"Who wanted what?"

"He also wanted to know the whereabouts of Alicia's sculpture."

"Okay. What you're telling me is a Russian fisherman, or maybe several, are looking for Alicia's sculpture. Alicia sent it to Chicago, only she didn't, so it's still on the island. But the FBI are aware of this, so my dear, it looks like everything is under control. Relax and call a babysitter. At a decent hour, which this is not."

"It's not under control. The FBI agent called before I knew where the sculpture was. But I told the rest of those callers it was back on Jellicle Island. Well, I didn't tell the rude guy. David Jones, also known as Fredrick Lewis, is mixed up with this and my two best friends."

"Earth to Tess."

"They're building a missile."

"My adorable children have destroyed your mind."

"It has to do with Cuba. I watched 'The Cuban Missile Crisis' on the History Channel the other night."

"That was thirty years ago. Not current."

"The Russians didn't succeed because they tried to bring the missiles in on ships where they were observed by the Americans. They intended to set them up in Cuba and aim them at America. Kennedy stopped them. Khrushchev lost."

"Now you've really lost me. Jellicle Island is not Cuba."

"But if you put a missile on it, you could do some serious damage to the East Coast."

"Do you know how big a missile is? I think someone would have noticed on little Jellicle Island."

"Maybe not a SCUD missile. Where's the Penney's catalog? Last year's '93 Christmas catalog."

"Penney's is selling SCUD missiles?"

Tess knelt by the side of the bed and pulled out a child-mangled, ripped and worn catalog and began thumbing through the pages. "Listen to this. ‘Fifteen space vehicles combine to form three different machines—land warrior, air warrior, and space warrior. Combine all fifteen to create the towering terror machine, on and on… die cast metal parts.’”

“Keep reading. I think you’ll see it says something about for ages four and up.”

“Die-cast metal parts. Don’t you see, Michael? Turn on the TV. Get the *Today Show*. There’s got to be something on the news.”

Maybe we’ll just not allow you to watch anything—cartoons, the History Channel, news.” Michael zapped the remote control.

“Good Morning. This is Monday, September 5, 1994. In the news this morning, Russian dissidents are picketing the United Nations building requesting the UN recognize eleven independent countries in the Commonwealth of Independent States.

“The dissidents seem to be proclaiming an alliance stronger than the former USSR. After a brief stop at the Oceanographic Institute on Cape Cod, President Clinton will address the UN’s opening session on Wednesday. Spokespersons at the White House consider the dissidents’ united stance an aggressive retreat from conciliation.”

“This is even worse than I imagined.” Tess leapt off the edge of the bed where she had been perched.

“Where are you going?” Michael asked as he turned off the television.

“To call Alicia.”

“She’ll be thrilled you woke her up to tell her she’s got the key to a Russian missile locked up in her sculpture.”

“I’m sure Seth McCalister will be interested.”

“Who?”

“The FBI agent.”

“Tess, for God’s sake. Don’t get yourself arrested as a crank.”

“Cranky bear, cranky bear.” Tess looked down at Katy who stood in the doorway in a sagging wet diaper.

“Change you daughter’s diaper. I’ve got a phone call to make.”

The telephone woke Seth McCallister, who rolled into a sitting position on Alicia’s sofa and stretched his aching muscles as he hurried into the kitchen to lift the telephone from its receiver.

“So,” he listened to the breathless voice on the other end of the phone talking rapidly to Alicia, “Michael thinks I’m spending too much time with small children and cartoon shows, but hear me out.”

McCalister listened patiently but incredulously. He wished he could have a transcript of this call, but they hadn’t considered tapping the Barrett phone. He needed a cup of coffee.

She made an interesting point about names. Telephone directories are filled with real Peter Smiths and David Joneses, but people do say their name with a certain authority that’s lacking when it’s not their name.

He had a nephew who played with Transformers. Die-cast metal. Put them all together… possible, possible. The artist’s eye had been drawn to the unique qualities of the metal she’d discovered on the beach. Maybe it had fallen out of the sky, part of a satellite. But she said she’d found it in a crate that had come ashore. And the Russian, had he come ashore with it?

Tess continued her story. “Think about the metal, Alicia. When Katy dumps all the puzzles around here, I get frantic. I started labeling the backs of them, putting all “ones,” or “PPP” for Pound Puppy Puzzle, labeling each piece to the same puzzle. Think about it. Was anything inscribed on the metal you found?”

“Yes. Yes, there was. There was a tiny set of numbers and geometric figures etched on one side.”

McCalister listened carefully. Tess continued.

“That’s it. Now, there’s an FBI agent named Seth McCalister. He called me about the sculpture, and sooner or later he’s going to get in touch with you.”

“He’s here right now.”

“He’s there? At six o’clock in the morning?”

“I’m under surveillance.” Alicia realized too late she probably wasn’t supposed to have admitted that. “Sounds pretty wild, Tess, but he’s here and I’ll tell him your theory.”

“I feel much better knowing he’s there. I’m really worried about you and Beth. You know my sense of intuition. I think you’re in danger. Please stay in touch. Bye.”

The connection ended. McCalister waited for Alicia to hang up and then he did, too. He walked into the hallway in time to watch Alicia descend the stairs. She was all legs topped by a fuchsia sweater that reached the hem of her shorts.

"Good morning. My friend in Chicago just called with a wild tale, but I think I need a cup of coffee before I delve into it."

"Good morning. I was listening in. I'm here on official business."

"And what if that had been my boyfriend?"

"I'd have been disappointed."

She maneuvered past him into the kitchen and began grinding coffee beans. She filled a teakettle with water and poured the ground coffee into a filter nestled in a glass carafe.

"Your friend's come up with an interesting plot. Does she drop acid, or is this your standard barefoot and pregnant American mother?"

"Tess? She couldn't be more sensible, and she'd deck you for a description like that. She's bright and intuitive."

"Okay. You're bright and intuitive. Where would you hide a sixty-foot missile on a hundred-square-mile island?"

"You can commission aerial photos from the airport. A plane flies over your property, takes a photo and bingo, you've got a picture for your mantel. You could ask them."

"The United States does have a sophisticated satellite system. I think we'd have noticed something like a missile silo."

"Sometimes, when I take the ferry, I look back at the island at the water tower, I would think maybe it's a missile in disguise."

"Not likely, but keep thinking. The midget man missile is only forty-six feet tall, 37,000 pounds and four feet in diameter. Of course she mentioned a SCUD. That's a lot smaller. Any remote, inaccessible tracts of land you can think of?"

"The whole island is basically inaccessible tracts of land hidden behind trees up narrow roads."

"Okay, trees are a good cover."

"My friend Roger owns a lumberyard. He might know if someone has built any tall structures, if he delivered a lot of lumber to someone. I'll call him."

"No, we'll call on him."

"Would you like some coffee first?" Alicia handed him a mug.

"Thanks. I've got to make a phone call. I could end up selling toy robots, but I think your friend Tess may have stumbled on a serious threat to national security."

Alicia directed Seth to Roger's house. As the sandy road snaked back and forth through acres of dense brush, McCalister mulled over her friend's improbable theory. By the time they'd passed a fourth "turn-out," he realized it was possible for all sorts of clandestine activities to take place on a hundred-square-mile island.

"It's still early. I hope we don't wake them. They have a new baby."

"The FBI likes to wake people," McCalister mumbled. He down-shifted the rental, and the engine made an ominous noise.

"Slow down, you turn about… here."

He couldn't go much slower, but he did not see the gap in the thick bushes until he'd almost passed it. He swung into the opening and continued down a gravel road.

"How much further back is it?"

"A long way."

The engine grew louder. The road rougher. The brush denser. McCalister wondered what would happen if they met someone going in the opposite direction and there was no turn-out near. The roaring engine would warn them, he decided, before they were propelled into the brush.

"It's just ahead. Turn here." A narrow road appeared just as she spoke. He could have gone up and down this meager attempt at a road and never noticed the gap in the brush.

A small cottage appeared among the trees. The wood was still blonde in parts, but the graying shingles provided such a complete camouflage it was almost invisible. On the porch, a man sat in a rocking chair with a pink blanket bundling a tiny form barely filling one arm. He held a mug in his free hand.

"Alicia! What a surprise. Don't tell me you're looking for your sculpture. I took it to the Nortons' place."

"Hi, Roger. I'm glad we didn't wake you."

"Haven't slept in a week. I thought babies slept. I haven't had a decent three-hour stretch of sleep since she arrived. Right, little buddy?"

He smiled at his daughter, oblivious to McCalister until he stepped forward and, with one foot on the porch, flipped open his identification.

"McCalister. FBI. I need some information Miss Barrett thought you might be able to provide."

"Whoa, baby," Roger replied.

"Any unusual structure going up on the island this summer?"

"There's always some weird architecture going up around here. Houses. Not the quaint old New England Cape Codders."

"Any tall structures about the height of a four-story building? A silo, maybe?"

"Nooo." He rocked the baby back and forth. He reached forward and set the mug on the floor. "Unless those crazy geriatric hippies out at the corp place are up to something. But they haven't built any silos that I know of."

"The Core Place?"

"Corporation. Some big corporation bought a stretch of land up-island. I forget which corporation. The people who own it probably don't even know it's on an island. They just like to look at the numbers on their tax returns. So a bunch of old hippies are living up there, renting it. They say they're going to farm it. They spent the summer developing some kind of irrigation system."

"But no silos," McCalister frowned. "Nobody's talking about anything peculiar going on there?"

"Hell, everybody thinks they're peculiar. But last summer a fellow started milking sheep at the other end of the island. Now he's making a bundle selling some kind of fancy sheep cheese."

"Can you think of anything else? If nobody's building up, how about somebody digging down, deeper than an irrigation ditch."

"Can't dig down," Alicia said. "The island's filled with clay pits that fill with water."

"What's this about? Drugs?" Roger continued rocking the baby.

"No, not that. I'd appreciate it if you wouldn't mention any of this to anyone. And if you think of anything else, call me." McCalister handed him a card. "You won't get me, of course, but give the information to whoever answers."

"Cool," Roger replied as he studied the card.

Alicia and McCalister got back in the car. When McCalister turned on the ignition it screeched a high pitched wail.

"You'd think the rental company would do something about this," McCalister said.

"They will. They'll dump it the day after tomorrow."

"How do you know?"

"The kids go back to college, and cars like this go to the junkyard. It just has to make it through Labor Day."

"So do I, so do I. If you'd direct me to the airport, I want to take a look at this farm Roger mentioned. I'd just as soon fly over it as try to find it by land. I don't want to make anyone suspicious."

"You won't. Planes fly over the island all the time. It's funny how you can do something out in the open and everyone can look at it and never give it a thought."

"Any other ideas? Beside the water tower?"

"There is the windmill farm."

"I'd have sworn I turned here. Blueberry bushes all look alike, you know. Which way now, intrepid guide?"

"Take a right." They entered a paved road.

"When we get to the airport, I'll give you cab fare. I presume the island's got cabs at the airport. When you get home, be careful. The Norton place is under surveillance. Whoever wants whatever is in your sculpture is going to do whatever it takes to get it. I guess those dogs of yours will bite if they have to. I don't know how long my aerial scouting is going to take. Then I'll be back. We've got the sculpture covered. I'd like to see who we catch, using it as bait."

At the airport, Alicia walked to the only cab waiting in front of the terminal building.

"Hi, Alicia. Need a lift?"

"Hi, Al. Yeah, I do."

"I think I've got a no-show here. There are no planes coming in right now. Get in. Change your mind, or something?"

"No, my friend had a change of plans. We should have taken separate cars."

"Car-pooling never works."

Alicia laughed and got into the front seat. "I can ride up here, can't I?"

"This one's on me. You're lucky I'm here. I made a lot of money driving a cab this summer. Had an easier time of it than my brother. He's been helping some weird guys over at the windmill farm. He says they built a contraption that didn't look anything like a windmill."

Alicia was quiet. She wasn't in the mood to jabber.

Alicia waited in the house for McCalister to return. When she saw his car approaching, she stepped out on the front step.

"Well?"

"I don't know where they are, but I know who they are, and I think I know what they're planning to do. The ultimate act of revenge is about to be played if we don't find the launch site."

"What about the sculpture?"

"That's the key. I think it's the trigger or nuclear warhead or something for a damn missile. As long as we've got it, they can't launch. It took some digging to identify the Swahili speaking Russian at the consulate. I don't know who was chatting in Swahili with him. The babble about fishing treaties was a smoke screen."

McCalister pushed past Alicia and entered the house. He spread an aerial photo across the dining room table.

"We flew all over this damn island. I should have taken you with me. I'm so close to this I can touch it and taste it and feel it, but I can't see it.

"Seeing is supposed to be my specialty." Alicia leaned over the map.

"We flew over that corporation farm your friend was talking about. No silos there."

"What else?"

"I saw some jib sail windmills. Pilot said it was an environmental project."

"That's it! The guy who gave me a ride home from the airport mentioned his brother was working there, but they built something that didn't even look like a working windmill."

McCalister grabbed the phone. “Sullivan. Get your team over to the windfarm. That’s where the missile is. In plain sight. If they connect whatever the hell is in the sculpture to it, kaboom. It’s all over.”

“You’re going to the Nortons’ now to get it?”

“No, we’re going to go to the party as scheduled and keep an eye out for someone to show up. We want to catch all of these operatives.”

32 | What's done is done

Frank Norton pulled off the main road and headed to his house, turned at the fork and continued slowly. The road was deeply rutted from the summer rain and required cautious maneuvering.

"We should have ordered another load of gravel. I hope no one loses a muffler coming through here tonight," Mrs. Norton said.

"It's not so bad," Beth suggested.

Around the final bend in the road, they caught the glimmer of chrome in the sunlight. "Frank, there's a car in our driveway."

"Mom, did you order something for the party? Flowers?"

"No."

"It's probably some god-damn-day-tripper," Dr. Norton said.

"Frank, I wish you wouldn't swear."

"I'm sick of chasing people out of here. No one has any understanding of what the meaning of private property is. They get off the Sanctuary trails, throw their trash about. Found an empty Pepsi can on the path yesterday."

He pulled up next to the car and stopped. A man was sitting on the Nortons' back step. "Who the hell do you suppose that is?" Dr. Norton said as he got out of the car.

"Be nice," Mrs. Norton said.

"May I help you?" Dr. Norton said with a frown.

"Dr. Norton? Martin Vanderhoop, town police."

"What can I do for the town police?"

"I believe you're having a party here tonight." He nodded at Mrs. Norton who had joined them.

“We don’t need crowd control,” Dr. Norton responded abruptly.

“Just a few friends to celebrate my birthday. Who told you?”

“You’ve got a sculpture in there by Alicia Barrett?”

“Last time I looked. What’s this about?”

“I don’t really know, sir. I was told to keep an eye on the Barrett sculpture.”

“Oh, for God’s sake.” Dr. Norton unlocked the door and went in. Mrs. Norton regarded the police officer.

“Please come in, Martin,” she said with a smile. The telephone was ringing. Vanderhoop stood in the doorway, his tall frame filling it. Mrs. Norton hurried to listen to the conversation.

“Damnedest thing I ever heard,” Dr. Norton said as he hung up the phone.

“Could I have a look at the sculpture?” Vanderhoop asked.

“It’s up in the living room. Follow me.”

The four of them trooped through the dining room, back to the wide front hallway, and then up the oak stairs. The police officer paused on the landing to look out the tall, narrow window.

“You can see anyone coming off the main road from here, can’t you?” he asked. “And from the front, from the porch, you can see the beach, right?”

“You can see cars coming from the road, but you can’t see the beach. Too many trees this time of year. It’s a steep decline to the shore.”

“Have you been up this way before, Martin?”

“I grew up on the island, Mrs. Norton. Used to fish off the beach before it was part of the Sanctuary. Know almost all the native islanders, too. I know Alicia Barrett. She’s a good artist.”

They continued up the stairs, through the hallway, and into the living room, which stretched the length of the house. The windows overlooked the trees that descended toward the shore. At the far end of the room, between two high-back Victorian rocking chairs, stood the sculpture.

Vanderhoop walked across the room and stood looking down at the sculpture. “It’s no Winged Victory,” he said at last.

Frank Norton laughed. Vanderhoop bent down and fiddled with a strip of the metal. It didn't move. "Solid," he observed.

Beth edged forward and peered at it. Here at last was the elusive sculpture. It had never reached Chicago, she was relieved to see. How in the world did Alicia think she could have sold this thing? The Park West Arts and Crafts shop would have been its final resting place.

"You've got yourself quite a conversation piece, Mom," Beth said at last.

"I can't imagine why it needs a police guard, but I love the idea," Mrs. Norton said with a laugh. "In a couple of hours, we'll have a house full of guests, and I have lots of things that need cutting up in the kitchen."

"I'll help you," Dr. Norton said as she left the room. "Beth, you can keep Officer Vanderhoop company. Martin, as you can see we're in a good defensive position up here on the top of the hill. The porch is cooler. By the end of the day, this room gets mighty hot. Do what you have to do." He studied the sculpture a minute longer. "Can't say I understand any of this."

When he'd left the room, Beth asked Martin, "When does the FBI arrive?"

"You know about this?"

"I know the FBI is on the island. I don't know what it has to do with this sculpture."

"I was hoping you knew. I just know I've been ordered not to let it out of my sight until the FBI gets it. Oh, and they want to know who shows up for the party."

Beth was wondering that, too. She went downstairs to help her mother cut up radishes. She and her mother weren't on the best of terms, as she'd missed the second plane she was expected on, leaving Mrs. Norton at the airport for hours.

* * *

The first guests arrived promptly at five o'clock. Sue Ellyn Norton, resplendent in vermillion, sat on the wicker chaise watching the lights of a car wind through the dense fog. When it reached the back of the house, Sue Ellyn could see it was Alicia and she was not alone.

"Happy birthday," Alicia said as she handed her a small package.

"What's this? My dear, you've already provided more excitement than I could have dreamed."

"This is my friend, Seth McCalister."

"How do you do?" she said slowly, but her smile indicated she approved. She wanted to ask about the sculpture, but more guests were arriving. "Frank will get you each a drink," she said as she hurried to meet her friends.

Martin Vanderhoop kept his eye on the guests. He recognized most of them, and he knew that in other places they were important people. On Jellicle Island they were just summer people enjoying the last weekend of the season. He stood near the sculpture, but it didn't seem likely that anyone was going to run off with it. It was too heavy and cumbersome to be moved unnoticed.

Sue Ellyn greeted each guest enthusiastically. When Robert Cunningham arrived with his sister Margaret's boyfriend, she was surprised, but when he handed her a gift of freshly caught bluefish, she hurried to put it in the freezer.

Birthday gifts were left on the downstairs dining room table, and the guests admired the display of watercolors Alicia had provided as they climbed the stairs to the living room. Drinks in hand, Alicia and McCalister joined them.

"Hello, baby," Alicia said as she patted her sculpture. "Hey, Martin, anything new?"

"You tell me." He looked at McCalister. "Does this mean I can relax?"

"No, you know these people. I don't. Anyone look out of place?"

"No, not really."

Alicia scanned the room, too, observing Beth's parents' friends sipping their drinks and munching hors d'oeuvres. "Beth," she called out. "You finally made it!"

Beth looked beyond Alicia to her date. She'd come close to believing Rick would be Alicia's date. "Hi, Alicia. Admiring your famous sculpture, I see."

“Has anyone offered to buy it?” Alicia asked, ignoring Beth’s obvious curiosity about her companion.

“I thought you didn’t want to sell it.”

“Just curious.”

“The sculpture is curious, Alicia. What’s going on?” Beth continued, studying McCalister.

By seven o’clock, the last of the guests were saying goodbye and wishing Sue Ellyn a final birthday salutation. McCalister knew someone would come for the sculpture. He studied Vanderhoop. He was a sharp ex-marine on guard in a house perched on a ridge overlooking the shore with a surveillance team of FBI agents watching from the main road. Vanderhoop was familiar with the multitude of paths and trails to the beach and through the woods. There was no way anyone could get in unnoticed.

“Alicia, I’m going to ask you to go home. The party’s over, and I have a bad feeling about what’s going to play out in the next couple of hours. I’m staying.”

Sue Ellyn entered the room, plunked down on the sofa, and removed her shoes. Her husband stood in front of the windows, frowning. Vanderhoop stood near the sculpture scanning the woods.

“I see a car coming,” McCalister said from the landing window.

Dr. Norton started down the stairs.

“Just a minute, sir. I think you’d better stay here.” McCalister blocked his way.

“It’s a van,” Vanderhoop said. He drew his gun and bounded down the stairs two steps at a time and stood behind the door.

“It’s all right. I’m expecting someone,” Dr. Norton said. “God damn late, but I know who it is.”

McCalister switched off the outdoor light. Through the dining room’s wall of windows, he watched a van pull up into the front yard and stop. A door slammed.

Vanderhoop adjusted the pistol in his hand as someone rapped loudly on the front door.

“Who is it?” McCalister roared.

“Balloons,” a voice squeaked.

Dr. Norton moved past Beth and Alicia, who stood on the landing, and descended the stairs.

"For God's sake, step out of the way," he told McCalister and Vanderhoop.

"Come on, come on. Let him in."

Vanderhoop switched on the outdoor light and opened the door. The front step was filled with silver, gold, orange, red, and purple balloons.

"You're late," Dr. Norton growled.

"I got lost," came the muffled reply.

"Follow me. The guest of honor is upstairs."

A loud chorus of Happy Birthday jolted Sue Ellyn into a standing position. "What in the world is this, Frank? You?" She laughed loudly, and in her surprise, her studied Southern accent filled the air as thickly as the wildly fluorescent balloons.

"Get your boat shoes, Sue Ellyn. We've got tickets on the shuttle to Nantucket. We've talked about going for forty years. Tonight's the night."

"My God, Frank. I'm exhausted."

"Put on your shoes. You merely have to walk to the car. Beth's packed your bag. If you haven't got your second wind by the time we get there, I'll carry you off the plane."

"You old sweetie," Sue Ellyn drawled.

Frank Norton followed his wife into the bedroom to expedite the departure. Beth looked at her watch. It was seven-thirty. She'd forgotten to call Rick. She went to find the number in her purse and went into the den to make the call.

McCalister followed Beth and stood outside the room listening.

"May I speak to Rick Lewis?" she asked. The phone clanked on the bar.

"Hello?"

"Rick! It's here. It's in my parents' living room right now."

Frederick J. Lewis let out a breath of relief. "Who's there?"

"In a few minutes, no one will be here but me. My parents are getting ready to leave on a jaunt. There's the policeman, but since you sent him, I guess you can send him away."

"A policeman?"

"I know who you're with," Beth whispered. "The FBI."

"You said police? Who's there, FBI or police?"

"Both, I guess. Alicia didn't tell me, Tess did."

Frederick was not sure how to proceed. He was stuck between a couple of rocks and hard places—FBI and police, Beth and Alicia.

"Okay, I can explain, but I need you to come and get me. I'm at the Brews and Booze."

"I thought that sounded like a local number. Why didn't you just come to Mom's party?"

"Don't say anything to anyone. I'll be waiting for you." Frederick hung up and paid his bar tab.

"You're a patient guy, buddy," the bartender said. Frederick regretted he'd been noticed. He had a couple of phone calls to make. He went out to find a booth on the street.

* * *

"Change of plans," McCalister said to Alicia. "I'm taking you home. I want to make sure no one's waiting for you there."

"Okay, but after we check the house, maybe I should come back with you. I want to see my sculpture one last time, before you rip it apart."

"Probably not negotiable, but I might need you."

* * *

Dmitri struggled through the woods. The thin branches snapped in his face, and the dense underbrush grabbed at his feet. The air was thick with fog. Margaret's brother had willingly gone along with Dmitri's plan to get a free meal at the Nortons' for the price of a bluefish Robert had caught earlier in the day. Mrs. Norton welcomed them into the house, and they realized they'd crashed a cocktail party. The meal turned out to be hors d'oeuvres, but the two of them mingled with the guests and enjoyed the free liquor until Robert pointed out the policeman at the end of the room. Dmitri stared hard at the sculpture, but he dared go no further.

On the way out, Robert Cunningham pointed to the unmarked police car on the old beach road. He assumed it was a drug stake-out and opted to go home. Dmitri circled back from the Cunningham house to stand in the woods behind the Nortons' garage. The Nortons' cars were gone, but he stayed in the woods and walked back along the ridge to get a view of the second floor. Only the policeman's car remained in the sandy space by the side of the house.

He stepped out of the woods and hurried across the back of the house to where the garbage cans sat against the back entrance. He pried off the lid and lit a match, dropped it into the open can, then stepped back into the shadows.

* * *

Vanderhoop smelled smoke. He could see the smoke billowing past the window on the landing as he charged down the stairs. He spun around and snapped open the rear kitchen door and jumped off the patio to the garbage can.

Dmitri stepped forward and struck. Vanderhoop fell to the ground, his gun fell from his hand. Dmitri considered taking the gun, but the house was still. He possessed the sculpture now. It was still Labor Day. He'd make the delivery to Fyordorvitch and head to Nova Scotia before the sun rose.

He picked up the lid to the garbage can and extinguished the fire. He dragged the unconscious policeman around the corner of the house and into the woods. Then he walked in the front door, up the stairs, and into the living room. He picked up the sculpture and carried it out of the house to the woods, where he dropped it. The sculpture bore into the ground with a dull thump. He dragged it closer to the steep slope leading to the shore and let it roll down the ridge. It rolled over and nudged against a tree. Dmitri retrieved the crowbar he'd taken from Dr. Norton's garage.

He raised the shaft above his head and brought it down with all his force against the sculpture. His brain sparked with images as he felt the impact of the metal against the crowbar. He thought of the boy and his search for treasure, the artist sweating over the searing heat from the butane torch, and of Margaret. He saw the face of his father in his final days. He tore at the metal, and at last it gave way. He plucked out the heart of the sculpture. He hurried toward the shore where Fyordorvitch had agreed to meet him. It had taken Dmitri so long to hand over the cargo that Fyordorvitch was worried he'd changed his mind and was on the side of the Russian sailors who wanted détente, not the old guard looking for revenge.

* * *

Frederick pushed through the crowded street filled with tourists and islanders eager for one last summer celebration. He headed for the pay phone at the end of the wharf. He dropped in a quarter and then, after dialing, four more.

"Scully? I got what you want, but I want more cash. Not in a bank account, but wired to me here on Jellicle Island."

"Freddy, you're done."

Frederick J. Lewis was tired of the game. He just wanted out.

"I've got the sculpture."

"Too late. The island is crawling with Russians. And they ain't all on the same side. Walk away, pal. Let 'em fight it out." Scully hung up.

As Frederick walked toward the bar he could see a car double parked near the entrance. He opened the passenger door and got in.

"Where've you been? I've been here for a while."

"I've been here for a while, too."

"I'd have picked you up before the party."

"Not in a party mood, Beth. So how big is this sculpture?"

"About four feet tall. Heavy, too."

"Figures."

"So what's your plan?"

"You've got to help me get that damn thing out of there. I need it. Got to have it."

At the end of the main road, Beth slowed the car, easing onto the gravel road. The car nosed down into a hollow, and the fog swallowed them. The Norton house didn't materialize until the final bend in the road, when the headlights cast a beam across the back of it.

"Something's wrong," Beth whispered. The back door was open and swinging in the wind.

"Get the car turned around and headed out. I'm going in. You said it's in the living room?" Frederick had no stomach for this. He didn't have much of a plan.

The acrid smell of smoke hung in the damp air. He crept up the back steps and slid into the dark house leaving the door to swing in the breeze. In the kitchen he paused, uncertain. Skirting the microwave cart, he entered the dining room. Confused, his heart pounding, he listened and heard only the bam, bam of the back door.

He walked around the heavy Victorian dining room table and stood in the front hall. He stared at the stairs unwilling to begin the ascent to the living room. As he crept across the hall, his shoes squeaked on the floor. If someone was up there, they knew he was coming.

He took his time. On the landing, he studied the darkness outside. No moon. Deep fog. He wondered how heavy the damn thing was. Where was he going to take it, and what was he going to do about Beth?

"What's going on?" Beth was close behind him.

"Jesus. I told you to wait in the car."

She moved around him and climbed the second half of the stairway. Light suddenly filled the upstairs.

"The sculpture's gone!" she shouted. "Martin's car is out there, but where is Martin?"

Frederick looked out the landing window toward the road they'd just driven. The light from the house bounced back from the glass, but no light shone from outside.

"Someone's stolen the sculpture, and they're heading for the beach," Beth called out to him.

"How do you know" Frederick inquired wearily. He could walk away from this. Take the ten thousand he'd already withdrawn from the bank and disappear. He'd thought grabbing the sculpture and demanding another ten thousand would be a walk in the park.

Beth was standing in the dark looking toward the beach from the open living room windows. "I can hear them crashing through the woods. They're headed toward the Sanctuary, I guess, but they're not on the path if they're making that much noise."

"Someone's coming," Frederick started. "I can see the headlights."

Beth joined him on the landing. "No, too far to the west. That's Alicia's place."

"Someone's using a flashlight, you can make it out. There. Look."

Frederick studied the light as it faded in and out, obscured by the trees and then reappearing. If Beth knew the short-cuts Alicia had used, he could get ahead of him.

"He's headed for the pond, I think, and then to the road at the Sanctuary. Do you know a short-cut to get to the Sanctuary faster than the path and the walk up the shore?"

"Of course. I've been walking up and down these paths all my life."

Frederick checked the lights still visible from Alicia's direction. The house lights were off now, but a car's headlights shone. He went up the remaining steps to the living room, past the bathroom where Beth had turned on the light and the bright orange wallpaper burst in color like fire. The living room was dark.

"What the hell?" Frederick batted at a mass that floated above him as he walked into the dark room.

"Balloons. Dad gave them to Mom for her birthday." The balloons were bunched against the ceiling, their long ribbons dangled above Frederick's head.

"We've got to move fast, but there's something I've got to do first."

* * *

When McCalister drove back up the driveway to the Nortons' house, he noticed the black smudge that looked like an unearthly scribble on the gray shingles. A light was visible from the upstairs hallway. Vanderhoop was probably sitting in the dark guarding the sculpture, waiting for someone to come after it.

"Wait here," he told Alicia.

He headed for the back door. He touched the lid of the garbage can. It was hot. He saw marks in the sand and his eyes followed them into the underbrush where the policeman lay.

Sprinting up the back steps, he lunged into the dark kitchen where hours earlier he had studied the floor plan. The house was silent, and the light from the upstairs dissipated before it reached the bottom step. He crept up the steps, his gun drawn. The light was coming from the small bathroom papered with fishing labels. He moved quickly across the hallway and aimed his gun into the living room.

Something brushed against his neck, against his collar. The hair on his head stood up, snapping with electricity. He spun on his heels and jabbed. He punched a balloon that floated across the room. Switching on the light, he saw that the room was filled with balloons anchored to the chairs. From the outside, it must have looked like the room was full of people. A silver balloon, its ribbon wrapped through the elaborate cut-out woodwork on a Victorian chair, floated near the empty spot where the sculpture had been.

"What the hell?" McCalister let out his breath and holstered his Glock, checked the other rooms on the floor and reached for the phone. Then he hurried back to the car.

"The sculpture's gone," he told Alicia. "Someone went to a lot of trouble to make it look like the place was full of people. I hate to do this, but I'm going to need you to guide me through the woods to the beach. I'm thinking whoever's got the sculpture knows the roads are watched, and is meeting someone in a boat at the shore."

As he backed out of the driveway, he stared into the screened porch. The moon was beginning to break through the clouds, and he could see a balloon drifting slowly across the porch. "Happy Birthday" glowed in a fluorescent scrawl across its face.

A gunshot sounded clearly, echoing through the woods.

"What's the fastest way to the beach?"

"I've created my own path. It goes along the ridge, and with the moonlight we can see the path to the beach and anyone who's walking along the Sanctuary's trail. Turn left here."

"There's no road."

"No, it's a wide path. We can take the car about a quarter of a mile, then pick up my path. Look, there are tire marks. Someone has been through here tonight."

The path was smoother than the road. McCalister increased his speed. Overhanging branches slapped at the windshield as he drove.

"Stop. This is as far as the wide path goes."

McCalister shut off the engine. "Now where?" he asked. A cloud shut out the moonlight and blackness closed in again. Alicia got out of the car. The tang of her perfume hung in the air. He followed after her.

The earth beneath his feet was soft and spongy as they headed down a steep bank. When he stepped on a stick, it crackled with a sharp snap. He turned sideways to dig his feet into the loam. It was too dark to gauge the angle at which he was descending or whether the slope would level before they reached the shore.

Alicia stopped. McCalister, close behind her, put his hand on her back. He was surprised her skin was cool and her shirt dry. He was perspiring heavily. She pulled him toward her and whispered. "We're at the bottom now. There's a large dead tree uprooted just ahead. We're going to climb over it. Then the path descends again. We'll come out on the side of the hill overlooking the pond. From there we can see the trail and hear anyone on the path. It will sound like they're right next to us, but they aren't.

She started walking again. The sharpness of her perfume twitched his nose, and the softer smell of her hair and neck made him eager to finish this operation.

A voice sounded close by. A twig snapped. Then all was still again. McCalister caught the end of a branch in his hand and bent it back. Alicia moved back to where he stood.

"Someone's close," she whispered. "No one knows my path. They must be lost."

More thumps and cracks thundered in the dark.

"They're ahead of us. They're walking toward the shore." She pointed off toward her left. McCalister strained and heard the sound of a woman's voice. Below them a splash punctuated the silence.

"There's somebody over there, and somebody where that splash came from. Anyone familiar with these woods would know how to reach a little bridge over the stream. It's very narrow and shallow most of the way. Whoever it is, he's coming into the water at the deepest part." She stood still, staring into the darkness. "If you look over there…" she pointed to the right, "There's someone down there with a light."

A deep voice cursed in a foreign tongue. "Swahili?" she asked.

"Russian."

"I think whoever fell into the stream just ran into the overturned tree. It's may be five feet in diameter, and it was tall. It will take him a while to go over it or around it."

The woods were crowded, McCalister concluded. Frederick and maybe the woman's voice was Beth's, the Russian—the bwana fisherman, other Russians perhaps.

Someone had the sculpture or what was embedded within it. From the sounds coming from different directions in the woods, more than a couple of people were tracking it.

A flashlight shot a beam above their heads, and they instinctively ducked into the thick shrubbery. The light shot off in another direction. McCalister pulled Alicia down closer to the ground. She leaned into his face and whispered, "Just on the other side of the guy or guys with the light, there is a cutback to the main path. If we can get by them, we can get on the path and behind whoever is coming down the trail."

She started out in a hunched position, then shifted and began crawling on her hands and knees. McCalister felt the soft cool moss. He hoped Sullivan had taken down the windfarm and that the local law enforcement or other FBI agents were somewhere in the woods, too. From Washington, Jellicle Island didn't look this complicated.

"There's a thick wall of blueberry bushes over there," Alicia informed him. "If we stay low we can crawl past them. I think they're too busy with the tree to look around."

McCalister crawled over the spongy moss, but when it spread toward a tree, Alicia continued straight ahead over sticky leaves and exposed roots. McCalister could make out two burly figures hunched forward and tromping toward the shore. He hoped his back up team was in place.

He could hear voices clearly now. Alicia was a good guide. They'd come down the path behind the voices he'd heard from the top of the ridge.

It was the part of the job that defies description, the second before the gun is fired, the fugitive cornered, the spy trapped. The moment of intuitive response. McCalister stepped out onto the path and aimed the 9 mm Glock at the couple who were in front of him.

"FBI. Get your hands in the air."

Frederick spun around in surprise and stared up the path to where McCalister stood ready to fire. The moon broke through the clouds shining down on Lewis as if he were on stage. A shot rang out, coming through the woods not far from the woods where McCalister had seen the two burly figures. Lewis fell to the earth. Beth screamed and dived into the shelter of the bushes. McCalister stepped back into the woods and studied the outline of trees dense and silent in the spreading moonlight.

Just ahead of him the path opened onto the shore. He could see two figures at the ocean's edge. The moon was shining clearly now and a glimmer of light bounced off the metal clutched in the hand of one of them. Another volley of shots followed. The metal flew through the air. The figures raced towards the woods.

The tops of the trees began to sway. A hundred feet into the woods, hidden behind a boulder, Alicia pressed against the hard rock. Beth crouched next to her shivering. Twigs cracked. Then all was still. Far away an owl screeched, and an animal in its grip shrieked.

McCalister stepped onto the beach to pick up the shattered object. He could sense someone coming out of the woods behind him. Sullivan.

"You took care of the windfarm?"

"I'd like to take credit but when we got there, there were four bodies. Apparently the Russian fishermen figured out the plan and put a stop to it. I didn't expect to have a shoot-out in the woods. I should have brought my heavy caliber automatic weapon—the one with electronic laser lights."

"That was you over there in the stream?"

"I was tracking the fishermen who beat me to the windfarm. They were far enough ahead of me that they made it around the Point to the cove. Probably on a boat by now. We'll get 'em."

"As for the bwana, there are so many paths and trails up that ridge, he may have gotten away. We've got to get this piece of evidence to

Washington. The President's going to add a new paragraph to his speech."

"Would someone tell me what's going on?" Beth asked, her voice trembling.

"Rick wasn't with the FBI, was he?"

"*Ukungio Lichoni huujui,*" McCalister said with a shake of his head. "What gets in your eye is not visible to you." An old Swahili proverb. Mr. Lewis liked the easy life and couldn't figure out how to pay for it honestly and got suckered into a clash of ideologies.

"Frederick Lewis? Rick?" Alicia and Beth chorused.

"And then there were those who couldn't let go of the past. Old men who spent time in Africa and then in Cuba when Khrushchev lost the missile crisis. They thought up a cockamamie plan to build a missile piece by piece. They planned to launch it when the United Nations meets. They got lucky when the President added a trip to Cape Cod, because their missile didn't have the range for New York. We got luckier. If the son of one of their comrades hadn't had such a fondness for Swahili proverbs they might have succeeded. But then your friend Tess is one smart stay-at-home Mom. She connected the links."

Sullivan held the piece of twisted metal. "They had the missile assembled except for this one essential piece that was to be hand delivered to the site."

McCalister put his arm around Alicia, "You're a talented painter, but it's a good thing you tried your skill on sculpture. You're a damn good guide, too. I don't suppose there's a shortcut from here to the airport is there?"

"No. And now that I look at you, I realize I never mentioned the poison ivy."

33 | Secrets Are Things We Give to Others to Keep for Us

"Potato chips, nothing beats them for comfort," Tess said aloud to the empty living room. A large cumbersome Naugahyde sofa covered the south wall; a leftover from Michael's bachelor days. It was uncomfortable to sit on, sticky in the summer and now cold in the late afternoon of an autumn day in Chicago. At a right angle to it, a sofa bed in a now shabby brocade sat in front of the windows that overlooked the street. Tess glanced out as she waited for Alicia, Margaret, and Beth to arrive. She set the bowl of chips down and went back into the kitchen. The margarita glasses were rimmed with salt, and the pre-mixed drinks were cooling in the refrigerator.

Tess repositioned a pillow on the La-Z-Boy chair as Michael came down the stairs. "You know, Michael, the furniture in this room is awful. I'm going upstairs to make sure the kids are asleep and bring down a couple of fleece throws. There's nothing like something soft and snuggly to set the mood."

"Why so jittery?" Michael asked. "The kids are asleep and I'm headed for a guys' night out."

"A lot happened to all of us this summer, and I hope we can talk through it. Alicia's going to stay here overnight, and Margaret's going back into the city with Beth."

"Or after downing a couple pitchers of margaritas the ladies can spend the night in our living room on our lovely sofas. I wouldn't say a word." Michael popped a potato chip in his mouth. "I think I see a cab pulling up with your friends. I'm out of here. See you later."

"I'm glad Margaret and Alicia have arrived. Say hello to them on your way out."

Tess turned to study the room and followed Michael outside to greet her friends. As she walked toward them, Beth's car pulled into the driveway.

"Oh, boy. Here we go," Tess said as she turned to say hello to Beth while Michael spoke to the other two.

"Welcome. Whoever would have thought the Island girls would get around to having a reunion in Chicago?" Tess asked.

The front door opened directly into the living room without the pretense of a foyer. The three studied the seating arrangement. Alicia and Margaret chose the brocade sofa and sat down at either end. Beth eyed the La-Z-Boy recliner. "I've fought that thing before," she said with a laugh and settled onto the empty sofa. Tess retreated into the kitchen to fetch the drinks.

She marched back into the living room, stepping over the new Transformers scattered across the floor. She carried the tray of strawberry margaritas and set it down on the coffee table in front of Beth.

Alicia and Beth both reached into the bowl of potato chips at the same time and then laughed. Tess let out a deep breath of relief.

"There's three more bags in the kitchen and I've ordered a pizza." She poured the drinks and each picked up a glass, a moment of silence fell over them as they stared at each other.

"Here's to us," Margaret said. The tension eased and they all started talking at once, stopped, laughed, sipped their drinks, and when Tess sat down they moved a bit closer to each other and to the bowl of potato chips.

"I even managed to keep Margaret from wandering off to the International Terminal at O'Hare," Alicia began. "She hasn't even hinted whether she's heard from her Russian boyfriend. But, since Margaret knew all those secret paths we made as kids, after a summer of going back and forth to the beach with him, he knew them well, too. I'll bet he made it back to the Cunninghams', got Robert to take his boat out, and he's back on a Russian fishing trawler now."

"That would make Margaret's brother aiding and abetting a dangerous spy," Tess said sternly. "Margaret, you seriously didn't believe him when he told you he was a Russian fisherman?"

Beth took a deep breath, set her glass carefully on the coffee table and glancing at Alicia said, "Don't be too hard on Margaret. Alicia and I didn't have such great judgment either."

"I'm sorry, Beth, that Frederick got caught in the crossfire," Alicia said addressing the elephant in the room.

"He was a rat, but a charming one. It was a perfectly awful thing to happen. It's been tough sorting through Frederick's facts and fiction. I'm not sure if those Russian fishermen were aiming at him or he just got in the way of the shot meant for Margaret's friend."

"Seth says the Russian dissidents at the windfarm wanted revenge, but the Russian fishermen wanted détente," Alicia said. "It's hard to believe our little island was the setting for international intrigue."

Tess jumped in. "Ah, so it's Seth, now, not FBI Agent McCalister?"

"I'd like to think my Russian friend spent enough time on our island to reconsider his ideology. And I thank God my dearest friends didn't get hurt."

"Me too," Alicia and Beth said at the same time.

"I'm relieved you survived the summer, and the President had the opportunity to make an impassioned speech in favor of détente," Tess said.

"What's your next project, Alicia?" Beth asked.

"I'm thinking of sending sculpture to Chicago, Beth."

"That gives me an opening with the cute gallery owner, Mark Lyndenfeld. He said he'd like to see your sculpture—and I think see me, too."

"Hey! You said you were thinking of an international tour!" Margaret exclaimed.

"I am thinking of that, too. Watercolors and sculpture. I found my poor sculpture at the bottom of the ridge where your Russian boyfriend slammed a crowbar into it. It gave it a new dimension. Spread it out. Made it look like it could fly."

Commonly called *The Winged Victory*, the Nike of Samothrace (c200-190 BC) is a figurehead from the prow of a ship. With her drapery swept backward by the wind, she is the embodiment of triumph in victory.

www.ingramcontent.com/pod-product-compliance
Lightning Source LLC
Chambersburg PA
BHW070851250626
59CB00003B/1028